THE
GIRL
WITH THE
SCARLET
RIBBON

BOOKS BY SUZANNE GOLDRING

SUZANNE GOLDRING

THE GIRL WITH THE SCARLET RIBBON

bookouture

Published by Bookouture in 2022

An imprint of Storyfire Ltd.
Carmelite House
50 Victoria Embankment
London EC4Y 0DZ

www.bookouture.com

ISBN: 978-1-80314-011-7
eBook ISBN: 978-1-80314-010-0

For my lovely daughter Jen Jen, who found the wine window in Borgo San Jacopo and the memorial on Platform 16.

'Never trust the artist. Trust the tale.'
D.H. Lawrence, *Studies in Classic American Literature*, 1923

'What art can wash her guilt away?'
Oliver Goldsmith, *The Vicar of Wakefield*

PROLOGUE

FLORENCE

8 September 1943

Gabriella had tried moulding the potato dough into little dumplings the way her mother had shown her a hundred times. 'Lightly, girl, lightly,' Mama had said. 'Gnocchi need only the lightest touch.'

She rolled a long sausage shape on the floured marble counter, then pinched off lengths no bigger than the top of her thumb. But she still couldn't get it right. The dough looked yellow and shiny, compared to her mother's flour-dusted pillows, scored with a fork to capture the sauce. But if she didn't make the gnocchi, what would they eat tonight? There was so little flour to be had these days that they couldn't make pasta. But the basil was still growing well, so perhaps they could make pesto to add flavour to the bland but filling mouthfuls of fresh dough.

Even before the war started, supplies had become restricted. Everything was state property; everyone had their allocation. Gabriella grumbled to herself, but knew she was luckier than most. Since Grandmama died and her parents had moved from their house in Rome to live in their family's high-ceilinged palazzo in Florence, she had eaten well. Somehow, Papa's contacts were able to bring them fresh aubergines, peppers and onions from farms in the surrounding valleys.

Mama said they were better off in Florence and now the Germans were heading towards their previous home, she said she knew they had been right to leave. And Gabriella knew she wouldn't starve here like the ragged urchins on the streets of Rome. But without flour there was no spaghetti, no tagliatelle or, her favourite, orecchiette, little ears of pasta that captured a spicy sauce of sausage, Parmesan and rocket in their hollows.

Maybe if they were lucky enough to find more flour, Mama would teach her how to make pasta, the way she had been taught by Carla, the household's cook before she left the palazzo for the relative safety of her family's farm. And even if they didn't have meat or spices to enliven the sauce, they could use peppers or broccoli.

'Aren't you finished yet?' her mother called as she returned to the kitchen from the courtyard, in her arms a basket of ripe figs picked from the twisted tree that spread along one wall of the enclosed kitchen garden, ensuring all its purple fruit basked and ripened in the sun. Mama had to manage all the running of the house now, neglecting her art studio, where she had loved to paint and draw to the music of Puccini.

'It's so boring—' Gabriella began to say, but was interrupted by a sudden shout from outside. Her twelve-year-old brother, Riccardo, face flushed, chestnut hair flopping over his forehead, limped at speed past the door, yelling. 'Come and see, Gaby!' he shouted. 'They're coming. The Allies are coming!'

Gabriella jumped down from her stool, dusting her floury hands on her apron, and ran into the courtyard with its dry fountain, where the lamb was lying down in a shady corner, panting. Soon they would have to slaughter the beast. The garden could offer no more grass after the hot summer and fetching hay would bring suspicion. Who else had a prime source of meat fattening in their garden, who else might betray them for a joint of succulent lamb?

'Look,' Riccardo shouted. 'Over there, can you see?' He jumped up and down, pointing over the walls at the blue sky humming with the drone of aircraft. White balloons, looking like the jellyfish Gabriella had seen one summer in the sea long ago at the Lido di Jesolo outside Venice, when they had dined every night on spaghetti vongole on the balmy terrace of the Hotel des Bains, were floating down over the green hills around the city. 'See them over there? Hundreds of parachutes! The Allies are coming now!'

He clambered to the top of the wall for a better view and Mama shouted, 'Be careful you don't fall!' She was always urging him to be cautious because of his weakened leg.

Gabriella cursed her dress that wouldn't allow her to join him. He had all the fun, even though he was nearly two years younger than her. He was allowed to run errands around the narrow streets, while she had to learn how to manage a household, just because she was a girl. Mama was always reminding her to act like a young lady and forever fussing over Riccardo, ensuring he didn't overtire.

When she was very young, maybe as young as six, she had been excited by the thrilling words she and her school friends learnt when they were enrolled in the Fascist Youth as Figli della Lupa, the Children of the She-Wolf. She had repeated the stirring words, vowed to serve with all her strength, to suffer without crying out. She had made those vows, but as soon as she reached the age of nine all the girls were expected to behave like militant housewives, drilling with doll babies in their arms, learning first aid and childcare. The boys, with their black shirts, learnt how to fight and be soldiers. But Riccardo had not become a *balilla*, a young soldier, as he was educated at home throughout his sickly childhood when he was recovering from polio. Yet, despite his handicap, being a boy, he had far more freedom than she did.

There he was, waving his arms, on top of the ancient stone wall that linked the palazzo to the chapel. Shouting, making an exhibition of himself in his threadbare shorts and torn shirt, his withered leg barely hampering him in his excitement. Yet she was expected to be demure and decorous. The grown-ups came outside too, talking in loud voices, watching the paratroopers drifting down over the distant hills.

'They've moved fast since we capitulated yesterday,' she heard her father say. 'Thank goodness they're here already and our city and its treasures will be saved.' Being in charge of the Egyptian antiquities at the Museo Archeologico, all he could think of was saving his precious artefacts from both destruction and the thieving hands of the invaders.

'We shall be saved from the Germans after all,' Mama said. 'Merciful Mother, all shall be well. Our prayers have been answered.'

Gabriella looked away from the bright blue sky, noticing that the quiet family who hid in the stifling attic by day had also emerged. The mother was obviously pregnant and her twins, a boy and a girl of five or six, clutched her skirts and peered at the strangers around them. And the secretive men who crept out of the cellar in the night had also joined the throng in the courtyard garden scented with rosemary and lavender. Everyone was pointing and talking at speed about what this meant, since Italy had joined the Allies the day before.

She stood close to her mother. 'Do you think Uncle Federico will be able to come home now?' Her art historian uncle had not told the family where he was going, he had only said it was important work for Italy's cultural heritage. Riccardo missed his tuition in the great paintings of Italy and Gabriella missed him pointing out how auburn hair like hers was beloved by many artists.

'Soon, child. Let us hope the end is not far off now.' Mama hugged her daughter to her side, stroking her hair. Gabriella knew what her mother was thinking: *how can we keep this beautiful child safe?* She'd often heard her talking to Papa. 'She's only fourteen. She's still a child, but she's already beginning to show signs of maturity. And she's going to be a beauty with her unusual tawny hair and green eyes. The same colouring as my Great-Aunt Elena. We shall have to keep her close while life is still so unsettled with soldiers on the streets every day.'

Then, as the drift of white sails floating down the hills began to thin out and the drone of aircraft faded into the distance, everyone was startled by a loud knocking on the heavy studded door to the street. Papa answered and two half-familiar faces ran in, regular callers on their cellar lodgers. 'We're clearing out, right away,' they shouted, rushing to the basement steps.

'But we're going to be alright now,' Papa said. 'Haven't you seen them? The Allies are coming.'

'It's not the Allies,' the men shouted back. 'It's the bloody Germans.'

ACT ONE
THE CLOAK OF DECEPTION

Secrecy and Ciphers

ONE

LONDON

September 2019

Sofia stood back from the large canvas with its distorted figures. As always, there was the lamb, its neck oozing with what looked like dark, clotting blood, and, in the distance, over an impression of dark blue hills, floating white blooms like dandelion clocks. Her father's signature, these symbols, never explained, never expanded, but always present in all of his many paintings.

Since his not entirely unexpected death in February at the age of eighty-seven, she had come to feel the tremendous weight of responsibility for organising this retrospective exhibition. His life's work, or at least a representative selection of the majority of his works, was being curated along with those on loan from private collections. The negotiations with the Firenze Gallery in Bond Street had been finalised only months before his death and as Riccardo had become increasingly incapacitated and her mother Isobel more withdrawn, it had fallen to Sofia to handle the major part of the arrangements. Some of the work was on loan from galleries and individuals, some he had never sold, preferring to display them in his Cornish studio, which opened to the public twice a year.

'Have you decided which ones are for sale yet?' Phoebe Ackroyd, the gallery's elegant director, sidled up to Sofia. Today, while she was supervising the hanging of the paintings, she was wearing a sleek khaki boiler suit and immaculate trainers. Once she was schmoozing the buyers, she'd be in silky drapes and heels.

'No, I'll have to drag my mother up here. She can't remember which ones we sent here in the end. She's kept a couple of favourites, but other than those it's all down to her as she owns everything now and she's not sure about keeping the Cornwall studio open to the public for much longer. The biannual openings are always such a hassle.'

'Then if it's all clear-cut, no probate or other annoying little inheritance problems, we should be seeing a lovely rash of red stickers the minute we open. There's already masses of interest in this, you know.' Phoebe gave a satisfied laugh. 'I've even had some clients asking for a sneak preview.'

'I'll ring her later and see if she'll come up at the end of the week. She's down in Cornwall at the moment, but I can't see any reason why she can't get here soon.'

'Wonderful. There is one other problem though. You still haven't given me the copy for the brochure and the wall captions.'

'I thought you might ask for that.' Sofia felt the burden of this task weighing more and more heavily on her shoulders. Her mother seemed too reduced by her elderly husband's death to show any interest in this important exhibition. Sofia was not sure she could depend upon her to contribute to the detailed description and interpretation of the paintings.

'We're getting tight for time now. Normally we send out the catalogue with the invitations but we're already too late. With the opening on 15 October, I need to get copy to the printer no later than two weeks before, so we have time to proof and double-check.'

'I know. I'll have to get on with it. He hasn't made it easy for me though.' *No, he damn well hasn't*, she thought. No titles, no descriptions, just numbers. Like some bloody arrogant composer numbering all his symphonies. At least all the paintings were dated, but no titles, not a single one.

'I don't think it matters so much if we can't give them titles,' Phoebe said, standing back from the vast canvas, tilting her head this way and that. 'The numbers rather add to the mystique, don't you think? This one's Seventeen, isn't it?'

'Yes, there's always a tiny number next to his signature, so they're easily identified. Then the number and date it was completed are also on the back.'

'Very helpful. But that doesn't get away from the fact that we need a bit more detailed information. Serious collectors want to know why the artist created a particular painting, they want insights, understanding, interpretation. All part of the provenance.'

'Don't I just know it,' Sofia sighed. When had her father ever told anyone what had inspired him to paint a particular subject? Had he ever fully explained why he painted hills and valleys peopled with boys with bleeding ears and laughing girls? She could remember asking him once, when she was quite young, why the boys were hurt, and he'd given a little laugh, saying, 'They didn't like what they'd heard,' but he never said more than that.

Her earliest memories were of him taking her on his knee on the split leather sofa in his London studio, then carrying her across to one of his huge canvases and pointing out the colours. 'Yellow Ochre, Scarlet Lake, Prussian Blue,' he murmured, kissing her cheek. 'Remember that, my darling, it's how we spin our magic.' She would nuzzle his neck, smelling his fatherly scent of oil paints, tobacco and the cologne he always wore, which she later came to recognise as lemon and bergamot. And then her mother would break the spell, snatching her away for a bath, her supper and bedtime.

'Perhaps you and your mother could work on the descriptions together? It might be nice for you to get to team up and do that. A tribute to the great man.' Phoebe clapped her hands. 'Now I must leave you for a while. Roddy and Jez are manhandling the next lot round the corner. I'd better check on them. Think about it, won't you?' The text please, soon as,' she called over her shoulder as she marched into the next room to chastise her boys.

I'll think about it alright, Sofia told herself. But Mum's not going to be much help. She won't come up here willingly, I know she won't. I'll probably end up driving down there and dragging her back to Kentish Town.

Sofia was still living in the large Victorian house where Riccardo had painted early in his career and where she had been born. His studio was there still, spattered with paint, rejected canvases stacked against a wall, rags tossed onto a bench, brushes standing to attention awaiting his return, although he hadn't painted there for at least fifteen years. There was a similar scene in the now-quiet, abandoned studio in Cornwall. She imagined her mother opening the door expecting to find him there, contemplating his work, palette and brush in hand, listening to Puccini.

But neither studio, nor either of his homes, held clues to the meaning and content of his work. Although she could remember him employing models from time to time and even looking at photographs of the country and city of his birth, he didn't paint portraits, he didn't do life models, nor landscape. It seemed, she thought, as if all his paintings were sourced from inside his head, deep in his soul, and she knew that none of his notebooks, sketchbooks, letters or photos could help her.

Only he knew what his paintings meant, and maybe they were only ever intended to mean something to him and him alone. He never talked about his life or his childhood, apart from an occasional reference to a favourite dish prepared by his mother. Sofia knew he had been largely educated at home, because of his childhood illness, so it wasn't surprising he didn't talk of school friends; and, if he still had relatives in Florence, he never spoke of them.

Then she laughed to herself. He would think it an immensely funny joke if she just made up her own fanciful descriptions of his paintings. She wasn't talented in the way he was, but she'd studied art history, she could fake it, write her own interpretations of his work with or without her mother's help. Maybe that was the answer.

She was interrupted again by Phoebe, who marched towards her with a clipboard. 'I've just been checking,' she said, running her finger down a list. 'You remember how we decided to call this exhibition *Numbering The Years*? We've said that in his lifetime, Riccardo produced one hundred and eighty-two significant works, right? Well, accounting for those in private collections and allowing for the two your mother has hung on to, I can only make it a total of a hundred and eighty-one. I've checked the numbers – thank God he numbered them all, it makes it a lot easier – and I can't find Number Sixteen anywhere. You don't think she's tucked it away somewhere, do you?'

Phoebe tapped the list with her pen somewhat impatiently, while Sofia frowned and tried to think. Even though the paintings didn't have titles, their numbers were almost like titles in themselves. She felt she knew them intimately and could instantly picture Number Eleven, the one with a child crouched inside a straight-sided cave, his hand cupping his ear. Number Three was a dream-like garden with what looked like tall thin cypress trees, dark columns silhouetted against a pale sky filled with white balloons and boys with bleeding ears peering round the tree trunks. But a Number Sixteen didn't spring to mind at all.

Before she could answer, Phoebe snapped, 'Maybe it's better for us to leave the full list out of the catalogue. But if you can think of a good reason why I don't have details of the missing number, you will let me know, won't you?'

Sofia watched her stride off to her office. Phoebe's manner was irritating and at times unsympathetic; after all, this was her late father's life's work she was talking about and his death was still raw. She'd loved – no, still loved – him, her dear father, even if he had always been distracted and preoccupied. She thought for a moment about the sequence of paintings, trying to recall their details. Number Fifteen, she thought, was the one with a building, tied like a bursting parcel, spilling figures out into a crowded square. As for Number Seventeen, she could have pictured that one quite clearly even if it hadn't been hanging right here on the wall in front of her; it had a distinctive border of people tucked into beds, almost like in a dormitory. So was there also a Number Sixteen? And if so, what did it depict? But had it ever existed?

TWO

FLORENCE

12 September 1943

'I have my doubts myself, in these unsettled times when we don't know from one day to the next what life will bring, but your father wants you to continue attending school,' Mama said. 'However, I will escort you there and back every day.' She gave an exaggerated sigh. 'How I am meant to manage, with all I have to do, I don't know. But I must care for you in accordance with his wishes.'

Gabriella knew how busy her mother was. She no longer had help with cleaning and cooking. Carla, her grandmother's old housekeeper and cook, had fled to the countryside soon after the family arrived in Florence. It had sounded so grand when her father told her they were going to live in the Palazzo Rinaldi, but really it was just a big old draughty house, not a fine palace. And now, even though the family confined themselves to a few rooms of the spacious palazzo, floors still had to be swept and washed, clothes and bedding laundered, the garden watered and meals prepared.

'But you will have to help me whenever you are here.' Her mother hugged her. 'And I will teach you how to patch and darn. While this war continues, we shall have to make our things last.'

Mama had beautiful clothes, but she rarely wore them now, preferring simple cotton dresses covered with a long apron when she was baking and a paint-spattered smock when she was engrossed in painting in her studio, where she played recordings of Puccini operas on a wind-up gramophone. Gabriella had seen jewel-coloured dresses peering from beneath linen dust covers in her mother's wardrobe and sometimes crept into the bedroom to let the fine pleats of shimmering azure silk ripple through her fingers.

'That's my Fortuny,' Mama had whispered, slipping into the room and startling her. 'The pleats will stay like that forever. It was a present from your father on our honeymoon in Venice. We went to Fortuny's studio to see his designs. Oh, it was so hard to choose. The colours were like precious stones, my dear, topaz, emerald, sapphire, gorgeous, brilliant shades! And I brought it home in a round box, twisted and coiled like a snake. That's how they sent them out, you know. Just like a snake.' And she smiled as she lifted the dress from its hanger, then laid it on the white coverlet on her bed.

'How can it fit you?' Gabriella asked, looking at the narrow column of silk. 'It's so small.'

Her mother laughed and stretched out the pleats with both hands. 'It can fit anyone. It will fit you when you are older. It will suit you, with your rich bright hair.'

Gabriella stroked the dress with the tips of her fingers, wondering how it would feel to slide that gleaming silk over her head. 'When will that be?'

'After the war is over, when we are all together.' Mama slipped the garment back onto its hanger. 'And when you are taller.' She measured the dress against her daughter's height. 'You'll trip over it if you don't grow some more. I'd better feed you and make sure you will be able to stand tall in Fortuny.' Then she showed Gabriella how the slinky dress coiled in its hatbox and stowed the box away on top of her wardrobe.

And now Mama was taking off her apron to walk Gabriella to school along the Via Faenza to the Liceo classico, which she would have to endure until she was fifteen. It wasn't that she didn't like learning, really, she did, and she hoped her education could continue. But all her old friends were back in Rome. The girls here didn't welcome this red-haired newcomer and called each other comrades, *camerata*, in the manner of good fascists. They competed to earn badges and were aggressively self-confident.

Franca and Tina were the worst. Sisters only a year apart, daughters of someone Gabriella guessed was very important from the way they spoke and sauntered around the classroom. Soon after Gabriella had first started at the school, when she was nearly thirteen, Tina had grabbed her baby doll from her bag and dropped it on the floor, cracking it so hard one of the eyes was dislodged and rolled back in the doll's head. 'Oops,' Tina had said, laughing, 'that was careless. Now you've got a blind baby to look after.' She threw the doll back at Gabriella, hitting her in the chest. She'd accepted the slight, sensing that protest would only intensify the teasing, and since then she had let herself mutely melt into the background while the two of them showed the class how important they both were.

All the other girls looked up to them in fascination and fear. All that is apart from Stefanina, who was a year older and challenged their bullying ways with a mocking laugh. 'Watch it,' Tina yelled back. 'You're nothing but a *zingara*, a gypsy bastard,' added Franca. 'You can't tell us what to do.' Stefanina tossed her head and turned away, but all the girls knew that there had never been a father in her household, her mother was now dead and she had only her grandmother for company. Yet she acted as if she couldn't care less what the mocking sisters said about her. Gabriella wished she could be fearless like this sparkling girl with her black curly hair. But today, maybe she could catch the sisters' eye in a good way. They were both greedy girls and she had an offering for them. Unbeknown to Mama, she had taken four figs, two for each sister.

She waited until the break for lunch, when the girls were allowed to sit outside on the low walls that linked the cloisters around the square of scrubby grass, where a fountain pool was filled with thick green water. Franca always led the way, inspecting what each girl had brought to eat, taking a crust here, almonds there or, if she was lucky, a scrap of salami. The sisters halted in front of Gabriella and peered at her dry bread and hard Parmesan rind.

'That all you've got? Pathetic.' Tina went to swipe the food from her lap, but Gabriella pulled the napkin closer.

'She never has anything worthwhile,' Franca said. 'Come on. Someone's bound to have mozzarella or ham.'

'No, wait. I've brought something for you today.' The sisters turned back to her, the strange little Roman girl with the hair that glinted. 'I got them just for you. I've brought you ripe figs.' She uncovered the bundle hidden beneath her crust and revealed the dusky purple fruit, plump and tempting.

'I love figs,' Tina said, plonking herself down on the low wall. 'They'd better be ripe.' She grabbed one and bit off the remains of the stalk, then split the fig in half with her thumbs, revealing the shiny seeded centre. 'Perfect,' she said, sucking her sticky hands and biting into the rosy flesh, so the juice ran down her pimpled chin.

Franca squeezed her plump bottom into the space on the other side of Gabriella and she too helped herself to the fruit, taking two at once, as if she suspected her sister would steal her share. 'Where'd you get them?' she said. 'Can you get us some more?'

And Gabriella realised she had to be careful how she answered. Mama might notice if she took more fruit and the fig tree was now almost bare. 'I don't think so,' she said. 'The tree didn't have much fruit this year. But maybe a few late ones may yet ripen. I will watch out and if they look good, I will bring them for you.' She felt wary, but comfortable at the same time. The girls were leaning close to her and she was aware of the scent of perspiration and the underlying odour of garlic, as well as the strength of their well-fed bodies.

Tina unwrapped her napkin to reveal thin slices of prosciutto, a ripe bulbous tomato and a wrinkled peach. 'Here,' she said, handing the fruit to Gabriella. 'If they think I'm eating that, they can think again.'

Her sister peeled back her napkin. Her parcel was almost the same. 'She promised me mortadella today. And I don't want that!' She tossed a bruised pear into Gabriella's lap.

How could they have such abundance when everyone was struggling to find good food all over the city? Mama said the shortages were bound to get worse. Now the Germans were here they'd be requisitioning supplies for their troops and there were reports that they'd already raided the grain and oil stores of the villages around Siena to send back to their home country. Both girls looked extremely well nourished and Gabriella suspected they enjoyed raiding their schoolmates' lunches for a feeling of superiority, not hunger.

And then her suspicions were confirmed when Tina said, 'You stick with us, little Roma. We'll look after you, won't we, Franca?'

'You know who we are, don't you?' her sister said, nudging Gabriella's side with her elbow. 'Our poppa, he's a very important man. And now the Germans are here, he's even more important. He's helping them find all the troublemakers and he makes sure we have plenty of everything. So you stick with us and do what we say and you won't go hungry.'

'Our father is Major Michel Carisi,' Franca said, with a proud toss of her head. 'He commands a force of strong men who do everything he says. He says he has four saints helping him in his crusade. He's going to make sure the people of Florence know who's in charge.'

THREE

CORNWALL

September 2019

Sofia called out as soon as she opened the front door to the farmhouse. She thought her mother would have heard the car scrunch the gravel in the drive and be waiting to greet her, but she was nowhere to be seen. 'Mum, where are you?' she shouted, walking through the flagstoned hallway to the large kitchen, where the Aga tucked into the old chimney breast radiated heat even on a warm day of Indian summer.

Opening the stable door that led out onto the sheltered courtyard, she expected to see Isobel sitting in the stone corner seat that always caught the last of the afternoon sun, but it was empty apart from a drained mug and a paperback on the rickety table nearby. Perhaps she was outside gardening, Sofia thought, passing through the arched doorway to the walled garden that her mother took such pleasure in, where runner beans hung from hazel wigwams, raspberry canes bent over heavy with fruit and salads and green vegetables grew in ordered rows. But all she found was a rabbit darting out of the lettuce and a blackbird squawking inside the fruit cage.

She's slipping, Sofia told herself. *She never used to let the weeds grow like this and that rabbit has found a way in somehow.* And then she realised the gate armoured with chicken wire was wide open, so a family of rabbits could have cheerfully hopped in to eat undisturbed. She could see her mother beyond, standing at the far side of the field, looking out to sea, just as her father used to do, leaning on one of his many walking sticks.

'Mum,' she called. 'You had me worried. I've been looking for you.' She marched across the turf, close-cropped by a neighbouring farmer's sheep in return for mended fences and deliveries of logs. 'Did you forget I was coming today?'

Isobel turned round, hugging her long cardigan close in the fresh breeze from the sea. 'Oh darling, I was in a dream. No, I hadn't forgotten.' She brushed her wind-blown ash-blonde hair from her eyes.

Sofia hugged her and kissed her cheek. She was chilly, despite the sun. 'How long have you been out here? You're really cold. Let's go inside and get some tea.' She kept her arm around her mother, shepherding her back towards the house. 'We might still be able to sit outside if the sun hasn't gone from the courtyard.'

'I was sitting there earlier. I was reading, I think.' Isobel shivered a little. 'Then I thought I might pick the raspberries and I saw the gate was open. I must have gone for a walk.'

'You were just standing still when I saw you. Had you walked along the cliffs?'

'I don't know. I don't remember. I know I was thinking to myself, what did he see out here? He was always standing and watching and I thought maybe if I just stood there, I might know what it was.'

And Sofia knew she was thinking of Riccardo. He had always taken himself off for long walks and although in recent years his weakened leg had limited his travels, he had often just drifted out onto the cliffs and stood there for ages, staring at the sea, its unbroken horizon melding with the sky on days of grey. She knew he was letting his mind break free, float with the waves, the sea mist, the looming clouds. He would often shake his head as if waking from a dream and almost run back to his studio in the barn beside the house to transfer his thoughts to paper or canvas. She'd grown used to his introspection too, his inability to follow a conversation, hear an attempt to grab his attention or a question concerning anything as mundane as an offer of food or drink. That was his nature, his world. But was Isobel going to follow this pattern too, now he was gone?

As they entered the courtyard, Sofia immediately felt warmer. The thick, rough stone walls radiated the heat of the day and the sun was still lingering on the bench. 'You sit there, go back to your book and I'll be out in a minute with tea,' she said. Her mother sat down obediently and closed her eyes, lifting her face to the last rays of the day.

When Sofia returned, bearing a tray of tea and the saffron buns that had been her father's favourite, Isobel still had her eyes closed, but she wasn't asleep. 'Here we are, Mum, I've got lots to tell you, but let's eat these first.'

Isobel opened her eyes and stared at the buttered bun on the plate her daughter handed to her. 'He always loved these. I got them without thinking.'

'Oh, and I thought you'd bought them because I was coming. They're my favourite too, you know.' She bit into the bright yellow crumb, thick with creamy local butter. 'But I'd have been just as happy if you'd bought Jenny's scones.' Jenny B's, they agreed, was the best source of scones to eat with jam and cream, while Cornish Maid in Camelford had the best pasties, full to bursting with juicy steak and orange swede. Years of family holidays and rented cottages, followed by the excitement of eventually buying the farmhouse, had given them many opportunities to do their research on the pick of Cornish cuisine. And even after TV chefs and fine dining began to take over the old tearooms and chip shops, Sofia still associated Cornwall with such simple food.

Isobel broke her bun in half, then half again, popping a tiny corner in her mouth. 'I don't know why I buy them. But I can't get used to him not being here, I suppose. He was never in the way, always in his studio or out walking. It wasn't like I saw him every minute of the day. But I knew he was there. It seems so strange.'

Sofia took her mother's hand. It was still cold. 'It's early days yet, Mum. You can't be expected to get used to it in such a short time. Six, nearly seven months, it's nothing. You were together for nearly forty years. Of course it's going to take time.'

'Was it really as long as that? And of course I knew him before we married. Funny to think I married my teacher.'

'Whatever would they think of that now? He'd be in big trouble nowadays. Corrupting his students. He'd have got the sack and been in disgrace.' Sofia had always known that her mother had been in her first year of art school when she met Riccardo. But talking about it again seemed to be animating Isobel, bringing her back to life.

'He was so very handsome. All the girls adored him. I wasn't the only one, you know. But the others were very obvious, while I was quite restrained. He said that was what he liked about me, my modesty.'

'He adored you, Mum, always did. Bella, he called you. Did he do that right from the beginning?'

'I think so. He laughed about it – "bella Bella" was how he put it. I didn't mind. It was part of his character. Just as it was in his nature to be so challenging and demanding.'

Sofia knew what she was about to launch into. The career she had hoped to develop eclipsed, stifled by her husband's talent and fame. But why feel so resentful, Sofia thought, when the adulation brought invitations to the Venice Biennale, the Royal Academy, premieres, operas and other glittering events, all because of Riccardo's career and mysterious charm? The London home and this farmhouse were all purchased by his enormous success, so why did she still complain?

Isobel sighed. 'And I've been thinking all the time, thinking that now I have a chance to be myself at last. Now I'm no longer in his shadow, now's my chance. It's not too late, surely—' She broke off, fumbling for a tissue tucked up her sleeve, and her voice faltered. 'Then I feel guilty for thinking even for a second that I am glad he's gone.' And she bent her head to wipe her tears.

'Don't feel bad,' Sofia said, pulling her mother close to her. 'You're adjusting, that's all it is. You're bound to feel strange after such a long time.' But she knew what Isobel meant, as her life too had been shaped by his charismatic personality. Would she have studied History of Art without his persuasion? Would she have immediately involved herself in working as his assistant if he hadn't cajoled her into doing so? In her last year at university, when her boyfriend had left her broken-hearted, struggling to continue her studies, despondent at the thought of ever finding a job, it had seemed an easy, safe solution. But maybe she should have struck out and become more independent?

Life had always revolved around Riccardo. Had he been indulged as a child when he was recovering from polio? His stunted leg meant he could no longer walk great distances as he aged and he needed help to carry canvases, his portfolio and luggage. His whims, his needs, his intense work schedule, even his time out of the studio was determined by his need to see contacts, art critics and galleries. He had chosen the restaurants where they dined, the plays and films they saw, even the operas by Puccini and Rossini that played constantly in the house. But that was the nature of the artist, that was Riccardo, there could never have been room in his life for a talent equal to his.

'I feel so angry,' Isobel said. 'I feel such anger at how my life has been wasted.' She stood up and threw pieces of saffron bun on the cobbles beneath the dovecote for the birds to peck. 'From now on, I'm going to decide what I do and when I do it.'

Sofia watched her march inside the house. Although she had heard rumblings of resentment before, she hadn't been expecting this now. How was she going to persuade Isobel to return to London and help her finalise the notes for the exhibition? If her mother wanted to turn her back on her years with Riccardo, Sofia was going to have to honour her father's memory alone, without her help.

FOUR

FLORENCE

13 September 1943

Riccardo was scribbling in a notebook on a seat in the garden; a mixture of shapes, animals and words. It was the end of the afternoon; the sun would not set for another three hours, but the garden's high walls and cypress trees were creating a dusky light. Gabriella couldn't quite see what he was doing and she was so bored. Apart from school, she wasn't allowed to go anywhere on her own, Mama was so concerned about the German soldiers patrolling the streets with their fascist comrades. But despite his shortened leg, Riccardo had been sent on his own to the Mercato Centrale to see if flour had arrived today and then to the Museo with a message for his father, while she was escorted everywhere by her watchful mama.

'What are you doing?' she asked, twisting her head round to see the drawings emerging on the paper.

'It's hieroglyphs, Father says. Like the Egyptians did. They didn't have writing like us, they wrote with symbols. Look.' He held out the pages, filled with strange signs and words she could recognise underneath, like, *we shall have a feast when the lamb is killed.*

'Is that how the Egyptians wrote that? About the lamb?'

'No, I'm making it up. I'm using their kind of writing to create a code that no one else will be able to read. Then I'm going to send secret messages.'

Gabriella studied the pages. Riccardo was very clever and although he didn't attend school, because he had been so ill when he was younger, their parents were teaching him in their own way: history, the ancients, maths and art. He was only twelve, thirteen at the end of the year, but he was already a talented artist and had been allowed to watch his mother painting in her studio and use her pastels, watercolours and gouache from an early age. The lamb he had drawn in a coffin-shaped frame was simple but lifelike. 'Who's going to kill it?' she asked.

Riccardo shrugged. 'Mama and Papa say they can't bear to do it. But they're going to have to. We can't let it starve. It only had potato peelings and stalks of chard today. Anyway, it didn't come here to be a pet. It's meant to feed us for a long time, Mama says. I think Papa is going to ask one of the men in the basement to do the deed, in exchange for a share in the meat. They wouldn't be sentimental about killing an animal.'

'I thought they'd all left,' Gabriella said, remembering the flurry of activity underneath the house the day the German planes had dropped the parachutes. They rarely saw the young men who came and went at odd hours. Papa had told her and Riccardo their home was spacious enough to share with others who needed to work in the city, but it was best they never talked about the men in the cellar or the family in the attic. It was none of their business, he said.

'They come and go,' Riccardo said, turning his attention back to his drawings. 'Mama says they must be crawling through the sewers, they stink so much.'

'Why are they doing that?' She imagined the stench in the tunnels must be worse than the backstreets of Rome, where the gullys ran with putrid streams from the crowded tenements. Papa always said Naples was much worse, but she had never been to

Naples and wouldn't be able to go until this wretched war was over.

'It's so they won't be caught, stupid. Papa says they're partigiani and they'll help the Allies win the war. That's why he's letting them live in the cellars. They're the partisans and they hate the Germans and the fascists.' He bent his head once more to his work and Gabriella drew closer to get a better look.

'Maybe we could help them. Deliver messages using your special code.' She was desperate for something, anything, to relieve the boredom before Mama found some more tedious darning or cleaning for her to do. That afternoon when she'd returned from school, she'd had to beat rugs hanging on the line in the courtyard. Clouds of dust and fibres had choked her and powdered her clothes and skin, while her mother told her she had to hit harder.

Riccardo looked up. His dark brown eyes gleamed. 'Mama will never let us go anywhere near them, but we can find out what they are doing and keep a record of their activities.'

'How could we do that?' Gabriella had never entered the palazzo basement and had hardly ever seen the men up close.

'There's a place where we can listen to them. They won't be able to see us, but we can hear everything they say.' He closed his notebook and jumped up. 'Come, I'll show you.'

Gabriella followed him to his bedroom, a place she didn't normally visit. The ground-floor room was large, with glass doors that opened onto the garden, above the steps to the basement below. 'Do we have to go outside?' she asked, thinking they would easily be seen crouching by the entrance.

'No, come over here.' Riccardo pulled a chair upholstered in dark tapestry away from the wide stone fireplace, which must once have burned olive wood to warm the room during the cold, wet Florentine winters. He crouched down and squeezed himself into the large cavity.

Gabriella squatted down beside him so they were jammed tightly together in the space behind the chair. Riccardo put a finger to his lips and cupped his hand around his left ear, bending his head slightly. And then she heard it. The rhythmic pattern of male voices, rising and falling over the sound of wood on metal, the tell-tale noises of men cooking and eating.

Her brother pulled the notebook from his pocket and scribbled, then passed it to her. *If we can hear them, they can hear us.* She nodded and added a note of her own, then handed it back. *Is this the best place to listen?* He smiled and mouthed 'Yes,' then crawled out of the fireplace and beckoned to her to follow him to the far side of the room.

Gabriella stood up, dusted off her knees and joined him sitting on the side of his bed. 'Will they hear us now?' she asked, keeping her voice low.

'I don't think so, as I can't hear them clearly this far away. I sometimes hear faint sounds at night, but that's usually when they go out for hours, so the best time to listen is during the day.'

'Oh, but I have to go to school every day. I won't be able to come and listen to them.'

'Don't worry, they're mostly quiet in the daytime. I suppose if they're out all night, that's when they need to sleep. But around now, late afternoon and early evening, they're awake and they usually have a meal. Yesterday I heard them saying something about carrying a comrade through the sewers to the hospital. And the day before, I think they said they could hit the railway somewhere.'

Gabriella felt a race of excitement. This was so much more interesting than sweeping floors or beating carpets. This could be really important, but how could she be free every day? 'Mama keeps wanting me to do jobs for her. I won't be able to come and listen all the time. You'll have to do it without me.'

Riccardo saw her disappointment. 'I'll tell her you're going to teach me English. She'll let you off then. You still have your books from your school in Rome, don't you?' She nodded and he said, 'And if you can't join me sometimes, I'll put a secret note under your door so you know what's happening.'

'Not in hieroglyphics though, I hope. I'd never be able to understand it then.'

He frowned for a second, then his expression brightened as he said, 'We'll make up our own code then. A special one, just for you and me. Papa was telling me about secret messages – ciphers, they called them. You can do it by reversing the alphabet or using numbers instead of letters, all sorts of things. Even winding a message written on a long thin tape of paper around a stick.'

She listened intently, then said, 'Maybe we don't have to use the Roman alphabet. Papa once showed me how the Russians write. Their alphabet has more letters than ours. I wrote it out with the equivalent letters and sounds alongside them. I could write out a copy for you and then nobody else would be able to read it.'

Riccardo jumped off the bed and hopped up and down. 'Yes, yes, let's do it! When can you get it? We could start right away.' Gabriella joined him and they held hands, dancing round and round until they heard a shout.

Gabriella's shoulders drooped. 'Mama... She'll be wanting me to help her make a sauce or chop the vegetables. I'd better go.' She headed for the door, then turned back. 'I'll find the Russian and slip a copy under your door tonight.'

FIVE

CORNWALL

September 2019

'Shall I organise supper?' Sofia asked early that evening. She had already checked what supplies were in the house and was shocked to find the larder and fridge were not as well stocked as when her father was still alive. A dry piece of Davidstow Cheddar and a half-used pack of bacon were pretty much all there was, apart from the chilled bottles of tonic for her mother's gin.

'If you want, darling. I can't really be bothered to cook for myself these days. Thank God I don't have to make that damned spaghetti vongole all the time any more. Yet another thing I'm relieved to say is no longer my responsibility.'

'I can run down to the village for fish and chips then. That suit you?'

'I probably won't eat much of it, darling. You get some for yourself and I'll just nibble a chip or two.'

Sofia thought her mother was looking thin. All part of her anger-fuelled resentment and guilt perhaps. 'What about scampi? You've always loved scampi, haven't you? They're not too huge.'

'If you must.' Isobel poured herself a large gin and tonic with ice. 'And lots of tartar sauce,' she called out as Sofia was leaving the house.

Later, beside the crackling fire, eating from paper bags on their knees, which would never have been allowed in Riccardo's time, Sofia thought her mother seemed calmer.

'How long are you going to stay, darling?' Isobel said, finally screwing up the empty, greasy bag and tossing it into the fire. She had eaten every piece of scampi and several of Sofia's chips. 'There's a concert at St Endellion on Saturday. A young string quartet. We could go if you like.'

Sofia thought that wouldn't have been allowed in her father's time either. He liked loud operas and lots of them. 'Sounds lovely, but I think I ought to get back to London tomorrow.'

'But you've only just got here. Surely you can stay a little longer?'

Sofia shook her head. 'Not really. And actually, I want you to come back with me.'

'What on earth for? I loathe London.' She shook her head, sighing. 'I loathe here too. I need a change.'

'I'm sorry you feel that way, but I need your help. You haven't forgotten about the exhibition, surely? It's only weeks away and there's masses still to do.'

'I thought that Phoebe girl did everything. She makes enough on commission. She's in charge, surely?' Isobel swirled the drink in her glass, the ice catching the fire's light.

'Yes, she is, but she still needs our input on certain aspects. And you mustn't forget how important this show is. It's been long-awaited and there will be sales, of course. You're not going to tell me you wouldn't appreciate a little more income, are you?'

'Of course not. I just don't want to have to go to London, that's all. What does she want from us, anyway?'

Sofia took a deep breath. She knew her mother wasn't going to like this, but she plunged in. 'She needs descriptions, call them blurbs if you like, for all the paintings. She wants them for the catalogue and to display on the walls in the gallery right next to the pictures. And I think she's right. It's totally bonkers having nothing there but a number. At least a title would have given the critics and art lovers something to work with.'

Isobel threw back her head and sighed. 'It's all about him, isn't it? I feel I'm never going to be free again.'

'Mum, it's not much to ask. I can't do it on my own. Besides, maybe it would be good for you to get away from here. You said yourself you wanted a break. We could go somewhere different for lunch perhaps, somewhere Dad never went to.'

'As long as it's not Italian,' Isobel murmured. 'And I don't want to stay at the house. I want to be free of all the memories for a night or two. Book me a room in a lovely hotel.'

'If that will make you happy, I'll be happy to do that. Can you be ready to leave in the morning?' Sofia was foreseeing a tedious journey back to London if her mother was going to complain throughout.

'Of course I'll be ready, darling. You know I'm an early bird. I had to be with his demands for fresh coffee every morning before he started work. And now you're putting this on me as well. It seems I'm never going to be free of him. And I haven't even told you about his final imposition yet. Talk about last will and testament! It's too much, really it is!'

She slammed her glass on the little side table, ran across the room to the bureau and picked up a sheaf of papers. 'It's utterly ridiculous. He only went and booked a trip to Florence for this November. A whole week. He must have known he was never going to be well enough. It arrived the other day, with a note from the travel agent, saying that he specifically wanted me to go even if he was no longer here. He's booked the flights and the hotel, the whole darn thing. And he even planned the itinerary, day by blasted day! He's booked restaurants, listed the main sights and even booked tickets for the opera.' Isobel threw the documents back on the desk. 'That bloody man! He's still trying to run my life according to his ideas, even beyond the grave!'

That night Sofia lay awake, remembering her father. She was

always told she looked like him with her dark chestnut hair, but that was the only characteristic she'd inherited as she could appreciate art but not create it herself.

It was just like him, she thought, to plan a holiday without consulting Isobel. But he wouldn't think it was selfish, he'd have thought he was being considerate, thoughtful, taking care to select the best time to go, on the best flights, to stay at the best hotel. He must have known Florence intimately, so he'd have picked out the most important sights for her mother to enjoy. So why couldn't she see it that way, why did she have to keep saying he was trying to control her? Didn't she have any good memories of life with him?

Maybe we should just go, she thought. The two of us. If I can bear her protests that is. I'd love to see Florence, especially to see the highlights he'd chosen. And maybe we'd grow closer during that time. Or grow further apart if she carries on like this.

Next day, on the drive back to London, Isobel kept fiddling with the radio stations, finding nothing to her liking.

'Oh, just turn it off, Mum,' Sofia said. 'You're obviously not in the mood to concentrate on listening. And I think we should use the time to talk about this trip to Florence.'

'There's nothing to talk about, darling. I'm not going. I'm going to cancel it all and hopefully get a refund or a credit note.'

'Are you sure? If it's all booked and paid for, why don't we do it anyway? I'm sure he'd have picked the best places, you know what he was like.'

'But that's exactly why I don't want to go. Because he's chosen everything. It's like he's still here, ordering us around, telling us what to do. Isn't it enough that he did it for the whole of our marriage? I was never allowed to choose a restaurant, never permitted to book a play and certainly never an opera. He always had to be right and in control.'

'But you've got to admit, he had very good taste. And he did always choose well.'

'I suppose,' Isobel grunted, and folded her arms.

Sofia glanced at her mother. 'Have you brought the itinerary with you?'

'It's in my handbag,' she said, staring out of the side window at the passing fields of grazing sheep.

'Where's that?'

Isobel nudged the bag at her feet. 'Down here.'

'So why don't you get it out now and tell me what's in it? I'm curious and we might as well talk about it now to pass the time.'

'Oh very well, if you insist. You're beginning to sound more and more like your father.' Isobel sighed and pulled a large, crumpled envelope stuffed with papers out of her bag. 'But don't think I'm going along with this. I won't be persuaded.'

Sofia smiled to herself. She didn't mind at all being compared to her charming, persuasive father, who always got his own way with good humour and flattery. 'It's entirely up to you, Mum. But we might at least see what he arranged. It's all free if he's already paid for it.'

'Every day and practically every hour is accounted for,' Isobel grumbled. 'Oh no, I'm wrong, he's left the last day clear. Well, that's something, I suppose.' She unfolded the creased documents. 'Day One – arrive early evening, check into the Palazzo Alfieri, then dinner is booked for 8 p.m. nearby at Le Antiche Carrozze. Order the crispy octopus with garlic potato purée. Oh, for God's sake,' She rattled the papers and scrunched them on her lap. 'It goes on and on like that. This is where you go, this is what you must eat... It will be like having him dragging along with us and lecturing us all the time.'

Sofia tried not to laugh. 'I think it's rather sweet. You've got to admit, he was good company. He was never boring. Tiresome yes, but never dull.'

'Oh, I suppose so. I'll try to think of it as advice, not a command.'

'Good idea. Like a very well-informed TripAdvisor review or rather insistent tour guide. Imagine him walking in front of you with an umbrella or flag, like those group tours have.'

Isobel managed a slight chuckle. 'Knowing him, he'd want the biggest most colourful umbrella. One of those golfing jobs, all bright clashing stripes. He'd be striding ahead, rushing us to the next destination.'

'Are you saying "us" because you think we should go together?'

'No, I'm not being literal, darling, but I am thinking about it. However, when you see the detail that's involved in this timetable, you'll understand. He's told us when to visit the Duomo, where to buy ice cream, which route to take to the public gardens and to the market. He's included the station and – you'll never believe this bit – he's booked tickets for the Uffizi Gallery and specified which works of art have to be seen! Isn't that simply incredible! I don't think we'd dare deviate from his plan for a moment.'

'We could do the ones he picked out and then have a detour – see some others, perhaps?'

'As long as it doesn't make us late for everything else he's booked.' Isobel began laughing, a laugh that deteriorated into hysterical sobs.

Sofia took one hand off the steering wheel to pat her mother's arm. 'Don't get yourself in a state about it. We don't have to do it, but I think it would be interesting. Let's talk again when you've had a good night's sleep.'

MESSAGE ONE

Daed si bmal eht

SIX

FLORENCE

24 September 1943

Boys can be so annoying, Gabriella thought when she went into her bedroom after school that day. Two pieces of paper had been pushed under her door. Riccardo had obviously been listening more than once while she was stuck in her lessons.

She unfolded the notes and began to slowly sound out the Cyrillic letters as she tried to decipher the code she had suggested. It wasn't as easy as she had imagined, but she was fairly sure it said, '*They are going to rescue someone tonight and bring them back through the sewers.*' She felt her heart racing with excitement. This was better than she'd thought it would be.

The second one had scratchings-out, as if he wasn't sure he'd heard correctly and had to try again to write it down. It seemed to say, '*It must be tonight. No one survives the Villa Triste.*' She puzzled over this. Villa Triste? That meant the Sad Villa. Who would give a building such a strange name?

Then she heard Mama calling, 'Gabriella, are you back? I need you.' She stuffed the notes in the pocket of her skirt, left her school bag on the bed and went to the kitchen, where her mother was smiling. 'You'll be pleased with this,' she said, holding up a small bag of flour. 'Just this once, we can make pasta and you can choose what kind.'

'Tortellini, please.' Gabriella grabbed her apron, washed her hands, then stopped. 'But what can we put inside them? Do we have a filling?'

'I think we can spare a small pumpkin. I will prepare that while you are making the pasta.' Her mother poured half the flour onto the marble counter, made a well in the little pile shaped like a white volcano, added a beaten egg, then showed her daughter how to lightly mix the dough with her hands. When it was bound together, she told Gabriella to let it sit on the countertop for a while so they could finish making the filling: 'We want the dough to cool before we roll it out and the pumpkin must cool too before we fill the tortellini.'

The marble work surface was cold to the touch, but the kitchen was hot because of the cast-iron stove. 'Run outside and fetch me some sage leaves from the herb garden. You know which plant I mean? If you are not sure, smell it. You cannot mistake the scent.'

Although it was late afternoon in early autumn, the September sun still warmed their days. The herbs grew in the enclosed court-yard in a raised bed. There was rosemary, fennel, thyme and plenty of sage. She recognised the woolly, grey and purple leaves, but just to be certain she bent to crush a leaf in her fingers. The smell reminded her of lamb's liver served with a garnish of fried sage leaves and tender saltimbocca moistened with butter.

She picked eight leaves, hoping that would be enough, then peered through the archway at the open garden where the path was lined with pencil-thin cypress trees. The lamb was usually on his feet again by this time of day, having spent much of the hotter hours panting in the shade. She couldn't see him immediately, so she stepped through the arch onto the gravel path, her feet crunching the stones. He wasn't lying in the shaded side of the garden, nor beneath the trees. The grass was mostly short and wiry, but some longer shoots were beginning to emerge near the spring that trickled from the spout in the wall into a channel that ran around the garden. That was where he often found a few blades of new grass, but she could not see him – and then she saw the flies buzzing. She went closer. There, under the walnut tree that spread its branches over the grass, was a dark patch of moisture, that was what had attracted them.

Gabriella ran back indoors, clutching the sage. 'Where's the lamb? He's not there.'

'No, dear, he's gone.' Mama turned to her with a smile. 'But you'll be seeing him again very soon.'

'Soon? Why?'

'You like lamb, don't you, dear?'

'Yes, but...'

'Then soon you'll be glad he has gone and will be coming back to feed us all. We shall eat very well, very soon.'

'You mean you've killed him?'

'Not me, dear. I enlisted help. It was done today. We couldn't wait much longer. Even though the grass may have grown a little, we could never have found enough to feed him properly.'

Gabriella looked at the leaves clutched in her hand. The bruised sage emitted a strong scent and she was reminded once again of one of her favourite dishes. 'Will we have lamb's liver? With sage leaves?'

'I'm afraid not, dear,' her mother said with a shake of her head. 'That's how I was able to get the flour today. Our lamb is more than simply meat on the table. He is currency as well, in these difficult times of bartering to survive. I have a woman coming tomorrow to make salami – or as near as we can make it with the spices I still have. She will then take a good portion and in exchange she is bringing me peppers and artichokes in oil and dried tomatoes. That will be a great help to us, come the winter.'

'Lamb salami?'

Mama laughed. 'It can be made from any meat. I know pork is the most common, but you may be glad of it and may prefer it to donkey or horse, which is all they can get in some towns these days.'

Gabriella turned away in disappointment. She had missed all the excitement today then. The slaughter of the lamb, the departure of the liver and the overheard conversation in the basement. There was much to discuss with Riccardo.

After helping her mother roll out the thin pasta, then stuff and pinch the little parcels of tortellini, Gabriella went to find her brother. He was not in his room, as she had expected. She searched everywhere, then returned to the kitchen. 'I can't find Riccardo. Has he gone out?'

'No, my dear. He is painting in the chapel.' Her mother looked a little distressed. 'Unfortunately, he was there when the lamb was slaughtered. He shouldn't have been, but he is always so curious. I knew it would upset him. He is such a sensitive boy. He's on the stairs leading to the bell tower. I'm letting him use my paints.'

Gabriella ran off through the cloistered walk that linked the palazzo to the chapel, which her father had told her had been built centuries before. It was so quiet and her steps echoed on the flagstones as she entered. 'Riccardo,' she called out, 'where are you?'

Her mother had said the stairs, but she wasn't sure exactly where that was. Crossing the mosaic floor inside the chapel, she saw an arched door, partially open. She peered through and saw a winding staircase and, only a few steps above, bare brown legs, one sturdy, one shortened and weaker. He was standing on a box, silently painting an image in an alcove in the thick wall.

She went closer, a step at a time. He must have heard her approaching, for after a moment, without turning away from his work, he said, 'They told me it wouldn't hurt him.'

She stood on the step below him, looking up at what he had painted so far. He had sketched an outline of the creature, lying on its side, the garden's avenue of trees stretching behind. 'I saw the blood, in the garden,' she said. 'Was there lots of blood?'

He turned to look at her, brush in hand, his face was strained. She thought he must have cried earlier as his eyes were red. 'They didn't let it bleed much outside. Mama said they had to collect the blood for the *buristo* she is making tomorrow. I've already told her I won't eat it.'

Gabriella wondered for a moment about the *buristo*, then realised it was the salami her mother had mentioned. Not salami, but blood sausage. She'd seen it sometimes when she and her father had visited the *salumeria* to buy her favourite mortadella, the bulbous grey *buristo* looking unappetising compared to the other dark red sausages and pink hams wrapped in nets hanging on hooks from the ceiling. 'I'm not sure I want it either.' She paused and looked again at the picture he was creating. 'Do you think the lamb was frightened?'

'It was very quick. They came from behind and cut his throat. He never saw them, he was looking at me when they did it.'

'Who's them?'

'Two of the men from the basement. One held him down and the other held the knife. It was over in a second.'

'I wish I'd been here to see it.'

'No, you don't. He'd become our pet. If we were farmers and had many sheep, we would never have befriended him the way we did.' Riccardo sighed and hung his head. 'I didn't think I'd mind, but I did. It wasn't like swatting a wasp or killing a mouse. He looked at me with such trust, just before they cut his throat.'

'Is that why you're painting him?'

'I don't know. I think I want to remember how it felt, seeing it happen. I'm not good at writing essays, but I can draw and paint. Mama said I could do what I liked. And it is not an inappropriate image to have in a chapel – after all, Jesus was the Lamb of God – so it will seem like a holy image perhaps to others.'

'You're very good at art. Is that what you're going to do when you're grown up?'

He turned back to look at his work, then stepped down from his box and stood back. 'I think I will always want to paint the thoughts in my head. And Papa says if a man doesn't have to grow his own food for the table, then he should do whatever he's best at.'

'I don't know what I'm best at yet. I can't draw like you and Mama and I'm not good at history like Papa.'

'You're good at studying, like him. Perhaps you will study history and help Papa at the Museo.' Riccardo wiped his brush on a rag and laid it down beside the other brushes and some tubes of paint.

'Aren't you going to do any more?'

'Tomorrow. The paint has to dry now. It will take several days for me to finish it, but I can do it whenever I'm free. Let's go to my room and do some more listening.'

'I read the notes you left. The men are going to be very busy tonight.'

He looked serious and said, 'They're involved in very dangerous work. We must make sure our notes don't fall into the wrong hands.'

'Don't worry, I've hidden them at the back of my English textbook.'

Riccardo smiled. 'I knew you were good at something else. You're good at keeping secrets.' Then he began running, with his lopsided gait, all the way to his bedroom with Gabriella behind him. They ran through the door, slammed it shut, then fell onto the bed, panting and laughing.

Gabriella sat up and listened. 'I can't hear anything, can you?'

'They're probably still sleeping after disturbing their rest to deal with the lamb earlier today. They'll be awake soon, I'm sure.' Riccardo hopped off the bed and picked up a notebook. 'I'm keeping a diary too of everything we find out.'

'Is it in our code?'

'No, that's too difficult for me to do quickly. I've done it by writing the words back to front. It's a very simple cipher and could be easily broken, but at first glance it still looks like nonsense.'

'Let me see,' she said, holding out her hand. His writing was tiny but she could decipher it quite quickly, and recognised his brief account of earlier conversations. 'You must keep this hidden too.'

'I'm going to. I have a good hiding place.' He went over to the fireplace, bent down and reached up inside the chimney. 'Up here, there's a hollow space. It won't be found here.'

'What if you have a fire?'

'I doubt I'll be allowed one this winter. Mama says we shall all be cold this year. It's becoming difficult to get hold of wood. We'll only have a fire in the kitchen, in the woodstove.' He stood up, notebook in hand, then smiled and said, 'We are spies, Gaby. *Agente segreti.*'

She laughed at his description of their game and, at that moment, they heard the sounds of movement below them. The men were awake and soon they heard the clattering of pans as food was prepared, overlaying the murmurs of conversation. The children stooped to crouch in the fireplace, Riccardo ready to write down anything of significance. Then after a few minutes a delicious, familiar smell seeped up the chimney and into the fireplace. Gabriella recognised the aroma. The men were preparing her favourite dish: lamb's liver with sage.

SEVEN

LONDON

September 2019

The hotel Sofia had chosen was tucked behind Oxford Street, a short walk from the Firenze Gallery. Her mother was tired after their drive from Cornwall, so they agreed they would meet again for a late breakfast before tackling the subject of the exhibition.

'I hope you slept well last night,' Sofia said when she joined Isobel at the breakfast table the next day. Her mother was crumbling a dry croissant in her fingers.

'Oh, I don't sleep well these days at all. I thought it might be better, away from home where I wake thinking I can hear your father going out to his studio at some ungodly hour, the way he always used to. But it was just as bad last night. And London is so noisy. Bins and deliveries were clattering around at 5 a.m. just as I finally dropped off.'

'Sorry to hear that,' Sofia said, thinking she'd help herself to a large cooked breakfast at the buffet. She'd left the house in Kentish Town early without eating. When she returned to the table, Isobel was folding her napkin and finishing her coffee. 'Aren't you going to have anything else?'

She shook her head. 'I couldn't possibly. I'm feeling so tense this morning. It's the thought of this gallery, that Phoebe woman and having to look at his pictures all over again. I just want to get it over with as soon as we possibly can.'

'It might not be that quick. I don't think we can make up the blurb on the spot, but I'm sure once we get there you'll feel better. You want to help me write the descriptions, don't you?'

Isobel shrugged. 'Oh, what do I care? I won't be any use to you, darling. I've simply no idea what his paintings are about. He never talked to me about them, not once in all our years together. He just did them.'

'Didn't you ever ask him to explain? Ever ask him why they weren't titled?'

'Oh, very early on perhaps. All he ever said was he couldn't find the words to express his thoughts. He told me that's why he always had to paint what was in his head.'

Sofia was struggling to finish the food she had piled onto her plate. The scrambled eggs were dry and the bacon too fatty. 'But that doesn't mean we shouldn't attempt to analyse what he was trying to say in the paintings. The art critics have tried many times, haven't they?'

Isobel laughed. 'Tried and failed, darling. He used to think it was enormously funny. Look at this, he'd say – Waldemar thinks Number Twenty expresses the inner conflict of the artist at odds with the modern world!'

'But we've got to have a go. It will really help to add meaning to the exhibition. And the dates they were painted will help, surely? You might be able to tell me what was going on at the time and it could be relevant.'

'I'm not sure his work had any bearing on current events, darling. I think it was totally introspective. But we'll see.' Isobel dabbed at the corners of her lips with her napkin and laid it down.

Sofia pushed her plate away and stood up. 'But the year I was born, that's when he did his version of the Nativity, isn't it? That's about the only painting of his that is easy to understand, even though it's also full of his usual symbolism.'

'He was so afraid,' Isobel said. 'Such a difficult birth. You were dragged out of me protesting and I needed a transfusion. He thought he was going to lose us both.' She tried to smile, but it was faint and ineffectual. 'So the only time he related his work to us, to his life now, was when he thought he'd lose everything.' She gave a suggestion of a laugh. 'You could call it "The Madonna with the Bleeding Breasts".'

'Isobel, Sofia, so pleased you could both come today.' Phoebe waved her hands around the light space of the gallery. 'What do you think? Impressive, isn't it?' The paintings were spaced well apart, giving viewers room to stand and absorb their complexity. 'Shall we start?' She held out two clipboards, each bearing a list of the exhibits, with stamp-sized pictures and white space for notes. 'I thought we could jot down thoughts as we go round, if that's alright with you?'

'Fine.' Isobel shrugged. 'Whatever you want.'

Phoebe didn't seem to register her reluctance, but Sofia covered for her anyway, saying, 'It's a been a lot for Mum to take in, what with dealing with the solicitors and so on. We'll take a break if it gets too tiring.'

'Of course, you set the pace. I'll follow you,' Phoebe said and they moved to the first painting. 'They're not in numerical order, so this is Number Twenty-Five, painted in 1975.'

'I know that,' Isobel snapped. 'He was obsessed with bridges. This one, and about five after this, are all about bloody bridges.'

'Do you think perhaps he was referring to his birthplace? Could this be an evocation of his memories of Florence, maybe a bridge between the past and the present?' Phoebe's pen hovered above the clipboard and she began scribbling notes.

Isobel snorted. 'You can say whatever you like. Fact is, I don't bloody know. He never explained any of them. Kept it all to himself.'

'I think what my mother means,' Sofia said, 'is that we might be able to pinpoint events and possibly identify certain subjects, but we are going to have to rely on our own interpretations of the pictures. Maybe we can just take notes for now and work on the actual wording of the captions later, when we've had time to think about them?'

They worked their way through the first room, jotting down thoughts and suggestions, mostly from Sofia, while her mother sighed and looked bored. Then Phoebe's phone buzzed in her pocket. 'Sorry,' she said, looking at the message. 'I've got to leave you for a bit. I'll be back soon as,' and she marched off towards her office.

'Are you feeling alright?' Sofia asked, seeing her mother drooping. 'We can take a break for a bit.'

'I need to get outside for a while. Can we go somewhere for coffee? This is all a bit too much for me.'

They left Phoebe a message and walked through a nearby alleyway to a café bathed in September sun and sat outside. 'You don't have to do this if you really don't want to,' Sofia said. 'I can probably manage on my own. Do you want to go back to the hotel and lie down for an hour?'

'I might just do that, darling. Let's have lunch together though when we're finished. Just as long as it's not Italian and it's not with Phoebe.'

'Okay. We'll walk across to Chinatown – that dim sum place.'

'I'd like that, and then I might wander down to Berwick Street and treat myself to a lovely length of silk, perhaps.'

'Good idea.' Sofia drained her coffee cup. 'Oh, and there's one other thing Phoebe asked me the other day. She wants to know where Number Sixteen is. She doesn't have a record of it anywhere. Do you have any idea? It's not one you've kept in Cornwall, is it?'

Isobel shook her head. 'No, I've got the Nativity painting, as you know. That's Number Thirty-Five. And I've also kept Number Thirty-Two because that was painted the year we married. But I don't think I've ever seen a Number Sixteen. Maybe he never did one, darling. Maybe he lost count.' She gave a slightly hysterical laugh. 'He'd think we were all mad, trying to interpret his strange pictures. If he'd ever really wanted us to understand them, he'd have made sure we had all the information. There'd be typed descriptions on the back or in files somewhere. You know how he had to control everything. The simple answer is, he never wanted to explain his work. He wanted to be bloody mysterious and not at all helpful!'

EIGHT

FLORENCE

25 September 1943

Mama was flustered. 'I can't prepare supper tonight, I'm needed upstairs. Gabriella, you will have to finish the cooking for me.' She turned to her husband. 'And you must stay down here in case any patrols come round tonight. A raid is the last thing that family needs. All this too, on top of the day we've had.' Allied planes had bombed the north of the city earlier in the day, killing a large number of civilians. 'They made a pact not to destroy our city and now this.' She rushed away with a jug of hot water, a bowl and towels.

Gabriella had no idea what Mama was talking about, but she looked at the half-made gnocchi. Some were already formed into neat pillows, the rest had yet to be shaped. She could do that and if her mother didn't return soon, she could find the ingredients for a sauce as well. Tomatoes perhaps or a simple pesto, maybe broccoli if there was some in the larder.

She began forming the long thin rolls to make the potato dumplings, then Mama rushed back in again with two little children. 'Gaby, I want you to look after Sara and Nathan for me. Signora Giardino is having her baby upstairs and it's best the children stay with you for now.' She pushed the pair towards her daughter, then disappeared.

Gabriella had hardly seen anything of them before. The family had moved into the stifling attic in the early part of the summer and seldom left their cramped quarters, coming downstairs only in the cool of the evening to walk around the palazzo grounds out of sight of the other occupants. She slid from her stool, wiped her hands on her apron and said, 'Would you like to come outside with me, into the garden?'

The children both nodded and held hands as they followed her into the courtyard, still warm from the day and fragrant with the scent of rosemary and lavender. The last few figs hung ripe and purple from the tree, so Gabriella picked two, wondering if there would be enough to take later for her greedy school friends. 'Do you like figs? You can have these to eat when we've had a game in the garden.' Then she took one more for herself and put the fruit in the pocket of her apron.

Walking through the courtyard door and out into the tree-lined expanse of the main garden, she found the ball that Riccardo had been kicking around earlier. She took off her apron and laid it down carefully so the fruit would not get squashed, then tossed the ball in the air. Nathan chased after it and Sara followed and soon they were liberated, giggling and breathless, like normal children, not frightened rabbits rarely released from their secret burrow.

When they tired of running, Gabriella thought of another game: 'Let's play hide-and-seek. You two hide and I'll come looking for you. I'll count to a hundred.' She knelt down, covered her eyes and began to count. She could hear giggles and scampering feet, but soon all was quiet. 'I'm coming!' she called out and looked around the garden. They were nowhere to be seen and the light was beginning to fade, making dark, shadowy shapes all around.

She looked behind every tree and bush in the main garden, then under the benches and tables dotted around to catch the shade in the height of summer. She couldn't see either of them anywhere and began to worry that she hadn't looked after the children as well as her mother had expected. So finally, she began calling for them: 'Nathan, Sara, where are you?' Faint, muffled laughter reached her ears and she stood still, trying to locate the sound, then traced it to the wall around the courtyard.

Next to the arching fig tree was an alcove in the wall, where perhaps a small statue or trickling fountain had once stood. In the shadows she could barely see them, but the children were there, curled tightly together, huddling into the stone, their pale faces hidden but emitting smothered laughter. 'There you are!' she said, joining in with laughter of her own. 'But you hid together and not separately. I certainly didn't expect that.'

'Mama says we must always stay together,' Nathan said. 'We must never be parted.'

'We're twins,' Sara explained. 'Mama says we arrived together.'

'But I'm a bit older,' Nathan said, pushing his sister.

'Only by two minutes,' she retorted.

'You hid yourselves very well. I'd never have found you with the light fading. Now come and help me find the figs. I can't quite remember where I left them.'

The children ran ahead and shouted when they spotted the white apron gleaming in the dusk. They all sat on the grass to eat the ripe fruit, oozing juice and sweetness, and Gabriella said, 'You're very good at hiding. Have you been playing hide-and-seek a lot?'

Sara looked at her brother and said, 'Mama and Papa have made us practise hiding a few times. We have special places here and where we lived before.'

'She says we must be very quiet when we hide,' Nathan said, adding in a squeaky little voice, 'Like tiny mice, not a sound. We curl up very, very small.'

'But you weren't quiet when I called, were you? I heard you laughing and that's how I found you in the end. I don't think I could ever have found you if you'd stayed silent, so why did you laugh?'

'Because you're not German,' Sara said. 'We don't want the German soldiers to ever, ever find us.'

Gabriella was trying to digest this information when suddenly they heard a cry, a baby's piercing, angry wail, ringing out from the house. The children jumped up. 'Mama said we could go to her when we heard the baby cry,' Nathan said and they both ran inside.

As Gabriella followed, she hovered by the half-made gnocchi for a second, but then decided to run after the children, up the stairs all the way to the attic. At the top of the flight of steps, she saw Signor Giardino proudly holding a bundle and bending down low so his older children could see the puzzled red face. 'Meet your little brother,' he said. 'We shall name him Izaak.'

NINE

FLORENCE

27 October 1943

'Move up, Ginger Roman,' Franca said, plonking herself down on the low cloister wall at lunchtime and peering into Gabriella's small package of food. All around them, girls were gossiping, eating their lunches and giggling.

Tina pushed herself into a small gap on the other side of Gabriella, knocking a neighbouring girl with her elbow so her lunch fell off her lap. 'Oopsadaisy,' said Tina, watching the girl get up and scrabble on the paving to collect her scraps of cheese and ham. 'Nothing there worth having.' The girl walked away from her tormentors and Gabriella noticed Stefanina, the only girl not afraid of challenging the sisters, patting a space beside her on the wall and putting a comforting arm around the upset schoolgirl. But Tina was oblivious to Stefanina's darting glare of disapproval as she settled herself.

'You haven't got much today,' Franca said, after looking through the parcel then pushing it back into Gabriella's lap. 'Are they starving you?'

'No, there just wasn't much I could bring today.' She thought of the sparse supper they'd had the night before. Now the flour had run out, there was no pasta or gnocchi. They'd had to make do with polenta and greens seasoned with oil and garlic. Mama was rationing the *buristo* carefully, even though no one really enjoyed it. The cured meat was hung out of reach in the cool larder and, once it was sliced, her mother locked it under cover on a marble shelf. There was no way she could sneak anything like that out of the house.

'I might be able to get some artichokes or tomatoes next time,' she said. The vegetables were preserved in olive oil and although it would be messy, she thought if she made sure they weren't dripping in oil she could manage to wrap one or two in paper and a napkin. Hopefully they wouldn't make telltale stains in her pocket or her school bag.

'If you like,' Franca said. 'But we get plenty of those and lots of bread.' She was a solid girl, looking larger and more well-fed by the day.

'We had chicken last night,' Tina said. 'And our cook made lots of risotto, so we have arancini today as well as ham. Do you want one?' She offered Gabriella a golden bread-crumbed ball that she had already bitten into.

Even though the morsel was cold, it was still delicious. Gabriella nibbled the crisp crumb coating the creamy rice flavoured with strong Parmesan. She ate it slowly, bit by tiny bit, thinking it was a long time since she'd had risotto as rice was in short supply too.

'Have another one,' Franca said. 'I don't want all of mine.' She started to hand over an untouched arancini ball, then retracted the offering. 'What do you say, Roman?'

'Th-thank you,' Gabriella stuttered, holding out her hand.

'There you go then. You stick with us and you might get more where that came from.'

'We should take her home,' Tina said. 'Our little ginger pusscat needs feeding up and we've always got lots of food to spare.'

'Aren't your parents finding it difficult to get supplies?'

Gabriella asked. 'We haven't got any more flour at the moment, so we can't have pasta.'

'Poppa has his sources,' Franca said. 'He's in favour because he's doing such important work. We'll never go short of food.'

'What kind of work does he do?' Gabriella asked, thinking of Uncle Federico's knowledge of art history, which had taken him away to do something very important. Her father, as a museum curator, had detailed knowledge of the artefacts he exhibited, but his job brought them little extra food.

'Ridding the city of undesirables. You know, partisans, rebels, Jews,' Tina said.

'He has lots of help,' Franca said. 'Men are loyal to him and willing to work hard to clean up Florence as well as the rest of Italy. Poppa says his men are saints.'

'He works long hours and sometimes has to bring his work home with him, doesn't he, Franca?' Then Tina giggled, looking at her sister as if they shared a naughty secret.

'Won't your mother mind if you bring a friend home?'

'No, she wouldn't care. Anyway, she's not here. She's staying with our aunt in the mountains. Poppa has to go there some of the time, so she keeps the house ready for him. But there's no school there, so we must stay in Florence. Besides, it's so boring up there. Just goats and sheep. No one to talk to. Nothing exciting to see, like here.'

'Do you want to come back with us today?' Tina said.

Gabriella shook her head. 'I'd like to, but my mother will be coming to meet me after school. I'll have to ask her if I can go another time. Maybe tomorrow?'

'We'll see.' Tina shrugged. 'Should be okay.'

'Tomorrow might be more interesting,' Franca said with a knowing look at her sister. 'Poppa doesn't have many special guests at present.'

Tina giggled again and stood up. 'And tell your mother we will walk you home afterwards.'

'Will your father allow you out on the street in the evening?'

'Of course. He will tell Bruno to walk with us. We'll all be quite safe, no one would dare approach us.'

'My mother will also want to know where you live. She's very strict with me.'

'Poppa has a suite at the Hotel Savoy in the Piazza della Republica,' Franca said.

'Where the fairground is?' Gabriella was impressed. She longed to be allowed to ride the gaudy carousel, the rotatoria, but Mama said it attracted undesirable elements and climbing onto the revolving gilded horses was unladylike. They sometimes passed it, its tunes spilling out across the vast square where the Germans patrolled and rode on the merry-go-round when they were off duty.

'That's right. But we always have dinner at Villa Triste, on Via Bolognese. It's more interesting there, especially when Poppa is working.'

'And who is Bruno?' she asked, as her mother was sure to demand every detail before allowing her daughter out of her sight.

'Our cousin from Sicily,' Franca said. 'He's very handsome and very funny. He's allowed to escort us when we have to go out alone, if he isn't working.'

Villa Triste. The Sad Villa. Gabriella had heard that name before. She wondered how it had come to be called that. Why was it sad? Perhaps she would find out when she went there, if Mama would permit her to visit with her two new friends.

TEN

LONDON

12 September 2019

Sofia was somewhat relieved when Isobel agreed to take the train back to Cornwall. 'I've rung Mick's Taxis in the village, darling, and told him to meet me off the four thirty at Bodmin Parkway. That way, I'll be home well before six. I don't want you driving all the way there and back again, getting stuck in the traffic around Stonehenge as always.'

'If you're sure. And are you quite certain you don't want to help me with these captions any more?' Sofia had made a start but Isobel had shown no interest.

'You're perfectly capable of doing it all on your own, darling. You always did understand his way of thinking. Sometimes I thought you knew him better than I did. Real daddy's girl, weren't you?'

Sofia decided not to rise to this. Isobel had always implied that they had a specially close relationship and that she was envious of their bond. 'I'll do my best to make the descriptions meaningful and interesting, but I shan't be offended if you change your mind. I'll send you my drafts when I've finished. But don't leave it too late though, Phoebe needs to get the brochure and the captions printed.'

'I know, darling, I know. But I promise you, I have no desire to try and interpret his unfathomable pictures. You can say whatever you like.' She glanced at the departures board in the busy station, then gave her daughter a quick peck on the cheek. 'That's me, Platform Six. Don't hang about now, you get back to that gallery and start work.'

Sofia watched her mother's sprightly step as she trotted across to her waiting train, handbag on her shoulder, overnight bag with magazines, book and a prawn sandwich hooked over her arm. She felt the huge burden of responsibility for making the exhibition a success weigh heavily upon her and decided to start work immediately at home rather than in the gallery.

Back in Kentish Town, she thought she should have lunch before settling down to the difficult task of inventing a creative provenance for all the paintings. She'd joined her mother for breakfast at the hotel, but hadn't had much of an appetite so had only eaten fruit and yogurt. That was a mistake, she told herself as she peered into her almost-empty fridge. It would have to be cheese on toast again and a packet soup. The pine country-style kitchen, which had not been modernised in all the years her parents had lived there, was cold even though autumn had barely begun. But a patch of sun was glinting on the terrace outside, so she took her unimaginative lunch there to sit and think.

The late-Victorian end of terrace house was tall and thin, spread over five floors from basement to attic studio, and the garden echoed it, being long and narrow. At the far end was a rickety summerhouse where she had played as a child and where at one time her rabbit Bubbles had slept at night, safe from the local foxes. Her parents had never been active gardeners, but Sofia had slowly tamed the jungle since returning to live here after university, learning much herself and employing Jason once a month to prune, mow and tidy. But still tendrils of honeysuckle raced over neighbouring fences and lacy ferns and dark viburnum flourished in the mostly shaded garden, where ripe pears were now dropping from the solitary fruit tree laced with a scented rose.

Once her parents had established themselves permanently in Cornwall, she had shared the house with various friends and it had resulted in the relationship with Ed, which had fizzled out when her ill father needed more of her attention. But the house held more good memories than sad ones and she was content to stay until she knew more about her mother's plans.

Riccardo's studio was at the very top of the house, where one of the few modifications – Velux windows – had been inserted years previously to admit the light he needed to paint. Sofia climbed the flights of stairs and opened the door. It smelt of paint, turps and dust. The cool north light her father favoured filled the airy space where he had once spent the majority of his time, leaving the room only for snacks, loo breaks and sleep. When the daylight vanished, he often stayed up here for hours, contemplating a new canvas, making rough sketches for another composition, or sometimes simply lying on the wrinkled Chesterfield sofa with his eyes closed. If she ventured in when she was young, to find him lying there, he would pretend to be asleep, then suddenly startle her with a loud 'Boo!', making her squeal with delight.

The memory of his playfulness made her smile. He'd chase her around the sofa, then grab her and tip her upside down, and when she was upright again, she'd finger the ear lobe that was shorter than the other one, its ragged edge hard to the touch. She'd ask him why it was like that and once he'd said it was what happened to naughty boys and another time he said, 'I thought I was going to be a pirate when I grew up, but I turned into an artist instead.' And then she remembered how, if she had crept upstairs to see him, their games would be interrupted by her mother shouting from the floors below that it was time for tea, for a bath or to do her piano practice.

There must be something here, she thought, *that will give me some clues*. This was where the majority of his paintings had been produced. Some early ones had been brought from his home city of Florence and a few had begun life when he was teaching at the art school in Putney, where he had met her mother. But most had been created here, with a view of the grey rooftops, dusty lime trees and railway lines of Kentish Town. Hardly an inspiring sight and certainly not the subject of his richly populated canvases.

She turned her attention to the workbench that he used rather than a desk. A much-planed butcher's block, it was solid and rough, workmanlike, littered with papers, brushes and creased tubes of paint. She began sorting through the sketches and pads, hoping for clues that she could relate to specific pictures. Here and there she found a hasty life study, done to check the angle of a knee, the inflection of a head, the curve of a shoulder blade. On some of his drawings he'd scribbled a note on tone or colour, on others the name of the model or the date of the sitting.

But she couldn't relate any of this to the completed paintings. He never took photographs or carried a sketchbook in his pocket, and his finished pictures appeared to be unrelated to any of the material here. 'Oh, for goodness' sake,' she muttered. 'Couldn't you have kept a diary, made notes in your sketchbooks, anything, to give me even a tiny hint of what they meant? Every other artist did, from Leonardo to Rembrandt, so why didn't you?' She brushed all the papers to one side. None of them could help her. It seemed to Sofia that his paintings had largely emanated from whatever nightmares his brain had concocted. They were embedded in his memories and were extracted one thread at a time then woven into these bizarre creations of unrelated images.

She slumped onto the battered sofa, so old and so worn that the seat cushions had split, revealing hessian lining and wisps of horse-hair stuffing. 'I'm doing this out of respect for you and your work, Dad,' she whispered. 'You've got to help me.'

And then, as she idly picked at the coarse hairs protruding from the couch, she realised. He *was* helping. Florence, the city of his birth. The place where it all began. He'd told her often enough, hadn't he? 'My mother said I had always drawn and painted, even when I was very young. And by the time I was eleven, she was giving me the run of her studio.'

Of course – it was obvious. She had to start at the beginning, where he had learnt to paint and where perhaps the ideas that permeated a lifetime's work had started. She had to persuade her mother that they should go to Florence together. And then she groaned. The exhibition was barely three weeks away and his Florentine itinerary didn't start till November. There was no time to go now; she'd just have to write whatever she could and hope it didn't make a nonsense of all the work that was going on show in the exhibition.

Damn you, she said to herself, shaking her head. Why couldn't you have arranged this trip earlier? In fact, why didn't you just tell us about the pictures while you were still here, you arrogant bastard?

Then she paced up and down. It was getting late, the northern sky patterned with a fringe of pink and gold cast by the setting sun. You're not going to get away with this, she thought. I'm going to give Phoebe some ridiculous explanations just to get her off my back and then I'm going to Florence. I'm going to dig and dig, until I find out what you've been trying to tell us and the world all these years. You won't be able to hide yourself any more after that, will you?

ELEVEN

FLORENCE

30 October 1943

Gabriella didn't think she had ever seen such an abundance of food. The table was spread with platters of salami of every variety, olives, burrata and other cheeses, dishes of pappardelle with a rich ragù, chicken cooked in butter and succulent steak alla Fiorentina cut into strips. There was a dish of buttered gnocchi dotted with shavings of truffle as well, but Gabriella thought she'd had enough gnocchi for one lifetime.

'Is all this for us?' she dared to ask in a whisper.

'Course not,' Tina said. 'Tonight, Poppa and his men will eat here as well. But we're here first, so we can grab a share before they start. Go on, have whatever you want.'

Gabriella tentatively put a small spoonful of the meaty pasta on her plate, then a slice of steak and a little chicken.

'Have more than that,' Franca said, reaching across for a large spoonful of gnocchi for herself. 'The men won't leave anything for us, so take as much as you can.' She balanced large chunks of crusty focaccia on top of the pile of food, its oiled crust sparkling with crystals of rock salt.

'And don't forget there's dessert too,' Tina said, dropping a large crisp cannoli shell filled with cream cheese and studded with chopped pistachios on top of Gabriella's plate, along with a slice of schiacciata alla Fiorentina, the lemon-scented cake sandwiched with cream that had once been available in every respectable bakery in Florence.

Gabriella gasped at the enormous plate of food she was holding. Although she was hungry and her mouth was watering at the sight, she felt guilty too. Ordinary families thought themselves lucky to have boring polenta and greens day after day, while some were lucky to have even that. And what were Riccardo and her parents going to eat tonight? Would Mama allow them to have a little of the lamb salami?

'Come on,' Franca said, leading the way to a small anteroom through an archway off the dining room. 'We always eat in here, out of their way. They'll be coming in soon.' She pulled a curtain across the entrance, rattling the rings on its pole, and they heard male voices coming closer.

The girls hunched with their plates on their knees, sitting on dainty armchairs of pale blue watered silk with gilded frames. Once the setting for important meetings and glasses of frosted Campari garlanded with orange slices, the anteroom was now dingy, the suite stained, the upholstery ripped, baring tufts of stuffing. They could hear the men's loud conversation and Gabriella caught snatches she couldn't understand: *'Not meeting... target... more in hiding... He'll talk soon... No need for more...'*

She didn't ask questions and the two sisters didn't talk either as they were busy stuffing their mouths with food, barely pausing for breath. While their heads were lowered over their plates, she pushed the sponge cake and a piece of bread into the pocket of her skirt. She knew she would struggle to eat everything on her plate and she couldn't bear to waste such delicious food when she knew Riccardo would be eating so poorly.

Finally, the girls paused and put their plates on the delicate gilded table before them with a clatter of forks. 'Oof, I can't eat another thing,' Franca groaned. She glanced at Gabriella's uncleared dish, which still contained some ham, cheese and focaccia. 'Aren't you going to finish it?'

'It's too much for me. I'm not used to eating such a lot. Maybe I should put it back?'

'You can't do that,' Tina said. 'Poppa won't like it. But you can take it home if you like. Or,' she said, glancing at her sister with a mischievous look, 'we could save it for our guests.'

Gabriella looked at her with curiosity. Were people staying here and not at the hotel?

'Not tonight,' Franca said. 'It's too soon. You know what Poppa says: we have to be careful.' She stretched and yawned. 'Here, take it with you,' she said, wrapping the remains of the meal in a napkin and handing it to Gabriella. 'We'd better take this little Roman home now, don't you think?' She stood and stretched again, her school blouse straining over her fully-grown breasts. 'Come on, let's find Bruno.'

As they emerged from the hidden room, all heads turned towards the three girls. 'Aah, here are my piccoli angeli. Come here, cari.' A large swarthy man at the head of the dining table opened his arms wide to welcome his daughters and hugged them close. 'And who is your little red-haired amica?'

'This is Gabriella, from school. We think she needs feeding up. Don't you?' Tina pulled her friend closer, so her father could take her hand and stroke it in his big, meaty fist.

'Dear child, you are most welcome to eat with us,' he said. 'Our table always has plenty and Tina is right. My, you have such a tiny hand.'

'Poppa, she has promised her mother that we will make sure she gets home safely. Can Bruno escort us now?' Franca turned to smile at a young man seated at the far side of the table, who was chewing a mouthful of food. He wiped his mouth with the back of his hand and stood up, his chair scraping on the marble floor.

'Of course, mia cara figlia, he will go with you straight away.' Franca's father snapped his fingers and Bruno stepped forward to open the door to the hallway, gesturing for the girls to go through. 'Take care, Bruno. Don't lose them,' he said with a nod of his head.

Their steps echoed in the hall with its stone staircase climbing to the floors above. The conversation in the dining room resumed with laughter and in the lulls, as they proceeded to the front door of the building, Gabriella thought she caught a snatch of another sound from somewhere. Crying, groaning? She listened again, more carefully. No, it was only the raucous noise of the men still dining at the laden table.

TWELVE

FLORENCE

30 October 1943

Gabriella was not used to being out on the street as night was falling and became increasingly worried as they walked through the backstreets across the city towards home. The solemn tolling of bells around the empty city alarmed her: 'Mama will be cross that I'm so late. She told me there are severe penalties for breaking the strict curfew.'

'You needn't worry,' Bruno said, 'You are with us. We have permission to be out at this time. Don't we, girls?' He turned to his giggling cousins. 'We'll get her back safe and sound, won't we?'

When they reached the familiar street of Via Faenza, Gabriella pointed out where she lived and Bruno said, 'Very impressive. Such a big house. How many of you are living there?'

'Me, my brother, my parents and some lodgers,' she said, immediately thinking perhaps she shouldn't have added that last piece of information.

He nodded. 'Very interesting.' He turned to the sisters. 'And now we must say goodnight, mustn't we, girls?'

To her surprise, he then reached for Gabriella's hand. She thought he was just going to give it a formal shake, but he made a sweeping mock bow and kissed her hand. As he bent over it, she caught the scent of the highly perfumed pomade that the smartest young men liked to use on their hair. Then he put his arms around his giggling cousins and they strolled off, singing a patriotic song.

She knocked on the front door and her mother let her in immediately. She must have been waiting in the drawing room off the hallway, listening out for her. 'You made it back just in time, girl.' She sounded cross, but she looked relieved.

'They said it would be alright, they are allowed to be out this late.'

'Are they indeed? Alright for some, isn't it? Did you have a nice time?'

At that point, Gabriella thought it would help to smooth things over if she gave her mother the parcel that had been forced on her: 'There was loads to eat and I was allowed to bring some back with me.'

Mama opened the package and stared at the food. 'Don't you want it?'

'No, I ate so much, I'm still full. And I have a piece of bread in my pocket for Riccardo.' She didn't want to mention the cake as she wanted to surprise him.

'Go to him then. He's in his room. He's been painting nearly all day long. I'll share this treat with your father. Thank you, my dear. With gifts like this it might be possible I will let you accept another invitation to dinner.'

Gabriella ran off to find her brother, but when she reached his room the door was firmly closed. She knocked, calling his name and tried the door handle. There was a muffled cry, then she heard a scraping sound as if something was being pulled away from the door.

'I didn't want anyone coming in unexpectedly,' he said, opening the door and letting her through. 'I was in the fireplace.'

'Has anything happened today?'

'I'm not sure. There's been a lot of talking and some shouting. It sounds like different people have been coming and going.'

'Show me your notes in a minute. First, I've got a treat for you.' She put her hand in her pocket and pulled out the bread and the cake.

His eyes widened and he grabbed the food. 'Mmm, our supper was terrible. I hate the *buristo*. She fried chunks of it and it has such a sickly taste. I can't stand it and there is so much of it to eat. Mama thinks she has done well making provision for the winter, but if that's all we're going to have, I'd rather starve.'

'Well, you're not going to starve if I keep being invited to my friends' house. You wouldn't believe how much food there was.' She went on to describe the laden table and everything that she had been encouraged to put on her plate.

But when she told him she'd given their mother the remains of her meal, he groaned. 'No, Gaby, don't torment me. You mean I could have had that as well? I'd love some decent ham rather than that awful *buristo*.' He threw himself back on his bed in mock despair.

Gabriella laughed at him and said, 'I'll just have to stay friends with them then, won't I? Next time I'll see if I can bring you one of the cannoli, if there are any.'

He groaned again and said, 'They had those too and you ate a whole one? You didn't even bring me a little crumb of pistachio? I love pistachios.'

'I didn't know at first that I could bring the food home, did I? It was only when Franca made me take the leftovers that I felt I could. Next time I'll try to get you one and not crush it on the way back. Just think how it would have suffered in my skirt pocket! That sticky pastry all covered in fluff!'

He laughed too and finished eating the cake with exaggerated enjoyment, making sure no crumbs were dropped and lost. 'Now,' he said, reaching for his notebook. 'It's a bit messy, but I tried to keep up with what they were saying.' He frowned, peering at his scribbled jottings. 'I couldn't quite hear, but I think at one point they said something about finding a way into... I think they called it a place of Tristezza...'

'The place of sadness? How odd... Where I had dinner tonight is called Villa Triste.'

'And I'm pretty sure one of them said they're stepping up on the raids, and does the Giardino family know, and will they get out in time?'

'Is that all they said?'

'Not quite, but the rest of it was disjointed and a lot of the time they were grumbling about the Germans and the curfew. Oh, and something about them recruiting men for work. One of them said there was no way he was going to get caught and sent off to work for them.'

'We can listen a bit more tonight if you like. I can stay for a little while.' Gabriella stretched out on the end of his bed, feeling full of good food.

'No, I think they've stopped for now. Probably gone out. They'd gone quiet just before you got here, so I'm fairly sure there won't be anything else now.'

'Oh, that's a shame. I was looking forward to listening in.'

'Never mind. I've got another surprise for you.' Riccardo looked very pleased with himself. 'You know what else we need to be secret agents, don't you? Secret places to drop off messages.'

She frowned, puzzled by this development. 'What do you mean?'

'If I'm a secret agent and I have to deliver a secret message for someone to pick up, I have to drop it off in a hidden place. And then the other secret agent knows where to look and can collect it at a certain time.'

'Like a secret postbox, you mean?'

'Exactly,' Riccardo was jumping up and down in excitement. 'I thought of it today, when Mama sent me out yet again to see if there was any flour at the market. I knew there wouldn't be any, but she sends me to check day after day all the same. And when I was coming back, empty-handed, I had a brilliant idea!'

Gabriella was laughing, enjoying his enthusiasm for this new game. 'And just what is this so-called brilliant idea then?

He threw himself back onto the bed beside her and propped himself up on one elbow. 'We use the *finestra del vino*. You know what I mean, those little tiny doors in the walls of private homes? They're all around the city.'

She wasn't sure at first, but then she recalled noticing a miniature arched doorway in a wall near her school and asking her mother what it was for. She had replied, 'Anyone in Florence who makes their own wine is entitled to sell it by the glass through such a window. They're not used regularly now, because of the war and the curfew, but it is a very old custom here.'

'But how would you use them for messages? Mama said they're not in use at present. If they're not open, what will you do?'

'They're not being used to sell wine, but that doesn't mean to say they aren't ever open and being used for other things. The little outer door still opens.'

'So just what do you think you are going to do then?'

'Well, for a start, I'm going to test it out. Tomorrow, after you've gone to school, I'll slip a coded note to you in the wine window near your school. That one you saw. Then, when you leave to come home, you retrieve the message.'

'But what if Mama sees me and asks what it is?' Gabriella was aware of how watchful her mother was being. She might suspect a young man was trying to arrange a liaison with her attractive daughter.

'Just tell her it's a game we're playing. This way I can tell you what I've overheard during the day, you won't have to wait till you're home. And if she asks to see it, you can say we've made up a code and it just says meet me by the painting of the lamb when you get back. She won't mind that, she thinks I'm making a really good job of it.'

Gabriella clapped her hands with delight. He could sometimes be a really annoying younger brother, but now they were united in secrecy.

THIRTEEN

FLORENCE

12 November 1943

Gabriella tried to put some effort into singing the school anthem, the 'Giovinezza', but her heart was never really in it and she hoped her feeble voice did not betray her. Every morning, the whole school had to sing this patriotic song, as did all schools under fascism, spurring Italy on to greater efforts in the war and proclaiming how Mussolini was remaking Italy and its citizens.

Gabriella knew that boys would be expected to fight as they grew older, rising through the ranks of the Fascist Youth to become *avanguardisti* when they were fifteen, then joining the army at eighteen. Girls were expected to be good mothers and homemakers, loyal to the cause. At the end of this long anthem, their teacher shouted 'A chi la vittoria! – To whom the victory!' and all the girls would raise their right arm in the recognised dagger salute, the saluto Romano, and shout, 'A noi! –To us!'

Her new friends were among those singing and shouting the loudest. All the other students sang with lusty enthusiasm too, but Tina and Franca threw back their shoulders and held their heads high as they participated with fervent patriotism. She could tell they passionately believed in the words of the song, in the regime's mission and in the collaboration with the Germans. She knew that her parents longed for Italy to become free once more and for the Allies to succeed, but she tried to tell herself that loyalty was expected of her and that it would be better for her to follow her friends' example. Besides, her visits to the Villa Triste had become quite regular, with Mama's approval, largely because of the very welcome food parcels that she was able to bring home. Papa was grateful too, but urged her to be cautious if questions were ever asked about the occupants of the palazzo.

Last night she had returned with two crespelle alla Fiorentina, pancakes stuffed with spinach and ricotta. Mama had gasped at the offering, saying, 'How wonderful, one for each of us? Have you something for Riccardo as well? Oh, thank you, thank you.' She was almost tearful and Gabriella ran away to find her brother to give him one of the nut-studded cannoli before her mother could express any more emotion.

And she also hadn't wanted to stay long in her mother's presence in case she asked questions about her evening, for on this occasion, although she had been escorted through the streets after dinner, she had not been accompanied by Tina and Franca. Just as they were about to leave, their father had said, 'Stay with me, my piccoli angeli, we are going to have some fun tonight.' And they had both rushed to his side, laughing, while Bruno stepped forward to walk with her.

It was true, he was very handsome in his uniform, his black tasselled cap perched at a jaunty angle on his well-combed hair. He gave her his arm as they walked so she felt safe as they threaded their way through the dark, deserted streets. 'I am delighted I have been chosen to escort you,' he said. 'It is a task I greatly look forward to and every evening, when we come in to dinner, I wonder if I will find you there. You must feel very glad that Major Michel Carisi's daughters are your friends.'

'I am very fortunate,' she replied, thinking that it was safer to be their friends than their enemies. 'And I'm aware that I am privileged to be invited to dine with them.'

'We do well at their table, don't we?' He laughed and went on, 'Better than most of Florence, I'll bet. Polenta, if they're lucky, for most of them.'

Gabriella kept quiet. She didn't want to draw attention to the parcel of food in her pocket. She was anxious not to ruin this unequal relationship, which was so beneficial for her and her family.

'We get steak, salami, cheese, all the best and plenty of it,' he said. 'I don't mind telling you, before I joined them it was slim pickings back home. The best I could manage was *lampredotto*. Good old Uncle Michel, I say, letting me join him here in his work. With loyal fascists like him and our German friends, we will be triumphant.'

Gabriella had never had to eat *lampredotto*, the cheap tripe sandwich that used to be sold from stalls on the streets, but she didn't like the sound of it and said, 'Sometimes we have to eat *buristo*. That's not at all nice.'

'Aah, that's not so bad. I'd rather eat that. How'd you come by it?'

And Gabriella hesitated, uncertain how she should answer. If she admitted they'd kept a lamb and slaughtered it for themselves, questions might be asked. 'I think my mother saw a friend from the country maybe. I'm not sure.'

'Good for her. We all have to use our friends in these uncertain times. And you, young lady, need to eat well. You look better than when we first met. Quite the bella giovane donna.'

Gabriella could feel herself blushing. Although she knew he wouldn't be able to see her flushed face in the dim street, lit only by the rising moon, she didn't know what to say.

When they reached the palazzo, he reached for her hand, just as he had every time he had escorted her back home. But on previous occasions his sharp-witted cousins had been present and perhaps he'd thought he should be cautious. This time, instead of a comical bow, he bent his head to her hand and gave it a lingering kiss. Then as he stood and began to turn to leave, he tipped his cap at her and bade her goodnight.

She stood for a moment by the doorstep, watching him march away at a smart pace, then she knocked, hoping her blushes would have faded by the time Mama opened the door. But it wasn't her anxious mother, it was an eager Riccardo who pulled her inside, saying, 'Well, what have you got for us tonight?'

'You don't think you're getting first pick, do you?' she teased, offering him empty hands. He looked so disappointed, then she showed him the pancakes and the cannoli, but insisted they share it out with their parents.

Later in his room he lay on the bed, his mouth smeared with sweet ricotta, picking crumbs off the coverlet. 'Did you remember to pick up my note today?' he said. 'When you came out of school?'

'No, I couldn't. I told you not to do one today, because I was going straight back with Franca and Tina. I can only get it on the days I'm not with them, stupid.'

'I forgot. The men in the basement gave me lots of news today, too.'

'What kind of news? You shouldn't put anything really important in the notes.'

He shrugged. 'It'll still be there in the morning. You can get it then.'

'Mama might think it a bit odd though. She's been okay so far, but I don't want her to ask too many questions. What did the note say, anyway?'

Riccardo reached for his notebook. 'There was a lot of talking today and then more this evening. This morning, they said something about moving the women to a convent. Probably the one in the Piazza del Carmine. That's what was in the note. Then later on, I heard them say eighty women and children altogether.'

'I wonder what that means? They're all going to become nuns?'

'I don't know. I thought it was strange. And the other strange thing today was that the Giardinos came down from the attic and were talking to Mama and Papa for ages. They hardly ever come downstairs in the daytime.'

Gabriella eased herself off his bed. Tired and full of food, she was ready for her own bed. She opened the door to leave, then had a thought and turned back to Riccardo: 'It's so unfair Mama won't let me out on my own. You're allowed to go wherever you like, aren't you? Why don't you ask Mama if you can start walking me to school? Or at least for tomorrow, if she doesn't like the idea of every day. Then we can collect the note without her ever knowing about it.'

He agreed and she left, knowing that as she fell asleep, she was going to be thinking about the feel of warm lips on her hand and the scent of Bruno's hair.

FOURTEEN

FLORENCE

November 2019

As they were walking back to the hotel after their first full day in the city, Sofia thought this trip planned by her father was going to work out after all, even though it had got off to a bumpy start the night before when they went out to dinner at the restaurant he'd selected.

'I think we should order exactly what he stated in his itinerary,' she said. 'It sounds interesting.'

Isobel was reluctant at first, but she couldn't make up her mind and after turning the menu over several times, and as they were conscious of the middle-aged waitress tapping her order pad, she agreed.

'You've got to admit, he knew what he was doing,' Sofia said. 'This crispy octopus is delicious and who would ever have thought it would work with this garlicky mash?' She speared another chunk of the dark brown, succulent meat and dipped it into the potato purée. 'And he is so right about having Campari and soda. I don't like sweet drinks, so this is refreshing.' She swirled the bright red liquid with the slice of orange and ice cubes.

'He always was good on food and drink,' Isobel admitted.

'Though I hate being told what to eat nearly as much as being told where to go.' She sipped her drink and went on, 'I remember when he first persuaded me to try Campari. I'd been brought up on cream sherry and gin and tonic. He said my palate would appreciate the food so much more if the aperitif was the bitter side of sweet. Like him, I suppose.'

Sofia thought how right her father was. She'd acquired his tastes and had never taken even a sip of Harvey's Bristol Cream sherry, even at school parties where every kind of alcohol was smuggled out of parents' drinks cabinets. 'Well, if it all continues to be as good as this, I'm not going to complain.' The medium-rare steak Fiorentina with crisp potatoes that followed was equally good, accompanied by large glasses of deep red Chianti Classico.

In the morning they had a buffet breakfast quite unlike any hotel offering either of them had ever seen before. Crisp pancetta, creamy scrambled eggs, dishes of spinach, vegetables and fried potatoes laid out on a hotplate and piles of fruit, yogurt, breads, croissants and madeleines were there for the taking. Isobel popped two little cakes wrapped in a napkin in her handbag, despite Sofia's horrified glance. 'For later, darling,' she whispered. 'In case I'm feeling peckish.'

She seemed to have suddenly recovered her appetite, Sofia noticed, as her mother displayed a hearty interest in all the food, from the panini they ate at lunchtime to the ices they enjoyed in the parlour of Don Nino overlooking the black and white basilica of the Duomo, where they had marvelled at the intricate mosaic work. The square was bustling with tourists taking selfies, souvenir hawkers and circling pigeons hungry for crumbs.

'At least he didn't specify which flavours we should order here,' Sofia said, licking her pistachio ice.

Isobel managed a smile. 'He would have done if he'd been here, knowing him.' She glanced across at the glass counter above the vats of different flavours of brightly coloured ice cream and trays of intricately decorated patisserie. 'And he'd have had a scoop of coffee and one of caramel.'

She seemed happier now, even though their first call on the itinerary, to the Uffizi Gallery, had not been quite so successful. Perhaps we should have queued with all the other visitors and waited for the lift, Sofia thought, instead of climbing all those flights of steps. Her mother had to rest halfway up, insisting that she was perfectly capable of continuing to the top of the building, where visitors had to begin their tour.

After seeing the Botticelli *Venus* and Caravaggio's *Medusa*, as instructed by Riccardo, Isobel had been happy to find the next artwork on his specific list, The Madonna with the Long Neck. But when they had finally located the famous painting by Parmigianino, she had laughed hysterically, pointing at the principal subject, who did indeed have an unnaturally long neck, till Sofia ushered her away to the gallery's café. There, overlooking the waves of terracotta rooftops surrounding them, Sofia thought her mother seemed to be less tense and almost enjoying herself. After they'd drunk their coffee, they walked out onto the walled terrace, where clipped box cones grew like statues in large garlanded urns. Groups of tourists talked loudly and smoked, so they went to the furthest corner to look down over the roofs around the gallery.

'Maybe he did want to come back,' Isobel murmured. 'He always referred to Florence as "the city of my dreams". I always took that to mean he loved it here.'

Sofia took her mother's hand. 'Let's try to see it through his eyes. That must be what he intended by drawing up such a precise and detailed schedule.'

'He never talked in detail about his life here, you know. I suppose his childhood was difficult because of the war.' Isobel leant on the parapet, looking at the teeming crowds below. 'The only thing I do particularly remember him saying was how he regretted never being in Florence for the Scoppio del Carro. He said once it was the only thing he'd like to come back here for.'

'The what?' Sofia had barely any Italian, even though Riccardo had sung to her in his language as a child and taught her to count.

Isobel laughed. 'It's a crazy thing. Typically Italian. It means the explosion of the cart and it's some damn fool thing they always do at Easter, where a kind of rocket shoots out of the Duomo and sets off a cartload of fireworks outside in the square! Can you imagine what the modern risk assessment brigade would say if they got their hands on it? They'd have a fit and get it banned for good in seconds.'

'Is it still allowed to happen now?'

'I think so. I doubt the Italians would let a few little regulations stop them having a mad show like that. I believe it's a centuries-old tradition but it was stopped during the war years, when he was a child. I suppose that was why it registered with him.'

'Poor Dad. So he never got to see the fireworks here. Maybe that's why he loved them so much back home in Cornwall. Remember how he always insisted on going to the public display down in the village on Bonfire Night and at New Year? Yet he still loved letting them off himself on the clifftops. Loved seeing them against a starry sky.'

'He always was a bit of a child. I think perhaps all artists are. They learn to play with what isn't real and embellish it with their imagination.'

Sofia hugged her mother. 'You're right. Come on, let's do the next thing on the list.'

'Why do you think he wanted us to come to the Piazza della Repubblica?' The extensive square was bordered by restaurants and hotels, including the imposing Hotel Savoy. But the most prominent feature was the brightly coloured and illuminated merry-go-round twirling in the centre, piping fairground music while children rode the cockerels and unicorns on its dais. And in one corner a street performer was making a rhythmic racket of percussion on pans and lids, clashing with the hurdy-gurdy tones of the roundabout.

'Maybe it's another memory from his childhood,' Isobel said, looking at the compact guidebook she'd brought from the hotel.

'And apparently the old ghetto was situated here, before the square was expanded in the nineteenth century.'

Sofia stared at the gaudy carousel. There was something familiar about it. She tried to think what it could be. Then she clutched her mother's arm. 'Doesn't that look to you like the symbol in Number Twenty? You know, that painting that's all squares and dark windows?'

Isobel stared at the twirling funfair. 'It could be based on something like this, I suppose,' she said. 'Maybe he remembered it from years ago. I think there's been one here for a long time.'

They both stood watching for a while, until Sofia said, 'Come on, let's go back to the hotel. There's nothing else on the list for today, apart from dinner. So we can put our feet up and then freshen up before we go out this evening. He's already told us where to go.'

Isobel rolled her eyes at that last remark, then looped her arm through Sofia's.

When they reached the hotel and approached the reception desk to pick up their key, the charming concierge smiled at them. 'I hope you have had a pleasant day? And I have a letter here for you, Madam.' He handed over the key and an envelope with Isobel's name typed on the front.

Sofia handed it to her mother, who said, 'How odd. Who knows we're here?' As they walked away from the desk, she ran her finger under the flap, pulled out a single sheet of thick paper, then cried out and sank into a nearby chair.

'Mum, whatever is it? Not bad news, I hope?'

'Here, see for yourself.' She thrust the letter into Sofia's hands and sat there trembling.

Sofia stared at the writing. It was immediately recognisable. Her father's distinctive handwriting: thick black ink, strong downward strokes, though written with less certainty than he'd possessed before his illness, and his signature. It was dated only a week before he died. 'I don't understand. How...'

'He's following us! From beyond the grave! Will it never stop?' And Isobel began to sob, her face in her hands.

12 April 2019

Mia Cara Bella,

If you are reading this letter, it means that you have followed my wishes and are in my beloved Florence. And I hope that you are accompanied by our darling daughter Sofia, who I trust is caring for you now that you are alone.

By now, if you are complying with my precise instructions, you will have experienced something of the essence of Florence and will, I hope, have begun to understand why I loved this beautiful city so much. But I expect you will also be wondering why I never wanted to return to the city of my birth after I had left for England.

That is a hard question for me to answer, but I hope that gradually you will learn what happened here and how experiences long ago, experiences I have never been able to forget, have coloured my work throughout my career and, I suspect, made me a man who was not easy to live with.

You will have noticed that the programme I prepared, which at one stage in my final illness I hoped I would survive long enough to enjoy with you, la mia Bella, contains one clear day. Knowing you well, as I do, I expect you greeted the sight of that free day with delight, thinking you could have some freedom from my diktats. I am sorry to disappoint you, la mia carra ragazza, but I have made arrangements for that final day, which I dearly wish you to accept. Please honour my memory by following my instructions. I believe that day will be significant and you will learn much about my work and my tortured mind.

I know I never told you very much about my family and my early life, but I may have mentioned my sister, Gabriella Dvorak, who lived with me and my parents until I left the family home for good. She still lives there and will be expecting you to call on her on the day that I have left free. If for any reason she is indisposed and is unable to see you, she will contact you at your hotel as I have instructed her to do.

You are to meet her at 11 a.m. on that day at:

Palazzo Rinaldi, Via Faenza.

I trust you will respect my wishes, Carissima.

Il tuo amorevole marito,

Riccardo

MESSAGE TWO

Pirt loohcs eht rof yad ecin a

FIFTEEN
FLORENCE

13 November 1943

When it was time for the school's lunchtime break, Gabriella sat down in her usual place on the low wall and was immediately joined on either side by Tina and Franca, pushing themselves tight up against her on either side. 'You enjoy yourself last night?' Franca said as she pulled open Gabriella's lunch package and immediately shoved it back again. Mama had only been able to provide her with sliced *buristo* and cold polenta.

'Bruno took a while to walk you home yesterday. Getting friendly, is he?' Tina gave her a dig in the ribs with her elbow. 'Can't blame you. He's the best of the bunch.'

Gabriella felt her cheeks burning. She didn't like the way this was going.

'Anyway, we don't want to talk about that,' Franca said, leaning in close, her garlic-laden breath combining with the ripe smell of the *buristo*. 'We want to talk about this morning. Who was that with you, on the way to school?'

'My brother, Riccardo. My mother let him walk with me today. He might be allowed to escort me every day from now on. Mama is so busy, it would be a help to her and she normally sends him out on errands all over the city every day. Because he's a boy, he can go wherever he likes, but she won't let me go out on my own.'

She was aware that she was talking far too much, rattling away to satisfy her inquisitor, hoping she would want to talk about something else. But Franca said, 'Shut up. Just tell us why he was looking in that wine window across the road?'

Gabriella felt herself go icy cold. Riccardo had been running slightly ahead of her that morning. He'd reached the little window with its iron door first and had reached inside, then bent to peer and feel around the empty cavity. 'It's a game he's been playing,' she said. 'You know what boys are like.'

'Is this what he was looking for?' Franca held out a scrap of paper. 'What does it say?'

Gabriella stared at the note. She knew what it said but she also knew she didn't want to tell her. 'I've absolutely no idea. He's in a world of his own. Making up some crazy game.' She straightened out the crumpled paper. 'I can't even read this. It's not written in Italian, is it?'

Franca snatched it back. 'Tell him he should be careful. Someone might think he's passing coded messages to partisans. He could get into serious trouble.'

'He's only playing a stupid game. He gets bored because our parents won't send him to school.'

'That's not very patriotic,' Tina said. 'How old is he? He should be a *balilla* till he's fourteen, then *avanguardisti*, like Bruno, till he's eighteen.'

Gabriella didn't want Riccardo or her parents to get into trouble, so she thought quickly and said, 'I think it's because he was so ill when he was younger. He missed a lot of school and he's very sickly. His leg will never fully recover from the polio.'

'Huh, a crippled weakling then,' Tina said. 'He wouldn't be any use, after all.'

'He's missing out on all the fun then, staying at home,' Franca said. 'We've all got a big treat tomorrow. You've heard, haven't you, about our school outing?'

'Yes, but I didn't understand what they meant. What is a display of fascist justice and strength?'

'Wait and see. It will be so exciting,' Tina said. 'Everyone has to go. Maybe your brother could sneak in at the back of the crowd, but then he won't get a very good view. Not like us. We'll be right in the front row.'

The girls didn't tell her any more than that. Maybe it was just as well. She would never have been able to sleep if they had told her exactly what was going to happen. She just imagined a parade, some marching and patriotic songs.

In the morning Riccardo was allowed to walk her to school again. She'd told him not to deliver any more notes and he promised he'd stop. 'I'm not sure it's a good idea. Tina and Franca are very nosey and might ask awkward questions. You can tell me all the news when I get back tonight,' she said. 'I should have a treat or two for you because I'm going back to the Villa Triste with the girls after school. And maybe I'll have some news for you too. We have a school outing today.'

'I wish I had something happening today. Where are you going?'

'I don't know yet.' She thought for a moment. 'Maybe you should follow us. We won't leave until after school assembly. I think other schools are going too. It must be something good.'

She should never have suggested it, she thought later that night. Neither of them should ever have been there. All the school-children were marched to the Piazza della Signoria and lined up in groups. They were all encouraged to sing the 'Giovinezza' three times, their shoulders back, their heads held high, black tasselled fezzes on the boys, black berets for the girls, urged on by their teachers. Black shirts, white blouses all around her, jostling for a good view of the platform in the middle of the square.

Then, as they were coming to the end of the final verse of their stirring song, three young, handcuffed men were marched through the crowd by fascist guards, hauled up the platform steps and made to stand beneath thick ropes, which were looped round their necks and tightened. As the men had passed the rows of mesmerised children, she'd noticed how their faces were bruised and bloodied.

An announcement she couldn't quite make out was shouted from the stage, then there was a crash and all three men jerked on the ropes, their legs twitching. Gabriella was so shocked she couldn't make a sound, but all around her she heard the other children gasp, then cheer as they raised their fists in a patriotic salute. All but Stefanina, that is. She didn't cheer, she didn't salute. Her fists weren't raised, they were tightly clutched against her breast. She clenched her teeth, her brows furrowed with the ferocity of her glare. She was so clearly angered by this cruel, humiliating public display, she was boiling with rage and silent tears ran down her cheeks.

When they were all marched back to their classes, they filed past the dead men still hanging from the gallows and Gabriella looked away from the purple faces lolling in the nooses. 'Look how they've peed in their pants,' boys jeered, pointing at the dark patches on the men's trousers. 'Show some respect,' Stefanina snapped, marching ahead, unafraid of showing how much she disapproved of their coarse remarks and the whole merciless display.

Gabriella admired Stefanina's independence of spirit and wished she had the courage to show that she too was horrified by the executions. She couldn't forget that image. Death and humiliation were stamped on her mind and she couldn't concentrate on her lessons for the rest of the day. At the end of the afternoon, Franca and Tina grabbed her arms and walked the group as a threesome to the Villa Triste. 'Bet you never thought today would be as exciting as that, did you?' Franca said, hugging her tight.

'Why were those men hanged?'

'They were traitors, that's why. Poppa found out who they really were. People like that don't deserve to live, he says. We've got to root them out if we're going to win the war.'

By the time they reached the villa, Gabriella wasn't feeling hungry, and for once, the sight of the laden table didn't rouse her appetite. But she forced herself to take a portion of the food because she didn't want to disappoint Riccardo. As soon as the sisters had finished eating, she felt she couldn't stay a minute longer, but the men hadn't yet come into the dining room. 'I don't feel very well,' she said. 'I think I should go home early.'

'You can't go on your own, Poppa won't allow it. I'll go and call for Bruno now.' Tina ran off and Franca pushed a parcel of food into Gabriella's hands.

In minutes, Tina was back with Bruno, who was struggling to do up the buttons on his jacket over his broad shoulders and chest. His hair flopped over his forehead and he appeared to have been sweating. 'You've got to come downstairs right away,' Tina said to her sister. 'You won't want to miss this,' and the two of them scampered away.

'What a pair,' Bruno said with a wry shake of his head. He smoothed his hair and set his cap at the approved angle, then opened the door to the street. 'The girls told me you were with them in the piazza today,' he said as they hurried through the dark streets, the solemn toll of bells warning everyone to go home and stay there till morning.

Gabriella was quiet, wondering what she could say that wouldn't make her cry or feel sick again. She felt tears welling as she recalled the terrible scene with the young men dangling from the scaffold.

He turned to look at her properly, then stopped on a corner where the white light of the risen moon illuminated her face. With his hands on her shoulders, he turned her towards him and said, 'I can see you are sensitive as well as beautiful. These are harsh times and you should not have to see such things.' He gently traced the curve of her chin and tilted her face up so he could look directly into her eyes. He stared at her for a moment, then kissed her forehead. 'I will look out for you,' he said and they resumed their walk.

SIXTEEN

FLORENCE

13 November 1943

Papa opened the door that night. 'My child,' he said, hugging her tight. 'We have been so worried. We heard that the whole school was made to witness that terrible scene. I am so sorry you were made to go there.'

Mama emerged from the drawing room and put her arm around her. 'Riccardo rushed here afterwards to tell us. He followed all of you, when you left the school. He should never have been there either. I cannot understand why they think children should see such terrible things,'

'I didn't even know he was there. I never saw him. But there were so many of us.' Gabriella finally released the tears that had been threatening to burst out of her ever since the trap on the gallows had opened and buried her face against her mother's gaunt chest.

'You must stay at home tomorrow and not go into school. You should rest here. I can't bear to think of it. I wish we weren't forced to send you there, but it will be trouble for us if we don't. Thank goodness Riccardo has largely been spared.' Her mother stroked her hair, soothing her. 'Riccardo came back and began another painting immediately. I let him work in my studio for the rest of the day, but I think he may have gone to his room now. He will want to see you, I know.'

Gabriella snuffled and her mother found a handkerchief for her to blow her nose and wipe her eyes. 'He'll be hungry,' she sobbed. 'He waits for me to bring back food.'

'Go to him then. Give him whatever you have saved tonight. Don't worry about us, let him have all of it.' She kissed her daughter on her forehead, covering the earlier kiss from Bruno, and shooed her away.

Riccardo had blocked his bedroom door again. Gabriella knocked and called to him, but there was no response. She had turned and begun walking back along the corridor when she heard a scraping sound behind the door, then it opened slightly.

'Can I come in?' she said. 'I've brought some mozzarella and focaccia for you. There's steak Fiorentina too.' He didn't open the door any wider, but she could glimpse part of his face, pale with shadows under his eyes. 'Mama wants you to have all of the food tonight.'

His face disappeared, but the door didn't close, so she pushed it open and stepped inside. He was lying on the bed, his face buried in his pillow. 'I saw it all,' he said in a muffled voice. 'I was right at the back, but I saw everything.'

'I know. Mama told me. I saw it all too and wish I hadn't. And the cheering... They all cheered and seemed glad. All the boys and all the girls there, apart from Stefanina, the bravest girl in our school. It was terrible.'

He rolled over and looked at her. 'When they brought them into the square, I was so close. I saw their faces. They were young men and they'd been badly hurt. The guards had beaten them, cut them. I will never be able to forget it.'

He slid off the bed and stood up, a fierce look in his eyes. 'Their ears had been cropped, Gaby, cropped like they were no better than dogs, stray curs from the street!'

She was shocked. She knew that hunting dogs commonly had docked ears and tails, but men? When had men had to suffer such treatment? She had not been close enough to see their injuries properly, but she had seen blood on their faces and clothes. 'Shh, now, I know. I won't forget it either. I wish we hadn't seen it. But what can we do? We can't complain. Anyone who speaks up will be silenced.'

'They can't stop me painting,' he said, striding around the room, waving his arms. 'I can tell the world the truth through my work. But they won't understand what I am painting, they never will.' He picked up a canvas on which he had sketched the outline of a branch bearing plump purple figs, oozing dark red juice and golden seeds from gashes in their flesh. 'Everything I put in my paintings will have meaning and only I will know its true significance.'

Gabriella was impressed by her brother's courage as well as his talent. He was only twelve, but he was so wise and braver than she would ever be. 'Franca and Tina told me their father brought those men to justice but I don't know if that's true.'

'Major Carisi is very important, I know that much. Papa said he has influence. You must keep them close as friends. We may learn something and be able to help in some way.'

'Did you listen today or were you too busy painting?'

'I heard a lot of shouting this evening. They've gone out now, I think.' He consulted his notebook. 'There was something about a number of women saved. They thought they were Hungarian. That's all really. It didn't make much sense.'

Gabriella opened the parcel of food she had brought from the dinner table and laid it on the bed, like a picnic. 'I'm feeling a bit hungry now. I couldn't eat much earlier. Can we share it?'

Riccardo joined her and hungrily stuffed a chunk of bread with cheese and steak, then took great bites of his hefty sandwich. After chewing a solid mouthful, he said, 'I also heard Mama and

Papa talking about house-to-house searches. They are worried about the Giardino family upstairs and said they should help them move out of the city. But as the mother has a very young baby, she doesn't want to leave.'

'We hardly ever see them.' She thought for a moment, remembering her conversation with the two children the night their baby brother was born. 'Do you think they're all in hiding here?'

'You didn't know that? You didn't know they're in hiding because they are Jewish?'

At that moment, Gabriella realised she had only been worried about herself up to this point, selfishly concerned with her lack of friends at school. But of course she knew that anyone of Jewish descent was at risk, as others at school talked about it, including the two demanding sisters who had befriended her. 'What will happen to them if they are found?'

'They will be sent away to a camp and then east to work. Many Jewish families left the city before we came here, well before the Germans arrived. Papa says the Germans took around two thousand from the ghetto in Rome last month and are starting here now.'

She imagined being forced out of your home. Leaving Rome with her family hadn't been so bad for her as she knew she was going to a house she had visited many times. But going to an unknown destination where you might be expected to live with strangers and work in a strange country would be extremely frightening.

'I hope this house won't be searched,' she said. 'Do Mama and Papa think it will be?'

'They're trying to decide what to do. I know they're worried. There are severe penalties for harbouring Jews and partisans. They could be arrested or worse.'

And instantly an image of the hanging men flashed into her mind. What had they done? Why did they have to be killed rather than imprisoned or sent away to work? And what would happen to her and Riccardo if her parents were accused? Now the bread and cheese didn't taste so good, after all. She struggled to swallow the dry food and began to choke.

Riccardo thumped her on the back. 'Don't waste it,' he said. 'We've got to be strong for the fight ahead. This is war, Gaby, and we'll fight it on our terms.'

She coughed again, then punched the air and shouted, 'A chi la vittoria!' She laughed and Riccardo joined her in the triumphant response taught in school, 'A noi!'

SEVENTEEN

FLORENCE

November 2019

Sofia read the letter again once she and her mother were in their room, away from the concerned glances of the hotel concierge and passing guests. She found her city map and located Via Faenza. It was not too far to walk and was located a short distance from the station.

Isobel had dashed into the bathroom and Sofia could hear running water. When her mother emerged, she filled the kettle with fresh water, saying, 'I'll make some tea and maybe we can eat those little cakes you stole at breakfast time. You haven't scoffed them yet, have you?'

Her mother pulled the napkin package out of her handbag and threw it to the end of the bed, then pulled off her shoes and lay down, closing her eyes and moaning, 'Why is he putting us through all this? Why, oh, why?'

Sofia quietly made the tea and placed a cup on the bedside cupboard with one of the cakes. 'I'm sorry you're finding this all so upsetting. I know he didn't ever make life easy. And he's not giving up now, is he? I had no idea he had any family left here, did you?'

Isobel shook her head in reply as she sat up to eat the cake.

'Why on earth does he want us to meet his sister anyway? We don't even know if she can speak English, for goodness' sake.'

'If you'd done this trip with him, while he was still alive, I suppose it wouldn't seem quite so mysterious. Okay, you might have been rather annoyed at not being able to go off shopping, but it would have seemed perfectly natural for him to want to visit his sister after so many years of absence.'

'I just don't want to do it. What on earth am I going to say to her? I'm only here because my demanding husband, who's been dead for months, insisted and is still trying to control my life from the afterlife?'

'But aren't you just the tiniest bit curious? Even if you're not interested in meeting Gabriella, surely you'd like to see the family home, the place where he grew up? It sounds very grand. I didn't know he once lived in a palazzo. I know I'm fascinated.'

Isobel gave a one-shouldered shrug, her mouth turning down. 'Maybe a little. But what am I expected to say? Hello, my husband never told me anything about you? I barely even knew you existed?'

'Of course not.' Sofia sat down in one of the chairs by the large casement windows that gave a view across the river. Soft late-afternoon light made the distant hills a mist of green and birds flew in formation over the rooftops as the day began to end. 'I just think it will be interesting and you might learn something.'

'Huh, it's still all about him though.' Isobel sipped her tea, then said, 'Perhaps we could go but not stay very long. She must be terribly old, anyway. She might not even remember anything about his time there.'

'He doesn't say anything about the length of the visit, just the arrival time. And,' Sofia reached out for the letter again, 'this line he wrote – *I believe that day will be significant and you will learn much about my work and my tortured mind* – Wow, you've got to admit that's pretty compelling. Do you think he was tortured?'

Isobel closed her eyes and leant back against the deep square hotel pillows. She yawned and said, 'I just don't know. In the early years I tried to understand him and I did wonder if something had happened when he was young. But I grew tired of trying. All I could do was be there for him.'

'I'm glad you could, Mum. He did some of his best work after he met you.' Sofia slipped from the chair and gently lay down on the bed. It had seemed odd at first having to share a bed, albeit a very large one, with her mother. The concierge had apologised again on their arrival, referring to earlier emails requesting twin beds. 'Our condolences, Madams. We are so sorry Signor Rinaldi is departed. And our deepest apologies, Madams. There are no twin rooms. But you have the best in the hotel, with a view, as requested.' She could see roofs, spires and domes from the bed, but standing at the window there was a full view of the River Arno as it raced through the city.

Sofia closed her eyes and leant back against the pillows in the spacious bed that had given her a good night's sleep, feeling that they had walked around half of Florence on just their first day. Her feet and back ached and she could feel herself getting drowsier. Her mother was definitely asleep, but they could afford to rest before finding the restaurant that was booked for the evening.

She was drifting towards sleep when she found herself remembering the captions she'd written for the exhibition, which had been well attended and generated good sales, though not as good as Phoebe had hoped. Number Eleven, the picture of a single boy in what she thought was a cave, she had described as being '*an evocation of his solitary childhood, as an only child creating imaginary worlds*', but what did she really know?

When the show opened, the gallery filled with serious art aficionados peering at the paintings and captions, catalogues and champagne flutes in their hands. And one of the critics introduced to her by Phoebe had quizzed her, saying, 'What do you think is the significance of the Number Sixteen?' For a moment she had thought he was referring to the missing painting and had been dumbstruck for a second, and then he had repeated the question, adding, 'In every painting? Haven't you ever noticed? There's always sixteen of something or other. Trees, beds, boys, there's always sixteen of them. What does that signify?'

She hadn't been able to provide a convincing answer, muttering about her father's obsession with repetition. But now she suddenly she realised what the encounter with Gabriella could mean and felt wide awake. She reached for his letter again. He'd said *'learn much about my work'*, hadn't he? If only this trip had happened before the exhibition. She'd tried so hard to describe the paintings, but this might be the key she'd needed. This might reveal their secrets at last, but they were going to have to wait three more days to find out.

EIGHTEEN

FLORENCE

15 November 1943

In Gabriella's dream, Franca was shouting at Stefanina, who threw the stolen crust back in her face. And then she surfaced from her sleep to hear knocking, loud voices and the sound of Papa protesting. She slipped out of bed and stood with her door open a sliver of a crack to listen. She could hear the commanding voices of men in the hall and Papa reasoning with them, saying, 'We don't have any lodgers here, but go on, check if you must.'

She peered out into the corridor leading to the hall. Two men in the black and green uniform of the fascists marched towards the stairs and she heard heavy footsteps going up and up as far as the attic. As she watched, she felt Riccardo slip in beside her in his nightshirt. 'I hope the Giardinos have left,' he said in a whisper.

'We'll all be in trouble if they haven't, won't we?' She reached for his hand and held it tight.

Mama emerged from the hall, her hair tied in a bedtime plait over one shoulder, her arms crossed over a silky robe of jade green with pink peonies. 'Stay in your rooms,' she said, shooing them back inside the bedroom.

'Can I stay with Gaby tonight?' Riccardo appealed to his mother. 'I'd be too scared on my own.'

'Of course you can. These men will be gone soon. They won't find anything and then we can all try to get some sleep if we possibly can. Turn out the light and get into bed.'

Gabriella hadn't slept with her brother since they were very young, but tonight she wanted someone close to her, so she took his hand and led him to the bed. He was trembling, but her embrace calmed him as they snuggled under the covers and listened in the dark. Beneath the musty scent of his unwashed hair, she thought she caught a whiff of the turps he used to mix his paints and clean brushes in the studio. 'Do you think the Giardinos have gone?' she whispered, hearing thumps and shouts overhead, out of time with the rapid thudding of her quickened heart.

'I hope so. They'll be arrested if they are found.' Riccardo lay very still as they both listened to the continuing search, bracing themselves for the scream of a child, the pleas of a parent or the cry of a tiny baby. But they only heard the scraping of furniture across the floor, the slamming of doors and coarse shouts. After a moment, Riccardo slipped out of bed and stood by the window, only partially covered by curtains.

'Can you see anything?'

'I'm not sure. Come and look.'

She stood by his side, looking out at the shadows of the garden. The moonlight traced silver around the cypress trees and the clipped topiary. It picked up the white of the gravel on the path that hemmed the borders and criss-crossed the lawn, ending at the gate that only the gardeners had used in the past, so manure, compost and waste would not come near the occupants of the house.

'I think something is moving down there. Look, can you see?' He touched the part of the windowpane level with the view of the furthest part of the path.

And for a fleeting second, Gabriella thought she caught a flit of movement. She cupped her hands either side of her face to focus on the dark outside. It was no more than insubstantial shadows floating over the shining whiteness of the path, like the brush of a raven's wing, but it was something nevertheless. What was she really seeing? Was that the ripple of a dark dress, the rhythmic hop of little legs, the stride of a man? And like a star, guiding them away from the palazzo, a tiny bobbing light; and then it was gone as quickly as it had come.

Was it imagined or real? 'Do you think that was them?' She pressed her forehead against the window, straining for a further glimpse of the ghostly figures, her breath clouding the cold glass.

'Maybe, but we can never say we saw anything out there.' Riccardo shivered. 'I'm getting cold,' and he turned and ran to jump on the bed, pulling the quilt over his head.

Gabriella ran to join him, jumping on top of him, and burrowed down under the covers. The bed had lost its warmth, so she snuggled up to her brother and gave a tiny squeal when he pressed the soles of his cold feet against her legs.

Then they heard clumping steps on the stairs and in the corridor and Mama's voice, saying, 'No, please don't go in. My children are asleep.'

The door was flung open and a torch shone around the room, its beam falling on their faces. They kept their eyes shut, gripping hands beneath the bedclothes, trying to look as if they were in a deep sleep, willing themselves not to whimper with fright. After a moment, though it felt like an age, the door was slammed shut and they heard heavy steps on the tiled floor, marching towards the front door.

They heard the lock turn and the bolts slam fast, then a murmur of concerned voices. Mama gently opened the bedroom door and came to the bedside with soft slippered feet, so much quieter than the forceful men before. 'It's all over,' she said. 'You can stay here together if you like tonight.'

'Were they looking for the Giardino family? Will they be safe?' Gabriella propped herself up on one elbow to look at her mother, a slim silhouette backed by the light from the corridor.

'Yes, they've all gone. I hope they will all get away in time.'

'How did they get out without being seen?' Riccardo sat bolt upright. 'I'm sure we could see something at the bottom of the garden. Was that them?'

Mama sat on the edge of the bed. 'Forget what you may have seen, my dears, forget they were ever here. It's better that way.' She reached across to brush his hair from his face. 'Now try to sleep, both of you.'

After she left, they heard the faint sounds of their parents retiring upstairs. Gabriella lay awake, her brother twitching in his sleep beside her. She wondered how the family had managed to slip out of the palazzo without being seen or heard. Perhaps they had been hiding in the garden or the chapel all along. Perhaps they had been warned that the house would be raided tonight. And even if the twins had hidden well and been as quiet as mice, as they had demonstrated to her the night their little brother was born, how could a mother ensure that a baby didn't reveal its presence with its cries?

She closed her eyes, knowing that now her dreams would be filled with the sounds of a wailing baby and a mother trying to stifle its screams.

NINETEEN

FLORENCE

16 November 1943

If a boy kisses a girl on the forehead, is that significant? Gabriella wondered what it could mean. A kiss on the lips is definitely meaningful, but a kiss on the forehead? Twice now Bruno had given her such a kiss and told her she was beautiful. But she was only fourteen, fifteen early next July, and he must be nearly eighteen, quite grown-up and mixing with mature men all the time. Did he consider her still to be a child or was she now, in his eyes, a young lady who might be the object of his affections?

Gabriella lay in her darkened bedroom, trying to sleep, but she could feel the impression of his lips on her skin and she was beginning to feel she would like more. Tonight, when she and the girls had finished eating and had joined the group of men in the dining room, she had noticed how he smiled the minute she entered. He had such dark hair and such deep brown eyes. His teeth were very white, unlike some of the other men who probably drank too much coffee and red wine and smoked all day, so their teeth were stained and their breath was sour. When Bruno bent to kiss her, she smelt the manly scent of fresh sweat, his pomade and the wool of his jacket.

Yet again, her two friends had been encouraged by their father to stay behind rather than escort her home, so she and Bruno were alone for the entire time it took to walk the empty streets. 'Tina and Franca really love being with their father,' she said as they strolled back.

'It is not so much their father they love, but the company he keeps,' Bruno said.

'What the other men, you mean? The men who join you for dinner?'

'Let us say the girls like to hear their stories about their work.' Then he added, 'But you are different. I think it is better for you that you go home at this time. Those girls are coarse, like the thistles that grow by the roadside. And you are a delicate flower, a rose that would bruise and wilt if it had to join them in their rough games.'

He was being mysterious again and she hadn't yet understood what bonded the sisters with their father. Riccardo questioned her every time she returned from these outings and he was still so determined to fight in his own way, as he put it. So she felt she must ask Bruno more and said, 'Were you all very busy today?' The group had arrived later than usual, all laughing but looking tired and dishevelled, as if they had been working hard. She had noticed that a couple of them looked dirty too, as if something had left dark splatters on their shirts. She could not tell if Bruno's shirt was dirty, as he was always in uniform, the black shirt and the green trousers of an *avanguardisti*.

'We are always busy,' he said, putting his arm round her shoulders. 'There is much work to do in the city to put Florence in order. And of course, the war continues and we must strengthen our position with our German friends, now that many of our countrymen have betrayed our cause.'

Gabriella knew what he meant by that as her parents were always talking about how Italy had been a divided country since the first week of September. The Allies had invaded Sicily back in July and maybe that was why Bruno had had to leave his home there and join his uncle here. And since then, the Germans had been trying to maintain their hold on the northern half of the country.

'When do you think you will you have to go away to fight?'

'Not for a while yet. Maybe when I'm eighteen in the spring. But if we can't keep control here, we may have to move on sooner.' He squeezed her shoulder. 'I hope that won't happen. I want to stay here and walk you home every night. You don't mind me saying that, do you?'

'No, I don't.' She bit her lip and wondered if she dare say more. So she added, 'I'm glad it's just us, the two of us. I'm glad the girls aren't here.'

'Me too. I look forward to finding you there after dinner and being allowed to escort you home. And I want to protect you, keep you safe. You know that, don't you? Whatever happens, I will do my best to make sure you are safe. You can trust me and tell me anything that worries you.'

And she did believe him, she told herself, as she tried to fall asleep, still feeling his arm around her shoulders, his lips upon her forehead.

The next morning, Riccardo ran ahead of her on the way to her school. She'd told him not to leave notes in the wine window after Tina and Franca's discovery and he'd said, 'Very well. But that won't stop me using other windows.'

'But I won't know where you've left the notes, will I?'

'It doesn't matter. They're not for you, they're to undermine the regime.'

He laughed, then showed her the cartoons he'd drawn. A recognisable Il Duce with devil's horns and a tail, a German SS officer with frilly knickers instead of uniform trousers.

The drawings were very good and they were amusing, but she gasped when she saw them. 'You could get into terrible trouble with these.'

'I'll be careful.' He shrugged. 'Anything to show how wrong this all is.'

And as they approached the school, Riccardo hung back, knowing she was almost there and would soon be mixing with her school friends. But before she could be lost in the crowd of girls, Bruno approached her. He looked tired, as if he hadn't slept well, and his tie wasn't properly tied. 'Will you be coming back to the villa tonight for dinner?' he asked, looking concerned.

'No, I don't go every night and I always have to let my mother know the day before.'

'Then I won't see you for a few days. I'm going to be busy. Maybe don't go this week. I don't want anyone else walking back with you.' He smiled and patted her arm.

'But I haven't been invited yet anyway. I have to wait to be asked.'

He nodded in response and began to walk away, but turned back and said, 'You're not going anywhere near the Piazza del Carmine, are you?'

She shook her head and he said, 'Best avoided for a while, I'd say.'

What did that mean?, she wondered. Please, not another hanging, surely? She knew the square well; there was a large Franciscan convent on one side. That didn't sound like an appropriate location for an execution.

Riccardo nudged her. 'Why did he say that?'

'I don't know. And you shouldn't go trying to find out either. You don't want to go getting another nasty shock. Try to stay out of trouble today.' And she left him to attend her classes while he decided what he should do next.

TWENTY

FLORENCE

16 November 1943

Gabriella couldn't find Riccardo when she returned early from school that day, longing to see a friendly face. Tina and Franca had ignored her all day. They seemed to be involved in their own private joke, as they kept sniggering and nudging each other whenever she looked at them.

Mama was in the kitchen, shaping gnocchi again. She had very little flour and was using the smallest amount to mix and dust the mashed potatoes. She looked up when Gabriella came in and said, 'A pity you aren't seeing your generous friends today. We have a very poor supper tonight. I may fry a little salami to add some flavour, but I must be careful to ration our supplies. We are in for a long, hungry winter, I'm afraid.'

'Where's Riccardo? I've checked his room, the chapel and your studio. He's not in any of them.'

'I thought he was in the studio, painting.' Her mother looked puzzled and shook her head. 'That boy, he's coming and going all the time. I can't keep track of him. He's in a world of his own.'

Gabriella moved to sit on a stool near the stove. She was cold and wet and now that her mother no longer met her from school, she ran home as fast as she could. Riccardo was usually waiting for her if she wasn't due to go with her friends.

'If you're just going to sit there, you can make me some pesto. We need a fresh batch, not that there's much to make it with.' Mama nodded at the ingredients arranged on the table, next to the pestle and mortar that pounded the herbs and nuts with oil. 'We're out of pine nuts and the basil has stopped growing now it's so much colder. But there's parsley and a handful of walnuts. Go easy with the oil though – I've very little of that too.'

Gabriella settled herself with the mortar in her lap and began grinding the dry ingredients in a rhythmic motion, round and round. It was a soothing task, one she had accomplished many times, the herbs releasing their scent and flavour as she pounded. She'd often heard her mother say that pesto could be made from any combination of herbs and nuts, but she hadn't tasted this version before. Sometimes it was myrtle and walnuts or even rocket and almonds, but Mama didn't have a productive garden like many housewives, she only had fruit trees and herbs.

As she reached for a pinch of salt to season the mixture, her mother said, 'Go easy with that too. I don't know where we're going to get any more.' Then she gave a tiny laugh and said, 'Your father says when they start salting the mountain roads this winter, he fully expects there will be scavengers up there, gathering it up and selling it on. People will be that desperate for salt, even gritty salt.'

Just as she'd finished, Gabriella heard a noise from the hall, a click from the main door and footsteps running down the corridor. Her mother turned her head. 'That'll be Riccardo now. Go and ask him where's he's been.'

He'd run towards the chapel; she'd heard him running and caught a glimpse of him as he ran through the cloisters. 'Wait,' she called. 'Wait for me.' But he didn't wait, he kept running as if he was being hunted.

When she entered the chapel she couldn't see him at first because no candles were lit. Then she heard the striking of a match and saw he was standing by the votary, lighting an offering that cast a glow over his face, the rest of him cloaked in shadow. 'Why are you in here? Mama said you'd been painting again today.'

His answer, when it came, was muffled, as if he didn't want to speak aloud in this hushed place. 'I need quiet to think about the subject.'

'I'm sorry. I can go and leave you in peace if you want me to.'

'No, don't go. I just want a minute here.' He bowed his head and clasped his hands under his chin, then a moment later looked up at the altarpiece, depicting the Adoration of the Magi, in which a host of characters had pushed their way into the frame with a retinue of servants, horses and dogs. All wore elaborate, richly decorated Renaissance costumes and the whole scene was encased in a gilded carving. Only the Madonna and Joseph were simply dressed in plain robes and the infant Jesus wore nothing but a cloth around his loins, as he blessed a supplicant elderly man, maybe one of the Three Kings.

'Isn't it ridiculous?' Riccardo murmured. 'Beautiful and skilful but ridiculous. My paintings will always tell the truth, not dress it up like a grand opera.' He turned back to Gabriella. 'Come on, I'll show you what I'm doing, then I'll tell you what happened today.'

He limped from the chapel, leaving the votary candle to burn down, and she followed him to his room. The unfinished canvas was propped against a wall, its paint leaving a trace on the plaster surface and the tiled floor. He turned it round so she could see what he had managed to outline so far. It appeared to be a crowd of women, some crouching, others standing, their faces distorted. And in the foreground, a nun, or at least she thought it represented a nun; it was very like a large bird, a swan or a heron with outspread wings, she couldn't quite tell because of the absence of body colour in the figures.

'What does it mean?' she asked as she bent down to study his work.

'It happened today. I went there, to the convent. I know you said not to, but I thought I should. I couldn't get close to see properly, but there were people gathering outside, so I waited. I saw a large group of women being taken away. Fifty or so, I think it must have been.'

'Who was taking them?'

'They were marched off to trucks by German soldiers and fascists. They're working together, Gaby. And I heard someone say that the convent was raided last night and these women were the ones they were taking.'

'Were they the nuns?'

'No, silly, the nuns had given them shelter. There are still some other women there, but the Germans didn't want to take them.'

'Why not?'

'Because they are only taking the Jews. These women, and their children, were Jewish.'

'But why? And where are they going?'

He shrugged. 'No one knows for sure. I heard someone say they were going to Verona. But then another person said they wouldn't keep them there for long. That they'd soon be off to a place of no return.'

'But they can't have done anything wrong. They're not criminals.'

'Of course they aren't. And I think I saw Signora Giardino among them.'

'What, our Giardinos? The family who used to live in the attic?'

'Not all of them. Just her, the mother, with her son and daughter.'

'But what about her husband and what about the baby? He's only weeks old.'

'I didn't see any babies. Maybe she was able to leave it behind with the nuns.'

Gabriella thought of the last time she'd seen the family. The parents with their two children, five or six years old, the baby, born two months ago, wrapped in its mother's arms. They had come downstairs late one afternoon, to take the air and walk around the garden before dusk. Signora Giardino had soothed her baby, holding him against her shoulder and patting his back. There had been whispering conversations with her parents, while little Sara and Nathan tossed a ball across the grass. 'Planning to stay somewhere safer,' Mama had said, when she'd asked what they had been talking about. 'The city isn't the best place for them now. They'd be better off in the countryside, now she's recovered from the birth.' But had they gone to the convent that night the palazzo was searched, expecting to be able to hide away until the Germans left Florence?

'I hope they'll be alright,' she said, almost to herself.

'I'm not so sure. The fascists are keen on rooting them out. I heard whispers all around me in the crowd. People were saying there's good money to be earned, if you know where they're hiding. People are betraying them, Gaby. It's like Judas Iscariot is our neighbour. It's all around us. We can't trust anyone now.'

She thought he had finished, for he was silent for a moment, staring at his new canvas. 'You should include the guards in this picture,' she said. 'Show them taking the women away.'

But he appeared not to listen to her suggestion, bursting with passion as he said, 'And do you know what the worst thing is? What I think is so dreadful about all of this? Italians are helping the Germans do it. I thought they were only after the partisans, but they're not. They're hunting for Jews. People of Florence who love their country, who've lived with others of another faith for centuries, are helping the Germans find them and get rid of them.'

TWENTY-ONE

FLORENCE

20 November 1943

Bruno had told her not to visit for a while, but Tina and Franca were persuasive and Riccardo was always hungry, so Gabriella asked her mother if she could join them that evening. She knew Mama was also always grateful for the extra food as supplies were becoming harder and harder to obtain. Riccardo had had many fruitless trips to the Mercato Centrale and their attempts to grow winter vegetables in the garden were a miserable failure.

'If only I had grown up on a farm and not in this museum, lovely as it is,' Mama complained, 'then I might have a lush garden of kale and spinach instead of withered weeds. Even the parks, turned over to *orti di guerra*, are more productive than this arid patch. And now I'm being told people are making coffee from chicory and tea with dried hibiscus flowers. What use is being an artist in such times? If only my paintings could turn into real food to satisfy you all.'

But Gabriella knew that her mother was rarely working in her studio these days. She used to paint nearly every day, brush in hand, mesmerised by the image on the canvas and the melodies of the Puccini operas she loved. She was growing listless and uninspired, as she struggled to concoct meals with the little she had, mend and wash their clothes and traipse to the markets in the futile hope of fresh supplies.

And that evening, the table at the Villa Triste was as usual laden with platters of meats, fresh and cured, and dishes of pasta and rice. Gabriella felt hungry and ate well enough, although the girls still teased her for her small appetite. 'You'll never have a woman's figure if you keep eating so little,' said Franca, whose school uniform was growing tighter week by week. 'Depends what kind of figure you want, fatso,' jeered Tina, who was slender and small-waisted despite the vast portions she consumed.

At the end of dinner, when they returned to the dining room, Gabriella was disappointed not to see Bruno at the table, even though she knew he had said he would be busy elsewhere for a while. 'Poppa,' Tina shouted, 'Who's going to take Gaby back home tonight?'

Gabriella started to say she could find her own way home, but Major Carisi waved towards the end of the table at a swarthy man with a scar under his right eye and said, 'Saint Alfredo. You can do the honours.' A ripple of male laughter echoed the pronouncement of this name. 'But don't take too long about it. We have a long night ahead of us.'

'Can we stay with you, Poppa?' Franca laid her greasy head on her father's shoulder. 'Do you have more castor oil?'

Her father put his arms around her and whispered in her ear, making her giggle with delight.

Alfredo stood up with a scowl. Gabriella didn't like his disgruntled look, but could hardly refuse to be escorted by him. As they walked at a pace through the streets, she had to quicken her steps to keep up with his strides. Finally, she dared to ask him a question: 'Where's Bruno? Is he busy tonight?'

'Very, I should think,' the man grunted. 'All the guys wanted the job. We're taking turns at the prison.'

'When will he be back?'

'Soon enough. When they've had their fun. They'll be gone soon enough, anyway.'

She couldn't make sense of this. What fun was there to be had in a prison in these challenging times? And who'd be gone and where?

'Right, is this it? Very nice, lots of room to take in lodgers,' Alfredo said when they reached the palazzo.

'We live here on our own,' she said.

'I'm off then,' he grunted, leaving her without a kiss, thank goodness, and marched away into the dark, abandoned streets, to the sound of stray cats fighting.

She couldn't stop thinking about his remarks as her mother opened the door. Gabriella pushed a parcel of food into her hands and ran to find her brother. Riccardo was waiting in his room, wrapped in two sweaters and a pair of cut-down trousers. Mama was becoming creative with clothing as he grew. Gabriella tossed him rolls and cheese, then threw herself onto his bed: 'Has there been any news today?'

'Other than the fact I was followed, you mean?' He broke the bread and inspected the cheese. 'I lost them though. Ran through the market and hid in a church for a bit.'

'Who was following you?'

He shrugged. 'Dunno. Scruffy guy. So I didn't drop off any of my cartoons in the windows today. I'll see if he's around tomorrow.' He took a bite of the roll he'd stuffed with soft cheese, chewed a mouthful, then said, 'I went back to the Piazza del Carmine though. I wanted to look at the frescoes in the corner of the square. There's one of the Madonna and Child with two saints.'

'Are you thinking of doing a similar painting?'

'Mmm.' He nodded while he was eating. 'A version maybe. But an odd thing happened there. This old woman, really dirty, dressed in rags, came up to me while I was looking at the painting. She said, "If anyone is a real-life saint, it's that nun." I didn't know what she meant, then she said, "Saved a baby, she did. Hid it under her skirts." I asked her what baby, but she shuffled away before I could question her any more.'

'Perhaps the Giardinos' baby is still with the nuns then. Do you think they'll look after him?'

'They should, shouldn't they? Aren't nuns always kind to children and everyone who needs help?'

'I suppose, but they can be very strict teachers too.'

'But forget about that. After the old woman had gone, I walked across the square to the other paintings there and I was sketching in my notebook when I saw an old man sweeping and picking up cigarette ends and putting them in his pocket. He saw me looking and he smiled at me, like this,' Riccardo screwed up his face, so his top lip scrunched up under his nose. 'And while he was pulling such a comical face, he said, "They're all gone to the prison now".'

'You mean the old man said that?'

Riccardo's grimace relaxed and he laughed. 'It was very hard to understand him and he didn't have any teeth left – well, he did, but just two stumps.'

'Do you think he meant the women that were taken away from the convent?'

'I suppose so. What else could it mean?'

'The nuns? Did he mean the nuns have been arrested for helping?'

'I don't think so. I saw two of them come out of the main door and walk across the square, towards the market. I suppose even nuns have to shop for food sometimes.'

'They can't just live on the Bread of Christ, can they?' Gabriella laughed at her joke and Riccardo threw a roll at her, then dived under the bed to retrieve it, dusting it off and eating it with the remains of the cheese.

ACT TWO
THE ANGELIC SISTERS

Sisters good and sisters bad

TWENTY-TWO

FLORENCE

November 2019

Sofia had been scanning her phone for information before they left the hotel that evening. One of the instructions in Riccardo's itinerary was intriguing: *'Check what time the wine window in Borgo San Jacopo will be open, before you go to dinner.'*

Isobel protested, of course. 'We've walked round half the city already today. Do we really have to walk somewhere else before we can sit down and eat?'

But Sofia took no notice and when they found the window, she was delighted. A miniature arched doorway was set into the thick outer wall of a small café, the thickness of the stone creating a deep aperture and windowsill. 'It's just like the little doors Dad included in a lot of his paintings – and look, there's a bell too.'

Isobel refused to ring it, so Sofia inserted her hand to tug the dangling chain and in response was asked whether they wanted red or white wine, which they drank at the outside table on the street. 'I love this,' she said. 'And there aren't any others open these days. But just think how, years ago, these windows we've seen everywhere were all dispensing wine to thirsty passers-by.'

'I suppose your father must have seen them in use when he

was young,' Isobel said, sipping her wine. 'But I've no idea why he thought he should refer to them in his pictures. It's all still such a mystery.'

When they had finished, they began walking to the restaurant Riccardo had chosen and Sofia noticed how the grand austere frontages of many of the buildings that lined the streets of Florence hid enclosed courtyards, protected by thick walls and heavy outer doors. Nearly every property had the title 'Palazzo' this or that, so she began to think that perhaps his childhood home would have a similar design.

As instructed by Riccardo's itinerary, they went to the Obicà Mozzarella Bar, a short walk from their hotel. A narrow entrance off the street led to a large paved patio filled with expansive umbrellas, coned box trees and glowing patio heaters and, beyond that, a modern restaurant specialising in dishes featuring the region's cheeses and antipasti.

Despite the warmth of the heaters, they elected to eat inside. They struggled to choose from the wide range offered on the menu. 'What did Dad say we should have again?' Sofia asked. 'Did he tell us on his list?'

Isobel pulled the crumpled itinerary from her bag. 'He wasn't so specific about this place. It just says, *"try whatever you like, but make sure you have the Gran Degustazione and arancini."* Well, I know what arancini are, but I've no idea about this other thing.'

'I think it's a bit of every cheese they have, it probably means tasting platter,' Sofia said, studying the menu. 'It includes smoked mozzarella di bufala. Sounds gorgeous.'

When the sturdy rustic boards arrived at their table, bearing cheeses, hams, sun-dried tomatoes, peppers, roasted artichokes and olives, accompanied by a basket of crusty bread and crispbreads, they realised they had probably over-ordered. Sipping the local Chianti they'd requested, again as directed by Riccardo, to accompany the feast, Isobel said, 'We're never going to eat all that. At least I'm certainly not. You'll have to do it justice, darling.' She dabbed a breadstick into the creamy stracciatella and picked at an olive.

Sofia cut open one of the crispy golden arancini to let it cool a little before eating it. Molten mozzarella bound the grains of rice inside the crisp crumb. 'I couldn't help wondering – why didn't Dad ever tell you anything about this sister of his?'

Isobel gave a weary shake of her head, implying it was yet another mystery. 'Oh, I knew he had a sister, but he implied they'd fallen out years ago. He hardly ever mentioned her name. Only when he talked about living with his parents.'

'But he must have been in touch with her recently, earlier this year, that is. And he never said anything to you?'

'When did he ever reveal anything, darling? He would lecture and demand, but he never told us anything about himself, you know that. And he was fiercely independent.' She frowned, recalling all the slights over the years. 'I remember the time he was offered a very lucrative commission, the only one he ever received. It was for a triptych at one of those new universities, I can't remember which one,' she said, shaking her head.

'It would have made a huge difference to our finances at the time and would have established his reputation far earlier than he did. But he only got as far as making some sketches and then backed out of it. I only found out because I took a call for him at the studio one day. He was furious that I'd spoken to the university bursar and when I asked what was going on, he clammed up, saying they didn't understand. A long time afterwards I found out they'd asked him not to include his usual motifs, like the lamb and the boys with bleeding ears, so he'd turned them down and refused to ever work for them.'

'Oops, touchy, wasn't he?'

'I thought of it more as arrogance. I suppose you could say it was hurt pride, but he could never have been told what he should paint. He couldn't produce work to order.'

'He had his own vision, I suppose. That or nightmare, maybe. I rather admire him for it, for sticking to what he believed in. Don't you?'

Isobel sighed and took a sliver of bresaola and an artichoke glistening with oil. 'I won't deny he was brilliant. Of course he was. But I'm tired, darling. So tired of my life revolving around him. And just when I thought I might begin to be myself again, after all these years, here we are, still talking about him and what made him so bloody clever.'

Sofia tried to conceal her impatience. This wasn't going to get any easier. 'Look, now we're here, let's just enjoy ourselves. We won't talk about him any more. We've got three whole days before we have to confront whatever it is this sister might have to tell us. I know we've been given a programme to follow, but that's no worse than coming to any other unfamiliar city and doing the Ten Must-See Sights, is it? I wouldn't know where to start without some kind of guide and maybe we've actually inherited the best guide we could possibly have.'

She held out her glass. 'Let's toast Dad, difficult as he was. Let's toast him for showing us how to enjoy Florence. He put a lot of effort into creating this programme for us.'

Her mother actually smiled and clinked her glass against Sofia's.

'Tomorrow we're going to the Boboli Gardens, I think they're called, to enjoy the view and find the grotto.' Sofia looked at her map, folded on the table. 'I think we could walk across the Ponte Vecchio on the way and look in the windows of all the jewellery shops there.'

'We shall have to buy something for you, darling, for being such a good daughter while I'm being such an old grouch.'

'No, you're not. I'm so pleased to be here with you. We should both get a souvenir. Earrings perhaps. And then we've got the opera in the evening, so we can dress up with our new purchases and go out on the town.'

'If you say so. Though I wouldn't call the opera going out on the town exactly. *Il Trittico* might be hard work for you as you don't know it.'

'Have I not heard it? He was always playing Puccini, wasn't he?' Sofia could immediately picture her father painting in his studios, to a musical background of opera.

'Then it might be familiar. It's three mini operas and there's a death in all of them, with the last one being a row over a will. Such a cheerful evening's entertainment!'

'Sounds a bit like what we're experiencing now. Wrangling over what he's left us to deal with.'

Isobel then began to laugh, really laugh, and the two of them realised they could enjoy being together.

'Look,' Sofia said, looking through the restaurant window, 'it's dark out there now, but all the courtyard tables have lanterns and the heaters are working. Why don't we sit out there and have one last drink?'

They sipped prosecco sitting in cushioned rattan armchairs, watching the lit street outside, framed by the arched doorway at the far end of the courtyard. As they walked back to the hotel arm in arm, the wide thoroughfare of the Via Tornabuoni glittered with strings of early Christmas lights. Tourists roamed and took pictures of themselves inside a giant illuminated cage that was part of the festive decorations.

'This isn't so bad,' Isobel said, leaning her head on her daughter's shoulder. She had once been as tall as Sofia, but she had shrunk an inch or two in recent years. 'You're right. We must enjoy ourselves.'

MESSAGE THREE

Gnitiaw si niart eht

TWENTY-THREE

FLORENCE

5 December 1943

Mama called out to Gabriella from the kitchen as soon as she returned from school. 'You're in luck today. Come and see what I've managed to get for us.' She was preparing pasta dough on the dusted marble countertop, with a long, thin rolling pin. 'You can choose,' she said. 'Whatever kind you like. But we don't have much choice of a filling or sauce tonight.'

Gabriella was wide-eyed, staring at the wonderful sight. Pale creamy pasta that could be turned into a huge range of marvellous dishes they hadn't seen in a long time. 'How did you come by the flour?'

'You'll be pleased about that too. I know how much you hated the *buristo*.' Her mother noticed the face she pulled. 'Don't worry. It was awful, I know. None of us liked it, but it was all we had at the time. So I exchanged one for some flour. Not much, unfortunately, and pasta is an extravagance, but I thought you deserved it for helping us so much with your regular contributions from your dinners with your friends.'

Throughout her explanation, Mama kept pulling at the sheet of pasta, refolding it and rolling it some more until it was as thin as paper. Gabriella thought of all the dishes she loved and wondered what she could request for their supper tonight. Carbonara? But there was no pancetta and eggs were in short supply. There was unlikely to be meat or sausage for a rich ragù and no shellfish now no one could easily reach the coast.

One of her earliest memories was helping Mama make tagliatelle as the slender ribbons of pasta were the easiest shape for little fingers to prepare. They cooked the strips, which were uneven despite her mother's careful supervision, and tossed them with crisp pancetta and sliced chestnuts.

She pictured layers of lasagne, sandwiched with meaty ragù and creamy béchamel, spiky cavatelli capturing a spicy mix of sweet paprika, sausage and tomato. They wouldn't be able to have ravioli or agnolotti, which needed special fillings, as the larder was so empty. Then, remembering one of her father's favourites, she had an idea. Looking at her mother's sad and weary face, she said, 'Do we have any garlic and broccoli?' And when Mama's smile reappeared as she nodded, she said, 'Then can we make *corteccia*?'

'Of course, my dear. That's a really good suggestion. It will make this go a long way. And I can spare a little oil, some dried chilli and I think I still have a can of anchovies too.'

Gabriella clapped her hands in delight. 'Then we have everything we need.' She threw down her school bag and grabbed her apron. 'Can I start now?'

'I'll roll it just one more time and then we'll be ready. You fetch the ingredients for the broccoli pesto.'

Minutes later, Gabriella was sitting on a stool shaping the little pieces of dough. She pulled off marble-sized pieces of pasta and rolled them into thin sausages, about the length of her little finger, as her mother demonstrated. Then she laid her three middle fingers on top, pressed down and dragged the pasta back towards her so it curled, still carrying the indentations of her fingertips, to hold the sauce. Each piece had to be flicked from her hands onto the flour-dusted countertop so the shape wasn't crushed.

Meanwhile, Mama was chopping garlic and broccoli and

gently frying it in oil with a couple of anchovies and seasoning. When she began grating cheese as well, Gabriella was surprised, but her mother looked up and smiled, saying, 'You see how you have helped us? Every time you brought back a piece of pecorino or Parmesan, I stopped your father from eating it immediately. Aren't you glad? And it's thanks to you we have a little more to spare these days.'

For once, Gabriella enjoyed the cooking. Her pasta shapes were easily made – cavatelli, Mama called them – little hollows, designed to capture the well-seasoned pesto, thinned with a little of the hot water from the pasta's brief immersion. But when the family sat down to eat this treat of a dish, Riccardo wolfed his food rather than savouring it and seemed restless.

'Sit still, won't you?' his mother kept saying. 'Your sister has done well tonight, don't you think? Not only has she made us all a lovely supper, but it's thanks to her that it tastes so good. Without the food she brings from her friends, we might be eating this with garlic and oil and little else.'

'Well done, Gabriella,' Papa said. 'It's delicious. Reminds me of happy times at my family's farmhouse.' He stirred the oily pasta in his dish. 'Happier times, before all this.'

His wife patted his hand, looking at him with sad eyes as she tried to smile brightly. 'Those days will come again,' she said. 'And I've saved the rest of the anchovies. They will keep for a while in the oil, even though the tin is open. We can have some more tasty suppers over the next few evenings.'

'I've finished. Can I go now?' Riccardo had eaten all his pasta and slipped from his seat, but clearly still felt he should ask permission to leave the table.

'Go then, you ungrateful child.' His mother laughed and waved him off with an impatient hand. 'You can go and join him as soon as you're ready,' she said to Gabriella. 'I expect he's longing to show you his painting. I don't understand the subject myself, but he's really rather good.'

As soon as she had finished her last piece of pasta, Gabriella excused herself and ran to join her brother. He was crouching in the fireplace again and beckoned to her as she came into his room, putting a finger to his lips. She knelt down beside him and tried to catch the fractured sounds from the cellar. Trains, they seemed to be talking about trains. Tomorrow, she thought they said.

When the conversation stopped, they heard footsteps and the banging of a door down below. 'They've gone now,' Riccardo said. 'There won't be anything else till they're back. And I'm usually fast asleep by then, so I won't pick up any more information.' He looked at his notes, all written in his back-to-front alphabet.

'It sounded like they were talking about trains?'

'I think so. They keep saying the train is waiting to leave. I don't know what that means, but all the trains leave from the station, don't they? So I think I'm going to go up there tomorrow to see what's happening.'

'Are you sure you should do that? There might be a lot of soldiers there.' Gabriella felt uneasy, but couldn't think why.

He rolled his eyes. 'I'm only going to take a look. I'll carry a basket, so I can say I've been sent out for supplies by my mother. I'll look completely innocent, so they won't suspect me of snooping.' He gave her a simpering look as he hobbled around the room, pretending to hold a basket over his arm like a harassed housewife, and they both laughed.

TWENTY-FOUR

FLORENCE

6 December 1943

No one was waiting for her when school finished that day. Tina and Franca hadn't invited her for dinner and, although Gabriella looked up and down the street with its tall, imposing buildings, she couldn't see either her mother or Riccardo. This had never happened before. She was always escorted, she had never walked the streets alone, in Rome or Florence.

She had been longing for more freedom, to be able to roam as freely as her brother, but now she suddenly felt unsure. Yet what was the worst that could happen? She could be home in fifteen minutes if she went straight there. But then she thought, no, why not enjoy this moment of liberty and experience independence. And she remembered what Riccardo had said last night. He was going to go to the station today. She hadn't seen him first thing this morning and Mama had walked with her to school, before going to the market in a probably futile attempt to buy food – anything, whatever was available that day.

The station was not far away and she was sure she knew how to get to the vast, low concrete structure, a crouching monster spewing troops into the city. When she and her family had arrived in the city by train when they left Rome, it had seemed so grey and unwelcoming, and she had not been back there since. She hurried through the back streets, trying not to look directly at anyone, especially men. Mama often said, 'You are becoming quite beautiful, my dear. You will turn men's heads before long.' She didn't want to turn any male heads – well, Bruno's perhaps, but no one else's.

Pausing in a shadowy corner, she made sure her hair was tucked well beneath her black beret. Its colour always caused comment in a city where most heads were so dark, although redheads were not totally unknown; those from Sicily were called Normanne, a reference to their supposed French origin. The Germans were nearly all blonde and she was auburn. Strawberry blonde, Mama had often said when she was very young. She liked that term, better than 'ginger', which was how Tina and Franca always described her, calling her Ginger Girl or Ginger Roman in front of all their classmates. If they were feeling kind, which was rare, they referred to her as capelli rossi, which she preferred.

As she neared the station, she became more aware of guards, some German but mostly Italian fascists. She slipped through the entrance, wondering if Riccardo was still there. Then she realised she recognised one of the men. Alfredo. He looked different to when she had last seen him, but then he had probably been off duty after his good dinner and now he was in his black and green uniform, wearing a pistol strapped into a holster that spanned his broad chest.

Alfredo caught her eye and came towards her, scowling. 'Hey you, where do you think you're going?'

She hadn't expected to be quizzed; she felt her heart increase its pace so much it hurt her breastbone. 'My mother... she sent me... Um... she wants to know which trains are running...'

'What? Don't make me laugh. Doesn't she know there's a war on?' He bent over her and gave a coarse chuckle, almost spitting in her face.

What should she say? This wasn't the kind of liberty she'd longed for and suddenly she felt very frightened and vulnerable.

'My father's niece, from the south. We think she is trying to get here.'

'No chance. Nothing from down south now. Tell her to stay put.'

The sudden shunt of a train being coupled on the far side of the concourse caught her attention. As she looked across, she thought she saw Riccardo at the end of the row of platforms and Alfredo noticed and followed her gaze. 'Oh, that's my brother over there,' she said. 'I must go to him and he can walk home with me.'

'He's yours, is he? Right little nosey beggar he is. Nearly got a clip round the ear, if you know what I mean.' He gave a crude laugh and added, 'No, you don't know what I mean, but you tell him to keep away if he knows what's good for him. Now clear off, the pair of you.'

Gabriella took it to mean that this was the moment she should leave and walked briskly across the wide station hall to where Riccardo was slumped against the wall. His face was tear-stained and he had a bruised cheek. As soon as he saw her, he said, 'You shouldn't have come. It's not safe here.'

'Let's go then. We'll be alright together.' She took his arm and pulled him away, but he said, 'Don't draw attention to yourself, but look over there.'

She glanced across to where he'd inclined his head. A shuffling line of women was getting onto the train, but it wasn't a normal train carriage with slatted wooden seats, like the one she'd travelled on when she and her family had first come here or when they'd had rail journeys in cushioned carriages in the past. This one had solid wooden sides with sliding doors and the only ventilation came from narrow windows at the very top. Several of the women bore bruises and one had her arm in a sling. They were being pushed and jostled by guards, who seemed anxious to get them onto the train and out of sight.

'Keep walking,' Riccardo said. 'Don't let the guards see you've noticed them.'

'Who are they?' Gabriella turned again to look at the despondent women and realised she recognised one of them. 'Look, there's Signora Giardino. She's with the twins, but not the baby.'

'I think they must all be the women who were taken from the convent,' Riccardo said, looking back.

'But where are they going?' Gabriella couldn't stop herself turning around and Signora Giardino caught her eye. She cradled her arms as if she was holding a baby and smiled and nodded. Did that mean the baby was safe somewhere? Gabriella hoped that was the case and then, while she was craning to look, she suddenly felt a hand on her shoulder. It made her jump as she thought it was Alfredo again, but to her relief it was Bruno, in his uniform.

'You don't want to be seen here,' he said in a kind voice, though he wasn't smiling. 'There are too many guards around. It's not a good place for pretty girls.' He kept a firm grip on her shoulder, steering her and Riccardo towards the exit, then looked back at the sentries ordering the women onto the train. 'I'd like to walk you home, but I can't. I have to go. Be careful and I hope I will see you soon.'

Gabriella was sorry to see him leave. She would have felt safer if he had been able to escort them and she wanted to ask him about the strange train filling with tearful women. She'd glanced at the destination board but it didn't say when the train on Platform 16 was leaving nor where it was going.

TWENTY-FIVE

FLORENCE

1 March 1944

Gabriella peered at the drawings on Riccardo's desk, but struggled to understand what they represented. She could recognise the outline and monochrome patterning of the Duomo, the cathedral of Florence. But she couldn't understand why a bird appeared to be flying out of a door, its wings on fire.

'Whatever are you planning to paint now?' she asked her brother, who was now adding a carriage of some kind beside the building.

'It's the Scoppio del Carro,' he muttered, his head bent over his work. 'It's a centuries-old tradition in Florence.'

'"The explosion of the cart"?' she said. 'Why on earth would there be an exploding cart right next to such an important building in the centre of the city? How could that be allowed?'

'It's been happening for hundreds of years.' He threw his charcoal on the floor and screwed up the page he'd been working on into a ball and threw that, too, across the room. 'Papa said I would be able to see it one day. But they haven't done it since the war started and even though I'm old enough now to see it, I don't know if it will happen this year.'

'Tell me,' she said. 'Calm down and tell me what it is. I don't understand what on earth you are talking about.'

He paced the room, waving his arms around, demonstrating how a lit rocket in the shape of a dove flies from the altar into a cart filled with fireworks and back into the cathedral. 'Papa says he has seen it many times. There are sparks all over the Piazza del Duomo and it lights up the sky when all the fireworks explode! I want to see it so much, but nobody knows if it will be happening this year.'

'When is this supposed to happen?'

'At Easter, of course. They've been doing it for nine hundred years, but the war is spoiling everything now.' He kicked at the threadbare rug in front of the fireplace, tearing fibres from its thin pile.

'I still don't understand what it means, but it sounds as if it would be spectacular.'

He threw himself down on the bed next to her, making the frame creak and shake. 'Easter Sunday is April ninth. If they're going to do it, they must be getting the cart ready now. And I know where it's kept. Papa told me. It's not far away, in Via il Prato.'

Gabriella sat up straight, 'You're not thinking of going there, are you?'

'Why not? I really want to see if they're working on it now. If they are, then I might get to see it. Imagine it, Gaby, a painted and gilded carriage, pulled by four white oxen. It has a special name. They call it the Brindellone. It must be a grand sight!'

'I'd like to see it too. If we can find out if it's going to happen, I will have time to persuade Mama that I can go with you at Easter.'

Two days later, Gabriella was allowed out with Riccardo as her escort to visit the main food market, on the pretext of buying flour if they could. They headed for the stalls first, so they could maintain their cover story if they were questioned later. They were in luck, but could only get a small quantity of flour with their state tokens. Many stallholders had little to offer and a large number were closed altogether. The market hardly resembled the bustling thoroughfare it had once been, rich with glistening mozzarella and Tuscan beef, fragrant with coffee, marjoram and olives, and coloured with strings of sun-dried tomatoes, shining red peppers and deep purple aubergines from the local farms. Now it was a sad place, the grandeur of the building with its rusting iron colonnades, upper portico and staircases, echoed their steps in the empty, abandoned market halls.

'This way,' Riccardo said, darting out of the market and down the outside steps. 'It's not far to the Prato now.'

Outside, the streets were busy with housewives running home with meagre purchases, others hanging washing from windows high above. Old women sat in gloomy doorways and elderly men poked around in gutters for cigarette ends. Here and there a dog cocked its leg over rubbish on the flagstones and a canary trilled in a cage above them.

Then Gabriella realised she was familiar with the area. Mama had taken her this way a few months previously to visit the pharmacy established by the monks of the nearby church. 'I need some more herbal medicine and their balsamic pills,' she'd said. 'I'm almost out of them and if this war carries on, I'll be a nervous wreck. You'll enjoy coming with me. It's meant to be the oldest pharmacy in the world.'

Behind the modest street doors, Gabriella had gasped at the gilded interior, mirrors everywhere reflecting the chandeliers and casting light over the few customers. While her mother bought her pills, she studied the glass-fronted cases of bottles and tins, all bearing the name of Santa Maria Novella. The shop's rooms were fragrant with a familiar perfume and she realised she was picking up her mother's scent, which hovered around her person and her clothes. Then Mama stopped by the perfume counter and said, 'I'd better get some cologne as well while I can. Who knows what might happen, the way things are going?'

On the way out, Gabriella said, 'It smells of you in there. Such a lovely smell.'

'That's because I've always worn Acqua di Santa Maria Novella.' Her mother smiled at her. 'It's their oldest cologne, a perfume actually. It was made for Caterina de' Medici in the sixteenth century. Just think – I must smell like a princess from the past!'

They both laughed at the thought and Mama said, 'I'll have to use it sparingly, but I'll dab a little bit on you when we get back.'

Gabriella had treasured that little spot of perfume. She had insisted it should go on her wrist, so she could keep holding it to her nose, trying to work out what herbs and flowers had been used to compose this wonderful smell.

And now, she and Riccardo were about to go past the shop again. Perhaps they could peek inside, to fill their noses with those heavenly scents? But as they approached the pharmacy, they saw German uniforms. Two soldiers outside, idly chatting, and then an officer in gleaming boots stepped out.

'Let's cross the road,' Riccardo said. 'We don't want to get too close to them.'

They kept their eyes on the way ahead and didn't look at the men as they passed, but Gabriella felt their eyes upon her and heard laughing and words spoken in their harsh, guttural language: 'Schau dir diese Rothaarige an.' She couldn't understand what they were saying, but she was sure it related to her appearance and for the hundredth time she wished she didn't look so different and could be dark-haired like her brother.

TWENTY-SIX

FLORENCE

November 2019

For late November it was surprisingly warm and Sofia strolled with her jacket over her arm. 'Why don't we have lunch over there?' she said, pointing across the road from the Pitti Palace to a row of café tables with umbrellas in full sun.

Isobel pulled a comic face. 'Are you sure we're allowed, darling? I don't remember seeing that restaurant on his strict schedule.'

'Come on. He'd only put the walk to and from the gardens on his list. He must have thought he should give us some degree of flexibility. But we can go somewhere else if you'd rather.'

'No, I'm fine with this,' her mother said, taking Sofia's arm as they walked across to sit in the hot sunshine.

That morning, they had peered in the glittering windows of the tiny emporia on the medieval Ponte Vecchio, each shop like a miniature treasure chest, bound with ancient shutters and bolts that secured them overnight. 'We must come back over this bridge later,' Sofia said. 'And take our time choosing us each a souvenir.'

Then they had walked up to the extensive acreage of the Boboli Gardens surrounding the Pitti Palace to admire the view over Florence from the hillside. Domed and sloping tiled roofs stretched before them, forming a tapestry of umber, terracotta and sepia below the bright blue sky, set in the green valley. Behind them, in front of a steep series of terraces, a marble fountain splashed into a basin as big as the swimming pool in Sofia's local gym in London. Elsewhere, water lilies spread across other still pools, statues lurked in the shrubbery and paths wound their way down to an elaborate grotto with statues of Roman gods, all adorned with shells, which Riccardo had insisted was another of the important sights they simply had to see.

'Reminds me of the Botticelli *Venus*, standing in her enormous scallop shell,' Sofia said. 'And I can't help feeling that Dad had been here and knew this place really well. These craggy stalagmites and stalactites remind me of certain elements in his paintings.'

'His trees were never really tree-like,' Isobel murmured, her head on one side, looking at the sculpted forms dripping from the ceiling and erupting from the grotto's floor. 'I suppose he saw this when he was a child. It must have seemed quite magical to a young boy.'

'The Grotta Grande, they call it,' Sofia said, studying the small guide she'd picked up in the hotel. 'Oh, and gosh, this is astonishing, there's a secret passageway called the Vasari Corridor, that starts here in the grotto and leads all the way to the Ponte Vecchio and across the river to another palace. It says it was built by one of the Medicis in the sixteenth century so he could go from his palace to the seat of government at the time. And listen to this – the bridge originally housed the meat market but had to be moved out because the smell wafted up into the corridor. So the goldsmiths then moved in and have been there ever since.'

'Sounds like the lofty rich have always been above the hoi polloi,' her mother said.

Later, as they basked in the sun at their streetside table and studied the menu, Isobel said, 'I tell you what, darling, we should order ribollita. Your father absolutely hated it. He said he could never eat it again, that and polenta. I think maybe it's all they had to eat during the war. But we should try it and thumb our noses at him, figuratively, of course.'

'Ribollita...' Sofia said, finding it on the menu. 'Vegetable soup with beans, thickened with bread. Sounds filling. We won't need to eat much else after that. But I'm happy to give it a go.'

The soup was indeed filling, rather like a hearty minestrone with cannellini beans to bulk it out, in addition to the bread that had soaked in the broth to thicken it. 'There's carrots, potatoes, courgettes, celery, onions, some kind of cabbage as well, I think. I don't know why your father didn't like it.'

'How do you know he didn't?'

'I seem to remember we came across it once in one of his Soho Italian places. He said the name means "reboiled", so perhaps it just conjured up memories of stale soup kept going for days with extra bits thrown in from time to time. Like the old-fashioned stockpot on the stove at my grandmother's.'

With an ice cream and coffee afterwards, they both felt they had eaten enough and set off back towards the river and the bridge of goldsmiths' shops. Now and then, Sofia turned to point out the hidden passageway above them, running through the attics and upper floors of nearby buildings. 'It's not open at present,' she said, after consulting her phone. 'We'll have to come back in a couple of years when the restoration is complete.'

But when they reached the Ponte Vecchio they forgot all about the secret corridor, as they became entranced by the succession of dazzling jewellery displays in the windows of the little shops lining each side of the famous bridge. 'Dad didn't say we couldn't buy ourselves a treat,' Sofia said. 'I'm sure he would have bought you something, if he'd been able to do this trip with you. How about those?' She pointed to an expensive pair of emerald earrings in the window.

'Maybe something a little less pricey, darling,' Isobel murmured, moving along to the next shop, one of the tiniest on the bridge. 'I rather like the natural coral, actually. What do you think?' She pointed to a display of earrings created from polished clusters of orangey-red twigs of coral.

'Looks a bit like a small lobster.' Sofia laughed. 'But the deep reddish-orange colour is lovely. It would suit you.'

'Maybe not those very long ones. They'd catch on my collars and scarves. An inch or so looks about right to me.'

They entered the minuscule shop named after the owner, Anna Maria Formigli, who fetched the display from the window. Isobel held first one then another style to her ears and settled on the first pair she'd seen. She was smiling as they left, then said, 'If your father had been here, he would have chosen for me, I know it. So it feels liberating to be making my own choices at last.' She clutched her daughter's arm and they walked side by side over the bridge, still clustered with groups of tourists admiring the view of the river and the rows of shops, then returned to their hotel to prepare for a night at the opera.

TWENTY-SEVEN

FLORENCE

3 March 1944

Riccardo and Gabriella walked past the church where the monastery's pharmacy had originated, onto the open space of the Prato and then up and down both sides of the long, wide street.

'Do you know where the cart is kept?'

'Not exactly, but it must be here somewhere. Papa said it was always stored in a warehouse after the ceremony.'

'Perhaps they have taken it away to the country for safety.' Uncle Federico had told them that many works of art had been removed from the city's galleries and museums and taken to private villas and palazzos in the countryside. And Michelangelo's *David* was entombed with bricks, in case the roof of the Accademia collapsed if the city was subjected to bombing. Little damage had occurred so far since the autumn, but the citizens of Florence were fearful for their beautiful historic city.

Most of the tall imposing buildings along the Prato had pairs of heavy, studded wooden doors that had admitted grand carriages in centuries past. But now all were locked and bolted, shielding their occupants and their treasures.

Riccardo sighed with disappointment. 'We're never going to

find the cart, are we? But now we're here, we're not far from Piazza Tasso. Come on, I'll show you the fresco there. The paintwork is flaking away and I want to memorise it. Maybe one day I'll paint a copy, or maybe I'll even be able to restore it.'

He began running with his lolloping gait and Gabriella ran with him, till they reached the square lined with trees that provided shade in the high heat of the city's summers so neighbours could sit chatting on benches while children played around them. But as they reached the corner of the square, Riccardo put out his hand to stop her going any further. 'Wait,' he said. 'There's too many soldiers around here.'

She looked over his shoulder across to the far side of the piazza. Armed guards were shouting and herding a large number of men into the school. There seemed to be hundreds of men, both civilians and military, Germans and fascists. 'What's going on?' she whispered, although there was no one nearby to hear her.

'Stay right here. I'll see if I can find out.' Before she could protest, Riccardo was darting around the edge of the square, ducking behind tree trunks, tucking himself into doorways and alleys. She clung to the corner of the building, clutching the cloth bag that held the precious flour, wondering what she would say if she lost the shopping and returned without her brother, asking herself if she could find her way home alone. Apart from the large crowd surrounded by guards, the piazza was empty of residents, but she could see faces peering from shuttered windows and tucked behind doors, watching and waiting.

Then she became conscious of a woman standing close by. She too was craning to see the guarded throng, but kept a shawl drawn over her head and most of her face, as if she wanted to stay hidden. Gabriella looked at her and their eyes met. 'It is not safe here, for a pretty girl like you. Leave while you can,' the woman hissed.

'I have to wait for my brother to come back. He's trying to see what's happening.'

'They've been rounding up the men all night. Good men who want to free Italy from its oppressors.'

'What will happen to them?'

'They're holding them in the school there. But then they will take them away. They're saying they send them off to work, but that's not true. They won't ever come back.'

Gabriella looked again at the crowd, diminished now that most had entered the building across the square. 'Just the men? No women?'

'Not now. We were taken, but then they let us go.'

'You were taken prisoner?'

'Not for long. They thought we wouldn't cause trouble but little do they know.' The woman looked at Gabriella more closely. 'How old are you?'

'Fourteen. I'm fifteen in the summer.'

'You look much older. You could pass for seventeen. They'd like you, with your unusual red hair.'

Gabriella felt uneasy. Why did the woman want to know how old she was? She glanced across the square again. She could see Riccardo coming back towards her. 'My brother is over there. I'll go home with him.'

'Yes, you should go. They'll come this way soon.' The woman's shawl slipped from her head, revealing purple bruises on her cheeks and throat. 'But when you feel ready, if you want to help true Italians, not this lot,' she waved her hand in disgust, 'come back to the Oltrarno. Find the locksmith and say you want to be remembered to Bianca. Say you were a witness in Piazza Tasso this day and you wish to join those who believe the Arno flows in Florence. He will know what that means.'

Gabriella didn't understand. She turned to look for Riccardo, who was weaving between the trees, but by the time he reached her the woman had slipped away. 'Did you see that?' she said. 'That woman who was here? She talked about true Italians and freeing Italy.'

'Then she might have been one of them,' he said, cocking his head back towards the school, where the guards were now closing and locking the heavy doors. 'I know why they've arrested them all and there were women here earlier. They're all partisans, or so the fascists think. They've rounded up about three hundred of them and I heard them say they're keeping them here until the train is ready.'

'So they're not going to be hanged or shot?'

'No, but the locals are saying they are being condemned to a living death. That sounds worse, doesn't it?' He looked back over his shoulder. Some of the guards were coming their way. 'We'd better run.'

As they left, Gabriella noticed the fresco he had brought her to see, painted on the oblique corner of a nearby building. A Madonna and Child, flanked by Wise Men and shepherds, all with golden halos like golden helmets, making them look like holy guards or maybe guardians. The flaking patches of plaster gave the impression of crusted scabs on the once-bright and gilded figures, giving the sacred picture a leprous surface, and Gabriella thought it was as if the beauty of Florence was gradually being infected and decayed by the fascist regime and their friends, the German invaders.

TWENTY-EIGHT

FLORENCE

4 March 1944

Mama rarely met her after school these days and she seemed withdrawn, unhappy, speaking little whether she was cooking, trying to cultivate the garden or when they sat down for supper. She no longer played her opera recordings and she hadn't used her paintbrushes in months, so Riccardo adopted her studio – if he wasn't running around the city. He was still obsessed with the Scoppio del Carro and, as Easter drew nearer, had discovered the Pirotecnica Soldi workshop where the fireworks were made. He went there to spy whenever he wasn't painting, running to the market or slipping back to the Via il Prato.

Gabriella had not dined with her friends for a couple of weeks either. Tina and Franca had been absent for the last three days, but today they asked her to join them at Villa Triste the next day. 'You're looking skinny, Ginger Girl,' Tina said. 'We need to fatten you up.'

She accepted their invitation, although she didn't always enjoy their company, because she knew how much the extra food meant to her family. And mealtimes at home were not enjoyable with the reduced rations and her mother's melancholy, despite her father's attempts to encourage his wife to be optimistic.

As she walked home she thought how she wasn't the only one keen to eat well. A grubby girl in a ragged dress sat listlessly on a step, holding out her hand as she passed. An old woman offered a begging bowl, but didn't have the energy to rise from her seat. Even the pigeons, pecking at the cobbles, were unable to find much nourishment.

When she was nearly home, she saw a figure leaning against the wall of a house nearby and, as she drew closer, she recognised Bruno. He raised his head and smiled. 'I've missed you,' he called out, stepping across the road. 'Where have you been?' He looked tired and his usually pristine uniform was creased and spattered with dark stains.

'I've been invited for dinner tomorrow. Will you be able to walk me home?' She took the arm he offered and they stood out of sight of the palazzo.

'I should be, unless I get reassigned. But it's been very busy and I haven't had an evening off in a while, so I think I'll be there.'

'Good. I don't like it when Alfredo walks me back. He makes me feel uneasy.'

He frowned. 'He'd never touch you, so don't worry about that. But he's not to be trusted, so you should be wary.'

'Please try to be there tomorrow night. I want to go to dinner so much. We haven't had any good meals for a while, so I'm looking forward to eating well for once.'

He pinched her arm. 'You need feeding up. You're getting thin.'

'That's what Tina and Franca were saying.' She laughed.

'Those two – they certainly don't need more food. Even Tina is looking a bit plump these days.' He grinned. 'What a lovely smile you have. Those two are like young witches. But you, you are a beautiful angel.'

He looked into her eyes and Gabriella felt that he was getting close to kissing her on the lips. But it was daylight, they were standing on the street; it would not be proper. She would have liked it to happen, of course, but she knew she should not encourage him. So she said, 'I'm glad you were here to meet me. It's so boring in the house. Riccardo is always running off on his own and my parents are very busy. I don't have any real friends at school either.'

'But you have Tina and Franca. They are your friends, aren't they?' He peered at her, a smile hovering on his lips.

She shuffled her feet, wondering how best to answer. 'Yes, but they're not real friends. They're always teasing me. They call me Ginger Girl. I'm just a pet they can tease and torment. But it's worth it for the lovely food.'

He laughed loudly. 'Those two. The terrible sisters. Like the ugly sisters in *Cenerentola*. They are jealous of you and your beautiful hair.' He coiled a strand of her long hair around his fingers so the sun caught the glints of auburn and fiery gold. 'I love the colour of your hair. Look how it flames in the light.'

In that moment, she felt she could fall in love with him. She knew she was too young to be courted, but she felt a strong attraction developing between them, as powerful as the magnet that Mama used to pick up fallen pins when she was altering their clothes.

'Thank you. You are very kind. It is nice to know I have a true friend.'

'I am your friend, Gaby. You can tell me anything you like.' He squeezed her hand. 'And your brother, he is not good company for you?'

'He is always playing some game of his own. I used to join in, but he is very tiresome and rather childish. He's invented a secret code and writes down conversations he's overheard. Then he pretends he's delivering secret messages around the city. He sometimes leaves them in wine windows all over the place.'

'Aah, boys like to play at being spies, don't they? But he is a just

a child. He isn't doing any harm.' He stroked her hair. 'While you...
you are a beautiful young woman and have grown out of such juve-
nile games, I think.'

'You're right. He is a child. He dragged me all the way to Via il
Prato the other day, trying to find out if the Scoppio del Carro is
being prepared for Easter.'

Bruno burst out laughing again. 'Explosive materials in the
middle of a war? That's hardly likely! What an idiot. You would do
better not to go with him in future.'

'And then he insisted we went over to Piazza Tasso and I was
really frightened, seeing so many soldiers. What was going on
there?'

His expression instantly changed and he looked stern. 'Your
brother is putting you at risk. There was some serious trouble over
there. You don't want to be near people like that. Please don't listen
to him any more. Is he planning to take you anywhere else?'

'I think he wants to go back to the station again. Why, what is
happening?'

Bruno shook his head. 'Your brother is bad news. He should
not be encouraging a beautiful girl like you to take risks while the
war is still raging. You must tell me if he tries to take you anywhere
from now on. And maybe tell me what he is writing in these
messages. I want to keep you and your family safe.'

With a sinking heart, she realised how foolish she had been to
be persuaded by Riccardo. Mama had thought they were only
helping her by searching for flour in the market. She had not
known how far they had walked and what they had seen. If they
had been caught up in the crowd and not returned, she wouldn't
have known how to find them.

'You're right. I went out with him because I was bored, but I
can see now that it wasn't safe. I won't do it again.'

He squeezed her hand. 'Good. I want to be sure you won't
come to any harm.' Turning to leave, he said, 'I will definitely be
there after dinner tomorrow to walk you home. And perhaps if you

hear that your brother has plans for more adventures you will tell me, yes?' He replaced his cap and saluted. How handsome he was and how right he was that she had now outgrown Riccardo's games.

TWENTY-NINE

FLORENCE

November 2019

Sofia and her mother walked to the opera house by way of a bar recommended by the hotel concierge. 'They serve the best aperitivo,' she said. 'You will eat extremely well there beforehand.'

With their order of Aperol spritzes they were invited to help themselves to a buffet of cold beef, ham, roast potatoes, courgettes with tomatoes and slices of grilled aubergine. 'You'd be lucky to get a few crisps with a drink back home,' Sofia said. 'This is like a complete meal.' The bar owner did not look pleased when they left after only one drink, but they explained they had tickets for the opera and he bowed as if he too was giving a performance worthy of an encore.

As the lights in the auditorium dimmed and the music began to play, members of the audience were still drifting in and chatting to old acquaintances. It was, Sofia thought, as if the opera was simply the accompaniment to their social life. Or maybe they had been many times before and didn't need to hear every refrain.

'What did you think, darling?' Isobel said when the lights lifted for the interval after the conclusion of the first of the three short operas, the fading bars accompanied by cheers and whistles from the rapturous audience.

'I loved it and it's very familiar. I'm sure Dad used to play this first opera all the time. Was it his favourite?'

'I honestly don't know, but he certainly played *Il Tabarro* a lot. Not very cheerful, though, is it?'

'Unhappy wife, husband kills her lover. No, it's not.' Sofia looked at her mother. She didn't dare say it, but had her father sent them to see this opera because it was about a dissatisfied wife? Was there a message here, somewhere?

'Thank goodness we had those big plates of snacks with our drink beforehand,' Isobel said, when her credit card failed at the opera house bar. 'I don't know why it isn't working.'

'Maybe because interval drinks and antipasti weren't on Dad's itinerary,' teased Sofia. 'Perhaps we shouldn't go off-track again.'

Isobel laughed. 'I think we should go off-piste at every opportunity. I've toed the line all those years and now I want to make my own decisions. And for a start, I think we should only stay for the second opera and then leave. We've got to walk all the way back and if we stay for the whole thing, we won't get to the hotel until nearly midnight.'

'No, I think we should stay for the whole lot. When are we ever going to come to Italy again and go to the opera? We'll be quite safe walking back, however late. And then we can have a drink back at the hotel. Let's go mad and raid the minibar!'

They walked briskly back after the third opera, the story of the counterfeit will. Sofia couldn't see any immediate parallels with her parents in this, but still wondered if her father was sending them a message with his choice of entertainment.

'I think Riccardo booked this performance so we could have the complete Italian experience,' Isobel said as they hurried along, arm in arm.

'You mean the way the Italians were greeting their friends throughout and their cheers at the end.' Sofia clutched her mother tight. She could hear shouting across the street, a drunk, possibly. 'Hold onto your handbag, just in case,' she said. 'It's not far now.'

When they arrived at the hotel, the lobby was almost deserted but the receptionist offered to serve them at the bar. 'We won't have to empty the minibar after all, darling,' Isobel said, perching on a chrome stool topped with a cobalt velvet cushion.

'And better nibbles down here,' Sofia said, piercing an olive stuffed with pimento and taking a sip of her chilled prosecco. 'You know, I can't help wondering – why did Dad decide to organise this trip for November? Everyone I mentioned it to said November is the worst month to come. It's normally very rainy at this time.'

'I've no idea, darling. Who knows what was going through his mind when he decided to arrange this?'

'But then I couldn't help thinking that maybe it was because of this opera. They don't have long runs like plays or musicals, do they? Operas have short seasons. So it wouldn't have been featured in the opera house's programme at any time other than now. But why choose this particular opera? *Il Trittico* – that means the triptych, doesn't it? It's a term I'd associate more with paintings than classical music.'

'Honestly, darling, I haven't a clue. Maybe because he was especially fond of this work, perhaps. I really don't know.'

'But just think. The first one is about jealousy and betrayal, with the man killing his wife's lover. The second is the tragic death of the young nun, who has a treacherous sister, and the third one is about a man's inheritance being contested.'

'The last one's more than that,' Isobel said. 'The lead character, Gianni Schicchi, offers to impersonate the deceased. He pretends to be the dead man on his deathbed and instructs a notary of his final wishes in order to change the will. Bit like your father, don't you think?'

Sofia had been thinking the same thing, but hadn't been sure how to raise the subject. 'The deceased speaking from the grave, you mean?'

'It feels like that. I mean, I know it's not a question of contesting a will in our case. But still, the idea that your father's dead and yet is still making decisions for us feels very strange. I keep trying to tell myself that his influence is benign, that he is watching over us, wanting us to enjoy his birthplace, but I can't help feeling there's more to it than that.'

'I'm sure there's no hidden motive in this, Mum. For some reason, towards the end of his life he wanted to come back to Florence one last time with you. Then, realising he wasn't going to be well enough or even last that long, he still wanted you to come here. I expect he thought you would never do it, unless he made all the arrangements.' Sofia grasped her mother's hand and squeezed it. 'I feel he had a love/hate relationship with the city for whatever reason. I'm hoping we'll learn what it was, but at least in the mean-time we can have a wonderful time.'

'But to be so manipulative. Right down to the way that letter was delivered. He must have known how upsetting that would be. He must have made specific arrangements with old Carmichael, his solicitor.'

'I see what you mean.' Sofia thought of the many conversations and correspondence she'd had with her father's solicitor. 'He must have given him precise instructions, I suppose. I remember telling Carmichael we were coming to Florence.'

'He was probably given a copy of the itinerary then. But what if we'd switched hotels? Then what would he have done? That would have thrown him!' Isobel's words were slurring. She was getting tipsy as well as tired.

'It's a pity the opera house was so modern. I'd love to have gone to an old-fashioned theatre, all dark red velvet and gilding.'

'Then I'll have to take you to Venice, darling. Once we've got this extremely annoying trip over and done with, I'll take you to La Fenice. But right now, my bed is all I can think about.'

Later, Sofia thought her mother had fallen asleep as soon as her head hit the pillow. But as she turned out her bedside light, she heard Isobel shuffle and say, 'You're probably right. He chose that opera deliberately. Not a single thing about this trip has been left to chance.'

THIRTY

FLORENCE

5 March 1944

Friday could not come soon enough for Gabriella. She was longing to see Bruno again and because he had admired her auburn hair so much, she tucked her hairbrush into her school bag, so she could undo her plait in the evening and let her glorious long hair trail over her shoulders. She sneaked into Riccardo's room when he went off to the studio, found his notebook in its hiding place and stuffed it in her pocket. She would slip it back once she had shown Bruno. She was sure Riccardo wouldn't miss it now he was so obsessed with the Scoppio del Carro.

As before, the table at the Sad Villa was spread with a sumptuous display of food, not as varied as on previous occasions, but still more splendid than the dishes her mother was managing to produce. Delicious aromas of pancetta, truffle oil and courgette greeted her as she hovered with her plate, wondering what to eat first and what to smuggle back home. She ignored the gnocchi with spring vegetables as she was sick of potato dumplings, having made them time and again throughout the winter. Instead, she took a veal escalope, cooked with baby artichokes and prosciutto, and a serving of broad bean risotto. On one side of her plate, she placed slices of potato and sausage pizza, knowing how excited Riccardo would be to see his favourite food, while for her parents she took thick slices of ham.

'Fill up while you can, Ginger,' Tina teased. 'Poppa says we might not be staying here much longer.'

Gabriella immediately thought of Bruno. If the girls and their father were moving on, would he be leaving too?

'Why does he say that?'

'Because of the war, of course, stupid. Don't you know anything?' Franca sneered. 'It depends how it all goes. We might stay, we might not.'

'But wherever we go, we'll be the winners,' her sister said. 'We'll crush anyone who doesn't support us.'

'Will Bruno have to go too?' Gabriella didn't dare look directly at the girls in case they noticed her blushes, so she kept her eyes on her plate.

Tina shrugged. 'Who knows? Maybe, but he'll be going off and serving in the army soon, he's nearly old enough.'

Franca gave Gabriella a sly look. 'You like him, don't you?' The laugh that followed was crude and moist crumbs splattered from her mouth all over her tight blouse. 'Ha ha, you've got a crush on Bruno! Are you in love? Does he love you?'

Gabriella could feel herself reddening and she stammered, 'He's very kind. I just wondered if he'd be leaving, that's all.'

'Maybe we should help him walk her home tonight,' Tina said with a smirk aimed at her sister. 'See what they've been getting up to without us.'

'Let's see. We can decide later what's going to be the most fun.'

Gabriella felt a prickling chill crawl over her skin. She didn't understand much of the girls' life or their motivation, but she was beginning to understand their characters better and if she hadn't been tempted by the food and the opportunity to see Bruno, she thought she would have tried to discourage their interest in her.

At lunchtime that day, some of the girls had clustered around the ornamental pool in the school's garden, edged by the cloisters where the girls gathered to eat each day. The fountain no longer splashed into the pool, but it was still filled with green water. Tina and Franca were leaning over the stone rim, shrieking with laughter, while other girls were watching with horrified fascination. Gabriella moved alongside to see what was so amusing, but it was only when she knelt down beside Franca that she could actually see what was happening.

The pond was shimmering with tadpoles, like inky commas waving their tails, clustered near the edge of the water. And the sisters were fishing them out, one at a time, placing them on the stone edging, then holding the sides of each tadpole's tail and pulling it apart, so it split into three sections. They then released the maimed creatures into the water, where they attempted and failed to swim.

The sisters were laughing hysterically, 'Three legs isn't better than two!' Franca shrieked. 'They've got two legs and a willy now,' yelled Tina, scooping up another tadpole.

'Stop it, you're being cruel. They'll never be able to turn into frogs now,' one of the watching girls said, grimacing at the sight.

'Have one, then, froggy lover,' Franca said, throwing the tadpole in a handful of slimy water at her critic, soaking her blouse and hair.

'There's hundreds of them. Do you want the school full of frogs?' Tina jeered too, then stood up. 'I'm bored. Come on, let's see who's got something good for their lunch.'

The pair were about to leave but Stefanina stopped them. She stood her ground before the sisters, her eyes bright and piercing, and said, 'You two are the nastiest girls in this school. No one likes either of you!'

Tina shoved her full in the chest, knocking Stefanina off balance so she slipped and fell against the rim of the pool, grazing her elbow and soaking her blouse. But she didn't cry. She picked herself up as the sisters sauntered off to begin inspecting other girls' lunch parcels and yelled, 'One of these days you'll pay for your dreadful behaviour! Thank goodness I won't have to stay here much longer!'

Gabriella had stayed silent throughout that exchange, ashamed that she didn't dare intervene, like Stefanina. However sickened she was by their torture of the tiny tadpoles, she feared the sisters' retaliation. And now, as she sat with them eating the food provided by their father and his cohorts, she suddenly lost her appetite and felt she could not swallow another mouthful.

'What's the matter, Ginger? Don't you like your dinner any more?' Tina had noticed she was no longer eating.

'She's lovesick, that's what,' sniggered Franca. 'Pining for her lover boy.'

'Kiss, kiss,' smooched her sister, wrapping her arm across her face and kissing the soft inner flesh. 'I know, let's get her ready to meet her Romeo.' Tina took a large spoonful of aioli from her plate, grabbed the back of Gabriella's neck and tried to force the garlic mayonnaise between her lips. 'Here you are, darling, you'll smell lovely tonight.'

Gabriella struggled and tried to turn her head away, but Tina shouted, 'Franca, grab her. Get her mouth open.'

She felt the metal spoon pushing against her lips, bruising the tender skin, scraping her teeth as it was forced inside her mouth. When it was pulled away again, she tasted blood as well as the strongly flavoured mayonnaise and she spat into her napkin. 'Oh, dearie me, didn't we like it?' The sisters shrieked with laughter as Gabriella tried to clean the oily mess from her face, her blouse and her loosened hair. She knew she looked a mess, but she tried hard not to cry and bit back her tears and her retort.

After a couple of minutes, she said, 'I think perhaps I'd better go. I can walk home by myself tonight.'

'Oh no, we wouldn't want that, would we?' Tina said as she stood up and pulled back the curtain separating them from the main dining room. The men were in a celebratory mood, swigging wine, making toasts and singing.

'Poppa?' Tina called across to her father at the head of the table. 'May we walk our friend home now? And may Bruno come with us?'

The Major smiled to see his beloved daughters. 'Piccoli angeli, come to me.' He held out his arms to embrace both girls, while Gabriella waited by the curtained entrance. 'I think you may want to stay with the boys tonight. You don't want to miss all the fun, do you?'

The sisters squealed with delight and Tina said, 'You mean we have visitors again?'

'Yes, but we shan't have them here for long. They are due to leave us soon. So we must have fun with them while we can, mustn't we?'

'Ooh yes, can we go downstairs right away?'

'Yes, but Alfredo should go with you.' He beckoned to the disgruntled man, who reluctantly took a last gulp of his wine, put down his glass and followed the excited girls, who raced from the room.

Bruno stood and buttoned up his jacket. He was straight-faced, not wanting to look eager, Gabriella assumed. His lips lacked a smile but his eyes were smiling. As they left the villa, the Major called after him, 'And don't be long. We aren't finished yet.'

Once they were outside, Bruno took her hand. He must have already noticed that her clothes were stained and her face and hair were greasy, for he said, 'I guess those girls have been teasing you. Don't worry, you smell lovely. Aioli is my favourite.'

That made her feel a little better. If only she had kept her hair tied back in its plait, she thought. It was hanging in sticky strands around her face. 'They've been in an unpleasant mood all day. I'm quite glad to be leaving early.'

'So am I,' he said. 'The boys will probably have gone back to work by the time I get back, but there should still be something left for me to eat.'

'I've got some pizza in my pockets,' she said. 'I was taking it back to eat later, but you can have it if you like.'

'No, Gaby, you keep it. You need it more than me. I know your family is short of food. Eat it yourself or share it with your brother. How is he, by the way? Has he been up to his usual tricks?'

Then she remembered she had something else for him. 'I brought this,' she said. 'It's his notebook. All in code, like I told you. If you can let me have it back once you've read it. I don't want any harm to come to him, even though he can be very annoying sometimes.'

'Thank you. I'll read it and I promise I'll look out for him. He must be careful, with all that is happening in the city these days.'

As they walked through the deserted streets he stroked her hand and when they arrived at the corner of the building opposite her home and a nearby church bell chimed, he laughed, saying, 'Now it feels like you really are Cenerentola and must get home before midnight.' He bent to kiss her and as he aimed for her cheek, she turned her face a little so their lips met.

He pulled away hastily, then stroked her hair. 'Not yet, little one,' he said. 'When you are older.' He saluted and walked away.

As she watched him go, she felt conflicted. Was it because she was too young? Or too forward? Or did she simply stink so much of garlic that he couldn't bear to be so close to her? She felt her face burning and waited a moment for it to cool before entering the palazzo. She didn't want Mama asking too many questions, so she placed the wrapped pizza on the hall table and raced to her room to rid herself of her stained and smelly clothing and wash her hair.

THIRTY-ONE

FLORENCE

November 2019

Sofia noticed her mother taking particular care that morning as she dressed for their appointment with Gabriella. She saw her turning this way and that in front of the full-length mirrors that fronted the wardrobe, rejecting first one scarf then another until she was satisfied with her appearance.

'Mum, you look lovely. Are you going to wear your new earrings as well?' Isobel was holding various pairs to her ears, trying to decide which looked best. Was she really worried about meeting this secret sister? She needn't have been concerned about the way she looked, Sofia thought; her mother was elegant and still so good-looking. Her hair may have faded over the years into silver, but her hairdresser ensured she still carried off a sharp ash-blonde bob, just below her jawline.

'No, I don't think I'll wear the coral ones today. She'll think I've been a typical tourist. I'll stick with diamond studs.' She inserted the small stones Riccardo had bought her many years before after one of his first major sales. He'd always given her expensive gifts of jewellery when he'd done well with his paintings.

'I'm sure you needn't worry too much about what you're wearing. She won't mind.'

'I don't know about that. She comes from a good family. She may be one of those refined, elegant Italian women who always look as if they've just left the hair salon. Besides, I don't want to let your father down. And you shouldn't either. You aren't going like that, are you, darling?'

Sofia looked down at her feet. She was wearing her favourite silver trainers. She'd worn them the day before as well, though not to the opera the other night. 'They're very comfortable. But if it bothers you, I'll wear my black boots.'

'And leave that scruffy trench coat behind too. Wear your smart navy blazer. It's not going to rain today.'

Sofia rolled her eyes, but didn't say any more. Clearly her mother was becoming anxious about this meeting. What was it he'd written again? *Experiences long ago, experiences I have never been able to forget, have coloured my work throughout my career and, I suspect, made me a man who was not easy to live with.* And suddenly she too began to feel uneasy about this assignation. What were they going to uncover when they met Gabriella? What secrets could have been hidden when Riccardo left Florence, never to return?

She brushed her hair and tied it back neatly in a style her mother had always liked. If her father felt it was important that they followed his instructions and met his sister, then they would, whatever the outcome might be.

'I'm ready,' she said. 'Will this do?' She turned to face her mother. 'We're quite early, so we can take it slowly and maybe have coffee on the way. I spotted a little café the other day when we crossed the Ponte Vecchio. It's set right on the edge of the river, really close to the bridge. It must have a lovely view. Let's go there first.'

After strolling along the river from their hotel, they crossed the bridge lined with goldsmiths' shops and found the café Sofia had picked out. On a terrace dotted with pots of geraniums, herbs and salad leaves, they ordered coffee. It being a typically Italian establishment, their hot drinks arrived with complementary slices of homemade cake, scented with lemon and sprinkled with candied peel. 'I love how generous all the cafés are,' Sofia said, taking a bite of the cake. 'Everything you order comes with delicious free snacks, like that bar where we had a drink the other night before the opera.'

Sipping their coffee and gazing at the layers of shops and dwellings that made up the Ponte Vecchio, Sofia felt she could sense the medieval pulse of Florence beating beneath the modern face of tourism. Pots of red geraniums decorated every windowsill facing the river, reminding her that people really lived in this fairytale creation. The bridge had barely changed since the early days of its construction, with subsequent generations adding more and more layers to the structure, including the uppermost tier with windows that formed part of the Vasari Corridor.

'Such a pity that the corridor isn't open at present,' Isobel said. 'Maybe we'll have to come back again in a few years, when it's been restored. Don't you think it would be wonderful to walk in the footsteps of the Medici?'

'You'd be walking in the footsteps of Hitler and Mussolini as well, don't forget. Maybe that wouldn't be so wonderful. Such arrogance.'

'Well, darling, I still think it would be fascinating.'

'It's so beautiful here,' Sofia said. 'The Florentines must have been so anxious about their city in the war. They had so much to lose.'

'So did Britain. We lost Coventry Cathedral.'

'That's not quite the same. Sad, I know, but hardly in the same league.' Sofia finished her cake and leant over the balcony railings to look at the lower arches of the bridge. 'Dad must have been here during the war. He was born before it started, wasn't he?'

'Quite some time before, 1931. And I believe life was somewhat unsettled and difficult even when he was very young, before the war started.'

'Do you think that's what he meant in his letter then? That stuff about experiences long ago? Is he referring to something awful about his childhood?'

'I simply don't know, darling. He never talked about his early years.' Isobel shook her head. 'But yes, it could mean that.'

Sofia looked at her watch. 'We'd better go and find out. It's time we went.'

After recrossing the river, they walked through the city centre, passing gelateria displaying tubs of brightly coloured ice cream and sorbet, confectioners offering figures moulded in dark chocolate, while the strong scent of Tuscan truffles crept from the purveyors of dried fungi permeating the local olive oil. But as they neared Via Faenza, where they knew the Rinaldi palazzo was located, Isobel suddenly stopped walking.

'What's the matter?' Sofia turned to look at her mother, who was standing with her head bent, hand clamped to her forehead. 'Are you not feeling well?'

'I'm sorry, I can't do it. I simply can't do it.'

'Oh, come on, we're nearly there now. It's only another ten minutes at the most.'

'No, I can't. You go on without me.'

'Mum, let's sit down for a moment. We'll carry on when you've had a rest.' Sofia steered her mother towards a nearby bench. 'I expect you've got a bit tired, that's all. It's further than I thought, I know.'

'No, it's not that. I'm fine, darling. I just don't want to go there and meet her, this... this person I've never met, never really heard of before. She's going to ask me questions about our life together and our marriage, I know she is.'

'Is that what's bothering you? Don't be silly. I can steer her away from anything that might make you feel awkward.'

'No, don't you see? I'm afraid.' Isobel wrestled with a tissue in her hands. 'I'm scared, Sofia. I don't know what she might tell us.'

'She might not have anything to tell us. She must be very old.

She's older than Dad, isn't she? Maybe she won't remember anything from years ago.'

'Perhaps. But that doesn't make me feel any better.'

'We don't have to stay long, if you feel uncomfortable. But aren't you just that little bit curious? I know I am.' Sofia squeezed her mother's hand to reassure her.

'But she may tell us something that will change everything.'

'What on earth do you mean?'

'She may reveal something about your father that I'd rather not know. He could turn out to have been a stranger to me all his life. And then I might feel that my time with him, my marriage, didn't mean anything at all.'

Sofia threw her arms around her mother and held her tight. She was beginning to feel apprehensive too. She loved her father – no, she'd loved the father she'd known. Would she still love him the way she did if it turned out that the experiences he referred to were ones she'd rather not know about? She couldn't tell, but this might be her only chance to uncover his inner thoughts and maybe understand his strange paintings.

MESSAGE FOUR

Enog enoyreve sah erehw?

THIRTY-TWO

FLORENCE

6 March 1944

Gabriella was becoming used to finding no one waiting for her when she left school at the end of the day. She walked quickly, anxious to leave the taunts from Tina and Franca behind her. They had not sat with her in class or at lunchtime; in fact, they had distanced themselves, claiming she stank of garlic and asking who would want to be friends with a girl who smelt like that?

As she neared the palazzo, she was surprised to see a uniformed member of the fascists standing outside. If it had been Bruno she would have been elated, but it wasn't, it was the surly Alfredo. For a moment she hung back, hoping he would go soon, but when she saw him walk up and down the narrow paving and then return to the front door, she realised he was staying right there. She thought of leaving and walking around the streets for a while, but as she turned to go, her movement caught his eye and he looked across to right where she was standing.

'Hey you! Ginger girl! Come here!'

She felt her cheeks burning. It was bad enough suffering the insensitive taunts from the two ugly sisters at school, but to hear the jibe out in the street was humiliating. She walked towards him, hoping she could pass by and disappear inside the house.

She tried to brush past him, but he grabbed her by the arm. 'We've been waiting for you. You're wanted indoors. We have some questions for you. Come with me.'

He pulled her inside and took her into the elegant reception room, where Major Michel Carisi was reclining, legs casually crossed, on the eau de Nil watered-silk sofa, smoking a small cheroot. 'Aah, here's our little friend at last.' He patted the space beside him and she couldn't help noticing how his manicured and buffed nails contrasted with the wiry black hairs sprouting on the back of his hand. 'Come and sit down next to me, my dear. We need to have a little talk.'

Gabriella slid her school bag from her shoulder and did as she was told, sitting as far away as possible and smoothing her school skirt over her knees. She looked around anxiously. The house was very silent, no sounds of pans in the kitchen or sweeping in the courtyard. 'Where's my mother? Is she here? Does she know I'm back?'

'Do not concern yourself, my child. Your mother is being very helpful to us. So is your father.' He put the cheroot to his lips, as if he was thinking, and the tip glowed. The acrid smoke stung her eyes and she blinked and turned away, stifling a cough. 'Tell me, my dear, how long have you been living in this beautiful home?'

'We came here last year, in February. So I've been here for over a year.'

'And you are about the same age as my lovely daughters, I suppose?' he said, smiling, his eyes crinkling.

'I'll be fifteen in July.'

'Aah, you are growing up fast, quite the young lady. Perhaps you can teach my girls some manners, eh?' He laughed heartily and the growing ash from his cheroot hovered over the silk upholstery.

Gabriella could feel herself blushing again and lowered her head. She wished her mother would come into the room and sit nearby and hold her hand. And as if the Major could read her innermost thoughts, he reached for her hand, holding it and stroking the back with his large thumb.

'So you are old enough, I think, to understand how in these difficult times, it is important to know who is loyal to Italy and who isn't? So I want you to tell me – who lives here with you in this very spacious, beautiful palazzo?'

Her whole being was trembling as she tried to give him a clear answer. 'Just my parents, my brother and me.'

He released her and she made her hands grip each other tight, holding them close in her lap, willing the shaking to cease.

'Are you quite sure about that, little one?' He waved his arm towards the hall door. 'So many big rooms, such a lovely home, how can you be sure there aren't intruders hiding in the attic?' She heard Alfredo chuckling from his position by the doorway. 'Are you quite sure no one else has been living here?'

She thought about the Giardinos and the two little children who hid so well when they played in the garden the night their baby brother was born. She thought about the shadows she'd seen that flitted like moths in the night and the secretive men who lived in the basement. 'I think my parents took in lodgers at one time, but I don't know who they were.'

'And did you ever see these so-called lodgers? Or did they just stay in their rooms all the time?'

She wanted to deny all knowledge of the palazzo's other occupants, but somehow knew that it was better to give him a little of the truth than none at all. 'Well, I think sometimes they would come downstairs and walk in the garden at night. I only know that because I heard voices, but I never saw them. Because I have to go to school every day, Mama always makes me go to bed early.'

'Of course she does. Not that a beautiful young lady like you needs beauty sleep, eh, Alfredo?' Again, Gabriella heard coarse laughter from the scowling guard. 'And what about anyone else? Do you think any other people have been staying here?'

'I don't know. But I did sometimes think I could smell cooking in the basement.'

He looked at her with his piercing eyes like black beads as if he was trying to get inside her head and rifle through her memories. 'I see. That's rather what we thought. We have been all over the place and there are signs that the cellar has been occupied fairly recently. I expect your parents will be able to tell us a little more.'

'Where are they?' Gabriella hoped they were both safe and not far away. And she wondered where they had found her father. Did they know he was a curator and had they gone to the museum to talk to him?

'They are helping us with our enquiries for now. My four saints will persuade them. But don't worry, I am sure they will return soon.' The Major stubbed his cigar out on the silken arm of the sofa, then stood up and walked towards the door. But as he and Alfredo were about to leave, he turned and said, 'And tell your brother to be careful. He may be young still, but he is not too young to be of interest to us.'

Gabriella tried to rise from the couch after they had left, but her legs were shaking so. Her mouth was dry and she felt her breathing increase rapidly. The men had gone, but where was Riccardo and where were the rest of the family?

After another moment she felt steady enough to leave her seat and walked out to the hall with its chequered black and white tiles. Mama always placed an arrangement of seasonal leaves and flowers in a misty Lalique vase on the marble-topped console below a large gilded mirror. That morning, she had filled it with arched stems of pale lilac wisteria. Now the shattered vase lay in pieces on the floor in a pool of water with the wilted flowers. In the kitchen, the stove was not lit and the family's limited food supply was scattered across the terracotta floor, kicked and thrown from the ransacked larder.

She felt tears welling, but held them back. She could salvage some of the rice and polenta, the potatoes were still good and the last of the wretched *buristo* was untouched. She would do her best to clean up and keep busy until her parents and brother returned. At least she hoped they would return.

THIRTY-THREE

FLORENCE

6 March 1944

It felt strange and unsettling to be alone in the silent palazzo. Gabriella kept telling herself that the family would return soon from wherever they were and that her mother would be pleased to know she had tried to restore order.

Picking the grains of rice out of the polenta and the remains of the flour took forever. She did well salvaging the rice, but the rest was hard to separate and in the end she swept the two together and hoped she hadn't also collected a quantity of dust and grit from the kitchen floor. But the staples were so precious she could not bear to waste them and she was sure her mother would have done the same.

Luckily, their little supply of olive oil hadn't been wasted and two eggs remained on a shelf in the larder. Also, the salt jar had not been emptied; she knew that would have upset Mama. The salt had been given in exchange for clothing and had been painstakingly collected from icy country roads during the winter. Although her mother complained that their friend had collected grit as well as salt, she was grateful for the dirty brown seasoning and would have been in tears if it had been taken.

It was clear that preparations for supper had not begun before the house was emptied of its occupants, so Gabriella lit the stove with olive wood and set water to boil. She decided to make gnocchi with some of the polenta, so the eggs and potatoes could be saved for another time. Once she had spread the yellow paste out to set, she stepped outside into the courtyard to see what herbs were growing so she could make pesto of some kind. But devastation greeted her here too. The flourishing pots of herbs lay in shards on the flagstones, the plants wilting where they'd been kicked over.

At that point, Gabriella sobbed for a moment. The destruction was so pointless and cruel. Then she took a deep breath, told herself not to be beaten and found a trowel so she could replant the herbs in among the tall irises growing at the base of the courtyard walls. *There's no point in wallowing in tears*, she thought, *I have to save what I can.* And when she'd finished, she picked the bruised and wilted leaves from the basil, hoping the rest of the plant would recover.

All this work distracted her from her worries about her family for a time, but once she had done all she could in the kitchen and courtyard, she began to feel extremely anxious again. It was half past five and would soon be dark. The light was already fading and the garden was disappearing into deepening shadows.

She wondered whether to start shaping the gnocchi, but the polenta wasn't quite firm enough, so she lit the lamp on the kitchen counter and began chopping and then pounding the basil in the mortar. The rhythmic motion was soothing and she remembered her mother's instructions to pound it into a paste. She knew it wouldn't be that good without pine nuts or Parmesan, but with a pinch of salt and a little oil it would still add flavour to their meal.

And as she pounded, she thought she caught the flicker of a light in the corner of her eye. She looked up from her mortar and pestle and it happened again, a tiny spark through the kitchen window. The reflection of the lamp, she thought, but when she looked again she realised there was a light outside, coming from the chapel. Maybe Riccardo had been there all along, painting again.

He had finished his fresco of the lamb long ago, but he was always coming up with ideas for new pieces of work. Perhaps he was immersed in his work and had no inkling of what had happened here today and Major Carisi's words were nothing but an empty threat.

She took the lantern to help her find her way. The moon was rising, but it was veiled by clouds and gave little light. As she approached the chapel, she began to feel nervous. What if the guards had returned? What if it was Alfredo? Perhaps this wasn't a wise move after all.

She trod softly over the flagstones and the chapel door was ajar, so there was no noise as she slipped through. The light she had seen was coming from the altar, where the flames of the candles were waving to her. Someone must have lit them recently, for they hadn't burned far down. She looked around, but the darkness made it hard to tell whether anyone was lurking behind the pews.

The door to the tower was open and she went to the bottom of the steps and called softly, 'Riccardo? Are you up there?' She could not detect a reply but, holding the lantern, she went up the steps to just below his painting, where the lamb with its bleeding cut throat gazed at her peacefully. She called again, but still there was no answer.

Turning round and going back down the steps, she suddenly thought she heard a sound. She looked up the turret steps and then she heard it again. It wasn't within the tower, it was in the main chapel. A soft sobbing, so sad it pierced her heart, and she knew it was her brother and she had to find him.

She walked back towards the altar, stood there very still and listened. It was coming from the right-hand side of the chapel. It was coming from the confessional. She ran, trying not to douse her lamp, then pulled back the curtain. Scrunched up on the narrow cushioned seat, his knees drawn up to his chest, his arms wrapped tight around them, was Riccardo. She held the light close to see him properly. His cheeks were wet with tears and the shoulder of his white shirt bore a dark stain. She looked more closely: it looked like blood.

THIRTY-FOUR

FLORENCE

November 2019

Sofia reached out to the long metal bell pull at the palazzo entrance. 'I'm going to ring the doorbell now,' she said. 'Are you sure you're going to be able to do this?'

Isobel threw back her shoulders and removed her dark glasses. She'd retouched her lipstick and her mascara had not smudged with her tears. She took a deep breath and said, 'Come on. Let's get it over and done with.'

As the bell's ringing tone echoed inside, they heard clipped footsteps on hard tiles and the door was opened by a tall, bearded young man. 'We have an appointment with Gabriella Dvorak,' Sofia said. 'We are Isobel and Sofia Rinaldi.'

'Of course. My grandmother has been expecting you. Please follow me. She is in the garden, tending to her roses.'

They followed him through the hallway, where a striking arrangement of orange and purple bird of paradise flowers stood on a marble console table. An ornate gilded mirror reflected the sculptural blooms and Sofia caught sight of her mother clenching her jaw, showing her determination to retain control of her emotions.

Beyond the hall, through a salon with gilt furniture upholstered in eau de Nil watered silk, open French doors led out onto a walled courtyard, where a fountain played softly into a pool. 'She's through here,' the young man said, indicating an arched gateway in the stone wall just past an espaliered fig tree. 'Would you like me to escort you there and introduce you?'

'No, I think we can manage, thank you,' Isobel said in a curt tone, going ahead through the wrought-iron gate. Sofia followed her and they entered a long garden with an avenue of cypress trees, lawns and large beds of shrubs, which she took to be roses. On the far side, a figure was bent over some bushes, busy tending to them. As they grew closer, Sofia realised the woman was not only bent by her age, but had developed the stoop of one who has worked hard for many years and yet still works with a crooked body.

As she looked up at them approaching, Isobel announced herself: 'Gabriella? We are here at the insistence of my late husband, Riccardo Rinaldi. I believe you are expecting us. This is my daughter Sofia.'

'Isobel, Sofia, you are most welcome,' Gabriella said, tucking her secateurs into the pocket of her heavy canvas apron and removing her thick leather gloves to shake hands with them both. 'I am so sorry Riccardo has now left you. I would have liked to see him again one last time.' Her alert green and amber eyes were wreathed in fine lines, but they twinkled with curiosity.

'Hmm, we're only here because we've had to follow his wishes.' Isobel sounded impatient and not a little ungracious.

Sofia broke in, saying, 'My father's original instructions for this trip didn't say anything about coming to see you. The first time we knew of this was when a letter was delivered to our hotel. It was something of a surprise.' She noticed how Gabriella's eyebrows rose at this point and added, 'But not an unwelcome one.'

'I see. He was always one for surprises.' Gabriella removed the scarf covering her head, revealing close-cropped silvery hair. 'But come inside and we'll talk.' She walked stiffly, using a stick, pausing now and then to point out particular roses. 'The Rosa Mundi is my favourite and was the first one I bought when I replanted the garden here. But it flowers too early in the year for you to see it. By this time, Compassion is pretty much all I have left.' She stopped by a tall rose growing against the wall, with two remaining blooms, pink tinged with apricot. 'Smell it. Doesn't it remind you of the scents of summer, like strawberries and raspberries?'

They obligingly inclined their heads to sample the fragrance. 'Oh, it's lovely,' Sofia said. 'Have you grown all the roses here? All on your own?'

'I was alone at first, but then I had help from my husband and in later years I've had gardeners. I'm not as strong as I once was.' Gabriella laughed and continued her slow, slightly unsteady progress back towards the house. 'I fell in love with roses before I ever fell truly in love with a man. I promised myself that when the war ended, I would devote myself to roses and I became something of an expert.' She turned and waved back towards the garden filled with rose bushes. 'I have the largest collection in Florence, apart from the Bardini rose garden, that is. The largest private collection.'

As they reached the French doors to re-enter the house, Gabriella called out, 'Carlo, we will take our coffee in the salon.' They could hear steps some way off and then the tinkling of cups as the young man who had greeted them at the entrance appeared with a tray. 'We'll start in here,' Gabriella said, leading them slowly through and indicating they should sit opposite her. 'You'll stay for lunch, of course. My grandson, Carlo, is an excellent cook.'

Sofia glanced at her mother, who was frowning, and quickly said, 'That's very kind, but my mother has been finding this trip very tiring. May we see how she is feeling in a little while?'

'Of course. I quite understand. It must have been a very trying year for you, losing your husband after such a long marriage. And I understand how there is always so much to arrange after such a loss. And you have had an exhibition of his work to organise as well.'

'Oh, I didn't have anything to do with all that. That's the

gallery manager's responsibility. And my daughter's, of course.' Isobel sat upright, her stiff posture matching her curt replies.

'What my mother means is that we have a great relationship with the curator, Phoebe Ackroyd, at the Firenze Gallery,' Sofia said. 'She's incredibly efficient and has tremendous contacts in the international art market.'

'That's good to hear. I would have liked to attend the exhibition, but I fear I am not comfortable travelling so far these days. My city and my garden are the extent of my world now.' Gabriella smiled, sipping her coffee.

'But you've been to London in the past?'

'Oh yes, I attended your father's first London exhibition and until a few years ago, I also made a point of coming over to attend the Chelsea Flower Show every year in May. For the roses, you know.' She smiled, her face crinkling into soft creases, and Sofia could see that she had once been very pretty.

'Did you ever meet up with my father on those visits? He spent more time in Cornwall in later years, but always loved a reason to be in London.'

'Sadly, no.' Gabriella set her cup down with a little clink on the saucer. 'We never met again. He did not want to and I could not make him see me.'

Isobel leant forward. 'So when did you last meet him?'

Gabriella looked into the distance, as if seeing an angry young Riccardo. 'It was some time after the war. He was going to Rome, to study art. He was already a very capable artist, always had been really. I believe it was the autumn of 1950. And he only came back once after that, about four years later.'

'But why wouldn't he agree to meet you again? What happened?' Sofia grasped her mother's hand, wondering what they were going to hear next. In the silence before her question was answered, she caught the sound of a familiar piece of music playing somewhere in the palazzo, an opera perhaps.

Gabriella looked so sad. She took a lace-edged handkerchief from her garden apron pocket, untangling it from her secateurs, and twisted it in her fingers. 'He said he didn't want to see me ever again after I said he had to know the truth.'

'What did he mean by that? You know he told us in his letter that coming here would help us to understand him better.'

'Maybe it will.' Gabriella sniffed. 'I told him the truth, thinking it would relieve him of the burden he had carried for too long.' She shook her head. 'But all I did was pass the burden on.'

'Oh, for goodness' sake,' Isobel snapped, standing up. 'Can't you just tell us straight? My husband was a very difficult man. I put up with him all these years and he's subjected me to even more stress with his unexpected letter and sending me here to meet you like this. In his letter he referred to experiences long ago that he'd never been able to forget. Aren't you at least going to tell us what they were?'

'Mum, please, sit down.' Sofia put her arms around Isobel, coaxing her and caressing her shoulders to encourage her into sitting. Her mother was trembling and she could tell she was near to tears again. 'Gabriella, I'm so sorry. But you can see what a strain this year has been for my mother. Perhaps we should leave after all.'

'No, please don't go.' Gabriella held out her hand. 'I apologise for not being direct. But after all these years, it is hard to revisit times that trouble me still.'

'He also said that these experiences coloured his work and that visiting you would help us to understand his paintings and what he referred to as his tortured mind.' Sofia was determined they wouldn't leave without finding some answers.

'An interesting way of putting it. Yes, he was a tortured individual. Tortured from an early age. Not literally, you understand, although there was one incident that left a disturbing impression on all of us. Did he ever tell you what had happened to his ear?'

'His ear? Oh, you mean his misshapen ear lobe?' Sofia shrugged. Her mother was hunched and too tense to talk. 'He always joked about it. Said it was an ear piercing gone wrong.

Someone had tried to do it for him when he was an art student. A darning needle and a cork, he said.'

Gabriella shook her head and laughed. 'A good excuse. But it wasn't like that at all. His ear was deliberately cut.'

Both women reacted to this news with a gasp. 'By him, you mean?' Sofia asked. 'It was a gesture of despair, like Van Gogh?'

'No, it wasn't artistic solidarity,' Gabriella said with a wry smile. 'No, he was deliberately maimed as a warning, not to be so curious.'

Sofia held her mother close. Isobel was holding her hand over her mouth. 'Who on earth would do such a dreadful thing?'

'They were terrible times,' Gabriella said. 'Stay and I will tell you.'

THIRTY-FIVE

FLORENCE

6 March 1944

Gabriella shone her lantern over Riccardo, still crouched in the confessional box. 'What happened? Where are Mama and Papa?'

His sobs faded and he gulped before he could answer her. 'It's all my fault. I hope they come back soon, but I don't know what will happen to them.'

'Do you know where they are now?' Gabriella couldn't stop herself recalling the cold smile of Major Carisi and the ugly sneer from Alfredo.

'I think so. I heard the men talking about Villa Triste. That's where you go for dinner, isn't it? With your two school friends?'

She held the lantern higher so she could see more of him. 'Come back to the house with me. Those men left ages ago.'

He climbed out of the confessional and she put her arms around him. Although she knew she was older than him by more than two years, the difference normally felt hardly noticeable. But now, with him tearful, shivering from cold and shock, she felt maternal, soothing a distressed child. 'You can tell me everything when we're inside. I've lit the stove and made supper. We can eat very soon, then you'll feel much better.'

He sniffled, but did as she said, holding her hand all the way back to the house. Indoors, she sat him at the table, put water on to boil, then fetched another lantern so she could look at him more closely. When the light fell on his shirt, she could see that she had been right in her assumption. The stain was blood, quite a lot of it; but was it his?

'How did this happen?' she asked, touching the stained shoulder. He turned his head to one side and then she saw it: his ear had been cut. Not extensively, but it was ragged. The lobe had been torn away with a section of cartilage and had bled profusely. The wound was now crusted with dried blood.

She turned Riccardo back to face her. 'Who did this to you?'

His bottom lip trembled again. 'Alfredo,' he whispered. 'Remember what he said that time at the station about giving me a clip round the ear?'

She remembered only too well. 'He's a dangerous man, he shouldn't have hurt you.' She looked at the wound again. 'I'll bathe it with salt water, then find a bandage. I don't want Mama thinking I haven't looked after you properly.'

He sat still, wincing as she dabbed at the mutilated ear with a clean cloth, soaked in warm water mixed with some of the salt from the jar. Then she ripped a clean kitchen cloth in two and tied it round his head to cover the wound. A stain started seeping through the fabric and she knew the dressing would need changing several times before the cut healed, but it was all she could do for him for now.

Then she tipped the hardened polenta paste out onto the cold worktop and shaped it into pieces no larger than the top of her thumb. After only two minutes in boiling water, the gnocchi were ready to serve with the pesto and she pushed a small serving towards Riccardo. As she rightly guessed, he couldn't manage a full portion: 'It hurts to eat,' he said. 'Chewing makes my ear throb.'

'Just eat whatever you can. I expect it will be painful for a few days, but I'm sure it will heal quickly.' She couldn't eat very much either, even though neither of them had eaten for hours. 'Do you want to tell me how it happened?'

He stared at his bowl, then began to talk. 'It was this afternoon. I was in my room drawing and I heard loud knocking on the front door. Not a polite knock, really loud banging, like people were desperate for the door to open. Then I heard shouting and Mama was talking, but she sounded frightened. She kept saying, "I don't know anything. Why won't you believe me?" So I poked my head out and that Alfredo saw me. I remember he laughed at me. "That's the little tyke," he said, then he came for me and said he was going to teach me a lesson. He knocked me to the floor, held me down with his knee and then he did this.' Riccardo touched his bandaged ear. 'I think Mama may have seen him do it. I heard her scream. She shouted at them, "Leave him alone. He's only a child." Then Alfredo got up, kicked me and said I was a troublemaker and I'd had it coming to me.'

'What did he mean by that?'

'I wasn't sure at first, but then I realised they were taking Mama away and as they left, Alfredo turned back and waved something at me. It was my notebook, Gaby. He said, "Thanks for the tip about the sewers. We'll get the lot of them now." How did he get my notebook? I haven't been able to find it, but I'm sure I hadn't taken it out of the house recently.'

Gabriella felt a chill creep down to her stomach, despite the warm dumplings she had just eaten. With horror, she realised she had been fooled and in her foolishness she had endangered the lives of her family and others. 'You should go to bed now,' she said. 'Sleep will help you heal.' She guided him towards his room, stepping around the splatters of dark blood outside the door.

Gabriella hardly slept that night, even though she was aching with tiredness. She could not stop thinking about her stupidity and her mind jumped from the Villa Triste to the station, to the hidden sewers and back again. All those conversations she and Riccardo had heard, all those discussions they had recorded in their simple code. How stupid it had been to use such a basic cipher. Nothing was hidden and if the men from the basement were partisans, as she now suspected they were, their actions could easily be tracked and they were sure to be arrested.

And in the meantime, what of her mother and father? Were they still being held and questioned, or were they on their way to the station to be herded into one of those crude wagons? She knew she had to find out and as soon as it was light, she dressed herself. She ate a little of the cold gnocchi and drank a cup of hibiscus tea, then took a cup to Riccardo. She gave a light rap on his door and opened it slowly. He was still asleep, lying with his undamaged ear pressed against the bloodstained pillow. She would have liked to wake him and tell him what she was doing, but she thought he would have been determined to come with her and she didn't want to risk his good ear as well. She wrote a note on a scrap of paper and left it beneath the cup of tea. She knew she couldn't tell the truth, so it just said: 'Gone to the market. Wait here for me.'

Although it was early, only a quarter past seven, there was already life out in the streets, heading for the market. But Gabriella covered her hair completely with a tight scarf and went in the opposite direction, towards Villa Triste. She knew the way off by heart now, after all those awkward evening meals where she was torn between hunger and humiliation. When she arrived at the stern building, she knocked on the door. After a few minutes, she heard the light tap of footsteps and a woman answered: 'Can I help you?'

'Is Bruno still here?' Gabriella tried to look over the woman's shoulder.

'No. They've all gone down to the station this morning. Just as well, after all the comings and goings last night.'

'Oh, what a shame I've missed him.' She paused for a moment, thinking how to encourage the woman to drop her guard. 'Are you the cook who serves all those delicious dishes every evening at dinner? I don't know if you recognise me, but I've been quite a few times now, as a guest of the Major's daughters. The food is just wonderful.'

'Well, thank you. It's nice to hear a word of gratitude for a change. Those two girls wouldn't know how to thank someone if they paid them.'

'I've told my mother all about your excellent cooking and she was intrigued by your recipe for the veal cutlets with artichokes. She said she'd love to try it one day if we can ever get the ingredients.'

The woman beamed, her cheeks a rosy contrast to her grey hair. 'As a matter of fact, I'm making that right now. It's the Major's favourite. I start it early in the day because it needs to marinate. Really helps the flavour. Come inside and I'll show you and maybe you can make a note of the recipe.'

She opened the door wide so Gabriella could step inside, then led the way to the end of the hall to the steps leading down to the basement, where Alfredo and the sisters always disappeared on previous visits. 'Such a nuisance the kitchen being all the way down here. I have to carry all the dishes upstairs every evening. Up and down all night I am and those fellows are always getting in the way. No consideration.'

When they reached the bottom, the woman turned left to the kitchen, but Gabriella could hear soft moans and immediately turned right. 'You can't go in there!' the cook shouted after her. 'It's not allowed!'

But Gabriella had already entered the unlocked basement room, which was furnished only with a table, a chair with leather straps and a fireplace filled with grey embers and ash. Odours of human waste, stale cigarettes and fear permeated the stale air and the flagstone floor was slippery with blood and urine. The table was strewn with chains, bloodstained rags and a large pair of stained scissors, the kind used by tailors to slice through thick cloth. And in a corner, slumped against the wall with her hands behind her back, her ankles tied and a gag across her mouth was a groaning woman. It wasn't Mama, but she still didn't deserve to be here in this cruel place.

Gabriella didn't hesitate. She grabbed the scissors, snipped the ties holding the poor woman, undid the gag and helped her up. 'Can you walk? We've got to get out of here as quickly as we can.'

They stumbled towards the staircase, where the cook was standing and wringing her hands. 'You're going to get me in trouble,' she wailed. 'I'm not meant to let anyone in, ever.'

'Say I threatened you with a knife,' Gabriella said. 'Oh, and I really did mean that about the veal. It was delicious.'

They staggered up the stairs and out into sunlight. The woman was bruised and shaken, her dress was stained, but she was otherwise unharmed. She managed to croak, 'I don't know how to thank you.'

'Get away from here quickly. That will be thanks enough.'

THIRTY-SIX

FLORENCE

7 March 1944

As she ran away from the villa of torment and pain, Gabriella hoped the cook would not be able to describe her accurately to the Major's cronies. She was anxious to get as far away as possible and wondered where she was most likely to find her parents. The station was an obvious destination, but it would be closely guarded.

Pausing for a second to catch her breath and consider her actions, she noticed a dishevelled woman collapsed against a street fountain and instantly recognised her. 'Mama!' she cried, running towards the slumped figure. Her mother's face was bruised and bloodied, but otherwise she was not seriously hurt. Gabriella scooped water in her hands for her mother to drink and wrung her scarf out to wipe the grime and blood from her face.

'Where's Papa? Do you know where they've taken him?'

'Train, they said train,' Mama murmured. 'Tonight.' She grasped Gabriella's hand. 'Riccardo? Is he...?' Her eyes were swimming with tears.

'He'll be fine, Mama. I looked after him. Now I must get you home. Do you think you can walk?' She helped her mother up and they staggered back to the palazzo.

Riccardo was awake by the time they returned that morning, in pain but hungry enough to finish the previous night's supper. Mama took a cup of hibiscus tea, then said she wanted to lie down in her bedroom. After a minute or two Gabriella heard a horrified scream and ran up the stairs to find her mother crying over her dresses. All her beautiful clothes had been pulled out of the wardrobe and thrown on the floor.

Gabriella bent to pick them up, but her mother barred her. 'Don't touch them,' she shrieked. 'Can't you see they've all been defiled?' She pointed to the damp stains and the incriminating silvery snail track on the dark silk. 'I can't ever wear these again, not now those disgusting men have ruined them.'

'Come away, Mama, come and lie down in my room. You'll be able to rest there. And I'll deal with this when I return from the market and the station. I must go out while there's still a chance of finding Papa.'

She took her mother's hand and guided her towards her own unsoiled room and persuaded her to lie on the bed. Then she returned to the pile of clothes, picked up the dress stained with semen with the tips of her fingers and put that to one side. The rest she scooped up and took through to the scullery so she could clean them later. But before she left her mother's room she checked the box on top of the wardrobe. Thank heavens – the Fortuny was still there, coiled like a sleeping snake. If those vile men had known of its existence they would surely have taken the most valuable garment in the whole room.

The market had little to offer as usual and Gabriella settled for kale and polenta. It wasn't much, but she knew she had to take whatever she could find. She wouldn't be reaping the benefits of suppers at the Villa Triste any more. And briefly she wondered how much trouble she had caused for their talented cook. Maybe she would make an excuse, maybe she would leave the city and escape to relatives in the countryside. She hoped she hadn't made life too difficult for the woman, whose only crime had been to feed the villains and their cohorts so well.

Scurrying away with her cloth bag of provisions, she passed so many sad, worn faces, women in drab scarves and coats, despite the milder spring weather. They were probably hiding their ragged, unwashed dresses underneath. Soap was increasingly hard to come by and Mama had been trading their sugar ration for soap. 'I'd rather be clean than satisfy a sweet-tooth,' she'd said. Gabriella was thankful for her mother's cautious husbandry and thought she would clean those spoiled clothes as soon as she returned to the palazzo. Some might only require sponging and airing, others might need washing, but all should be fresh and wearable once they had been draped over the lavender bushes in the sunny court-yard and dried in the fresh air.

As she neared the station, crouching like a monstrous hunch-back in the shadow of the basilica of the soul-inspiring Santa Maria Novella church, after which it was named, she was aware of a greater number of soldiers than usual. She hung back for a moment, wondering if she dared go further and questioning her reason for coming here.

Dissenting Italians, classed as troublemakers or partisans, were mostly either hanged or imprisoned, but some were sent to Germany to boost the labour force and others were sent further away. She wasn't sure where they were sent, but she was sure it wasn't pleasant and that their chances of returning were slim. If Papa wasn't still in the city's prison, there was a good chance he might have been brought to the station along with other prisoners.

Come on, Gaby, she told herself. *You've got to find out. He might be here. They might be loading men onto the trains today. You can't wait, you've got to go now.*

She crossed the road to the station. It was packed with guards and a large number of prisoners. She scanned the rows of men being pushed towards the rough wooden carriages waiting at the platform. There were so many of them, how would she ever know if he was here? Dark heads, white heads, bald heads, all bowed and bobbing in a line, shuffling forward, flinching as German and Italian soldiers pushed and shouted, 'Affretatevi' and 'Beeile dich'.

No fond farewells for these battered men with bruised faces, broken noses and torn ears.

And then she saw him. She saw his distinctive hat, a black wide-brimmed fedora that he always wore when he left the house. He had a black eye too. He spotted her and edged to one side of the long queue to be nearer to her. He shook his head to signal that she should not approach him and she nodded and called out, 'Mama sends her love and says she is waiting at home for you.' He smiled with relief, showing he had understood her message, and she noticed that he had fewer teeth than when she had last seen him.

He was standing towards the end of the slowly moving column of prisoners, not very far from the station exit. The nearby group of guards were lounging, bored with the whole process of waiting for the men to leave. And among them, laughing and joking, she saw Bruno. Handsome Bruno, who had teased her and enticed her, then betrayed her. She knew she had been foolish and that it was her fault the notebook had caused so much trouble and risked the lives of her family, but he had gained her trust and he had used her naivety.

She knew exactly what she had to do next. She strolled towards him and his comrades, pulling the scarf from her hair, tossing her head so the fiery strands bounced over her shoulders, catching the light and their attention. 'Bruno,' she called, 'how lovely to see you! And all your friends here too!' She told herself she was not a schoolgirl of only fourteen and a half years of age, she was the beauty Mama fretted over and was anxious to protect; she was a siren like the Botticelli *Venus*, which she had only ever seen in a book of the Uffizi's treasures, when Uncle Federico taught her how Italy's artists prized striking colouring such as hers.

Bruno turned towards her; his customary warm smile was not present, his eyes were ice-cold. He stepped away from his companions and said, 'What the hell do you think you're doing here? Get out!'

But if he had hoped to scare her off, he was wrong. She stepped forward as his friends craned to see who was causing the disturbance. They grouped around him, laughing, slapping him on the back, saying, 'Girl trouble, eh? Who's this little beauty? You're a dark horse, keeping this one to yourself, aren't you?'

She smiled, she giggled, she tossed her head and she glanced across at the now unguarded line of prisoners, hoping her father would take the hint. She didn't dare look overtly, in case the guards realised men were slipping away, but over their shoulders she saw one and then another dart off and into the alleyways of the surrounding streets.

'She's just a schoolgirl, that's what. Same class as my young cousins.' Bruno's lips snarled. He was no longer the kind friend he'd been on those evenings walking back from the Sad Villa. 'She's got a crush on me. Stupid kid.' He pushed her towards the exit and she stumbled on the steps and fell to her knees in the street. As she picked herself up, she caught a glimpse of Papa's black hat bobbing through the crowds of weeping women gathered around the station. She covered her hair again with her scarf and raced after him.

THIRTY-SEVEN

FLORENCE

7 March 1944

Gabriella caught up with her father and they marched at a pace back to Palazzo Rinaldi. They were both anxious to leave the station behind them, but running might have attracted attention.

'Your mother will be very angry that you took such an enormous risk, my dear,' he said. 'But I have to thank you from the bottom of my heart. If you hadn't created such an effective diversion, I could never have escaped. If I'd tried to run off without your help, I'd have been shot on the spot.'

She looped her arm in his, still catching her breath after running from the station. 'Do you know where the trains are going?'

'There is talk of Germany and some say Poland. Others have heard that this is only the first leg of the journey and that the train goes to a holding camp in Verona, where prisoners are selected for work squads.'

'But why did they arrest you and Mama?'

'They said they knew we had collaborated with Jews and partisans. So that meant we were undesirables too. I tried to convince them that we'd never known who our old tenants really were and there was no longer anyone upstairs or in the basement, but they weren't satisfied with that. They were convinced we knew the names of all our former lodgers and where they had gone.'

'Riccardo thinks Signora Giardino and her children were arrested at the convent and sent away with other women from there.'

'That boy. Too inquisitive for his own good. I regret to say that his prying may have been the reason we were investigated. The men seemed to know an awful lot about the people who had been living in our house. They kept saying they had information.'

Gabriella felt a prickle of shame pierce her being, reminding her of her stupidity. But how could she tell her father that it was she and not Riccardo who was to blame? She kept quiet and clung to his arm as they hurried through the narrow streets between the tall buildings. It was almost noon and shafts of sunlight were piercing the shade, exposing the peeling paintwork of the green shutters and revealing their broken windows. The city was showing signs of war-weariness as much as the people, but here and there was a vital sign of life, a caged bird singing in the sun, a pot of basil sprouting new leaves, a red geranium brightening a windowsill.

At home, Mama had roused herself and was boiling water in the kitchen. She sobbed on her husband's shoulder, telling him how brave their daughter had been. 'And she cared for Riccardo last night too. His poor ear... I've stitched it but it will never be the same again.'

Gabriella began preparing food for the family, simmering whole potatoes to make gnocchi again. Her father had not eaten since the previous morning. The prisoners had been given a bucket of water but nothing else. 'Your poor teeth,' his wife said. 'Those brutes, hauling you away like that.'

'It is nothing, I was lucky. Two men died in the night from their beatings. I expect more will die on the trains and in the camps. Thank God Gaby came to the station. I could not have slipped away otherwise.'

'And I didn't know what was going to happen in that terrible Villa Triste last night. They hardly touched me but they had a man strapped into a chair and a poor woman tied up on the floor. I can't bear to tell you about it. The man in charge, that Major, he invited his daughters to watch! They could not have been any older than Gaby. And they laughed and encouraged the interrogators!'

Gabriella knew she was referring to Tina and Franca. It confirmed what she had begun to suspect. Those sisters had been reared by a cruel father in an atmosphere where cruelty was admired. They were capable of anything.

'I was lucky,' Mama said. 'They threw me out on the street when they realised I had no information for them, but the other poor souls...' She looked as if she was going to sob.

'Don't, my love, don't dwell on what is gone,' Papa said. 'We must think carefully now. I doubt they will come back for you, but my name was on a list when they arrested me at the museum and they may well search for me. I don't think it is safe for all of you if I stay here, so I am proposing to leave the city tonight. I will head to our farm first and then go north to the mountains. I will try to get a message to Federico and join him in his work.'

On hearing her uncle's name, Gabriella was alert. They had not seen him for over a year, although letters had arrived from time to time, reassuring the family that he was well and that they would be together again once the war was over. When the family had first arrived in Florence, he'd just said he was going to be doing important work for the future of Italy. But what could he, an art historian, and Papa, an Egyptologist, possibly do to help the nation? She knew they both believed in saving Italy's treasures from the invaders, but right now it seemed to her that ordinary citizens were more in need of direct action and supplies to help them survive than the preservation of historic works of art and artefacts.

'Vincenzo, you must take supplies with you. We may not have much, but you cannot know how quickly you will reach the farm. You may have to hide along the way.' Mama stood in the larder doorway, shaking her head. 'Gabriella, when you have finished cooking, please run to the panetteria and buy whatever you can. Here, take the tokens, and be prepared to pay extra if they have more under the counter.' The family had avoided the black market up to now, but clearly, Papa had to have food for his journey. 'It will only be their usual coarse brown bread, but it will do for now,' she said.

'It will be white bread again for me soon,' he said. 'They're bound to be producing their own flour down at the farm.'

Later, as Gabriella ran back from the baker's, she wondered if Mama would want to leave Florence too and enjoy the plentiful food on the farm. But if she wanted to go, she'd insist on taking her son and daughter with her and now Gabriella had other plans. Since she had caused the disturbance among the guards at the station, she knew she had a special power. It had been exercised once again, with almost disastrous consequences, just now at the baker's.

At first, he had insisted he couldn't supply her with any more bread than the allowance to which the family was entitled, but then she had let her scarf slip from her head and as her brilliant curls fell to her shoulders, she had said, 'Are you quite sure?' He had reddened and dipped under the counter, bringing up a second loaf, which he passed over to her. As she reached for it, his other hand grabbed hers and he said, 'And what do I get in return?' She knew exactly what he was thinking and she pulled away sharply, slamming the coins she had ready down on the counter. 'You get paid,' she said and quickly left the shop with the extra bread before he could protest.

She knew it was a dangerous ploy, one which might lead her into circumstances she wouldn't be able to control perhaps, but she felt it was the only weapon a girl on the brink of maturity had. She just had to be sure to use it sparingly and carefully.

On her return, Papa had packed a small bundle. 'I won't take much,' he said. 'A large case might arouse suspicion and I can't risk being searched and asked for papers. I'll get as far as I can in daylight, then lie low till dark.'

'Are you sure you shouldn't wait till tonight?' Mama was fretful, near to tears.

He shook his head. 'I can't risk being picked up after curfew. Once I'm out of the city, there will be fewer checks, I'm sure. We have many friends here, so I can find somewhere to rest in safety if I must wait. But my main concern now is to be sure you will all be safe once I've left.'

He kissed his wife and held her close. Then he kissed Gabriella on the top of her head. 'Bless you for what you did. Look after your mother and tell your brother to stay out of trouble.' Then he slipped out into the street and they both stood watching him swiftly disappear.

Mama began to cry again, so Gabriella urged her to sit down while she prepared their food. 'Has Riccardo eaten again?' she asked.

'He says it hurts too much to eat. Perhaps you can persuade him to join us.'

The potato gnocchi were only going to need a couple of minutes' simmering, so Gabriella went to find him before she finished cooking. He was lying on his bed, drawing again. An ugly man with a beard, snarling, a knife in his hand. He looked up when she entered.

'Come and eat,' she said. 'You must be hungry now.'

'No,' he mumbled, his head lowered over his work. 'I don't want to eat – it hurts.'

'What if I make something you don't have to chew? I can make you soup, maybe stracciatella? We can spare an egg for that.'

He rolled to one side and looked at her. The sight of his bruised face and his livid ear sent a stabbing pain through her veins. 'It was all my fault,' he said. 'I'll never forget that.'

And again, she felt the pain of her guilt and knew that she had to find a way to make amends. She held out her hand to him. 'Come on, you have to keep your strength up for the Scoppio del

Carro. If it doesn't happen this year, it will happen again some time and you will need to be strong enough to push your way through the crowd to see it all.'

He managed a weak smile and took her hand. She pulled him to his feet, then they walked along the corridor together.

THIRTY-EIGHT

FLORENCE

November 2019

'What a terrible thing to happen,' Sofia said when Gabriella had finished telling them how Riccardo's ear was mutilated. 'He was only a child then, wasn't he? Twelve, if that?'

'He was just a boy. A very clever, imaginative boy, already destined to become a truly great artist, but a boy all the same.'

'I don't quite understand,' Isobel said. 'I can see that being injured like that would be traumatic and terrifying, but is that the burden you mentioned?'

'There is a connection, which will require further explanation.' Gabriella managed to stand, with the aid of her walking stick. 'I can tell you more if you are staying for lunch.' She gestured towards the garden. 'It is warm and sheltered in the courtyard, so we can eat outside.'

Sofia turned to her mother. 'I'd like to stay, but how do you feel now?'

Isobel gave an exaggerated sigh. 'I suppose we can. We've come this far and I still don't fully understand what Riccardo said in his damned letter, so we might as well stay.'

'Thank you,' Sofia said, turning to her hostess. 'We'd love to. That's very kind of you.'

'Come, I'll show you where you can refresh yourselves and then we shall eat together and talk some more.'

'What beautiful plates,' Sofia said, admiring the pattern of yellow lemons with a blue border, when they were seated at the outside table.

'Some of my family's possessions survived the war. We loved these plates and often used them in those days. I thought you would appreciate seeing them today to get a feel for how life was then. We didn't always have much to eat, but it was always served in style.'

Carlo brought bread and olive oil to the table, but declined to join them. 'He wants to see to his dishes,' Gabriella said. 'Do you like the schiacciata?' She indicated the crusty, knobbly strips of thin brown bread in front of them. 'I told him I wanted you to experience the true flavours of Florence today. This kind of bread, with the first pressing of this season's olive oil, is typical of what we used to eat, although during the war it was all in short supply. The Germans requisitioned much of our oil and grain for themselves.'

A small portion of tagliolini with white truffles followed, then a dish of wild boar stuffed with mushrooms, served with a black truffle sauce, spinach and peas. 'I'm sure you didn't eat this well during the war,' Isobel said, savouring the fragrant dish.

'Nor before the war either,' Gabriella said. 'But this is typical of the region at this time of year. We ate well before Mussolini and we ate well again afterwards – eventually. Riccardo, I remember, enjoyed his food. I used to bring back treats for him when I dined with some friends at that time.'

'He was very particular,' Sofia said. 'He had an opinion on every Italian dish and he even gave us detailed instructions on what to eat and where to eat during our stay here.'

'As always,' Isobel said. 'He always took charge. But he had a great dislike of polenta and ribollita. Said he was never going to eat them again.'

Gabriella laughed. 'That's because those two foods were often all we had to eat. There wasn't much choice at certain times. We were luckier than most, because we had the garden here. It wasn't full of roses then, it was full of vegetables, thanks to some wonderful people who lived here with us.'

'Was this whole place just for you and the family?' Sofia waved towards the tall house behind them.

'It was a house full of life at one time when my grandparents were alive. When we moved here from Rome, in the middle of the war, there was just my father's younger brother, Uncle Federico. Then the servants left to go to their families in the countryside and my uncle went away on important work to save the city's heritage. But my father wanted to stay here to protect the museum artefacts for as long as he could.'

'And do you live on your own here now, with your grandson?'

'No, the palazzo is no longer one dwelling. I split it into apartments many years ago. I needed more income than my rose-growing could provide. I kept a few rooms on the ground floor for myself and I have the gardens. I could be happy with just one room as long as I could keep my garden. And Carlo is staying here while he studies at the university. He is a great comfort, but we have some other help too.'

'So this place belonged to my father's parents, my grandparents?' Sofia asked, wondering who would inherit this beautiful property.

'It belonged to the family of my father and his brother. In truth, your father was entitled to half the property. I tried to make him take his share, but when he refused I put the proceeds from creating the apartments into a trust. I said I would never touch his rightful inheritance so one day that portion will be yours.'

'Please, I didn't mean to imply...' Sofia felt uncomfortable. 'It's more that I'm interested in my father's family and all the things he never told me.'

'He never discussed his past with me either,' Isobel snapped. 'I thought he was just trying to be mysterious or that he had fallen out with his family. Now I'm beginning to think he was always difficult, just as he was throughout our marriage.'

'He was always obsessed with his work, even when he was young,' Gabriella said. 'When I think of him, I see him forever bent over his sketchpad, furiously drawing or standing before a painting, trying to judge if he'd got the angle or the light right.'

'Sounds like Dad,' Sofia said. 'He was immersed in his work right to the very end. You mentioned a sketchpad. Do you still have any of them here? I've had a terrible time trying to describe his paintings for his last exhibition. He never explained them, just gave them numbers.'

'He took most of his sketches with him when he left, but there are a few, I think. And of course there are his paintings in the chapel here.'

'More paintings? Can we see them? Are they staying here?'

'They will always have to stay here,' Gabriella said. 'They're not canvases, they're wall paintings. Frescoes. Our mother allowed him to paint the walls of the chapel when he ran out of canvas during the war and immediately after. He may have been young, but they are still very good.'

Sofia felt excited about this new evidence of her father's early talent. 'And do they show signs of the way he was going to develop later on? His distinctive artistic style?'

Gabriella nodded. 'There are elements, I think. But of course this was very early in his career. He was just a boy then.'

'But considering the way his reputation developed and the interest the critics have taken in his career, it would be important to have a record of these works as well. We'd love to see them, wouldn't we, Mum?'

'I suppose so, darling. We might as well while we're here. But we're still no nearer to understanding what on earth he meant in his mysterious letter.' Isobel sighed and sipped the Chianti that had been served with the wild boar. 'I'm not sure that we're learning anything at all.'

'Perhaps it will become clearer later,' Gabriella said. 'And now we have dessert: Carlo has made us another traditional autumn speciality.' She turned her head as he arrived with a dark cake sprinkled with pine nuts and raisins. 'Castagnaccio! It is made with chestnut flour and oil and is found all over Tuscany at this time of year. And with it, we shall drink *vin beato*.'

Slices of sweet cake were passed around the table, served with a spoonful of ricotta topped with chestnut honey. The tiny glasses of dessert wine were the perfect accompaniment, Sofia thought. 'I'm sure I can taste herbs in the cake as well?'

'A little rosemary,' Gabriella said, pointing to the bushes sprawling in the courtyard. 'We have always had it growing here and I can remember it appearing in just about every dish we cooked years ago.'

When they had finished their cake, Gabriella said, 'Come, I will show you where Riccardo began his career as a famous artist.'

They walked with her along the side of the palazzo, through shaded cloisters that led to a chapel with a heavy wooden door. Inside, the light was dim, but candles burned on the altar and a couple of votives were lit on the offertory stand that was layered with the molten wax of many prayers. The musty scent of centuries of worship mingled with the smells of candle wax and incense, reminding Sofia of times when her father had taken her to services in the Our Lady, Help of Christians church in Kentish Town, as well as school trips to Westminster Abbey.

'Surely that's not one of his?' Isobel pointed to the gilded trip-tych above the altar.

'No, we think that may be by a student of Brunelleschi,' Gabriella said. 'But Riccardo admired it greatly and I think he found it spiritually inspiring.' She moved towards a little door to the side and hovered unsteadily with her stick.

'Let me,' Sofia said, darting forward and turning the handle. The door opened to reveal a spiral staircase within a turret.

'It's in here, his first major painting. You'll see it if you go up a few steps. I can't go with you. I find this narrow staircase too difficult these days.' She turned away so they could pass through the doorway. 'I'll sit down and wait for you.'

Sofia looked at her mother. 'Are you alright doing this? I'm excited to see his first important piece of work.'

'We might as well, now we're here.' Isobel followed her daughter and they walked up the curving steps.

As the stair twisted around the centre of the tower, they came face to face with the wall painting, lit by daylight streaming in through an arched window. 'Oh, my goodness,' Sofia gasped. 'It's the lamb he always included in his pictures. Look at it! We've seen it before, haven't we?'

Isobel leant forward to look at the appealing eyes of the creature that seemed to be begging for mercy. 'The bloody lamb. So this is where it all started.'

'But what does it mean? Why was he always painting a lamb with its throat cut? Is it a religious message of some kind? I don't understand.' Sofia ran back down the steps and into the chapel. Gabriella was sitting to one side, her head bowed in prayer, but when she heard their steps, she looked up.

'I know,' she said. 'You want to know why there is a lamb. I don't know for sure why he continued to use it as a symbol, but I can tell you that there was once a real lamb and Riccardo was present when it died. I think perhaps that was when he first began to lose his innocence.' She paused, looking reflective, and, after a moment, continued. 'We were both children when it all began, but we left our childhood rapidly behind. Come sit with me and I will tell you all about it.'

MESSAGE FIVE

Ecnerolf ni swolf onra eht

THIRTY-NINE

FLORENCE

12 March 1944

It was a sign she was recovering from her ordeal, Gabriella thought, as her mother left the house to visit the market, her basket over her arm. She must be feeling stronger and, although it might be frustrating when there was so little to buy, she would see neighbours and exchange snippets of news; and perhaps she would be in luck and return with flour or rice. Kale and spinach were sprouting in the garden, despite their poor efforts at cultivation, so there was always something to add to the monotonous diet of polenta and potatoes. Their supply of olive oil was dwindling and eggs were increasingly hard to find, but they were managing. In the evenings they chatted over their meagre supper, imagining how well Papa was faring on the farm, eating crusty white bread made from home-ground flour, pasta with the first peas and broad beans of the season and plenty of freshly made burrata.

When Mama returned from her outing, she carried bread and rice, but she also had news: 'They are saying that over three hundred men were sent off by rail in cattle trucks on the eighth. I hadn't realised they had arrested quite so many.'

Gabriella pictured again the sad shuffling queue of beaten,

defeated men. 'I saw them all lined up in the station. And Papa would have been on that train with them if I hadn't found him in time.'

Her mother shook her head sadly. 'They're all decent, loyal men. All Italian patriots, unlike the brutes colluding with the Germans. But there is nothing we can do to stop it.'

Gabriella hugged her. 'We must be strong and wait for their return,' she said, but all the time she was thinking, *can I tell her what I am planning? Is this the right moment? I feel sure she will try to stop me.*

She had already persuaded her mother that she should no longer attend the school. It was not hard to convince her. 'Those girls you saw in Villa Triste, the Major's daughters, they were always teasing me in class. I wanted to be friends with them at first and be invited to dinner, but now I'm afraid they will threaten me if I go back to school.'

'Of course you mustn't return. Such terrible, cruel girls. I saw how they behaved that dreadful night I was taken to that awful place. You must stay well away from them. They are extremely dangerous.'

'If I don't have to go to school, I can help you here and keep Riccardo company. I think he needs to leave his work sometimes and play outside.' Gabriella put water on the stove to boil, knowing her mother might listen to her plan over a cup of chicory coffee.

'If you can, Gaby. His ear is recovering, but his mind isn't. I don't mind him drawing and painting so much, he is incredibly talented, but yes, it would do him good to run around again. He was always so active before, despite his disability, such an amusing, inquisitive boy.'

'He was desperate to find out whether the Scoppio del Carro would be happening this year and so wanted to see the warehouse where the cart is stored. He hoped he might pick up some clues there, but we never found it.'

'Well, why did he never ask me? Of course it isn't going to happen in the middle of a war. Explosives could never be allowed in the middle of the city at this time. But I have known the Soldi family for many years. I will send a message and ask if it would be possible for you both to see the famous cart. But I doubt the white oxen that pull it will be there now. I'm sure they've been sent off to graze in the valleys in the countryside, where they will be safe from hungry, butchering troops.'

'Oh, that would be wonderful. I'm sure it would cheer him up enormously. And I'd go with him, of course.'

'Grazie mio caro, you are a great comfort to us both. And I realise now, since your brave actions in saving me and your father, that perhaps I have been too restrictive. I know I can trust you to look after yourself now and you may have more freedom. But please be very careful. You have blossomed into a beauty and are sure to attract attention.'

Gabriella blushed and hung her head. Mama reached out to her and lifted her chin with the tips of her fingers so she could look at her: 'You really are very beautiful, my dear, and will catch the eye of every man who sees you. In these uncertain times, some of them will not have honest intentions and your honour may be at stake. Do you understand what I am talking about?'

Gabriella could not stop herself from blushing even more. She nodded and said, 'I think so. Girls at school have talked about what has happened to some of their older sisters and cousins. And I've heard people at the market talking about the women who were taken from the convent and held prisoner. The guards attacked many of them.'

Her mother sighed and blew on the hot coffee her daughter had just poured. 'My dear, it pains me to think how you have had to leave your childhood behind so quickly. But I fear that is inevitable in wartime. Many serving soldiers will try to act honourably in difficult situations, but there are some who will use the chaos created by the unrest to satisfy their urges. It is tragic but true. You must, as I say, be very careful.'

'My dear Mama, I understand and I respect your concern for me. You have always protected and cared for me with respect and tenderness. But in these extraordinary times, even one as young as I must do what they can to help our country and I would like to try with your permission.' Gabriella paused for breath before continuing, 'The day that Riccardo and I saw the prisoners being herded into the school in Piazza Tasso, a woman spoke to me. She had just been released, along with a number of other women, but I could see from her bruises that she had been beaten, so I have every reason to believe that her message was genuine.'

'What did she tell you?' Mama looked so old and weary, quite unlike the vibrant elegant artist Gabriella remembered from the years before the war.

'She said one day, when I was ready, if I wanted to help true Italians, I should find the locksmith in the Oltrarno and say I wanted to be remembered to Bianca. Then she told me to say that I had witnessed the events in Piazza Tasso and that I wished to join those who believe the Arno flows in Florence. She said the locksmith would know what that meant.'

'What a strange message. And you think she was sincere?'

'I do, Mama. She'd been arrested too, but she had been released. She disappeared as soon as Riccardo found me again. I want to go to the Oltrarno, to the locksmith, to find out what it means. If I can help our country in any small way, I feel I should.'

Mama clasped her daughter's hands. 'You are very brave, my dear. I cannot stop you from going. So you can go with my blessing, but please God you return and you stay safe.' She took another sip of the ersatz coffee and pulled a face. 'And please God may we have good espresso again one day.'

FORTY

FLORENCE

13 March 1944

Gabriella did not want to be accosted by any men, German or Italian, on her walk to the Oltrarno district, so she wrapped her scarf tightly over her head and set off through the narrow streets to cross the river by the Ponte Santa Trinita. This wider bridge was safer than the Ponte Vecchio, which always attracted crowds of soldiers looking at the view that had been admired by Hitler. Pairs of guards manned all the city's bridges, but the two on duty took no notice of her with her empty basket.

How fawning, she thought as she crossed the bridge, to adapt the centuries-old Vasari Corridor that linked the Pitti Palace in the Oltrarno with the Palazzo Vecchio, especially for the visiting dictator. Mussolini had ordered the enlargement of the central windows in the section that spanned the Ponte Vecchio so his ally would have a better view. It seemed as if the treasured cities of Italy were destined to become the playthings of Europe's dictators. Papa certainly thought so and with his museum colleagues had worked hard to protect their most precious exhibits or remove them elsewhere for safety.

She carried an empty basket to convey the illusion that she was on a mission to find fresh vegetables but inside she rehearsed what she should say if she was questioned. If she was stopped before she found the locksmith, she and her mother thought she should say she was searching for food supplies. But if she was questioned once she had found him, she was to say she hoped he could cut a copy of the key tucked in her pocket.

Safely across the bridge, she decided to criss-cross the alley-ways and streets on the southern side, looking out for the street vendors that had sprung up all around the city, offering black market goods or even just a few eggs laid by hens in a courtyard, or dried tomatoes preserved from last year. Everyone was selling whatever they could to get by. Near a dingy leather shop she saw an old woman dressed in the black of long widowhood, sitting on a step with a selection of dried beans; she was wizened and so was her produce. Gabriella approached her and crouched down beside her to ask, 'I'm looking for the locksmith. Do you know where that is?'

Milky, red-rimmed eyes peered and sized her up. 'There's two of them around here. Do you have money?'

'I do for the right answer.'

The crafty old woman's toothless smile told Gabriella that she understood and she held out her hand. Gabriella let a couple of coins touch her palm, but held them tight until she had an answer.

'Via Toscanella is safe. The Germans favour the other one.'

Gabriella didn't ask about the 'other one'; she didn't want to meet any Germans if she could help it. She thanked the old woman and quickly found the street mentioned. It was very narrow, with high-walled buildings on each side, the yellow plaster patchy, the green shutters and doors peeling flakes of paint. The locksmith conducted his business in perhaps the smallest shop in the whole thoroughfare, little more than the width of its narrow entrance. Through the doorway she could see the walls and ceiling were festooned with locks, hinges, padlocks and bolts of all sizes, some shining bright, others rusted with the patina of antiquity, perhaps salvaged from abandoned buildings.

She stepped inside this passageway of a shop and in the dim light saw a wooden counter at the far end, where a grey-haired man sat stooped on a stool, filing an enormous key. It looked like the kind of ancient key a priest might keep on his belt to unlock the door to a chapel, or a medieval baron might use to lock an iron-banded coffer. He didn't look up, but she thought his eyes slid to one side to check who had entered his burrow, which smelt of rusted iron, oil and years of dust.

'Excuse me,' she said, 'May I speak with you? Bianca told me to come and find you.'

At that, his head lifted and turned slightly. 'Really? Why's that then?'

'I met her at the time of the incident in Piazza Tasso.'

He turned to face her and stared hard with unblinking eyes.

'She said if I wanted to help true Italians, I should find the locksmith in the Oltrarno. Is that you?'

He stood up, placed the key on the counter and wiped his hands on his dirty brown apron. 'Did she say anything else?'

Gabriella's mouth felt dry and she tried to swallow, but coughed for a second. 'She said I should say I wished to join those who believe the Arno flows in Florence.'

The locksmith laughed. 'Well, it does, doesn't it? Stupid girl.'

Gabriella didn't know if he meant she was the stupid one or Bianca. She felt herself blushing again; her cheeks were hot and she felt too warm after her walk through the streets. She pulled at her scarf and her bright hair tumbled down over her shoulders. 'She said you would know what that means.'

He laughed again and shook his head. 'I know what she means alright. It means she's found a right one here.'

She was confused. Had she found the right locksmith? Was it safe for her to be here? She hesitated and began to think she should leave, but then the man said, 'Come through, my dear. We can't be seen talking here.' He stood aside and waved her behind the counter, then strode to the front of the shop and locked the door.

Beyond the shop itself was a back room filled with tools and a bare, rickety staircase, which led up to another narrow room with a table and chairs, where he obviously prepared simple meals, judging by the blackened pan she could see. 'Sit there,' he said, 'and drink this while we talk.' He poured two tiny tumblers of Chianti and lit the overhead lamp, making the glasses glow like rubies.

'Firstly, my name is Enzo. Now, have you any idea why she might have picked on you and told you to come here to see me?'

Gabriella thought for a moment as she sipped the wine. 'She could see I was concerned about what was happening in the square that day. Then she commented on my age and said I looked older than I really am and she said that "they" would like my hair. And because she talked about true Italians and because many of the prisoners in the piazza that day were partisans, I assumed she was interested in people who can help with the resistance.'

'Good girl. How old are you?' He studied her closely while she answered.

'Fifteen.'

'No, really.'

She hung her head a little. 'Fourteen and a half. I'm fifteen in the summer.'

'You're a bit on the young side, but she's right. You look older. You could easily pass for seventeen at least.'

'That's what she said.'

'Have you ridden a bike before?'

Gabriella was surprised by this unexpected question. 'I used to have a bike in Rome, but I haven't ridden one for nearly two years.'

'Well, it's something you don't forget. Might be useful if we need you to go a bit further afield.' He downed his wine and offered her another glass. She shook her head, so he poured just for himself. 'You know it could be dangerous, don't you?'

'I've seen what's going on. I know they're ruthless. So I'm prepared to take a chance.'

'Well said.' He studied her face for a moment, obviously testing her nerve as well as her patience. He gave her paper and a pencil. 'Give me your address so I'll know where to find you.'

Gabriella hesitated, then wrote down the details. As she pushed it back across the table to him, she said, 'My mother and brother live there too. I don't want them involved.'

'They won't be, I promise you. But just so we know we can trust you, I want you to do a little something for me on your way home.'

She felt a knot in her stomach as she anticipated what this might be, knowing how the baker had behaved and how the soldiers had gazed with hungry eyes upon her hair. 'What do you want?'

'Take this note and on your way back, find the *finestra del vino* in the Borgo San Jacopo, halfway along between the two bridges. It will be open and you must ring the bell there three times, slip this inside and go on your way. Can you do that for me?'

'Of course I can. Is that all?' Gabriella felt a huge wave of relief that it was such a simple task.

'Make sure you aren't seen and check you aren't followed when you leave here.'

'When will I know how I can help?'

'You will hear alright, mio caro. Trust me, you will hear very soon.' Then he stood and went across to a cupboard at the back of the room. 'Here, have these, then if you are stopped, you will have a legitimate reason for being out on your own.' He placed a handful of sprouting potatoes in her basket. 'Now be on your way and be careful.'

FORTY-ONE

FLORENCE

13 March 1944

It was just as Enzo had said. The iron door that protected the little arched window was open. Inside, above the deep stone ledge, hung a bell on a chain, with another short chain hanging from the clapper. Gabriella could just about see that the room beyond was dark and empty. She hovered by the opening for a second, looking around and checking no one was watching her. The narrow street was empty and she hoped inquisitive eyes weren't spying from nearby windows, but all the shutters appeared to be closed, hiding the occupants away from the city's troubles.

She reached for the chain and rang the bell three times. There was no other obvious sound once the echoing chime had faded, but after a moment she thought perhaps she could detect a faint shuffling inside, like the hushed sound of felt slippers taking cautious steps on the tiled floor. She placed the folded note on the ledge under a piece of broken terracotta tile that must have been left there for the sole purpose of holding money or messages. Then she walked swiftly away, along the street, back to the bridge she'd crossed earlier.

Of course she was curious to see who collected the note, and couldn't resist looking back over her shoulder a couple of times, but she saw nothing. And she'd been just as curious to know what the note said. She'd taken a quick peek soon after leaving the locksmith. All it said was: *Follow this one. Check she's for real.*

It made sense, she thought. Anyone could have gone to the locksmith offering their services. Choosing someone young who appeared to be innocent would be a perfect cover for infiltrating a clandestine organisation. She knew many Italian citizens were so desperate for money and supplies that they were turning in their neighbours if they suspected their involvement with the *Resistenza* or if they thought they were harbouring Jews. The fascists, both Italian and German, paid their informers well and there were rumours that gangs like the one run by Major Carisi were recruiting common criminals to assist them in their searches, raids and brutal interrogation. She shuddered to think how her mother might have suffered if she had been kept for much longer in that vile basement.

On her swift walk home, she looked over her shoulder now and then, but couldn't see anyone obviously following her. There were other figures roaming the streets, but most were outside simply because they were desperate to find supplies.

Mama was anxiously waiting for her, but was pleased when she showed her the potatoes. 'Wonderful,' she said. 'We can grow more from these. What a generous gift. Maybe we shan't miss the Villa Triste so much after all.'

'Grow more? Not eat them?'

'See the shoots sprouting? These will grow into potato plants and their roots will grow many more potatoes. Even I know that. I was shown by our gardener when I was a child. And we don't need to plant the whole potato, we can just cut off the sections that are sprouting and what's left we can cook and eat. I'll dig a trench for them today.'

Gabriella laughed at the thought of her artistic mother digging in the garden. 'Are you sure you can get these to grow? You didn't have much luck with most of the vegetable seeds you planted before.'

'These will be easy. They are already growing, we just have to water them.' She sighed. 'We may be glad of them come the winter if this war continues much longer. I hear it is very bad in Rome now.'

'I remember it was getting hard there when we left. Women and children were begging for food in the street.'

'They'll soon be begging here too, if the Germans keep taking stores from our farmers for their own countrymen. They'll strip us bare, so we must eke out our supplies carefully. If we end up surviving on nothing but polenta we'll all end up suffering from pellagra, like the peasants used to.'

Gabriella had heard this term before, usually flung in a derogatory fashion at girls at school who suffered from bad skin, but she also knew that in reality it was accompanied by diarrhoea and dementia. The poor disease, others called it, so were they now poor? 'Do you think we'll all get ill eating polenta?'

'Not if we try to keep eating a variety of vegetables. We might get thin, but we can try again to grow our own supplies. We are fortunate in having a real garden, so we must use the space we have. And there are edible weeds that our gardeners, when we had them, used to hoe from the soil. Dandelions taste like rocket and we'll let the nettles grow too. The young shoots are like spinach when cooked and we can use them for soup as well.'

Gabriella smiled at this mother, once so used to fine food, who had been brought up in wealthy households with servants to manage all the household chores. She'd told her often enough, 'Before times changed, the palazzo had heated radiators, so it wasn't cold in the winter like now. Your grandmother's handyman, Ugo, kept the charcoal boiler going in the basement. And the garden was always well tended, the laundry was washed downstairs and the floors swept. Your grandmother didn't have to do a thing but play her viola, embroider and attend the opera.' And now Mama was learning to grow vegetables, subsist on supplies once considered fit only for peasants and mend her own stockings, while neglecting her painting.

'Perhaps I will be able to collect more food for us if I am accepted by the partisans,' Gabriella said. 'They must reach out into the countryside and have access to sources among their contacts. But that's not the only reason I want to do this. I do really want to help after what happened to all of you.' She didn't dare tell her mother why she felt so responsible, so she told her about her first successful mission and they both laughed when she said, 'I wondered if a hand might suddenly pop out of the window and grab the note before I could run away!'

'Or perhaps a hand offering you a glass of wine,' Mama said. 'And it will be very helpful if you are lent a bike. Do you think they will let you keep it here?'

'I've no idea. He simply asked if I could ride one.'

Her mother began carving up the sprouting potatoes, putting all the chunks with shoots to one side and the remains of the vegetable into a pot of boiling water to cook. She held up a piece with purple sprouts, saying, 'See this? Each piece will make a whole plant and each plant will grow many potatoes. If that's not miraculous, I don't know what is.'

'I'm glad it makes you happy, Mama. I just wish I could help Riccardo too. Is he in his room?'

'No, I've persuaded him to go back to my studio. The light is better in there and he can use any of my materials. He wanted to try charcoal and pastels today on paper.'

Gabriella turned to leave the kitchen, then stopped and said, 'I don't want to tell him what I might be doing. The less he knows, the better. It's serious now.'

'I understand, my dear. He came close to being very badly hurt and we don't really know anything about the people who might be using you.'

'I just have to trust them.'

'But you know what they say – *Fidarsi è bene, ma non, fidarsi è meglio.*' Mama gave her a knowing look.

Gabriella knew the old saying well. *Trusting is good, but not trusting is better.* But who could say who could be trusted? And was this the only way she was ever going to be able to atone for her betrayal of her brother's trust?

FORTY-TWO

FLORENCE

November 2019

'His life was harder than I ever realised,' Isobel said, dabbing at the corners of her eyes with a tissue. 'I should have had more patience.'

'Don't upset yourself. You couldn't have known. He never shared his past with you, so how could you understand?' Sofia kept her arm around her mother, comforting her as best she could.

She turned to Gabriella, who looked tired after telling her long story and even older, if possible. 'I can see that all of this was upsetting, but I don't see why he turned against you? Nothing you have told us so far explains the burden you say was passed on.'

'There is much more to tell. So much happened in those years. We were so young, we didn't really understand the consequences of our actions. And even the youngest could not be fully protected from the horrors that raged around us. And when we thought we were all saved at last, when the Allies finally arrived, there was such unrest on the streets that when we eventually emerged from the gardens where we had sheltered, we were confronted by bodies and rubble at every turn. No one could escape the full horror of conflict.'

Gabriella paused and sighed. 'That was when we really

suffered. Many starved to death in the weeks after the Germans left, because it was impossible to get supplies of food. And there was no electricity or water for many in the city, so those who didn't starve were infested with lice because they couldn't wash themselves or their clothes.' Her eyes closed as if the horrific scenes of the past were once more there before her.

Sofia was growing concerned for their elderly host. 'Gabriella, I can see you are finding all this very tiring. I don't want to tire you out even more. Perhaps we should call it a day and let you rest.'

'No, there is so much more to tell. So much more.' Gabriella grabbed hold of Sofia's wrist. Her grip was surprisingly strong for such an old woman. 'But perhaps your mother would like to rest and return this evening?'

'Mum? What do you think?'

Isobel shrugged and sighed. 'Why hear only half the story? We still don't fully understand my difficult husband. I'm willing to come back, if that suits you.'

'We'll do that. We'll go back to the hotel and put our feet up for a while.'

Sofia gave Gabriella her hand to help her rise from the seat in the chapel. They walked together at her slow, unsteady pace back to the palazzo and left her in the care of her grandson.

'Are you sure you'll be okay to return this evening?' Sofia asked her mother as they walked back to their hotel. 'You must be finding it quite tiring too.'

'I'll be fine,' Isobel said. 'I'm nowhere near as old as her. If she can manage, I'm sure I can. Besides, this could be our only chance to hear what she has to say. She must be nearly ninety, she can't go on forever.'

'I think she said she was a year or two older than Dad. So that would make her about eighty-nine. She's pretty good for her age, don't you think? She might be a bit slow on her feet, but her mind is sharp as anything.'

'But is she telling us the truth? Or is it her version of the truth or what she thinks she remembers?' Isobel snorted. 'I'm not going to believe every word she says and neither should you.'

'I'm not so sure,' Sofia reflected. 'Her accounts so far ring true to me. They certainly tie in with certain elements of his work. I wish I had the exhibition catalogue with me. I'd like to ask her about all of the paintings and see if she has a better explanation for each of them. My descriptions were simply wild guesses.'

'You did your best, darling. I'm very grateful to you for taking on that immense task.'

Sofia slipped her arm through her mother's. She felt closer to her than she had in a long time. Isobel was starting to sound less resentful of her husband's challenging ways. Perhaps further revelations this evening would help her to finally come to terms with him and with their married life.

When they returned to their room later that afternoon, Sofia was grateful the hotel was so quiet. As it was situated right on the north bank of the Arno there was little passing traffic. She made two cups of tea and once they were refreshed, she and Isobel lay down on the bed and quickly fell asleep.

Sofia woke after a short nap, but her mother was still sleeping, so she sat in the armchair by the window, watching the light fading over the rooftops. She found the exhibition details on her phone and reread the descriptions she had painstakingly written before she had had any idea of what lay behind the paintings. In one, she'd said the use of the lamb motif symbolised *the loss of the innocence of childhood*.

How right I was, she thought. I suppose it's obvious, because a lamb stands for purity, but it's closer than I could have imagined. Poor Dad, growing up with such a sensitive nature in the midst of so much conflict and hardship. He was so kind and generous to me and I never gave any thought to what his formative years could have been like. Now I'm the one feeling guilty. I should have asked him to tell me about his childhood while he was still here.

Sofia was deep in thought, gazing out of the window as the lights began appearing on the far side of the river, when Isobel woke with a start: 'How long have I been asleep? We need to go very soon, don't we?'

'Gabriella said seven, so I'm going to have a quick shower and change. We've bags of time.' As Sofia ran the shower, she thought again about how little she knew of her father's early life. So far, the revelations about the past, while somewhat disturbing, still did not fully explain his work or his controlling attitude. But she wondered what more would be revealed as the evening wore on. And suddenly a thought occurred to her. If it felt appropriate, once they had heard everything Gabriella had to tell them, should she rewrite the descriptions of his paintings – and more to the point, maybe even produce a book of his work, expanding on the background to them? It could enhance their value; it would certainly add to the interest shown by the art world and collectors. The exhibition had resulted in some sales, but not as many as Phoebe had expected.

After a quick towelling dry, Sofia ushered her mother into the bathroom and phoned Phoebe in London. She answered to a background buzz of noise. She was clearly entertaining, or at least in a bar with friends. 'I've got a question for you,' Sofia said. 'Have you got a minute?'

'For you, always. How's it going in Florence? Is your mother behaving herself?'

'It's wonderful and she's fine. But listen, if I happened to find out a lot more about my father's past... if I happened to uncover things about his upbringing, his history, that cast more light on the development of his work, what would you say?'

'Huge opportunity. The more we know, the more we can publicise. Do you think you're on to something?'

'Possibly. We've met up with an old member of the family. Someone who knew him when he was a child. She's told us quite a bit already and we're meeting for dinner tonight.'

'Fabulous. Dig up all you can. Maybe make some notes? Or record the conversation on your phone.'

'I'll try. Oh, and she's shown us his first ever real painting. Done during the war, when he was about thirteen.'

'Oh my God, really? Does she want to keep it? Can you get your hands on it?'

'Afraid not. It's a fresco, firmly attached to the wall of the family chapel.'

'That's a shame. Then make sure you take photos. Get it all on record. We'll see what we can do with it when you're back. You've got me thinking already – book, documentary – it might even help us get that deal with MOMA in New York...' There was a sudden buzz of noise in the background and Phoebe became distracted. 'Ciao, must go now. Give my love to your mother.'

Sofia could hear the shower running. She wouldn't tell Isobel about this conversation. It might not go any further – or she might be on the brink of discovering things about her father she would never want the whole world to hear.

FORTY-THREE

FLORENCE

15 March 1944

Gabriella still hadn't heard any more from Enzo. Should she return to the locksmith's shop? She was growing impatient and woke each morning wondering if a message would arrive that day. He had said she would hear soon, but when would that be?

She voiced her concern to Mama, who said, 'No, you should wait quietly here. You don't want to draw attention to his shop. If they have need of you, they will let you know. All in good time.'

'But the days are so long now I'm no longer at school. By the time we've run to the market and done whatever we can in the garden and the laundry, there's so little for me to do to fill the day.'

'Well, today's different. You can go with Riccardo to see the Scoppio del Carro cart. I've heard back from Mario Soldi and he will be there today at ten to show your brother around.'

'That's wonderful. Riccardo must be so excited. I'd be happy to go with him.'

Her mother looked worried. 'He's not as pleased as I thought he would be. He hasn't left the house since that terrible day. It's as if all the joy and curiosity that he once had in abundance has left him, poor child.'

Gabriella felt as if her mother had just confronted her with evidence of her betrayal, but she only said, 'I'll go to him now. He mustn't miss this opportunity. It will be good for him to go out and he's so curious about the cart used in the Easter ritual.'

As they walked together to the Via il Prato, with clear instructions this time on which of the many barred entrances protected the famous cart, Gabriella was painfully aware of the change that had come over her brother. The once mischievous boy, his dusty brown knees grazed in tumbling games around the palazzo grounds, was subdued. His mother had cut his thick brown hair to make it easier to dress his wounded ear, which was still livid and swollen. She no longer applied a dressing, but bathed it twice a day in salt water and said it was healing quickly.

'We may find out whether they have plans for the fireworks this year after all,' Gabriella said, trying to provoke some interest in him. 'Or if they think they should hold off until the war is over, we may get some idea of when they will start preparing the cart for the ceremony again.'

He was still sullen and quiet, his hands in the pockets of his shorts, his head looking down at the flagstones as they walked, his old boots scuffing the paving. She tried to see his expression, to get some inkling as to what he was thinking or feeling. And eventually she heard him muttering.

'What did you say?' she said. 'I can't hear you.'

'Nothing will ever be the same,' he mumbled. 'It won't ever happen.'

'I still can't hear you properly. Speak up.'

Then he stood still, right in the middle of the paved street, and shouted at the top of his voice: 'This city is never going to be the same again.'

'You don't know that. The war will be over one day. Everything will go back to how it once was.'

'It can't. I'll never forget what happened. What I did.' She noticed how his face was reddening and his chin was trembling.

And in that moment she felt the painful realisation that he was infected with guilt for what he believed he had caused to happen: his injury, his parents' arrest, his father's departure, the arrest of who knew how many others and their deportation on those crude trains to some unknown destination. She knew it wasn't his fault, but she couldn't bring herself to say that she was the guilty one, not him. All she could manage to tell him was, 'Shh, you aren't to blame for anything. Come, calm yourself.' She threw her arms around him and after a moment of struggling against her, his tense body relaxed and he sobbed.

'You still want to see the cart, don't you?'

He was able to nod his head against her shoulder.

'We're nearly there now. But we're early, so we can sit down for a moment till you feel ready. I really want to see it too and one day we'll see the real thing exploding in front of the Duomo, I'm sure. You'd like that, wouldn't you?'

He nodded again, then pulled away from her, wiping his nose on the darned sleeve of his sweater. They sat down on the edge of a dry fountain bowl, feeling the warmth of the spring sunshine on their faces, drying his tears. Pigeons pecked at their feet, hoping they had brought crumbs, but there was nothing to spare in the city. Everyone ate every scrap for themselves.

When they reached the warehouse entrance, Gabriella told Riccardo to ring the bell and soon they heard quick footsteps on cobbles and the harsh withdrawing of bolts. A small door opened in the heavy studded gates and a tubby, older man peered at them. 'Welcome, my young incendiario – forgive me – and incendiaria,' he said, adding the feminine version of the word for arsonist in deference to Gabriella. 'Please follow me.'

They stepped over the door's raised threshold and Signor Soldi locked the door again and waved at them to follow him across the courtyard to the buildings on the other side. 'We store the Brindel-lone, the famous cart, in here,' he waved at a large barn, 'and when the oxen are brought up from the country, we prepare them in there,' he waved at the stables. 'They have to be washed and brushed till they are the purest white, then they are decorated with garlands of flowers on their heads, just like Vestal Virgins.'

'How many oxen are used to pull the cart?' Gabriella was curious, picturing the lumbering, flower-decked beasts harnessed to the cart, threading their way through the cobbled streets of the city.

'We always use four, but we bring in six, just in case one of them is not fit on the day. It is a special occasion that one day and we cannot afford to have a lame or sick beast.' He led them to the barn and lifted the great iron bar that held the doors shut. 'And here we have the Brindellone, our centuries-old cart.'

At first they could not see it clearly. It was a tall, tiered structure on wheels, a little like a painted wedding cake, Gabriella thought, with its four segments topped with a kind of turret bearing a crown. But as the man flung the doors open wide and held them back with great iron hooks, sunlight streamed into the barn, revealing just how shabby the legendary cart had become. Dust motes hovered in the sunbeams illuminating the once-grand, castellated structure, now veiled with thick cobwebs. It stood abandoned, unused, on the floor of beaten earth scattered with wisps of straw, scented not with the whiff of cordite but the must of beetles and mice.

Signor Soldi sighed. 'You're not seeing it at its best. We normally repaint it every year and repair the damage done by the fireworks the previous Easter. But now...' He shrugged as if to say, what was the point in doing anything at all in these unsettled times?

But at that moment, Riccardo finally came to life. He stepped forward to stroke the body of the cart, its wheels and the fretwork of turned balustrades bordering each level. The upper tiers were far above him, but he stood back and gazed at the scorched paintwork of faded blue, gold and red. 'I could help you repaint it,' he said, pointing to the carved heraldic reliefs that embossed the six panels forming each part of the tower.

Signor Soldi gave Gabriella a quizzical look and she said, 'He may be young, but he is already a talented artist. I know he could be useful.'

'Perhaps, but it is a great treasure. This cart is over four hundred years old. The tradition stretches back to the eleventh century. It is not something for an inexperienced hand to toy with.'

'I'm sure he appreciates that. But will you consider his offer of help?' Gabriella felt that Riccardo desperately needed to be absorbed in a project. The Brindellone could be the very thing to distract him.

He shook his head as if pondering this idea. 'His mother, Baronessa Rinaldi, is a very good artist. I suppose she has been teaching him?'

'Ever since he was very small. She is convinced of his talent and has given him the run of her studio and her materials.' Gabriella paused for a second, wondering how much personal information to divulge to this old family friend. 'But she paints little herself these days.'

'Aah' – he nodded sympathetically – 'in hard times an artist either cannot stop or cannot start. There are no compromises for true artists.' He stepped towards Riccardo, saying, 'Young man, you want to become a great artist like your mother, eh?'

'I paint and draw all the time. May I make some sketches while I'm here?' He held out the sketchpad he had just pulled out of his pocket, along with a couple of sticks of charcoal. 'I'd like to copy the designs painted on the panels if I may.'

Signor Soldi patted his shoulder. 'Of course you can. It gladdens my heart to see you taking such an interest in our heritage. We have all been deeply saddened by the need to postpone the Scoppio del Carro yet again. Never in all its history have we been without its blessing. With it not being possible again this year, that will be four years our harvests have not been blessed by the Church with a magnificent display from our cart.' He fetched a sturdy stepladder from the side of the barn and placed it in position for Riccardo. 'Here you are. Be careful climbing up, but it will help you see more of the upper parts.'

Gabriella was so pleased to see her brother animated again. He climbed the ladder and stood with his knees pressed against the top strut, balancing on his good leg so he could sketch the patterns. 'It's quite badly damaged up here,' he said.

'Every year we have to make repairs,' Soldi said. 'Some years are worse than others. This time is not so very bad. But we must make it good before we can paint it again.'

Riccardo took notes on the colours as well as the carved designs. 'And do you always use the same paints? The colours that are still here in patches?'

'More or less. And we try to replicate the traditional designs on the woodwork too.'

Riccardo stepped down from the ladder and moved it round the other side of the cart. 'It's even worse over here,' he said. 'The medallions are partly broken and the paint has completely burned off.'

Signor Soldi seemed impressed and smiled at Gabriella as they both watched the once sad and deflated young boy absorbed in his study of the paintwork. 'He is the image of his mother. And out of respect to her I would be happy to allow him to help us restore the cart. We may not be able to resurrect our lives at present, but this small gesture would give us all hope for the future.'

Gabriella felt a huge sense of relief that she may have helped her brother find such an appropriate distraction from his misery. His face was brighter, she thought. This was just what he needed, to help him heal and forget.

'Young man,' Signor Soldi announced. 'I shall appoint you as my youngest apprentice. We may not be allowed to perform the ceremony this year, but we can make preparations for the day when it can once again be towed in all its splendour into the Piazza del Duomo. As of tomorrow we shall begin the repairs and then you will assist with the repainting. I shan't be able to give you any work until the damaged parts are restored, but if you would like to watch how we go about repairing the cart, I would be delighted to show you what we can do. Starting tomorrow, the Brindellone shall be restored to resplendent glory!'

Riccardo jumped down from the ladder, clapped his hands and shouted, 'Yes! To the glory of the Brindellone!'

FORTY-FOUR

FLORENCE

5 April 1944

It was two days before Good Friday when at last it happened. Gabriella had almost given up thinking about the locksmith and his promise, but that morning, when she was dressed and sat brushing her hair, her mother called out, 'Someone's just delivered a note here for you.'

She rushed into the hall. Slipped under the front door she found a folded piece of paper bearing her name. She opened it out and read the tiny writing inside. In one column there was a list of ten addresses scattered around the city. The other half of the sheet carried the following instructions:

Go to Gianecci Armetti in the Mercato Centrale at 11 today and ask for fresh porcini from Firenze. Then do as he says.

She showed the message to her mother. 'What do you think I should do?'

Mama glanced at the message and said, 'The market is a very public place, so you should be safe. But I will come with you, all the same, just to be sure.'

· · ·

The central market in Florence was not far from the station. There were several stalls that usually sold dried mushrooms and fresh ones were also available from the vegetable stands. But these days both fresh and preserved produce was scarce and when Gabriella and her mother arrived, they scanned the few dealers, wondering which one related to the mysterious note. 'I'd better let you go ahead,' Mama said. 'They might become suspicious if they notice you are accompanied.'

Gabriella began browsing the rows of stands, most of which were closed and shuttered while others had very little on display. At last she spotted the merchant's name featured in the note: *Gianecci Armetti – Funghi Secchi*. A few strings of garlic, tomatoes and mushrooms hung from the stall's ceiling and dried porcini, looking like withered leaves, were displayed in a basket. A smell of forest mulch and twisted roots filled the air, reminding her of autumn risottos and the forager's chicken her mother used to make before the shortages. An old man dressed in a grubby, collarless shirt and dark brown coat sat on a rickety chair in a corner of the stall, his face shaded by his battered felt hat as he sat picking at his nails with a small penknife.

'Signor Armetti?' Gabriella said in a hesitant voice. He didn't seem to hear her, so she stepped forward and lowered her head, trying to see if he had noticed her.

He didn't look up, but in a low rasping tone said, 'What do you want?'

'I've come to ask for fresh porcini. Do you have any today?'

He raised his head to look at her. 'No, I don't have any. Everything here's dried. Can't you see?'

She looked around his stall and then she remembered the exact wording of the note. 'I meant to say, fresh porcini from Firenze?'

And at that point, she noticed his eyes narrow. 'Why didn't you say that in the first place? I don't have them here, but you have the addresses?' She nodded. 'Then go to each one, ring the bell in the *buchette del vino* and when you hear someone answer, you only have to say two things. "The Arno flows in Florence"; and then say, "the new Vasari is complete." Have you got that?'

'Yes, I think so. Is that all?'

'It's enough. Now go before anyone sees you.' He waved her away and bent his head again to attend to his long yellow nails. But just as she was about to step away from the stall, he said, 'Here, take these,' and he handed her a crumpled brown paper package.

Gabriella turned to leave and caught sight of her mother walking towards the entrance and running down the stairs. She had obviously been watching over her all the while, which made her feel reassured that she had found the right place.

Outside the market, she caught her mother's arm and said, 'Walk with me for a moment.' Once they had turned a corner, away from the pedlars and beggars hanging around the market area, she said, 'I just have to deliver a spoken message to all the addresses in the note.'

'Is that all they want you to do? Shall I come with you?'

'No, you go home and wait for Riccardo to come back from Signor Soldi. He'll be hungry when he returns.' She opened the paper package and saw what she was hoping for: porcini. 'See what you can make out of these.' She pressed the parcel of dried mushrooms into her mother's hands, pecked her cheek, then left.

By the end of the afternoon, Gabriella's feet were aching. The wine windows she had to find were located all around the city. She tramped from Piazza San Lorenzo to Piazza Santa Croce and across the river to the Oltrarno and back again. At each address she found the *buchette del vino* was already open, as if the occupant was expecting a customer for their home-pressed wine. Some had little, studded wooden doors, others iron grilles, but all were open in anticipation of something. And each had a bell, whether hanging from a chain or sitting on the sill of the window, waiting to be rung. She hadn't been told how many times to ring the bell this time, so she gave each bell a tug or a shake and from somewhere in the depths of the inner room she would hear a response of some kind.

At the first wine window, a small arch edged with stones of grey granite, the ringing of the bell elicited only a grunt and some distant shuffling. She waited a second or so till the person seemed closer to the opening, then she spoke. She thought she might hear a word of thanks or a spoken acknowledgement, but the only reply was another grunt and the shuffling sound moved further away.

By the time she reached the final window, fairly close to where she had found the locksmith in the Oltrarno, she no longer expected any conversation or to see a face. Everyone was silent, accepting the message but not giving her anything in return. She was tired, footsore, hungry and thirsty as she neared her last desti-nation. In future, she thought, I will arm myself with some suste-nance for these journeys.

She was just about to cross the road and stop at the window when she caught sight of a man hovering. He wasn't in uniform, but he was old enough to be signed up to fight or sent away to work. Most men of his age weren't loitering on corners. The only men seen in the streets were either soldiers or those past their strength and no longer of any use. And it seemed to her that she may have seen him more than once that day, so she carried on walking on her aching feet, despite her desperate desire to stop and rest.

Gabriella walked around the block, ducked through an alley-way, cut along to the river and then took a right turn back into the Oltrarno and found the street she had walked earlier. She could no longer see the man and, once she had satisfied herself that this particular street was quite empty, she felt it was safe to ring the little brass bell she could see sitting on the sill. And unlike all the other nine addresses, this time the tinkling brought a real person to the window. A tiny old lady, barely tall enough to reach the sill, peered up at her as she delivered her message, then said, 'Take care, little staffetta. Here is something for your trouble.' The woman pushed a small basket containing two eggs across the sill. 'God go with you,' she said and turned away out of sight.

Gabriella stared at the white eggs as she began slowly trudging home. She was so hungry, she was tempted to suck one from its shell, just as she'd heard some peasants did. But then she thought of her mother and brother and of the dishes that these precious eggs could help them make. *Rafanata* perhaps, though maybe the potato cakes would not be that good in the absence of pecorino and pancetta. Aioli would be an extravagance; or maybe Mama would prefer to add an egg to her stracciatella, giving the light vegetable broth additional goodness.

She was so absorbed in thinking about the ways this unexpected bonus could be used that she didn't hear the man behind her. Suddenly a hand clamped her shoulder and a voice said, 'What d'you do to earn those then? They black market?' She was so startled, she jolted forward and only just managed to stop the eggs falling out of the basket. Then the hand reached over and snatched the basket from her. 'They'll be safer with me,' he said. 'Don't want to go wasting good food, do we? Run along now.' He pushed her so she nearly stumbled again, and, as she recovered and stood upright, he left. He marched in the opposite direction and Gabriella was left stunned and tearful. He didn't know her, she'd never seen him before, but, clad in the black and green uniform of the fascists, he claimed superiority over ordinary citizens, no matter how hungry they were, and he had the right to take whatever he wanted.

FORTY-FIVE

FLORENCE

5 April 1944

When Gabriella returned, she could hear her mother humming in the kitchen. It cheered her to hear this happy sound; it meant that Mama was recovering well from her ordeal and growing stronger by the day.

'Is that you, Gaby?' her mother called out, emerging from her work, wiping her hands on her apron. 'You look exhausted, child, come in and sit down.' She put her arm round her daughter's shoulders and walked her to the chair near the back door, where the warm spring air, scented with the courtyard's purple iris, fused with the steam from the stove. 'Here, drink this coffee. I don't think it's much better than the chicory, but see what you think. It's made from roasted barley.'

Gabriella sank onto the chair and sipped. The brew was still bitter, but it was a slight improvement on *caffè d'olanda*. 'Tell me what happened today,' Mama said, sitting down with a small cup beside her.

And Gabriella could not help herself, she burst into tears and spluttered, 'I had eggs for you but a fascist guard stole them.'

'My dear, I'm so sorry.' Mama's hand stretched out to stroke her arm. 'But he didn't hurt you, did he?'

She shook her head. 'No, but I was thinking how happy you'd be to see I'd brought back fresh eggs. We could have had *rafanata*.' Her sobs prevented any more words.

'No more tears, Gaby. As long as you are unhurt that is all that matters. Eggs would have been very welcome, but your safety is more important.' Mama clasped her hand, reassuring her that she didn't grieve for the eggs. 'Now tell me what you had to do, if that is permitted.'

So she told her mother about the messages, her long trek around the city and the final confrontation with the thief. 'I think another man had been following me as well and then the guard ran off once he'd stolen my eggs.'

'Do you think you will have to undertake a similar task again?'

'I have no idea. I don't even understand what the messages meant. What is the new Vasari? I've heard about the old one, though I've never seen it, but what is the new one?'

Mama was thoughtful. 'I was invited to walk the Vasari Corridor many years ago. My uncle was a trustee at the Uffizi and he was involved in reassessing the works to be displayed in their section. I must have been fifteen – yes, a little older than you are now, I think – and I was invited with my parents to walk the entire length of the passageway. We entered through a doorway at the back of the grotto in the Boboli Gardens. I thought it was all very exciting – a secret corridor that spans the whole city!'

'So what could they mean by a new Vasari? They can't have built another passageway connecting buildings, can they?'

'No, nothing obvious to the outside world. But perhaps there is a network of interlinked houses, maybe a route through attics and over roofs or underground through the cellars.'

'And if the partisans are no longer able to use the sewers as they once did, then this would give them an escape route?' Gabriella pictured the nest of rats their Roman gardener had once disturbed, sleek, fat bodies zipping across the grass into hollows under shrubs, followed by his fierce, little, excited dog.

'It is possible. But I think the less you know about it the better. That way, if you are ever stopped and questioned, you really can claim to know nothing. You are doing important work now and there will always be a risk.'

Gabriella felt reassured by her mother's caring words and sipped some more of her coffee. 'Did Riccardo wonder where I was?'

'Not at all.' Mama shook her head with an amused smile. 'He has been with Signor Soldi again all morning. They haven't started repainting the cart yet, but I can't tell you what a difference there is in him. He is so full of joy again and when he came back, he went straight to the studio to work on the sketches he had made. I am so glad he has a zest for life once more. And I have news too. We are going to have help and we are going to make the garden more productive.'

Gabriella was astounded but pleased to see the change in her mother. She was animated and determined, so different from the sad broken woman of only a short time ago. 'What, we're going to have a gardener?'

'Not one, but four. I decided that it is ridiculous for us to have all this space to ourselves. We cannot use all the rooms, so I have arranged for us to have lodgers again.'

'But is that going to cause trouble for us?' Gabriella worried that giving houseroom to more partisans or Jewish families might bring the household under further scrutiny.

'I hope not. They have been referred to us by the priest Don Leto Cassini, whose work has saved many Jews from this city. He was himself arrested and sent to prison for a time, but that has not dimmed his enthusiasm for good work. Giving this family shelter will benefit all of us. I have little knowledge of cultivation, but I have more than enough rooms to spare.'

'When will they be coming?'

'Tonight. They are refugees from Hungary but they have been staying at the convent for some time.'

'Were they there when the convent was raided?' Gabriella remembered that those who could claim they were Hungarian were spared deportation.

'I believe so, and the mother was arrested and held for a time with those who were sent away. They may be in need of our help, Gaby, but I hope that in helping them, we will be helping ourselves too. I certainly feel more positive myself, knowing we can assist and give a home to these people.'

'But will they bring food with them and how will they cook?' Gabriella was painfully aware of how little they had just for themselves and how her mother was struggling to find fuel for the stove.

Mama held her head high. 'We don't need grand furnishings and possessions. There is much here that can be sold, bartered or burned. We need food much more than grand antiques or jewels. We can afford to invite this family to share our kitchen and our meals.'

Then Gabriella noticed how bare her mother's hands were. She still wore her wedding ring, but the large square-cut emerald had gone: 'You sold your beautiful ring?'

'I exchanged it, my dear. What need do I have of such a ring now? Instead we have a sackful of polenta and a small bag of flour. That is far more useful to us these days.' She laughed and it was not a bitter laugh, as if she regretted the loss of her ring; it was carefree, showing how little she minded now for the treasures she had inherited.

'Then we can give this family a welcome meal of gnocchi,' Gabriella said. 'They may as well get used to it until we have something better!'

ACT THREE
THE INHERITANCE

Legacies and a lifetime of guilt

FORTY-SIX

FLORENCE

November 2019

'Would you mind if I came back tomorrow morning and took a photograph of the painting in the chapel?' Sofia and Isobel had only just arrived at the palazzo for dinner, but she wanted to make sure she had secured this opportunity before events took a turn.

'Just that one?' Gabriella looked refreshed. She had changed from her earlier gardening slacks and blouse into a bright silk Pucci shirt in emerald green and turquoise, over black capri pants. She may have been old and stooped, but she was still very stylish.

'Oh, of course, you'd said there was more than one?' Sofia hadn't thought to ask earlier in the day, the lamb painting had been such a surprise after their long lunch and subsequent conversation.

'Oh yes, my mother allowed Riccardo to do several. It was the only way she could keep him occupied. He'd used up all her canvases and started painting over ones she'd started and then discarded. I can't tell you how insatiable he was.'

'I'd like to photograph all of them, if you don't mind. Tomorrow's our last day, but our flight isn't until late afternoon, so there'd be time if I came early in the morning.'

'You must come back. I'd like you to learn everything you can about him, while you're here.'

'Are you sure, darling? We have to allow time to check in. You know I don't like to be rushed in airports.' Isobel was a nervous flyer and always wanted to double-check every last detail.

'We've plenty of time. You don't have to come with me. I'll let you have a quiet morning, so you don't feel stressed.' Sofia was already thinking what a coup this was and could almost hear Phoebe's gasps of excitement in her head – *Fabulous, what a find! We must definitely think about a book – the discoveries – the art tour – I can see it already.*

'No, darling, if there are more paintings then I'll have to come with you. It won't be the same if I only see photos. I want to see them for myself.'

Sofia frowned, knowing this would slow her down, but she couldn't deny her mother the opportunity to see all of her husband's hidden early works. After all, she had supported him throughout his career and probably should be credited with ensuring that he had gained such international acclaim.

'But first,' Gabriella clapped her jewelled hands, 'an aperitif.' Carlo magically appeared in the elegant drawing room with frosted glasses of ruby red liquid, clinking with ice. 'Negroni sbagliato. I hope you like it. I used to love to drink negronis but I can't take drinks of such strength any more, so this is a tame version for an old woman. It's Campari with Asti Spumante.'

Carlo sat down with them and Gabriella said, 'I have given my grandson a night off. He is going to join friends tonight. I said after giving us such a splendid lunch today we would be happy with a cold selection of his specialities for dinner.' She clinked glasses with Carlo and, once he had downed his drink quickly, kissed him on the cheek and waved him away: 'He has heard my stories often enough. He doesn't need to hear them all again.'

After they had chatted a while, Gabriella led the way to the adjoining kitchen, where a feast was laid out on the scrubbed wooden table. Various salami and hams, mozzarella, salads and more crusty bread. 'I thought we'd eat here in comfort – and because this was where many of our childhood dramas occurred, it seemed appropriate for us to be here in this room. It has changed little since those times. We have refrigeration these days and the old wood-fired range has been replaced with a gas cooker, but other than that, it is much the same as it always was.'

Sofia glanced at the shining copper pans, the large earthenware storage jars, the bunches of herbs that hung from an iron frame chained to the ceiling. 'This is lovely. And what a spread Carlo has left for us. It looks marvellous.'

'He loves going to the Mercato Centrale to shop for us. Have you been there?'

'We've been following the very strict itinerary my husband organised for us,' Isobel said in a crisp tone. 'Unfortunately, it didn't allow for spontaneity, so no, we haven't been to the market, or probably many other places that ordinary visitors manage to see.'

'Perhaps you will find a moment tomorrow. It isn't far away.' Gabriella eased herself into a kitchen chair by gripping the arms on both sides.

'I rather doubt it. We're quite surprised that today wasn't planned down to the last minute. Typical of him to keep control over everything we've been able to do. Story of my life.'

'I'm sorry to hear that your marriage to my brother was so challenging.'

'He was extremely hard work. I know it sounds ungrateful, but it's true. He was a very difficult man.'

'I'm sure he didn't mean to be unkind. Perhaps after all he'd experienced he just wanted to be sure life turned out well. He may have meant it for your security and well-being.'

'It's all very well, but he wanted to control everything!' Isobel heaved a choking sigh, sounding near to tears, and leant on the table, her head in her hands.

'What my mother means,' said Sofia, hastily coming to the rescue, thinking her mother was going to ruin the evening by being emotional, 'is that he always thought he knew best. He wasn't being uncaring, he just liked to ensure that everything was right.'

Gabriella sighed, 'So much had gone wrong. What started as a game went so very wrong.'

'You need to tell us more, don't you? Is there much more to tell?' Sofia felt nervous. Was this evening going to end in tears for all of them?

'There's so much more and we are going to need fortification,' Gabriella said. 'Please eat, drink, so we can sustain ourselves for the rest of the story.'

'I'm not sure I want to hear any more.' Isobel was screwing up the napkin lying folded on the table.

'Don't worry, Mum, I'm here. We can do this together.' Sofia took the bottle from Gabriella and half-filled her mother's glass.

'It started with friends, school friends and a girl who was lonely,' Gabriella said. 'We should choose our friends wisely, but unfortunately I didn't. And when I did meet true friends, it was hard to keep them close by.'

MESSAGE SIX

Sbuts etteragic dna sevod gnimalf

FORTY-SEVEN

FLORENCE

5 April 1944

The Dvorak family arrived just as dusk was falling, when the first bats flitted over the palazzo garden in the lowering light. They were all very subdued, the two girls of seven and eight, Lili and Jazmin, clinging to the side of their mother Hanna, while their taller and older brother Bela stood sullenly behind them.

Mama led them upstairs to the rooms she had allocated on the first floor. Large spacious rooms that had once been the master bedroom, dressing room and study, with a separate bathroom. When she returned to the kitchen, she was smiling and said, 'Hanna says she has never known such a grand home and the two girls think it is a fairy tale to be living in a palace.'

'And the boy?' asked Gabriella, 'Will he be trouble?'

'I think not, but poor boy, he is confused and angry. He is at an age where he feels humiliated by events, powerless to help. After their trek from Hungary, they had thought they were safe in the convent until that raid, taking all the Jewish women and children away. Imagine witnessing that, seeing the harsh treatment those brutes dealt out. And their mother was taken too, at first. They must have all been terrified. Being here, working with his mother in the garden will be good for him. She is a farmer's daughter and is used to working on the land, so we are very fortunate to have them here.'

When the newcomers came down for supper that night, Hanna presented a basket containing a clutch of young, tender artichokes. '*Carciofo*, from the convent garden,' she said. 'Bela and I have been working hard in their garden and they will have an abundance this Easter.'

Mama thanked her and picked one of the little purple- and green-leaved vegetables from the basket. 'We always used to roast them whole with lamb. But I fear we shall be short of Easter lamb this year.'

'We shouldn't have killed him,' shouted Riccardo. 'We should have kept him for Easter.'

The two little girls looked startled and clutched their mother's arms.

'Don't worry,' Mama said. 'My son is rather excitable,' and she gave him a fierce, admonishing look. 'We had a lamb that grazed in the garden, but we could not provide for it through the winter. But had it lived, it would no longer be lamb!'

'It would still have been good meat though,' Riccardo said, 'not gnocchi.'

'We shall be grateful for whatever can be spared,' Hanna said. 'The day after tomorrow is Good Friday, so we have one day in which to source supplies for an Easter feast. Bela is a very brave, intrepid boy and he will see what can be found.' Bela nodded his silent response, while his mother continued, 'And I will inspect the garden and find out what you have here and make plans.'

Gabriella liked the sound of this and liked Hanna even more when she said, 'City people do not always understand the country ways of survival. There is much to be found for free if you know how. I will show you what to look for.'

And finally Bela spoke too, in his uneven, newly broken voice: 'I can get pigeons for us to eat too.'

'Really? There are not so many now nobody has crumbs for

them.' Gabriella thought how in Rome, before the war, a carpet of pigeons would fly from her feet when she ran to the Colosseum.

'How will you catch them?' Riccardo jumped up and down. 'Do you have a net?'

'No,' Bela said. 'But I have a catapult.' He pulled the device from his pocket and pretended to take aim at this cheeky boy opposite him.

'Can I have a go?' Riccardo lunged for the weapon, but Bela pulled away and stuffed it back in his shorts. 'It is not a plaything,' he said gruffly.

His mother laughed. 'He is an expert. He shot squirrels, rabbits and pigeons on our farm, to protect our crops.

The meal passed, with conversation about the dishes that could be made if the garden became productive again. Riccardo befriended Bela by showing him his drawings of the Brindellone and explaining the Easter tradition of previous years. Soon, the surly boy was engrossed in trying to understand how religion and pyrotechnics were linked in Florence.

Gabriella listened to the discussion between her mother and Hanna as they enthusiastically discussed possibilities for cultivating the garden and their favourite recipes. Hanna was clearly the more competent gardener and cook, but Mama was showing she was eager to learn and made up for her lack of knowledge by also offering to adapt some dresses for the two girls, who barely spoke during the meal.

Were Jazmin and Lili just shy or were they shaken by their experiences? Gabriella couldn't quite decide and thought it best not to ask too many questions about their life in recent months. They were pale and thin, not starved but clearly lacking nourishment to grow with vigour. Their hair was cropped to their chins, presumably their mother's solution to infestations on their travels with other refugees. She thought how they must have been so frightened by the raid on the convent and their mother's arrest. 'I can show you round tomorrow, if you like,' she said. 'There's lots to see here and Riccardo's done a wonderful painting of the lamb in the chapel too.'

'I'd like to learn to paint,' Lili whispered and her sister nodded, indicating that she wanted to as well.

'Maybe Riccardo can teach you then. He is very talented.'

The young girls both glanced at this animated boy, his paint-spattered clothes and the ragged ear crusted with scabs. 'How did he hurt his ear?' Jazmin asked.

Gabriella hesitated. She couldn't tell them the truth. It was far too alarming, much too brutal a story. Instead, she said, 'He was being silly. He fell against a window and it broke. Serves him right, stupid boy.'

The girls giggled, putting their hands over their mouths to smother their laughter. Such sweet little girls, so unlike that pair of cruel sisters she had known, who she now hoped never to see again.

FORTY-EIGHT

FLORENCE

10 April 1944

The arrival of the Dvorak family had brought a miraculous change in circumstances, Gabriella thought. Not only was Hanna resourceful, she was also generous and was encouraging her mother to be bolder and more determined to make the most of their circumstances.

The new lodgers may have seemed quiet and reserved at first and they were still polite and unassuming, respecting the right of the owners of the property to have privacy, but they were all able to contribute enormously to everyone's quality of life. On Good Friday, they all attended church, where the crosses and statues were draped in black. The atmosphere was solemn and subdued, but the following day, Hanna announced that she and her children would go in search of the 'Easter feast'.

'I doubt there will be much to find,' Mama said. 'But if Bela manages to bring back a few pigeons, we shall be most grateful. In normal times we'd also have boiled eggs and bake a Colomba Pasquale.'

Gabriella's mouth watered at the thought of the dove-shaped cake similar to a panettone, sprinkled with crunchy nuggets of sugar and almonds. How wonderful if they could have a dish of pigeons followed by a baked dove, she thought, then decided she had to share the joke with Riccardo. She found him in the art studio, working on a painting that featured the Brindellone. He had only sketched out the form so far and was surrounding the cart with doves and weeping women.

'What are they doing in your picture?' Gabriella peered at the figures. It wasn't a very joyful Easter scene.

'I was thinking about the service yesterday and how sad Mary must have been to see her son dying on the cross. And then I thought about the women taken away from the convent. It feels as if there is sadness all around us this weekend.'

'But Hanna and her children are going out to see what they can find for Easter. Please don't be downhearted. They may return with pigeons and maybe the makings of a Colomba Pasquale. Won't that be funny? We'll have birds to roast and stew and a sweet dove cake!'

He smiled at that and said, 'You're right. We must try to make it a good Easter, even though the Scoppio del Carro won't happen this year. I've been asking Signor Soldi how they make the Colombina, the dove that lights the fireworks. He says it's sculpted out of papier mâché and they have to make a new one every year, because it's always damaged when it sets the display alight.'

'Maybe we could make our own flying dove in honour of the ceremony?'

Riccardo's eyes lit up and he laid down his brush. 'I think I could make it out of wire and paper. I've never seen the real Colombina, but I know it's white and carries an olive branch. It contains a firework that's lit by holy fire at the altar. I wonder if I could make a model dove to carry a flame?'

Gabriella could see how excited he was becoming at the thought of creating his own display. 'But you must be careful. It sounds dangerous. You will have to do it outside.'

'Don't worry, I'm never going to risk this family's safety again.' He began searching for materials and as Gabriella left him, she knew he was still thinking about the danger to which his parents had been exposed and that he still felt it was his fault. She knew she should tell him it was all her doing, but she could not bring herself to do so. Besides, she told herself, while he had been running around the city, having freedom and playing his game of *agente segreti*, she'd had to go to school, enduring the spiteful attentions of Tina and Franca so she could return with delicious treats. So she was not at fault and now she was contributing to the vital work of the resistance, while he was still wasting his time painting and pining for a firework display. She had more important things to do.

When Hanna and her children returned that afternoon, they were tired but triumphant. 'My time at the convent has been well spent,' Hanna said. 'The nuns have excellent connections all around the city and so we have been able to find lamb. Not much, but enough for paprikash tomorrow.'

'And we have eggs as well,' squealed Jazmin. 'We're going to boil them and colour them.'

'Easter eggs for everyone,' echoed Lili, hopping up and down.

'What about the pigeons,' Riccardo asked Bela, 'did you shoot any?'

'We have those too,' Bela said, holding out his hands, each fist holding three birds. 'We can eat them tonight with the fresh turnip greens my mother has gathered from the convent garden.'

'And I have been busy too,' Mama said. 'We shall have a Colomba Pasquale after all. It may not have grains of sugar or almonds on top, but it will still be shaped like a dove. I found the old baking tin Carla used at the back of the larder and I've used some of our flour.'

The two little Hungarian sisters clapped their hands at the thought of the wonderful cake, then Lili said, 'Can we boil the eggs now, so we can paint them when they are cool?'

It seemed to Gabriella that the scene in the bustling kitchen was helping everyone to forget the war and deprivation on their doorstep. While they were busy and had supplies, they could put the misery from their minds and stop worrying about what might happen next for a day or two. Maybe this was the Easter Peace, the new life that the festival promised, she thought.

When Sunday came, Hanna's daughters were very excited and skipped all the way to church. They fidgeted in their seats, but were quiet and well behaved during the service. Riccardo was restless too and when they left the church he ran ahead, saying he had to get ready.

Mama and Hanna were occupied in discussing how they were preparing the lamb with artichokes. 'Such a pity there is no paprika,' Hanna said, 'But your garden has mint and rosemary and that will add flavour.' As they all walked back, it could almost have been an Easter stroll before the war. The spring sunshine, the prospect of a good meal, gave Gabriella hope, despite the presence of armed guards in all the piazzas where citizens of the city gathered. After the service, she'd overheard gossip about the difficulties the Allies were facing. Troops were struggling to make progress beyond Monte Cassino and her mother said it was as well they were no longer in Rome, which would bear the brunt of the fighting next.

As soon as they reached the palazzo, Riccardo was hopping up and down, saying, 'I have prepared a surprise for us. Come into the garden right away.'

The two mothers were reluctant as they wanted to concentrate on their cooking, but seeing how excited he was, they relented. 'We can't come for long if you want a good dinner cooked for you,' his mother said.

'Come out into the main garden, but stay near the wall,' he said and ran off again.

'I've no idea what he's up to,' Mama said. 'I just hope it won't take very long.'

The next minute they heard him shout from somewhere up above them and then they heard a sliding sound from behind and a white object flew over their heads. Gabriella realised Riccardo had managed to stretch a taut cord or wire from the top of the palazzo to the corner of the lawn. And whizzing down this angled trajectory at great speed was a model dove. Its outspread wings were angled as if in flight and it held a twig of something in its beak. But she caught only the quickest glimpse of it as it zoomed past, burst into flames and then dived into a wheelbarrow at the end of the garden.

'Brindellone,' screamed Riccardo from the top of the house. 'We have our own Scoppio del Carro.'

But Mama did not applaud him. She suddenly leapt into action. 'That damn boy will set the trees alight,' she said, running to fetch a can of water. Hanna joined her and they ran to the flaming barrow, which was full of dry leaves under one of the cypress trees.

Bela and his sisters were screaming, not with terror, but with laughter, as the two women ran around complaining how dangerous this escapade was. Riccardo rushed outside, yelling, 'Did you see it? Did you see my dove? Wasn't it brilliant?'

He ran towards the flaming wheelbarrow and his mother scolded him and then gave him a slap, catching his wounded ear. He sank to the ground and then she sank down too, with her arms around him: 'Oh my darling, my darling, I'm sorry. I didn't mean to hurt you. Here, let me look.'

Everyone rushed over to the still-smoking, dampened cart, a smell of acrid smoke filling the air. Riccardo was crying and now the little girls began to cry too, upset that this display had ended so dramatically. 'It needs more stitches,' Hanna said. 'The wound has reopened and it's bleeding. Why don't I take him to the convent where they have the skill to do it properly?'

His mother pulled away and tried to brush off the blood that had seeped onto the shoulder of her blouse, then she too began to cry.

'I wanted to give you all a wonderful surprise,' Riccardo sobbed. 'But it's all gone wrong, like everything I do.'

'Shush, darling,' his mother said through her tears. 'It was wonderful. You are very clever to invent a way of recreating the display. Clever, clever boy.'

But Gabriella stood watching silently. Yet again, his imagination had almost caused a disaster. When cypress trees caught fire, they burned so ferociously, so quickly, like flaming tapers to oil; it would have been over in an instant, but the damage would have been irreparable. And she wondered: even if Riccardo's ear could be restitched and heal, could his mind ever recover?

FORTY-NINE

FLORENCE

14 April 1944

A week after Good Friday, Gabriella received a present. The doorbell rang early one morning and when her mother opened the heavy door, she found a bicycle had been propped against the front gates, but the messenger was nowhere to be seen.

'I think this must be for you,' Mama said as they both examined the bike. Its black frame was scratched and rusty in parts, but the tyres were good and the basket attached to the front contained several potatoes and a couple of onions.

Gabriella began emptying the basket and found a creased scrap of grubby paper beneath the earthy vegetables. She smoothed it out and read,

Collect your instructions from the buchette del vino in Borgo San Jacopo. Do not cover your hair.

Mama was reading over her shoulder. 'Uncovered hair? That must mean they want you to distract someone, I think. You are certainly very noticeable. But I don't like the sound of that.'

Gabriella was already excited at the thought of riding a bike again, and to reach the window mentioned, she'd have to cycle across one of the city's bridges and over the river. 'It says don't cover, but it doesn't say don't tie it up. I could plait my hair or pin it back.'

Her mother tucked the offending hair behind Gabriella's ears, then held it in a tight bunch. 'It's so long and thick. Maybe plaited and then pinned around your head. That would look more modest, I think. It won't attract so much attention.'

She had to sit very still in the bedroom while Mama fussed over her, tightly braiding the wavy auburn hair, then securing it with what seemed like a hundred hairpins that stabbed her scalp. Gabriella peered into the mirror on the dressing table. She no longer looked like herself; she was not used to seeing her hair so restrained. Even at school she had never tamed it with more than a single fat plait hanging down her back between her shoulder blades. 'There you are,' her mother said, when she'd jabbed the last pin into the woven hair. 'That should last you on your errand. When do you have to go?'

'It doesn't say, but I think as the bike was delivered so early, I should set off right away. I don't yet know what they will want me to do, but I imagine I'm to cover some distance or perhaps make a delivery.'

Her mother fussed some more, insisting she should eat before leaving and giving her a chunk of bread and water in a flask, as the day was beginning to grow warm. Then she kissed her daughter and wished her luck. 'I just want to see Riccardo before I go,' Gabriella said. 'I want to see if he'll recognise me with my new hairstyle.'

She ran to the studio, where she knew he would be working before he went to the warehouse to watch the progress on the cart. His ear had been restitched by a nun at the convent and was beginning to heal better than before, although it was still weeping and sore.

'What do you think?' she shouted as she burst through the door. 'Different, isn't it?'

He was startled and nearly dropped his paintbrush, but he quickly recovered and said, 'It's like a halo, wound around your head. Like an angel, no, a Madonna.' He walked around her, examining the way the hair was captured and tucked away. 'I must do a quick sketch. Stay right there.' He fumbled for his charcoal, then she heard it scratching the paper as he drew her in profile from both sides, from the front and from behind, murmuring, 'How white the neck that holds the crown...'

'Aren't you finished yet?' She was growing impatient, desperate to set off on her adventure. 'I have things to do, I've got to go.'

He turned back to his painting, laying down his sketches. 'It's important to remember. I must never forget...'

And she realised he was lost again in his world of images, dreams and nightmares. He was absorbed in his work and did not look up as she slipped out of the studio door and out to the bike. She'd thought she had forgotten how to ride, but as she wheeled forward and lifted herself onto the saddle, it was as though she had been cycling the streets of Rome only yesterday.

The flagstoned surface of the roads near the palazzo made the old bike wobble at first, but she grew more confident as she pedalled and by the time she reached the smooth surface of the nearest bridge, the Ponte Alla Carraia, she was thoroughly enjoying the feeling of pure freedom. The morning air was fresh and she was glad she was wearing a sweater and jacket, but the sun was bright with promise in a clear blue sky. She could feel the breeze teasing little wisps of hair around her forehead, despite Mama's efforts to tame every curl.

In the middle of the bridge she slowed down and stopped. She could see two German soldiers on the far side and knew she would have to pass by them; it would look suspicious if she turned round. Besides, to reach her destination she had to cross the river at some point and probably all of the bridges were being patrolled. She leant her bike against the parapet and removed her jacket. It wasn't that she was too warm, but she knew her young curves were more obvious under her sweater alone. She folded the jacket and placed it in the basket, then wheeled the bike towards the men.

Once they had noticed her, they straightened up, shoulders pulled back with military authority. 'Halt. Was hast du da?' one of them said in a harsh tone. His comrade reached into her basket, pulling out the jacket, then he picked up the flask and shook it. She knew it sounded like it contained liquid and he smiled and said in a softer tone than his companion, 'Ist es Schnaps?' His blue eyes twinkled with amusement.

She shook her head and laughed. She knew what he had asked and she answered, 'No, it's just water. I'm on an errand for my mother and I may get thirsty.'

He returned her smile and let her repack the basket, then said, 'Geniesse diesen schönen Tag.' She nodded and resumed her walk with the bike and as she did so, she heard the gruffer soldier say something about 'Rothaarige'. She knew 'rot' was red and realised they were talking about her, but whether it was complimentary or not she could not tell.

Once she was over the bridge, she was tempted to turn left and cycle alongside the river, but that route offered fewer opportunities for diversion if she felt unsafe, so she took the second left instead, into Via di Santo Spirito, which she knew would lead straight to her destination. There was less sun in the high-sided street and fewer people, probably because most at this time of the day were anxiously scouring the markets for supplies. With food becoming so hard to find and expensive to buy, the streets were no longer scented with the delicious smells of vegetables roasted with garlic, pasta fragrant with truffle oil and freshly baked bread, but reeked of unwashed clothes and blocked drains.

When she reached the little arched window in Borgo San Jacopo, its door was again open and she could see the chain for the bell. This time she hadn't been told how many times she should ring it, so she clanged the clapper twice, then waited. She heard shuffling steps entering the dark room within, then a woman about

Mama's age peered at her through the tiny aperture: 'Sei tu quello dai capelli rossi?'

Gabriella nodded, then turned round so the woman could see her auburn hair properly. 'Yes, that's right. I'm the redhead. My mother made me wear it like this.'

The woman sniffed as if she thought interfering mothers were no help to the cause. 'Well, I guess you're the one they said would come. So go to the locksmith. You've been there before, haven't you?'

'I know where it is,' she answered, turning her bike round to leave, thinking *they could have saved me some time and sent me straight there*. But the woman called out to her, saying, 'Here, take these for your trouble.' And through the window she pushed a handful of tender young artichokes and a couple of sugared frittelle on a greasy piece of paper. Then the inner window shutter was slammed shut. Gabriella grabbed the precious food, placed the vegetables in her basket and ate the frittelle immediately. She'd had a meagre breakfast of bread and ersatz coffee and was already hungry. The fried dough balls weren't the best she'd ever had, probably because ground almonds were now impossible to find, but the sweetness and hint of lemon in them gave her the energy to continue.

After a sip of water from her flask, she began cycling again towards the Oltrarno district. She saw very few passers-by on her way there, but as she approached the shop, she saw two German soldiers looking in the window. She couldn't go in while they were there, so she cycled around the block again and up to the piazza, until she saw them strolling on the opposite side. She raced off again immediately, arriving breathless at the shop, where the door was open and waiting. As she was looking over her shoulder to check she hadn't been followed, Enzo the locksmith called to her, 'Come in with your bike and shut the door.' He was sitting at the back of the shop as before.

'I was worried I might have been seen.'

'They've been past twice today, but hopefully they won't come this way again. Nosey Nazis. Lean your bike against the counter and come upstairs.'

She followed him up the rickety staircase and there at the table was a young woman in a red dress with sparkling eyes, a young woman even more mischievous and alluring now she was no longer wearing her drab school uniform, her beret replaced by a scarlet ribbon threaded through her curly black hair. Gabriella gasped aloud: 'Stefanina! What are you doing here?'

'I wondered if it might be you, when Enzo said the new girl was a redhead.' Stefanina turned to the locksmith at her side. 'You're right, she is very pretty. But that hair needs to come down. Weren't you told that?'

'The message just said not to cover my hair. It didn't say I couldn't tie it up. It was my mother's idea and she insisted.'

'Ha, mothers, aunts, grandmothers, they all worry so about our honour,' said Stefanina, laughing, rolling her eyes and tossing back the wine that Enzo had poured. 'How are we to win this war if we can't distract those stupid Nazi noodles? Sit down here, next to me. Before we leave today, I'm going to teach you how to flirt.'

FIFTY

FLORENCE

14 April 1944

'It's best if we just walk past them, looking innocent,' Stefanina said as they strolled towards the Santa Trinita bridge. 'There's usually guards at this end, but sometimes they're on both sides and you never know when they're going to want to take their time.'

Gabriella tried to remember all that her friend had told her as she'd removed the pins from her hair in the upper room at the lock-smith's shop. 'Smile, flutter your eyelashes, giggle. Twirl your hair around your fingers and jiggle your shoulders. They're all young, missing their girlfriends and home cooking. They're so easy.' Stefanina laughed, demonstrating how she would lean forward, revealing the shadow between her breasts, how she would slip the scarlet ribbon from her hair and toss her curls, how she would make the skirt of her red dress swirl around her knees.

It wasn't much different, Gabriella thought, to when she had created the diversion at the station, the diversion that had freed her father. She practised tossing her long hair over her shoulders and thought it would have made more of a show if she'd been cycling, the breeze wafting her hair in the sunshine so it glinted in the light. And if she'd been riding the bike, her legs would have been more visible too. But Stefanina insisted they walk side by side, wheeling the bike between them. 'We look good together, don't you think? One dark, one red? Which of us will catch their eye first?'

And Gabriella tried not to think about what was buried at the bottom of the bike's basket. She'd caught a glimpse as Enzo placed a wrapped bundle beneath the piece of stinking salt cod with its thin covering of muslin. The *carciofo* were scattered on top, their purple and green leaves looking like exotic flower petals. But it wasn't vegetables that lay at the bottom of the basket, it was guns, she was sure. She'd seen the dark metal and the shape of the barrels.

As they neared the bridge, Stefanina said, 'Oh good, they're on the far side. That means they will get a good eyeful as we walk across and with luck, your hair will blow in the wind to tease them.' Out in the open, above the fast-flowing River Arno, Gabriella's tawny mane lifted in the breeze and though she knew it was doing what was required of her, she thought how tangled it would be when she came to brush it out that night. *And what am I going to say to Mama, when she sees me returning like this?* But at least she'd saved the precious hairpins, stowing them in her skirt pocket.

She shaded her eyes as they drew closer to the men and Stefanina did the same, saying, 'Don't worry. They're only boys, ordinary soldiers. They'll be easy.'

They were just about to walk past when one of the men said, 'Darf ich in ihren Korb schauen?' He indicated the basket and pushed the artichokes to one side, revealing the fish beneath. 'Was ist das?' he asked.

His fellow soldier peered at the basket and then pulled away, making a face and saying, 'Es ist das stinkende Fisch!'

The first boy stood back and smelt his fingers, then shook his head. The girls laughed and Stefanina said, 'We use it to make bacalao. It is delicious. Don't you like it?'

'No, it stinks. We like good fresh *Kabeljau*, not this stinking dried stuff.'

His friend laughed too and then said, 'Aber ich mag diese roten Haare.'

Gabriella giggled as she had been instructed and Stefanina took the handlebars of the bike and began to take a step forward. 'Mama will be angry if I don't get this to her right away. You can stay and talk if you like.' And she wheeled away with her secret still safe inside the basket.

'You like the stinking fish too?' The young soldier reached for a curl of Gabriella's hair, sparkling red, orange and gold in the brilliant sun overhead.

'Once it's prepared, it's delicious, but I know it smells awful like this.'

His friend also reached for a lock of this bright tawny gold, so close she thought she could smell the onions on his breath, but the first boy knocked his hand away. 'Not with your smelly fishy fingers you don't!' And that gave Gabriella an opportunity to pull away from both of them and, with a final dazzling smile and toss of her head, she began walking away, turning for just a second to flutter her fingers as they watched her go.

But where was Stefanina? And where was the bike with its precious cargo? By now, she cared more for the artichokes and the salt cod than the hidden guns. *Mama will welcome both of those if I'm allowed to get them safely home.* But neither her new friend nor the bicycle were in sight.

She trudged back along the streets she had cycled earlier that morning, thinking about the loss of the vegetables and about her mother's reaction to her unruly appearance. *Maybe I'll run straight in to see Riccardo and say he wanted to draw me with my hair unpinned.*

Deep in thought, she wasn't aware of steps creeping up behind. Suddenly two pairs of arms were flung around her. 'Here she is,' yelled Franca, breathing garlic into her face. 'We've missed you, little ginger girl, haven't we?'

'Why haven't you been to school lately? You bad Roma,' Tina said, pinching her cheek. 'You need feeding up again.'

'Yes, come back with us. We still have lots of food to spare.'

'I can't. My mother is expecting me back very soon. I have to help her as she hasn't been well.' Gabriella wanted to escape as soon as possible. And what if they took her back and the cook saw her? Would she remember her? Remember the girl who helped a prisoner escape?

'There's lots of food and it's even better than before,' Franca said. 'That stupid old cook left us and we've got a proper chef now.'

'He'll feed you up, even if we go back right now,' her sister added. 'Come on, let's go.'

They both linked their arms through hers and forced her to walk in step with them. Gabriella knew there was no point in resisting; she had to accept they could do anything against her will. Franca was even heavier than before, weighing on her arm like a great sack of polenta, and Tina, though wiry, was tall and strong.

'Bruno won't be there though,' Franca said. 'He's gone off to be a proper soldier now. We'll have to find you a new boyfriend, won't we?'

'Who do you think she'd like best? Alfredo?' Tina said, then giggled and went on, 'I know, what about our visitor? The new friend we met last night. Let's take her to meet him.'

Gabriella was relieved she wouldn't have to face that thug Alfredo who had harmed Riccardo, but was this other man going to be worse? Since Bruno's betrayal she knew no one associated with the sisters and their powerful father could be trusted.

'Oh, she'll like him.' Franca shrieked with laughter.

As the stark frontage of the Villa Triste loomed in front of them, she felt a deep sense of trepidation, remembering her last encounter with the harsh sisters. They had always enjoyed teasing and humiliating, but now she could sense how much they relished inflicting pain too. Their father, and the men with whom they associated, all used brute force to control, to get answers and to eliminate those who were opposed to their regime.

'Let's eat first,' Franca said when they were inside, pulling Gabriella along with her down the stairs to the kitchen. 'Marco,' she called out, 'we've brought a friend back with us. What have you got for us to eat?'

An elderly man with strands of greasy grey hair plastered to his scalp was chopping onions. He wiped his hands on his stained chef's whites and opened his arms in a friendly greeting. 'Little ones! Welcome back. You are hungry after school? You want frittelle, arancini? Sit here and I make for you.'

He turned up the heat on the large range stove and placed a deep fat fryer over the heat. 'I have them ready,' he said, opening a large cold cupboard, which Gabriella quickly realised was a refrigerator. She had never seen one before, but Mama longed for one to keep food fresh longer. The waft of cold air she felt when he opened the door matched the chill of fear she was already feeling, aware that in the bite of a mouthful, the sisters could shift from feeding her delicacies to causing her harm.

The fried treats were ready in minutes, the dough balls sprinkled with sugar and the arancini with grated Parmesan. Tina and Franca grabbed them, breaking them open to cool a little before stuffing their mouths. Gabriella knew they would taste delicious, but she was too tense to even think of eating. When the two girls had had enough and there was only one of each ball left, Tina wrapped them roughly in a napkin and pushed it into Gabriella's skirt pocket. 'For later,' she said, through her mouthful, splattering sticky crumbs over her blouse.

'Come on,' Franca said. 'Come and meet your new boyfriend.' She pushed Gabriella from her seat, grabbed her arm and pulled her away, out of the kitchen and across the corridor. Gabriella knew where they were going: she had been there once before.

FIFTY-ONE

FLORENCE

14 April 1944

The door to the room across the passageway was bolted this time. Tina drew back the heavy bolts with a loud clang and in the slight echo that followed, Gabriella could hear a low murmur and a groan as Tina flung the door open. At first the room was in total darkness, but as the light from the corridor filtered inside, two bodies became visible and the sour smell of human waste wafted towards them.

'We've brought a new friend for you,' Franca shrieked. 'If you're nice, we might let you have a kiss.' She switched on the lights and the flood of the stark white beam revealed the room's occupants, both squinting and turning their heads away from the sudden intrusion. They could not shield their eyes from the light because their wrists were tightly bound.

There was a woman slumped on the floor against the wall. Her feet were bare and bloody and her ankles were lashed with twine that bit into her flesh. Seated, or rather collapsed, on the sturdy armed chair was a naked man, his neck, legs and wrists fastened with leather straps. His face was battered and bruised, his ears had been partially severed. Gabriella could never have recognised him, he was so injured, but she knew that this was the work of Alfredo, the same man who had sliced off a portion of Riccardo's ear.

'No, no, I want to go home,' Gabriella whimpered. 'I don't like it here. Let me go.'

'But Bruno isn't here any more. You've got to have a new boyfriend,' Tina said. 'Now let me introduce you properly. This is... oh, I've forgotten again, what's your name?'

The man groaned in reply. He could not form words, his lips were so swollen, his teeth so broken. 'That's not very helpful,' Franca said. 'Let's see if your friend can remember,' and she turned to the frightened woman on the floor slick with blood and urine, then kicked her.

'I don't know,' the woman cried. 'We don't know anything. Please let us go.' Tears streaked her dirty, bloodstained face and she tried to shuffle back from Franca's twitching foot, but fell onto her side.

'You're no help,' Franca said, giving her another kick. 'I'll have to ask him myself. I'm sure he told us when we were helping Poppa last night, but silly me, I'm so forgetful.'

She picked up a pack of cigarettes lying on the table in the middle of the room. 'I always like to smoke after I've eaten,' she said, striking a match, 'it helps my digestion.' She lit the cigarette and inhaled, blowing the smoke away with plump, pouting lips. Despite her coarse features and bulging body, she smoked with elegance, aping the glamorous actresses she must have seen striking languorous poses in films.

Tina laughed at her sister's pose as smoke spiralled in the filthy room. 'I want one too,' she said, but didn't move away from the door to help herself to the pack.

'In a minute,' Franca said. 'I'm the eldest so I go first.' She circled the table, looked down at the trembling woman on the wet floor, gave her another half-hearted kick, then completed her circuit by standing in front of the groaning man. 'If you don't tell me your name so I can introduce you to this lovely young lady, I'm going to have to help you remember, aren't I?'

Gabriella felt sick but was emptied of the will to move. She desperately wanted to leave this hellish basement, she didn't want to witness the girls' fun, but at the same time she felt she had to know how far they were prepared to go. She closed her eyes and wished she could disappear, and then she heard Franca speak again.

'Well, if you're not going to tell me, maybe this will help. It usually does.' The next sound was a scream of utter agony. Gabriella opened her eyes to see Franca pulling the red ember tip of her cigarette away from the poor man's arm. A livid sore spoke of his pain, alongside other burns made previously.

'Let me, let me,' yelled Tina, leaving her position by the door and rushing to the table.

Gabriella did not wait. This was her only chance. While the two sisters were engrossed in their hideous game of torture, she slid away, ran up the stairs and burst out the main door into the street. She ran as fast as she could and as soon as she was out of sight of the Sad Villa, she threw up in a gutter. As she spewed and then sobbed, she reached into her pocket, hoping for a handkerchief, and her fingers felt the parcel of food Tina had stuffed in there. She pulled out the bundle, wiped her mouth on the napkin and threw the whole lot into the puddle of vomit.

She could not eat from their table ever again. Their food could never taste wholesome; it was seasoned with cruelty and treachery. Those girls may have attended a conventional school, albeit one imbued with fascist ideology, but their real education had taken place at the Sad Villa every evening after dinner. As she turned away from the mess she saw the hungry pigeons fluttering down from the rooftops to eagerly peck at this unexpected find.

Gabriella ran most of the way home, stopping now and then to check she wasn't being followed, catching her breath and feeling sick whenever she looked behind her. Never again would she allow herself to be caught by those two. The extent to which they had been participating in their father's interrogations was shocking, but she was even more shocked by their arrogance. She could tell they didn't care how much she knew about their disgusting antics. Like the arrogant Italian and German soldiers on the streets of Florence, they knew they would not be challenged and could do whatever they liked, however cruel and inhuman.

When she returned to the palazzo, she ran straight to her room, washed her face and brushed her tangled hair. She didn't want her mother to see her dishevelment or her distress; Mama might grow even more anxious about her safety and decide to curb her freedom to cycle and help the movement. Once she felt more composed, she went looking for Riccardo. His room was empty but another painting was propped near the fireplace. It depicted a white dove, wings outspread and aflame, bearing a branch of bloody thorns.

She found him in the studio, contemplating a new picture. He stood back from the paper, charcoal idle in his hand, tilting his head and then leaning forward to smudge a line he wanted to correct. It was in the early stages of composition, but she could see what he was planning as it echoed the picture in his room. The white dove was flying above a maiden with braided hair wrapped around her head, holding an offering of pigeons with their breasts torn open to reveal dark hearts.

'You've let down your hair,' he said when he realised she had joined him. 'Why did you unpin it? Put it up again so I can check how it looks.'

She shook her head. 'All those pins made my head ache. Anyway, I need help to dress my hair like that. Mama did it for me. Has she been asking for me?'

'No, she's been busy. She and Hanna went to the convent, I think, with the children. Not Bela though. He's been trying to kill more pigeons.'

Gabriella sank into the old leather armchair in a corner of the room. The wrinkled upholstery had split in places and as she curled her legs around her, she picked at the horsehair spilling from the torn leather. 'Do you think one day we'll have forgotten this time, these months of war?'

Riccardo turned to her, 'We'll always have reminders of this time, Gaby,' he said, lightly touching his maimed ear. 'I can paint over an image or rub out a sketch, but I'll never forget what I have seen. Those who remain will have to remember to tell the stories of those who have gone.'

And Gabriella closed her eyes as she tried to erase the pictures of the Sad Villa, the bruised woman and the tortured naked man.

FIFTY-TWO

FLORENCE

November 2019

'Whatever happened in the end to those awful girls? It's simply shocking to think their father encouraged them to take part in such brutality.' Isobel had barely touched the tempting spread of food on the table while Gabriella was telling them about her escape from Tina and Franca, but now she took great gulps from her glass of Chianti.

'They left Florence before the Allies arrived, to join their mother in the mountains. Their father was killed in a shootout with American forces, but I never heard what fate befell those two girls. Nothing good, I hope. I'd hate to think they both made good marriages and lived long and happy lives after their cruelty. They were willing participants in their father's wicked deeds but I can see how they were reared to think that his methods were appropriate. They didn't think there was anything wrong with their cruel behaviour.'

'So dreadful,' Sofia said. 'You were lucky that they didn't turn on you as well that time.'

Gabriella shook her head, as if she was trying to rid herself of her horrific memories. 'When I got home I didn't tell my mother everything, but then she already had a good idea what went on in that awful villa, because of the time when she was arrested. That's why, when I told her I didn't want to go back to school, she didn't disagree. They had never really been my friends, I was just a bit of fun for them. It was unfortunate I met up with them again.'

'And did my husband, Riccardo, know about these awful girls? Did he know about the interrogations?'

'He was aware of a little, but I tried to spare him. He was so traumatised by his painful injury and the arrest of our parents that I wanted to protect him.' Gabriella sighed and looked sad. 'But no one could be fully protected from horror during that time. It was all around us, nearly every day. We had both seen the deportations from the station and people were being sent away even after the rail lines were bombed. Nothing stopped the horror.'

Sofia could see in Gabriella's expression, and the tone of her voice, her pain at remembering the distress of a young boy faced with the destruction of lives and property. She began to fully realise how much her father had overcome to go on to live a normal and truly successful life. This made her feel even more proud of his achievements and she glanced at her mother, who was crumbling a crust of bread on her plate, deep in thought: 'Mum, don't you feel it was amazing that Papa survived all this and became such a wonderful artist?'

Isobel sighed. 'I feel tremendously sad. I wish I'd known and we'd been able to talk about it together. Not knowing all this, I just felt I was faced with a difficult, demanding man I didn't truly understand. I feel guilty now for misjudging him.'

'You mustn't ever think that, my dear,' Gabriella said. 'You are not guilty of anything. You supported him throughout his career and gave him your love and a wonderful daughter.' Her voice was sincere, pleading. 'I am the guilty one, it was entirely my fault.'

'But you were little more than a child yourself,' Sofia said. 'You'd had to leave your friends behind in Rome, when you were young, then your father left and your mother was distressed. It must have been very difficult for all of you. I'm not surprised you turned to those awful girls initially. You needed friends.'

'That's true. And after a time I found real friends, not ones who used me, although I met them because they needed my help.' Gabriella shifted in her seat, sipped her wine and went on, 'My dear, would you mind fetching the dessert from the dresser over there? I told Carlo to leave out a bowl and clean plates.'

Sofia rose from the table as instructed and they all ate portions of sliced golden peaches baked with fragrant amaretto, sprinkled with toasted almonds. 'What are you going to do when Carlo leaves? He is the most wonderful companion for you, cooking and caring for you like this,' Sofia asked.

'I am very fortunate. But maybe my granddaughter will join me. She will start her studies next autumn and I would love to have her living here. It suits us all and since my husband departed, I have so enjoyed having company in the house.'

'Did you meet your husband here in Florence?' Sofia realised that so far his name hadn't been mentioned.

Gabriella smiled and her face lit up with happy memories. 'I met him when we were both very young. We shared so much together. Bela, my dearest Bela. We had two wonderful children and now I have six grandchildren altogether. That to my mind is as great an achievement as your father's artistic career. Wonderful children who have gone on to study, train and help the world. Doctors and lawyers, all of them. It is good to make amends for all the damage that was done in the past.'

'They must be a great comfort to you,' Isobel said, reaching for Sofia's hand. 'Just as my daughter is to me.'

'I have my roses and the friendship of many, but it is reassuring to have a strong, young person here. I dread to think how long I might lie among the rose bushes if I fell. But then if I were to die beneath my roses, I'd die happy!' She gave a reflective smile and added, 'Though maybe not completely happy, as sudden death is hard on those left behind. I'd rather be like Riccardo and have time to prepare.'

'How can you say that?' Isobel snapped. 'If he'd died suddenly he wouldn't have been able to arrange this ridiculous trip. His death would have been a shock, but I wouldn't still be following his orders as I had to do throughout our married life!'

'Mum, don't upset yourself. You've both lost husbands. It's not about who is right or wrong.' Sofia turned to Gabriella. 'Please don't take any notice. We're very grateful to you for your hospitality and your honesty in telling us so much we didn't know before.'

'I understand, my dear. It takes time to grow used to being alone again. I have had ten years. My Bela passed away far too soon. He was always a good person and I miss him still. We shared so much and he was there at my side when the dearest friend of my youth was taken from us. I must tell you about her, as I fear her life also had a significant impact on Riccardo. Let me tell you more about Stefanina.'

'Stefanina?' Isobel's voice was almost a whisper. 'Was she an old girlfriend of his? I always wondered. When Sofia was born I suggested we call her Stephanie, but Riccardo said he would not be able to bear to hear that name spoken every day for the rest of his life.'

Gabriella gave a sad smile. 'I can understand why. She was not his girlfriend, but I know she made a deep impression on him. She was the bravest person I ever met, right to the very end.'

FIFTY-THREE

FLORENCE

14 April 1944

Gabriella was woken from her sleep in the studio by the slamming of the front door and her mother's voice calling, 'We're back and we have news.'

She shook herself awake and then she and Riccardo went to the kitchen, where Mama and Hanna were unpacking a basket on the scrubbed table. Jazmin and Lili ran out into the garden and Bela followed, his rounded shoulders drooping, his slingshot trailing from his hand.

'Well done, Gaby,' her mother said. 'You've brought us such good treats this time.' Gabriella noticed the package of salt fish and the artichokes on the table. 'I must start soaking the cod right away. It really needs a whole day in water. But what a delight. Clever girl!'

Gabriella was puzzled. Did that mean the bike had already been returned, or just the goods in the basket? She didn't want to press for details, fearing her mother would be concerned to learn that she had lost the bike. And she certainly didn't want her to question how the rest of her day had been spent. She shook her head and said, 'You said you had news? Is it good news?'

'Hanna will tell you,' Mama said, busying herself with washing the fish and then placing it in a deep dish filled with cold water to soak.

'We have arranged to help the convent open a soup kitchen,' Hanna said. 'In return for helping them to cook, as well as working in the convent garden, we will all be able to have a midday meal there every day. There will also sometimes be vegetables to spare that we can bring back here.'

'We must do what we can to help,' Mama said. 'We are far more fortunate than many in this city. We have a roof over our heads, we have a garden, which will soon produce plenty, and if we are ever short, then there are goods here that I can trade. Gold and jewels are all very well but they won't fill stomachs by being hidden away.'

Gabriella thought of her mother's heavy rings, now never worn, the collar of pearls with a diamond clasp and the carved coral earrings with gold settings. Her mother was prepared to make so many sacrifices to keep everyone healthy, so the least she could do was continue with the work she had been asked to do. She left the kitchen and walked to the front entrance. The bike was there, where she had originally found it, leaning against the wall. So Stefanina – or someone else – had brought it back once the task had been safely completed. Gabriella grasped the handles and wheeled the bike into the hallway, thinking it would be safer inside than remaining where any passer-by might borrow it. As she did so, she realised the basket was not completely empty. At the bottom was a layer of white muslin, similar to that which had wrapped the salt fish. She pulled it out and saw a small note underneath on a scrap of paper. The writing was not the same as that on the note this morning. She read:

I will come for you tomorrow morning at nine o'clock. Tie your hair loosely. S.

Who was S? She assumed it must be Stefanina, who she'd last

seen walking away with the bicycle in her red dress and matching ribbon, while she herself amused the German guards. Perhaps this time they could stay together and then she'd feel she had some protection. Stefanina was bold and strong, she'd never be cowed by the cruel ugly sisters.

The next morning, Gabriella told her mother she was expected to run another errand by bike. 'I'm pleased it is going well so far,' Mama said. 'But be vigilant and if you ever feel uncomfortable about the jobs you are being asked to do, you must decline. I would not want you to put yourself at risk, however important it is.'

'I'll be very careful, I promise. But I'm happy to do whatever I can to help free our city and our country,' Gabriella said as she finished tying up her hair in a loose plait over her shoulder, then added a scarf as well in case she felt the need to completely cover her bright hair. She kissed her mother goodbye and went to wait outside with her bike.

As the chapel clock chimed nine, Stefanina arrived. She looked even more alive than she had the day before, with a fresh scarlet ribbon tied on top of her black hair. Her full mouth shone with the sheen of scarlet lipstick as she smiled in the early sunshine. 'You ready for another adventure? Shall we go and tease some more stupid soldiers?'

Gabriella thought the soldiers were an easier target than the sisters she hadn't been able to avoid yesterday, so she smiled and nodded. 'Let's go then. What are we going to do today?'

As they began walking down Via Faenza towards the central market, Stefanina said, 'Today is easy. We are going to pick up some copies of the anarchist paper *Umanità Nuova*. We'll hide them in your basket under some dirty washing and then we're going to deliver them to our supporters.'

Gabriella had once heard Papa talk about the newspaper, saying it had been shut down by the government for urging partisans to fight fascism, but that it was rumoured to be circulating again under the title *Risorgiamo*. 'Is it allowed?' she asked, wondering how risky today's mission was going to be.

Her companion shrugged and laughed. 'No, but who cares? People need to be kept informed. The regime can't stop us criticising them. We're not going to be forced to keep quiet.'

Stefanina looked as if she could never be told to be quiet. She was the naughty girl at the back of the class who was always giggling, whispering stories to her friends. The bold girl who wasn't afraid to confront bullies. And she must have lots of friends, Gabriella thought, good friends, not ones like Tina and Franca. And then she felt she should share her concerns, so her new friend would understand if she saw them again and wanted to avoid that pair of sisters. 'On the way back yesterday, I met two girls I used to know in school. I didn't want to meet them and they aren't really friends. Their father consorts with several men at the Villa Triste.'

'The Sad Villa? You know it?' Stefanina spun round, looking alarmed.

'Yes, I've been there with them several times. And they forced me to go with them yesterday.'

'What happened? Did you see anyone there?' She grabbed Gabriella's arm and stopped walking.

How could she describe the horror she had seen? But then how could she not? It was a relief to tell someone, especially someone who might have the sense to understand. 'I did, but it was so horrible.'

Gabriella began to cry, but Stefanina shook her shoulders and said, 'There's no time for tears. Just tell me what you saw. It might not be too late. I know it's where that Major Carisi and his brutes interrogate their prisoners. They're doing the Germans' dirty work for them.'

'A man and a woman in the basement. They were both tied up and badly hurt.'

'But they were both still alive? Did you get their names?'

'Yes, they were alive when I left. They were going to force the man to say his name, but he could barely speak. I never heard them say who the woman was. I managed to escape when the girls, those awful girls, lit cigarettes and—'

'I know what they like doing. I've heard about those two girls. We all have. They're Carisi's daughters, aren't they?'

'Yes, their father is the Major. They say he is very important.'

'Huh, he thinks he is, so do all his cronies. They think they are so important, they call themselves The Four Saints. Thugs, the lot of them. They'll get what's coming to them eventually.' Stefanina was frowning, then said, 'Were they guarded? And was the door locked?'

'It was bolted, not locked. And the only other person there was the cook. He's quite old.'

'Right, then listen to me. I have to get this information passed on immediately. You must carry on without me. Go to Borgo San Jacopo as before, collect the newspapers and deliver to addresses they'll give you.'

'But what if I'm stopped? What should I say?'

Stefanina was already running up the street, but turned and shouted, 'You won't have to say anything! Just let down your hair and flirt!'

FIFTY-FOUR

FLORENCE

15 April 1944

'If you are stopped and questioned, say you are trying to find soap,' the middle-aged woman in Borgo San Jacopo said after handing her the newspapers. 'And I'm sorry I have to give you this to hide them.' She passed Gabriella a stinking pair of filthy trousers to fold on top. 'They won't want to rummage through those. Too afraid of catching typhus, they are.'

Gabriella hoped she wouldn't catch any germs or lice either. 'And where am I supposed to take them now?'

'Here's the list, but if you're stopped don't let them see it. Push it under the trousers. Post the papers through the wine windows at these addresses. The last one will take the dirty laundry off you and with luck might have something for your trouble too.' The woman gave her a rare smile before closing the little door to her window.

Gabriella set off to locate the delivery points and, as she began to find them and complete her round, she started to rid herself of the horrors of her encounter with the evil sisters. She began to enjoy riding the bike in the fresh air, despite the feeling of deprivation everywhere in the city.

But at the last address, she was in luck. 'Well done, my dear,' the old woman said. 'Now pass over that nasty dirty washing and I'll deal with it. Whatever would we do without brave girls like you?'

'I'm very happy to help, but Stefanina is much braver than me.'

'Aah, that saucy miss. She's a bold one! Been a little rascal ever since she was a child. She loves to take risks, that one! Her poor dear departed mother would turn in her grave, knowing what she's up to now.' The woman turned away from the wine window into the darkened room and Gabriella thought she must be about to close the little door, but she turned back and handed over a basket of red onions and a damp bundle of muslin. 'Get straight home if you can and keep that cool. That's mozzarella, that is, fresh from the farm last night. Now be off with you. And you and that minx Stefanina take care,' she called out as she shooed her away and shut the little arched window.

Mama will be pleased, Gabriella thought. They hadn't had mozzarella for quite some time. She cycled quickly, feeling pleased that her mission had been accomplished without incident, and, as she approached the Ponte Sante Trinita, she realised she might pass the soldiers who had stopped her the day before. She could see them on the far side of the bridge, but she wasn't concerned; she had delivered all the papers and if they stopped her now, she had nothing to hide.

This time she decided to cycle past them, rather than walk. As she neared them, she pulled the band from her plait, so her hair spilled across her shoulders and rippled in the breeze in waves of gold and red. She gave them her most brilliant smile and had almost passed them when she heard a shout: 'Hör jetzt auf oder ich schiesse!' She didn't know what it meant, but the tone was harsh and as she looked back over her shoulder, she could see a gun pointing her way.

She skidded to a halt and wheeled her bike back towards the guard with his raised gun. His companion, the kind solider who had been nice the day before, beckoned. 'I'm sorry,' she said. 'I didn't realise I had to stop every time. I thought you might remember me from yesterday.'

'Oh, we do, but our orders are to check everyone crossing the bridge. Are you carrying more stinking fish today?'

'No, but I have stinking onions.' She didn't want to mention the cheese. It was far too precious.

'Let me see.' He poked among the onions, squeezed the muslin bundle and recoiled as some milky moisture oozed out. He shook his fingers in the sun to dry them. 'You may go now. Perhaps we shall see you again tomorrow.' He smiled, his blue eyes crinkling beneath blond eyebrows so fair they were barely noticeable. 'Good day to you.' He turned to his companion and Gabriella wheeled the bike away.

She hoped he hadn't seen what she had just noticed at the bottom of her basket as he rummaged in the onions. There was one newspaper left, one clandestine publication, banned by the fascists and obviously still viewed with suspicion. What would she have said if he'd pointed it out? It's just there to line the basket, it's going to light the fire when I get back? It could have meant answering more of their questions, it could have got her arrested. Once she was over the bridge, she cycled home quickly. It seemed even the simplest mission was fraught with danger.

When her mother and Hanna returned from their morning's work at the convent, they were both thrilled to see Gabriella's finds. 'We'll eat well tonight,' Mama said, already making plans for dinner. But when she saw the paper at the bottom of the basket, she was alarmed: 'I hope you weren't being asked to deliver this subversive publication?'

'No, it was just there to line the basket.'

'I'm throwing it in the stove right now. We don't want to be caught with this in the house, it's far too dangerous.' She snatched it and was about to shove it in the range, glowing with hot embers, when Gabriella grabbed it.

'No, let me look at it first, then I'll let you get rid of it. I won't keep it.'

'Alright, but promise me it will be burnt by the time we have dinner.'

Gabriella assured her and took the dusty paper, damp and stained with whey from the cheese, to her room. It was mostly full of articles she couldn't really understand, but one part really spoke to her. It was an open letter to all Italian women, saying:

And to succeed in this battle, we will fight alongside men, never conceding anything, never yielding, so that our children can live in a time in which men can truly be men.

I wonder if Stefanina has read this, she thought. She'd never concede or yield. *But can I subscribe to this too? Am I brave enough? I feel I must try, otherwise I will never make amends for endangering my family.* She felt the pain of her guilt heavy on her shoulders. She knew it would never completely leave her, but she might be able to lighten the burden by serving her friends and fellow compatriots.

Gabriella tore the page with the letter from the newspaper and tucked it under her mattress. She would keep her promise to Mama to burn the rest of the paper, but that didn't mean she couldn't keep these inspiring words.

FIFTY-FIVE

FLORENCE

6 June 1944

Some days that summer, within the walls of the palazzo garden, it was almost possible at times to forget the war and the city's hunger. The lawns had largely been given over to the growing of vegetables, thanks to Hanna and Bela, who had dug away the scrawny turf and turned the soil. They had already harvested early potatoes, peas and spinach and many more crops were steadily growing under their watchful eyes.

And around the city where roses were scenting the air, Gabriella sometimes found breathing the perfume and admiring the lush plants momentarily banished thoughts of hardship. Spare time was rare, but now and then she could cycle freely around the streets, especially to various public gardens, which, despite the growing of vegetables in the public *orti di guerra*, were still abundant in flowering trees and shrubs. In the terraced Bardini Gardens near the river, she loved to walk through the wisteria tunnel, where handfuls of dangling lilac flowers hung like bunches of grapes from the entwined branches.

And now, since the middle of May, the roses were in bloom everywhere, even on the few bushes that had been permitted to stay at the palazzo. 'Take Riccardo out with you,' Mama said. 'He spends far too much time in the studio. Since the work for the Scoppio del Carro finished, he has hardly left home. He needs fresh air.'

So Gabriella persuaded him to go with her to the Rose Garden off Piazzale Michelangelo. 'Bring your sketchbook with you. As well as plants, the garden has a wonderful view of the city. We'll take my bike and I'll let you have a go.' He'd never asked her why she'd suddenly acquired a bike, he was so immersed in his own projects and dark thoughts, but he agreed to go with her.

'Now we've finished restoring the Brindellone, I've nothing to look forward to,' he said, his hands in his pockets, as they wheeled the bike along the northern riverbank.

'But you still have your drawings and paintings. Are you running out of ideas?'

'No, but I keep wondering what's the point. Who's ever going to see them?' His worn boots scuffed the paving as they walked.

'Don't worry about that. Keep practising. You are going to be a great artist one day, I'm sure of it.'

She let him ride the bike between the bridges while she walked quickly to catch up with him. They had to cross the river at some point and she wondered whether to use the Ponte Sante Trinita, but she didn't want to keep seeing the same guards every day. They might become too familiar. So she told Riccardo they should go as far as the imposing Biblioteca Nazionale, then cross the Arno via the Ponte alle Grazie. When they reached it, that too was manned by a pair of guards, but they took little notice of a teenage girl and a young boy strolling over the bridge. With her startling hair well wrapped up in a tight scarf, she did not attract their attention that day.

As they climbed the winding paths up from the Arno, the sweet scent of the roses enveloped them. Even though the Giardino delle Rose was no longer at its peak, they were still surrounded by full-blown roses in every shade of pink, yellow and white, from magenta to blush, from primrose to coppery gold.

Gabriella kept stopping to smell the different flowers, trying to decide exactly what perfumes the silky petals were creating: 'This one has a hint of lemon, I think, and that one is more like peaches on a warm day.'

But Riccardo didn't bury his nose in the petals; he was transfixed by the panorama of the city from this high viewpoint, gazing at the jigsaw of tiled roofs, the bell towers, the domes and spires of Florence, with a backdrop of blue hills. 'Our city is so beautiful,' he murmured. 'That pattern against the sky, the colours... ochre, terracotta, creamy white and rust. I must remember all of it.' And he squatted on the grass with his pad, sketching and noting the various tones and the overlapping shapes.

Gabriella was so pleased to see him wholly absorbed by the scene. He seemed peaceful, less anxious, so she wandered about the rose beds, enjoying the colours and the scents. Like the rest of the city, the rose garden was neglected. There was greenfly on stems and yellow leaves with black spots littered the ground, but in spite of this the roses, like the people of Firenze, bravely fought to flourish. Many of the shrubs still bore labels, so she could learn their names, and she began to feel the bushes were individual personalities, not just plants, and that they were fast becoming her friends.

Perhaps when the war was over, when there were no longer food shortages and life was more settled, the vegetable beds in the palazzo garden could be replanted with roses. Gabriella lingered over her favourite, Rosa Mundi, tracing her fingers over the cerise flower, streaked with white, that looked as if Riccardo had splattered his paintbrush across the petals. And she scooped up handfuls of spent fallen blooms to fill the basket of the bike, so she could dry them and remember the colour and scent of the garden through the winter.

As the sun reached its peak, she felt thirsty and thought she and Riccardo should leave this peaceful garden. They walked down the hill and back towards the river, keeping to the shadier parts of the streets. Both felt carefree, Riccardo because he had new material for his paintings after his morning's work, Gabriella because she hadn't thought about the dangers of the city once while exploring the garden of scent and colour. Even within the city streets she carried a sense of hope as she caught the strong perfume of jasmine trailing over a wall.

But as they approached Piazza de Rossi they noticed a commotion ahead of them. They could see people being helped onto a truck by German and fascist guards, and a watching crowd was angrily rumbling. Riccardo wanted to get closer to find out what was happening, but Gabriella held him back: 'Wait, we don't want to get caught up in it.'

'No, I want to see. It doesn't look like the last time in Piazza Tasso when they arrested all those partisans. You can see these people are all very old.' He crept along the path towards the gathered crowd, sticking close to the wall, and Gabriella followed very slowly with her ticking bike.

When they reached the outer edges of the gathering, people muttering in low tones to each other, a man yelled out, 'You German bastards, can't you leave them alone to live out their days in peace?' His answer was rough hands dragging him away and the sound of agonised cries as he was beaten senseless out of sight.

'Who are they putting on the truck?' Gabriella asked a pinch-faced woman standing nearby, a baby on her hip, pressing its face to her breast.

'They've raided the old people's home. They're all very old. Look, that poor man can barely walk.'

Gabriella saw a bent elderly man shuffling with two walking sticks, followed by a shrunken old lady wrapped in shawls, despite the warmth of the day, hunched in her wheelchair. 'Are they taking everyone away from the home?'

'No, not all of them. Only the Jewish inmates. The Germans are saying Mussolini failed to do the job properly for them.'

Gabriella looked again, trying to understand. As the elderly residents were loaded onto the truck, she noticed one or two were tearful, but most simply looked dazed and bewildered. What was the point of it? What use were these old citizens to the Germans? They couldn't be made to work for them, could they? 'But why are they doing this?'

'Cleaning up, they call it. The Germans are doing it everywhere. Rumour is they're killing them all off. They hate the Jews. They emptied them out of Rome last year. Two thousand in one day. There won't be any left in Italy at all if they carry on like this. I don't see why they have to take them. They've never done us any harm, have they?'

Gabriella remembered the ghetto in Rome, where ancient ruins towered between tenements of yellow and ochre and the streets were paved with stone setts worn smooth by centuries of passing feet. She had walked there with Papa and he had explained that the Jewish community had been there for hundreds of years.

'And it's not just the Germans doing this filthy work either,' the frowning woman said, holding her child close. 'Look, there's that Major Carisi. Him and his thugs love causing trouble. They're the ones who've been searching out the Jews and the partisans and handing them over to the Germans. Some say they get paid for doing their dirty work. Judas money, I call it.'

Gabriella peered between the shoulders of the angry crowd and saw the Major there. His broad, well-fed chest strained the buttons on his uniform, his dark hair was slicked beneath his cap and his tight lips half-smiled with smug satisfaction. She tightened the scarf around her head, tucking stray wisps of telltale hair beneath the cloth. She didn't want Tina and Franca's father to see her.

She pulled Riccardo close to her to whisper in his ear, 'We should get away before they notice us.' He looked anxious, but turned with her to walk back the way they had come. As they left the scene, they heard a guard shout, 'That's the last of the Jewish pigs. We've got the lot of them.'

. . .

Gabriella spread her rose petals out on a tray near the warm range to dry, then went to find Riccardo. He had gone straight to the studio as soon as they returned from their outing. She found him sketching again, but not the happy scenes he had been drawing while they were in the rose garden. The page was filled with tearful faces seen through the spokes of a wheelchair.

'I counted them, Gaby,' he murmured as she crouched down to see what he was doing.

'What did you count?'

'The old people they were taking away. There were sixteen of them altogether. It must be an unlucky number. This and the trains that go from Platform Sixteen.'

She laid her arm round his shoulders. Should she tell him none of this was his fault? That she was the guilty one, not him? Or that she was trying to make amends by working secretly with the partisans? No, she couldn't tell him anything at all. The less he knew the better. His injured ear was close to her cheek, healed but still maimed. It would never be whole again. She kissed his poor ear and he looked at her.

'What's that for?'

'For being so sensitive and clever,' she said. 'Now I'm going to see what's left in the larder for lunch.'

She went through to the kitchen. Her rose petals no longer appealed to her. Their colours were fading as they dried, the scent had all but disappeared and they seemed to her now to be withered fragments of death.

FIFTY-SIX

FLORENCE

November 2019

Sofia and Isobel were stunned by the latest instalment of Gabriella's story. Finally, Isobel managed to speak: 'Old people, who should have been left in peace. Horrific.'

'Did you realise at the time what was happening?' Sofia was trying to put herself into the minds of her young father and his sister. 'Did you all know what the Germans were intent on doing?'

'I don't think any of us really knew until afterwards, did we?' Gabriella sipped her wine. 'Neither us nor the world, until it was over.'

'I suppose that's true,' Sofia reflected. 'Who could ever have imagined such terrible acts of cruelty.'

Gabriella sighed and continued, 'Although I was growing up fast then and Riccardo, despite his age, was confronted with horrific events, neither of us fully understood. I doubt that the adults did either. There were rumours of course, but who could believe that a civilised nation would want to eliminate such an ancient, cultured race?'

'And to take the elderly...' Isobel's voice was faint, near to tears.

'I can picture it from what you have told me. My grandmother was in a home when I was young. It was kind and gentle, totally respectful. That's how the old should be appreciated for all they have given during their long lives.'

'It's so awful,' Sofia said. 'It makes me think the Germans were going around Europe mopping up every pocket of Jewish life, however big or small. Yet they were in the middle of a war! How could they consider the removal of a small number of elderly Jews to be so important? I can't get my mind around it.' She shook her head in despair and gulped the last of her wine.

'And Riccardo, he was little more than a boy, and he saw all this?' Isobel dabbed at her eyes with a tissue.

'We both did. And of course this incident at the old people's home was also reflected in his paintings. Everything he saw in those terrible days was branded onto his memory. None of us could ever forget what we saw and heard, but for Riccardo it had to be incorporated into his work. How else was he to cope with the horror he had seen?'

'So this particular occasion is echoed in some of the images in his paintings?' Sofia was reflective, running her thoughts through his many works. 'There are iron bedsteads in one or two...'

'And a wheelchair in Number Eighteen too, I think,' Isobel said, also trying to think of the many significant symbols in his long lifetime of work.

'When I look at his paintings I see his interpretation of those times, again and again,' Gabriella said. 'I can see how it coloured every subject he painted, even right until the very end with his final piece of work.' She leant back in her chair; she was tiring.

'It's getting late,' Sofia said. 'You must be tired of us asking so many questions.'

'No, not at all. I'm glad we have been able to have these conversations. Your father was a very talented man and if this is helping you appreciate how wonderful he truly was, that makes me very happy.'

'It just makes me sad,' Isobel said, sniffing to stifle a sob. 'So sad that there was so much I didn't know.'

'But why do you think that was?' Sofia frowned. 'Why did he keep all of this hidden? It would have added so much to the interest in his paintings. I can't see why he wanted to be so secretive. I mean, Picasso was open about the inspiration for *Guernica*, so why couldn't my father have spoken out?'

'Hmm, because he always was bloody difficult,' Isobel snapped. 'He was never going to hand it all to us on a plate, was he? Look at how manipulative he's been with this trip. He could have spelt this visit out in the itinerary. He didn't have to employ subterfuge with the delivery of his letter to the hotel, did he? But oh no, always one for the dramatic gesture, he was!'

'Mum, please.' Sofia rubbed her mother's hand. 'It's more likely that he thought the more you knew about this arrangement, the more you'd think you had time to refuse and duck out of it.'

'I can't answer for my brother's motives,' Gabriella said. 'All I can think is that he tried to bury the guilt and the pain. Had he been open, then he would have had to face the guilt he carried, although it was never his fault. Remember, he always thought that his notebook had caused his family to be endangered. And maybe he feared that acknowledging the pain would break him, so he developed this carapace of creativity, to protect his heart.'

'I find it all so terribly sad,' Sofia said. 'I suppose these days we'd have labelled him as having post-traumatic stress disorder. And to think, he bore it alone for over seventy years. I wish he'd shared his thoughts with us. All those times when he'd be lost in a trance in the studio or on the cliffs in Cornwall... it makes me wonder what horrors he was seeing. I'd always thought he was concentrating on whatever he was working on at the time, but now I can't help thinking he was reliving the nightmares.'

'We all saw things no one should ever see in those days,' Gabriella said. 'They were dangerous, unsettled times. Even those who kept to themselves could find they were suddenly caught in the crossfire. And for those who were prepared to take risks, the odds were not at all in their favour. Have you seen the plaque in Via dei Pandolfini honouring Alessandro Sinigaglia? No? He was a black Jewish communist partisan.' With a wry smile, she added, 'So he scored badly on all counts with the fascists.'

'Go on,' Sofia said, engrossed by everything she was saying.

'He was shot five times in the back by fascist blackshirts under the command of Major Carisi. They didn't even arrest him, they just shot him in the street, then gouged out his gold teeth. Brutal thugs, they were. Anyone could have witnessed that execution, but they didn't care who saw them. They thought they had complete autonomy.'

'That's who's in Number Twenty-Nine, isn't it?' Isobel turned to her daughter, transfixed. 'There's a black man with two gold teeth in his hand.'

'Yes.' Gabriella laughed. 'Riccardo gave him back his gold teeth. He didn't see that incident for himself, but it was talked about throughout the city. The callousness, the sheer arrogance of those blackshirts, thinking they could conduct themselves like that. There was no limit to what they were prepared to do, they had ultimate power over us. The four main culprits in Carisi's gang were known as The Four Saints and they were ruthless.'

Sofia gasped. 'Saints? That explains something else. The haloed figures in some of his paintings. I could never understand why they were robed and looked like disciples or the Three Kings, but were holding bloody knives and scissors, not gifts of gold, frankincense and myrrh.'

'They were the saints of torture and assassination, not iconic religious figures.' Gabriella seemed finally drained. She slumped, a reduced figure in her armed chair.

'Such terrible times,' Sofia said with a sad shake of her head. 'We're grateful to you for talking about them so frankly. But now I think we must thank you and leave you. I'm sure this has been quite exhausting for you.' She stood and reached for her jacket on the back of the chair. 'May I still return tomorrow to take pictures of the frescoes?'

'Of course. Come as early as you like. If there is time we can talk again.'

'Surely there isn't more to tell, is there?'

'Oh, there's much more.'

'Then I must come too,' Isobel said.

MESSAGE SEVEN

Niatnuom eht ni pu em yrub

FIFTY-SEVEN

FLORENCE

17 July 1944

Every brick and tile of the city was baked in summer heat, even the shadows wilted, and no one ventured out into the red-hot streets in the middle of the day, preferring to conduct their business in the cooler hours of early morning and evening.

Stefanina had left a message, saying, 'Meet you in Piazza Tasso at 7 p.m.' She didn't say why, but lately there had been a lot of messages to deliver to various parts of the city and the last time they had met in person, she had said, 'The radio's playing up. It's hard to keep everyone in the know.'

Gabriella had not been back to that particular piazza since the time she and Riccardo had seen the mass arrests, but as she cycled there she thought it must be safe to return. So many had been taken back in March, it would surely be quiet there now. But when she arrived, the square hummed with life after the heat of the day. Children were running and playing, dogs were chasing each other, parents and grandparents were sitting on the benches or had brought chairs outside their homes to breathe the cooler air of evening. It felt as if the war had departed for a while and normal life was returning, where neighbours gossiped and parents scolded after the labours of the day.

She wheeled her bike around the square until she found Stefanina sitting at a table under a lime tree, her hair tied back with a fresh scarlet ribbon, drinking red wine with two young men and another girl about her age. They were softly singing 'Bella Ciao', the favourite song of the partisans.

'Here she is.' Stefanina jumped up and introduced her to her friends. 'Our newest recruit on wheels. She has been a great help to us.'

Hands were grasped and shaken and then Gabriella was invited to sit with them. 'Do you need me to help you with something this evening?'

'No, no, I just wanted you to meet some of our comrades. And I thought they would like to meet our beautiful red-haired staffetta.'

'I'm Alessandro,' one of the young men said. 'I can see why Stefanina has given you the job of distracting the guards, with your lovely hair.'

'Yes, Stefanina knows she's not going to turn any heads with her dark peasant colouring,' said the other girl, laughing, her deep grey-blue eyes sparkling.

'Careful, Norice,' the second man said. 'You know what a quick temper she's got.'

But Stefanina only laughed at her friend's gentle jibe and Gabriella could see that the banter was just that, the teasing of good friends, united by their cause, briefly relaxing in the balm of the piazza after a day of scorching July heat. She felt welcomed by these companions, accepted as an equal, although she was sure she was much younger than them. And for the first time since she had fallen prey to Bruno's charm, she began to feel that she might make real friends in the city.

Then Alessandro said, 'It's a shame we've only just met. Marcello and I are heading for the mountains tomorrow night. We figure if the Allies break through soon the Germans will retreat north and that's where we'll hole up and pick them off.'

Gabriella felt sorry that the new friendship was going to disband so soon, but she didn't show her disappointment, just said, 'I think my father and uncle may be there too somewhere. They've been gone a long time.'

'They'll be fine. There are plenty of sympathisers up there and many places to hide. The farmers are all on our side. Hey, Marcello, we'll be fed well up there, won't we?' His friend held up his glass and they all pronounced a toast to the intrepid partisans amid much laughter.

But after a while, in the midst of the joking around the table and while families were still allowing children to play one last game before bedtime, a truck roared into the square and men leapt out with guns. Mothers immediately grabbed the hands of little ones and ran to their homes, others stumbled as they raced to safety and Stefanina jumped to her feet, saying, 'Quick, inside.' She darted into a doorway that led to a courtyard, grabbed Gabriella's hand and pulled her up some steps inside the building, while the others followed.

They had only gone a short way out of sight when shots began to crack in the cool of the evening. Screams echoed and Stefanina ran to a window overlooking the square. 'Italian militia and Germans,' she spat, watching the chaos.

Gabriella felt sick as the firing continued and blue-grey smoke, the colour of Norice's eyes, drifted across the piazza. When the shots ceased, two of the men strolled towards the crumpled bodies lying where they'd fallen as they'd run to safety. One was a small child, a boy of maybe five years, not a threat, not a fighter, just an innocent child.

It felt as if the whole world was silent after the ruthless barrage of shots, then Stefanina spun round. 'Where's Alessandro?'

'I thought he was right behind us,' Marcello said. 'I'm going back out.'

'No, don't. They might start shooting again.' Stefanina turned back to the window. 'They got him,' she said, her voice wavering. She took a deep breath, almost choking on her grief.

Gabriella glanced down into the square. Alessandro was lying there. One of the guards gave his body a careless kick, then walked away. Her new friend, so recently met, so recently gone.

'We must go,' Stefanina said. 'We mustn't be found. They may start searching the houses.'

'What about the bike? I left it leaning against the wall outside,' Gabriella said.

'Don't worry. It doesn't matter, we'll come back for it. We must get away from here now. There is a way out above us. We'll use a section of the new Vasari. Come.' Stefanina sniffed, wiped her eyes on the hem of her skirt and walked back to the staircase. She began climbing up and up, till she came to a small door. 'Through here, but be careful. Some of the floorboards might be rotten.'

They all crouched and followed her into the dark, dusty attic. The stifling oven temperature made it hard to breathe and Gabriella felt cobwebs clinging to her hair as they crept through the narrow space till they came to another door and another baking attic. Ribbons of light filtered through chinks in broken tiles and dust danced in the rays as they crept through these secret roof spaces. A panicked fluttering as one of the doors creaked open revealed a mess of startled pigeons and other lofts held scuttling creatures she couldn't see but thought she could feel, crawling over her skin.

She wished she could cover her nose to avoid the musty smells of decaying things, but she had to use her hands to grasp roof joists as they scrambled through the filthy, hot voids over splintering boards. She realised that Mama had been right to guess that the new Vasari Corridor was comprised of linked roofs and attics. Eventually they came out through a final door onto a flat section of roof open to the cooler air of dusk. They leant on the tiled slopes, panting for breath after escaping the assassins like rats scuttling through the sewers.

The sky was tinged with gold and pink and Gabriella could see the sun would soon be setting. The dark shapes of swallows, *rondini*, whirled high above and darted into crevices in nearby buildings with their piercing cries. She began to think that her mother would worry if she wasn't home before dark, but she didn't want to concern her companions, given all that had just befallen them. However, Stefanina seemed to read her mind, because she said, 'You might not be able to get home tonight. After that raid, they're going to be picking on anyone out on the street this evening. We're not far from the bridge now, but you'd still have to cross the river and there will be guards posted everywhere. I don't think that you should attempt to get back after dark on your own.'

'What do you think we should do then?' Gabriella had never stayed out after curfew and she knew the penalties for those who risked being on the streets at night. The sounds of shouting and gunfire were as common at night-time as squalling cats and screeching owls.

Stefanina shrugged. 'If it seems there are going to be more raids, we'll have to stay up here. We have friends below, so I'll run down and check what's going on. I'll come back with water and maybe some food. We'll be safe here till morning.' She smiled, but it was a weak smile, marred by the tear tracks that scored her dusty cheeks and the cobwebs that veiled her black curls.

FIFTY-EIGHT

FLORENCE

18 July 1944

'My dear girl, I have been quite frantic with worry.' Mama rushed to hug her daughter, then held her at arm's length, checking she was unharmed. 'Knowing you were going to Piazza Tasso and hearing the news on the streets today, I have been beside myself.'

'So you heard what happened?' Gabriella sank onto a chair in the kitchen, near the open back door, where scents of rosemary and lavender baked by the heat drifted towards her. She was hot and thirsty after walking all the way back from the Oltrarno district and now it was mid-morning, the sun would soon send a searing blast of heat into every corner of the city. Stefanina had managed to find water, but there had been no food since late last night.

'It is all everyone can talk about. Five shot for no reason. Four men and one of them a child too. Where is the sense?'

Gabriella noticed Riccardo slip into the room and stand next to his mother. Had he heard the news too? Was this going to feature in another of his pictures? 'One of those killed was our comrade,' she said. 'A young man, Alessandro. One minute we'd all been sitting together around a table in the square and the next a truck roared in and they began shooting.' Her head sank into her hands.

'It was so sudden and so terrible. We watched from an upper window and then crawled through one attic after another to get away.'

'My poor girl,' Mama said. 'Here, drink this.' She gave her a cup of cool hibiscus tea. 'Why did they have to shoot them?'

'No reason. Tension is rising, Stefanina says. It was a random act of aggression and they knew that Piazza Tasso was a place where partisans often gathered. But apart from Alessandro, I doubt any of the dead was a threat to them. Certainly not the child.' Tears slowly trickled down her grimy cheeks and she brushed them away with the back of her hand.

'Five dead, you said?' Riccardo stared at her. 'How old was the child?'

'He couldn't have been much more than five, I guess. He just didn't run home fast enough.'

'Five and five,' Riccardo murmured, turning away and leaving the room. 'I must remember.'

Mama shook her head in despair. 'Is his art helping him? I just don't know. He is obsessed with recording every incident.'

'It's his way of trying to make sense of it all. Let him do it. At least it means he stays here almost all the time and is safe, unlike the little boy last night.'

'That's right, he should be safe here. But what about you? It's no longer safe for you out there. Please don't undertake any more errands. Stay here.'

Gabriella drained the cup of tea and looked directly at her mother. 'If I'm asked, I will have to go. How can I not, when so many are putting their lives at risk? But right now, I don't have the bike and I'm in need of a wash and a rest. A bare rooftop doesn't make for a very comfortable bed.'

'Of course, my dear. You must eat first, then sleep. I can make zucchini fritters quickly for you.' She began grating the courgettes, then beat an egg to combine the pale green and white young vegetables. 'Thanks goodness we have a productive garden and the extra supplies from the convent. Hanna is there again today with her children and has promised us something substantial for tonight. I've no idea what she will manage to produce, but she is so resourceful.'

The smell of cooking and her mother's chatter was comforting after her experiences over the last few hours. She felt drowsy and her mind roamed over the events of the night. They had all eventually managed to doze on the flat roof, but it was like sleeping on top of a cooling oven, as every surface had absorbed the full force of the sun's heat at its height and was still warm.

In the middle of the night, she had woken suddenly from a dream in which she thought she'd heard more shots. Jolting awake, she'd opened her eyes to see Stefanina and Marcello entwined in a groaning embrace with gasps and moans of pleasure, their bodies lit by the moon. Who could blame them for snatching a moment of joy in the midst of this unsettled time? With Alessandro gone in a second and Marcello due to leave for the mountains, they might never see each other again. She kept quiet, closed her eyes and managed to drift away once more.

In the morning, she felt stiff, aching from her night on the hard surface of the roof and longing for her mattress and pillows in the palazzo. It must have been very early, just before sunrise, as the sky was pale and birds were twittering. The air felt fresh and cool and Stefanina was leaning over the parapet that edged the roof. She turned when she heard Gabriella yawn and said, 'Good sleep?'

'Terrible. I thought I heard more shots in the night.'

'There was the odd one in the distance. One of our snipers hopefully, picking off a damned German.' Stefanina bent down to pick up the water flask. 'Here, have a sip. That's all we've got left.'

Gabriella took a mouthful. It wasn't particularly cold but it was still refreshing. Then she realised they were alone on the roof. 'Where are the others?'

'Marcello had to get going. Norice is following him. She's decided not to stay, she thinks it's better to get out now.' Stefanina pulled a red ribbon through her hair and tied a bow to one side.

'Are you going as well? To the mountains?'

'What, miss all the fun? No, I'm staying put. I want to see how the Germans cope when the Allies push through. It won't be long now.' She stood confidently with her hands on her hips, scoffing at the suggestion she should run away from the enemy. 'I'm going to do whatever I can to make sure they don't ruin our beautiful city. After what they did last night, I'm going to face up to them.'

'But what do you think I should do? And should I go back to Piazza Tasso today to retrieve the bike? It's far too valuable to abandon it.'

'Don't worry about it. If we need you again, you'll hear from us. And if we think it would be useful, we'll get a bike to you. I expect that one is long gone now.' Stefanina picked up the water flask, shook it and poured a little on the skirt of her cotton dress, then wiped her face with the wet cloth. 'Here,' she said, 'make yourself respectable. You look like a dirty angel after crawling through all that filth.'

Gabriella followed suit, though she was more tempted to drink the water than wash with it, her throat was so dry. But she wiped her eyes and around her mouth and felt fresher, then combed her tangled hair with her fingers and tied it back again with her sash.

'That's better,' Stefanina said. 'I'm going now. You should wait an hour or so and then make your way home. It's better that we aren't seen together this morning, after the trouble last night.'

As she embraced her friend briefly, Gabriella caught a reminder of the rough meal they had shared last night, pasta with oil and garlic, overlaid with the scent of earthy perspiration from their frantic escape through the filthy attics. For a short while they had all been together, united by grief for Alessandro and the other four victims, bonded with shock and fury at the Germans and Italians who had staged the massacre, for that was what it was.

'We'll never forget the night of the Piazza Tasso massacre,' Stefanina said as she waved goodbye and ducked through the low door that led to the stairs. Gabriella had stayed for a while, gazing down on the street, seeing her friend's bright red dress darting away from the building, weaving in and out of the pedlars coming out to trade in the cool hours of morning.

And now Mama was shaking her shoulder, waking her from her rooftop dreams, saying, 'Eat first, then sleep.' Then she put a dish of crisp fritters into her lap.

FIFTY-NINE

FLORENCE

18 July 1944

The hum of a distant plane and the corresponding boom of large anti-aircraft guns was what first alerted them. When they went outside, white leaves were falling across the courtyard and garden, across the roofs of the city, as if autumn had come early. White leaflets printed with a message for the people of Florence were fluttering through the hot air:

> *The city's liberation is at hand. Citizens of Florence, you must unite to preserve your city and to defeat our common enemies... Prevent the enemy from detonating mines which they may have placed under bridges.*

'Everyone's talking about what to do when the Allies arrive,' Mama said.

'But we'll welcome them gladly, won't we?' Gabriella, fresh from her nap and her bath, didn't understand why her mother and Hanna were looking so worried.

'Of course we will, but it may not be that simple. There might not be a smooth transition. The Germans won't give up easily.'

'There could be bombing,' Hanna said. 'We should think about where we can all shelter if things get risky. What about your cellar?'

'That would be the easiest place for us,' Mama said. 'There's the remains of our wine stored down there and we've got some old wine flagons we can fill with water. They'll be very heavy but if there's extensive bombing we'll lose the water as well as electricity.'

'Bela can help. He is very strong.' Hanna patted her son on the back, while her two little girls just looked on, chewing their fingers.

'What about people who aren't lucky enough to have cellars? What will they do?' Riccardo had joined them, with a sketchbook under his arm as always.

Gabriella thought of the many residents of Florence who lived in tall tenements, in single rooms or flats. They would be extremely vulnerable to any airborne attacks on the city as the Allies tried to force the Germans into retreat. Marcello and Norice might be safe in the mountains, but where would Stefanina take shelter?

'Many people will have to stay in the churches and other large public buildings,' her mother said. 'They are sure to be safe there as the Allies will never knowingly destroy the architecture for which the city is famous. They have always promised not to damage our legacy here.'

It was strange to be discussing the liberation or fall of Florence just as they were about to have dinner that evening. Mama told Gabriella to use the best hand-painted plates. 'Let's enjoy them while we can,' she said. 'They're hardly ever used.'

Gabriella carried the plates outside and laid them out on the large wooden table in the courtyard. The walls and paving were still radiating heat but it was less oppressive than the kitchen filled with the steam and heat of cooking. She peered through the archway at the main garden; poles strung with beans, glossy purple aubergines and fat bulbous tomatoes filled the beds Hanna and Bela had created in the once-smooth expanse of green lawn. These would need water too, so she hoped that if they could not leave the cellar for some time, their vegetables wouldn't die of thirst.

'We have found a new way of eating courgettes,' Mama announced, approaching the table with a dish held aloft. 'They have been so prolific, but they can become a bit tedious, so we are going to have tiella rice tonight. It's a wonderful dish that makes a very little rice go a long way.'

Everyone gathered to sit down, scraping chairs on the paving stones, crushing the creeping thyme and marjoram growing in the cracks, so the air filled with the perfume of bruised herbs as well as the tempting aroma of the baked dish topped with cheese. 'What's in it, apart from courgettes?' Gabriella asked, leaning forward to inspect the new recipe.

'It can be made with mussels as well,' her mother said, spooning a juicy portion onto Hanna's plate, 'but they are a distant memory, as is any seafood these days.'

'But what's in *this* dish?' asked Riccardo, looking suspiciously at the oozing mix of golden rice topped with thin slices of zucchini.

Hanna laughed at his uncertain face, saying, 'Taste it and see. They are all ingredients you've eaten before and enjoyed.'

Gabriella took a forkful from her helping. She could taste onion, garlic and tomatoes and there were thick slices of potato at the bottom of the dish. The overlapping circles of courgette were golden brown with the Parmesan cheese scattered over the top. She could tell her mother had been sparing with the salty cheese, but then they were lucky in these hard times to have any at all.

'It should have more cheese really,' Mama was saying as she began eating her serving. 'Not just on the top, but mixed with the rice.' She sounded disappointed with her creation, so everyone told her they loved it.

'It's a really useful dish,' Hanna said, knowledgeably. 'You could make this with any vegetables in season. And such sparing use of rice too. We're all going to feel very full after this.'

'I'm glad you like it,' Mama said. 'And as there are so many courgettes ripening at present, we can spare some flowers, I'm sure. If anyone can lay their hands on a little cheese to make a stuffing, we will enjoy eating fried flowers one evening.'

The two little sisters looked very puzzled and Lili said, 'We're going to eat flowers?'

Their mother laughed and said, 'Lots of flowers are good to eat. Maybe another time I will put nasturtium petals in our salad.' She put a couple of leaves of lollo rosso on her daughters' plates, then passed the salad bowl to Riccardo, who also hadn't helped himself to green stuff.

As the two mothers discussed ways of stuffing the courgette flowers – 'Just breadcrumbs and lemon will do' – and – 'Maybe with a few pine nuts?' – Gabriella thought how nearly like normal life this civilised supper was. Had it been only yesterday that she had witnessed the shootings in Piazza Tasso? Only last night that she had slept on a roof above the street and woken to see lovers embracing?

The table spread with a white cloth, the plates with their hand-painted borders of bright blue and yellow, the bowls with their paintings of fat lemons, the watered wine in crystal glasses: it could have been a pre-war summer garden party. In this sheltered, balmy courtyard could they forget the threat beyond these walls, the imminent advance of other armies and the turbulence that would surely follow? For a moment or two it was possible, and when Mama placed a bowl of ripe peaches on the table, picked that day from the espaliered trees that spread their branches against the sunny walls of their own garden, Gabriella felt she could rest for a while and forget the horror of the previous evening. But when she glanced at Riccardo, his pinched face, his maimed ear and his determination to draw even as they sat together as one big family, she wondered if he could ever forget, even for a minute.

And as that moment passed, they heard distant shots. They faded quickly, but in that second, each and every one of them was wide-eyed; they stopped eating and sat with open mouths, their ripe half-eaten peaches held in trembling fingers, while sticky juice dripped onto the table.

SIXTY

FLORENCE

November 2019

Sofia returned to the palazzo early the next morning. She left the hotel before breakfast, telling her mother she would be back by lunchtime. Isobel said she would pack, check out and rest before their flight home. She seemed to have forgotten that she had said she wanted to accompany her daughter to see the remaining frescoes.

Carlo answered when she rang the doorbell. 'My grandmother told me to expect you. She is not an early riser these days. Would you like to take coffee and a little something to eat before you go to the chapel?'

Sofia was grateful for his thoughtfulness and followed him to the courtyard, where they had eaten so well the previous day. The morning was fresh and chilly, but it was clear that before long the sun would warm the old paving stones and walls where they had taken lunch.

'I will take Nonna a tray in a little while,' Carlo said, sipping his coffee. 'She is very tired today. I believe she talked for a long time last night.'

'She has an excellent memory. Her stories were fascinating, but very troubling. I'm sure it was hard for her to tell us as much as she did. She must be digging up some distressing memories.'

'She always tells me she does not want to forget anything. What is it that your Dickens wrote? It was the best of times...'

'...it was the worst of times,' Sofia concluded. 'She met your grandfather, but she also lost friends during those years of hardship. Last night she gave us a graphic account of a shooting when a new friend, Alessandro, I think she said, was killed along with other men and a child. It's hard to believe, now, that this lovely city was once in the midst of a violent war.'

She finished the almond pastry and coffee he'd served. 'But if you don't mind, I'd really like to get on and take photos of the frescos in the chapel. I had forgotten there was more than one, till your grandmother mentioned them again last night.'

'They are not obvious. I will show you before I leave for the university.' Carlo led the way through the cloisters again and pointed out six more paintings on the chapel walls in half-hidden shadowy nooks and alcoves. He lit a candle for the votary stand, then left her in the cool chapel scented with the musty smells of piety and prayer.

After he had gone, Sofia took several shots, struggling to get good images in the dim light. But although the photos were not perfect, each picture contained elements with which she was familiar, ones which she had come to know well in her father's later work. The pathetic lamb peered from behind a tree trunk or lay below a shrub, the boys with bleeding ears ran away and the white blossoms bloomed. It was so clear to her, and would be to any student of his work, that this was where his original ideas had been born as he attempted to make sense of the chaotic time in which he was living then.

It didn't take long at all and she had the whole morning to fill, so once she felt she had a full record of all the frescoes, she rang Phoebe. 'It's even better than I thought,' Sofia said. 'It turns out there wasn't just one wall painting in the chapel, there's seven altogether.'

'Amazing! And are you sure they can't be transported?'

'Absolutely not. They're painted directly onto the plaster.' Sofia stroked the lamb before her, painted in soft chalky paint on the chapel wall.

'Some Banksy murals have been lifted from walls. We should check it out.'

'You'll see when I send the photos I've just taken. They are incredible though. Definitely his and definitely an indication of how he was going to develop. It's a more literal, realistic style than he adopted later on, but you can certainly see elements of his mature work in these. Anyway, I think viewing them *in situ* would give authorities on his work more of a feel for the way he grew as an artist.'

'Do you think it would be worth me coming over some time?'

'Let's talk about it when I'm back. It would certainly be a good idea to get some good professional pictures taken. The light in the chapel is terrible and I've only got my phone camera, but I've done my best for now.'

'This is so exciting! I can see this becoming a big, big story. It will definitely make the market prick up its ears. I can just see it now.'

'I'm glad you're pleased. And I've also been learning a lot about my father's early years. It's going to give us a lot of material to play with.'

'Wonderful. Talk soon.'

As she finished the call, Sofia realised she was not alone. Isobel had slipped into the chapel. 'It sounds like you are planning to cash in on your father's early trauma and tragedy. Are you sure that is the right course of action?'

'It's all part of his legacy, Mum. This is an important find. Can't you see that?'

'I'm finding it all so very difficult. I'm not sure any of this has really helped me come to terms with the way he was. I need time so please don't rush into anything. That Phoebe woman can only think about how she's going to get her greedy hands on more fame and money. I'm more concerned about how all this leaves us feeling about your father.'

'I understand that, you know I do. But I have to make the most of this opportunity to record this material. I'd never forgive myself if the place burned down and I hadn't taken these photos. You can see that, can't you?'

'I suppose so. But you know none of this has really helped, has it? Do you think you've gained any insights into the meanings of his pictures? Really?'

'I'm beginning to understand them better, I think. But there's still one big question I have for Gabriella.'

'More questions? How much more is there to know? How much more can that poor woman tell us? She was exhausted by the time we left her last night.'

'I want to talk to her about the descriptions I had to write for the exhibition. I had to guess what he meant by those recurring symbols of his. I'd like to go over some examples and see what she thinks.'

'And is that all? Will we then be able to leave here?'

'No, there's one more thing: I want to ask her why he never titled his paintings, but only gave them numbers. And then I want to ask if she has any idea why there is no Number Sixteen.'

SIXTY-ONE

FLORENCE

20 July 1944

Gabriella checked outside the palazzo every day, hoping there would be a message waiting for her or that the bike had been returned. But perhaps Stefanina had changed her mind. Maybe she had decided to join Marcello and fight in the mountains, in honour of their dear friend Alessandro, and they were feasting on stewed rabbits and creamy sheep's cheese. And if she was still in the city, she hoped Stefanina was safe, that she was bewitching a German or fascist soldier and that her flirtatious ways would protect her from harm.

Riccardo was not good company for her. He was working obsessively and had turned to painting over old canvases as he was running out of new ones. 'I'll do more in the chapel next,' he said, 'but if we have to move out, I won't be able to take wall paintings with me, so I have to do as many as I can that can be transported.'

Gabriella couldn't see how he was ever going to be able to shift all the many works he had produced. If they had to evacuate, how could they carry all their possessions and food, let alone his artworks? He would be limited to his sketchbooks and little more.

She turned to helping her mother, Hanna and Bela prepare the cellar in case they needed to shelter down there. Spare blankets, cushions and flagons of water were all taken down the steps where the previous tenants' hard beds stood bare and waiting for occupants. Lili and Jazmin were told to play in a shady part of the garden, making mosaics out of stones, pebbles and broken shards of pottery to distract them from the anxious preparations. Gabriella joined them in the shade during the hottest part of the day and helped them make a watery pond with an island that they could pretend they would escape to. 'Like Capri,' she said, describing how she had once gone there with her parents, remembering the glittering turquoise sea and their boat trip to the Blue Grotto. 'The sun shines through an underwater cave and it shines like sapphires,' she said, shaping a leaf as a boat to sail on the miniature pond.

The following day, after a night of occasional distant gunfire, Mama said, 'We must stock up on supplies while we can. Who knows how hard it might be to find enough food before long?' They all agreed to go out early in different directions, before the day became unbearably hot, but the little girls were to stay at home with Riccardo.

Gabriella wished she had the advantage of her bike – she would have enjoyed cycling with the early morning breeze in her hair – but she set off on foot towards the market area, as there were always likely to be street traders nearby as well as the regular stallholders. Many other residents seemed to have the same idea and the streets were thronged with tired faces, empty baskets in their hands, searching for basic supplies, while some, more famished and shorter of funds, resorted to begging.

'Concentrate on the staples,' Mama said. 'We can keep harvesting our vegetables and fruit, but we will soon run out of flour, polenta and rice. But whatever you see, you should buy. Especially eggs.'

As she walked the streets, gradually warming as the sun crept over the city, Gabriella wondered if Stefanina loved Marcello. She hadn't noticed any particular affection between them as they had all laughed and drunk wine before the massacre, nor while they were creeping through the dirty, choking, vermin-filled attics. But if you made love with a man, you surely loved him, didn't you? Or had she really loved Alessandro and was being comforted by Marcello? In these strange times it was hard to know what was right and what the moral code for women was any more.

Lost in thought, she didn't notice the figure behind her, the figure who crept up and grasped her around the waist. 'Still lovely, Cinderella,' he breathed in her ear. 'In fact, even lovelier than before.'

She knew the voice and she knew the face. Almost five months had passed since she had distracted him and his fellow soldiers at the station so her father could escape. Bruno had a tight grip on her arm, escorting her along the street, making her walk faster than she wanted. 'You're hurting me,' she said. 'And I'm trying to do the shopping. Leave me alone.'

'Oh no, not this time you don't. Little minx. You caused us a lot of trouble that day at the station. Don't pretend you didn't know what you were doing. You're going to have to pay for that.'

His tone was hardening. She knew she would have to turn him round, use the skills she had practised with Stefanina. 'I thought you'd gone off to fight,' she said, smiling. 'Your cousins told me you'd left the city.'

'Well, now I'm back. I'm needed here. This is where all the action's going to be happening very shortly.'

'I'm glad to see you're back. I really missed you. I loved our walks in the evening after dinner.' She felt his grip relax a little bit.

'It was nice while it lasted, until I got what I needed.' He spun her round to face him and grasped her chin, tilting her face up towards his. 'But now I need something else. I've got a taste for women after my special duties recently.'

She couldn't answer back. She was beginning to suspect his motives. They had moved away from the busier area around the market and turned into a dingy side alley. Rubbish littered the gutters and there was a sour smell of rancid rottenness.

He gripped her more firmly again and pushed her into an open doorway, into a dark hallway at the bottom of a staircase, then forced her back against the wall. 'Teasing me with your hair and your smiles. You knew what you were doing so you can make up for it now.' He pulled at her skirt and her underthings, all the while holding her tightly round the neck. She tried to push him away, but he was so tall and so strong. She was beginning to think she might have to close her eyes and just hope it would all be over quickly when she felt him jolt and fall onto her shoulder, then he sagged at the knees and fell to the floor. Blood trickled from his temple and, as he slumped on the filthy tiles, she realised Bela was standing in the doorway, his slingshot dangling from his hand.

'Quickly,' he said, reaching out for her. 'He might not be dead, just stunned. Come with me.'

She straightened her clothes and stepped over Bruno's body, breathless with shock. 'Were you following me?'

'Not at first, but I saw him marching you away. I thought I should keep close by. Come on, we'll go straight to the convent.'

They walked swiftly; running might have aroused suspicion, but Bela was anxious to get her out of sight as soon as he could. 'He might have been with comrades. Maybe he noticed you and told them he was going after you. We can't risk you being seen.'

Few words were exchanged as they rushed through the streets. Gabriella tried to cover her hair with her scarf as they sped, and when they reached the convent Bela led her into a sheltered corner of the garden, where jasmine and honeysuckle crept over an arbour. 'Wait here, you'll be quite safe. I'm going to explain to Sister Maria what has happened and then fetch my mother.'

Gabriella leant back in the perfumed shade and closed her eyes. She could hear the buzzing of insects and the tolling of the convent bell, and drifted into the safety of dark sleep.

She was shaken awake. 'How long have I slept?' she asked in a drowsy voice, yawning and rubbing her eyes.

'Not long at all,' a soothing woman's voice answered. Gabriella opened her eyes properly and looked up. A tall dark figure stood before her, silhouetted against the brightness of the sunlit garden. 'I'm Sister Maria. Bela told me what happened. I let you rest for a short while, but I think you should come with me now.'

Gabriella stood up, but her head felt light and her legs trembled. 'You are still experiencing shock,' the nun said. 'But thank the Holy Mother, it wasn't anything worse. Thanks to Bela, you were saved. He has great courage.'

They began walking towards the cloisters on the other side of the garden, passing a trickling waterspout, in the shape of a conch shell held by a lead cherub. 'You have running water,' Gabriella marvelled, letting the tips of her fingers pass through the thread splattering into a lead trough.

'It's spring water,' the sister said. 'You can drink it. The water comes straight to us from the hills and is always pure. It has never run dry and helps us maintain this wonderfully productive garden.'

Gabriella realised her throat and mouth were parched and cupped her hands to gulp the sweet water. When she had drunk her fill, she said, 'Did Bela really tell you what he did? That the man might be dead?' She felt herself trembling again.

'He did, my dear. He saved your life as well as your honour. He regrets risking the loss of a life and will confess. But it was for the greater good. He knows that.'

Inside the convent, Sister Maria led her to a bare cell with a simple white bed, on which was laid a plain white gown. Gabriella looked at the crucifix hanging on the whitewashed wall above the bed and made the sign of the cross.

'Bela has taken a message to your mother and will return when he can. For now, we think it best you stay here and rest.' She showed Gabriella the pitcher and bowl where she could wash. 'When your assailant's absence is noticed, they will come looking for him. It is possible they will come here so you must appear to be one of us.'

At that point, Gabriella realised that the gown was a novitiate's habit and that she would be disguised as a sister from the convent.

'But I am afraid that your appearance is most distinctive and you will be hard to hide.' Sister Maria pulled a pair of scissors from within the folds of her habit. 'So I regret to say that we think you must lose your lovely hair.'

Gabriella stared at the sharp steel shears. She thought how she had been told to use her glinting red hair to distract the soldiers and then she laughed and kept laughing. 'Cut it all off. I don't care, take it all.' She turned her back to Sister Maria, removed her scarf and tossed her loose hair back over her shoulders. She felt the nun gather it up in thick strands and heard the sharp snip as the blades hacked each handful close to her scalp.

'In normal times we could sell your beautiful rich hair. The wigmakers have always prized the pure hair of novitiates. Such a shame not to see it put to good use. But in the circumstances we'll have to burn it right away. Such a pity.'

But Gabriella didn't feel sad. Her hair had helped and then hindered and now it was gone.

SIXTY-TWO

FLORENCE

21 July 1944

Gabriella was roused by a bell in the early morning, followed by the sound of chanting. The convent was waking. She rinsed her face and mouth with water from the jug in her cell and slipped into the cool white gown, scented with cleanliness and purity. Her head felt strangely light and she ran her fingers over her shorn pate, cut so close to her scalp it felt like the velvet of a rabbit's ear. Sister Maria had taken her own clothes and scarf away, but had left her a white skullcap to cover what little remained of her hair.

She left the cell and walked through the cloisters into the garden, more alive at this early hour than in the heat of the day, with birds flitting in the trees and flowering shrubs. A frog glistened in the channel beneath the overflowing water trough and a bird came down to drink, throwing back its head with each sip.

The hazy light filtering through the leaves of the trees held the promise of another scorching day and she wondered if she should leave the convent before the sun was higher. She felt she had failed her family, not being able to return laden with goods for their stores. Had her mother and Hanna been able to find enough supplies, if the city was soon to be under siege? And had Bela returned safely with a message, or had he been apprehended on the street? Then she began remembering the firm grip round her neck, the probing fingers tearing at her clothes. She shut her eyes, shuddering. Questions began to fill her mind, so she had to sit down in the scented arbour and think calmly.

It felt so safe here, this world of plainsong and prayer, surrounded by a lush, irrigated garden. Perhaps it would be better to stay here, she thought. Maybe a life of seclusion, rather than racing around on a bicycle, would suit her better. She closed her eyes again and thought about whether she could live the rest of her life in a white cell, in a white robe, in purity and peace.

After a few minutes, she heard the bell ringing again and Sister Maria came into the garden and saw her sitting there. 'Come and take breakfast with us,' she said, leading Gabriella into a hall, where the nuns took bread and water in silence, sitting at a long trestle table, bowing their heads to murmur a response to the Grace. Afterwards, the sister led her away to her office overlooking the garden and said, 'We've had confirmation that your assailant did not survive. Bela's shot was accurate and deadly.'

Gabriella did not feel surprise or shock. She had guessed as much. 'Will they come looking for him then?'

'I don't think they know how the young man died. But the Germans are not a forgiving race. There may be repercussions. In the past they have been known to execute ten men for every German assassinated and in some regions they have burned down whole villages in retaliation.'

'Do you think that could happen here?'

'Let us hope the Germans have more pressing matters on their mind than the death of one reckless soldier. Besides, he was not one of their own. If he had been German, you can be sure they would be scouring the streets. It's Carisi's cronies you have to worry about. The man was a nephew, I believe. You and Bela must be very careful.'

'I wonder how Bela is feeling now. He's only ever shot pigeons and rabbits before.'

'He would do well to keep his slingshot hidden for now. They may not know exactly how that man was killed, but they will pick on anyone they suspect.'

Gabriella wondered if her past connection with Bruno would be questioned by the Major or his daughters. What if he'd said he was going to find her again? Or would they come looking for her? She didn't want to see any of them and the thought of staying safely in the convent felt more and more appealing to her. Perhaps if she made herself useful, she could stay while she decided what kind of future she wanted. 'I must do something to help, to repay you for your kindness. I really appreciate being able to rest here a while.'

Sister Maria smiled in a very knowing way. 'You are welcome to stay as long as you like, but I suspect your mother will want to see you safely returned soon. She has been a great help to us with her friends. I expect they will be here again this morning to tend the garden. Why don't you water the beds until they come?'

Gabriella was glad to have a task to divert her. The gully from the water trough ran around and across the garden, with pools at intervals, so water was close to hand. Dipping a watering can into the nearest reservoir, she began by irrigating the beds with striped green courgettes and emerging yellow pumpkins, then moved on to the bulbous tomatoes, which would receive the full benefit of the sun as it came round. Twiggy frameworks supported vigorous bean plants, their tendrils clinging to the branches as they climbed, hung with the purple, green and yellow pods that would deliver cannellini, borlotti and fava beans to be dried for use during the winter months.

A lizard scuttled away from the sprayed water and sparrows flitted down to the damp earth to search for bugs. She was totally absorbed in her work when she heard Mama calling, 'Gabriella, I can't see you. Where are you?' She was hidden by the lush growths all around her and stood up so her mother could see her.

Mama rushed over to her, arms open wide. 'There you are, my

dear. Oh, I've been so worried, but here you are. Bela told us every-thing.' She shook her head. 'Poor boy, he's very upset.'

'Is he here?' Gabriella tried to look beyond her mother to see if he was emerging from the cloisters. She so wanted to thank him for his bravery.

'No, we thought it better if he stayed out of sight for a while. Hanna is sure he has often been seen around the city, potting pigeons. They might think it was him.'

'So Bruno is definitely dead?'

'It would appear so. That means Bela is very much at risk – if anyone realises the fatal blow was caused by a stone. But I doubt it would be possible to tell. He could have been hit by anything or he could just have fallen.' She came closer and took the watering can from Gabriella's hand. 'But tell me, were you touched? Did he harm you?'

'No, Bela acted just in time.' Gabriella hung her head, remem-bering the feel of his insistent fingers on her thighs and inside her knickers. 'He saved me,' she added in a whisper.

'Thank God. You were lucky. You could have been ravished or murdered. It is happening everywhere. Women can fight, but men have this one dreadful power over them. I'm so relieved to know you were spared.' She kissed her daughter and held her close. 'Now, I've brought fresh clothes. Sister Maria destroyed what you were wearing yesterday, just in case your dress was recognised.'

'She has been so kind. I've felt so safe here.'

'But you want to come back home, don't you? We all miss you very much.'

Gabriella thought for a moment. She was tempted to stay in this peaceful haven, where she wasn't reminded of her guilt by the daily sight of Riccardo's haunted eyes, but her family needed her. 'Of course. It's restful here, but I'll come back with you. I miss the children too and I want to thank Bela.'

They went to her cell so she could change into the clean clothes her mother had brought. And when she removed the white cap, Mama gave a gasp and covered her mouth with her hand. 'What have you done? Your beautiful hair, it's all gone.'

Gabriella rubbed her hand over her velvety scalp, soft as a pony's muzzle, and laughed. 'It was always such a nuisance, all that washing and brushing out the tangles. Now I'm free!'

'But it will grow again, slowly, won't it?' Mama appeared so crestfallen, staring at her once-radiant Titian daughter, looking like a homeless street urchin who'd been scalped to defeat lice and fleas.

'I expect so, but maybe I won't let it grow very long. Anyway, it wasn't me who cut it off. It was Sister Maria. She thought it was too distinctive and I'd be safer like this.'

'You're certainly not going to attract attention looking like that,' her mother said, managing a feeble laugh. 'Thank goodness for Sister Maria. She is so quick-thinking. Did you know that she saved the Giardino baby when the convent was raided? His mother ducked down and put her child on the floor and Sister Maria hid it under the skirts of her habit.' Mama sighed. 'Poor boy, who knows where his mother is now, but at least he's alive.'

Gabriella tied a black scarf over her naked head. 'I'm ready now. Let's go home and give them all the fright of their lives when they see how I look.'

SIXTY-THREE

FLORENCE

21 July 1944

Whipping the scarf from her head, Gabriella spun round in front of the little girls, saying, 'What do you think of my new hairstyle?' Their faces changed from smiles of greeting to tearful in a second.

'Why have you cut off all your lovely hair?' Jazmin reached out to stroke Gabriella's head.

'It got very dirty and tangled,' she replied. 'So it all had to come off.'

'You look like a boy,' Lili said, running her hand over the soft stubble.

'Good. Then I can run around like the boys do and go anywhere I like!'

'In our old home, Mama said our hair would all have to be cut off if we caught lice. But I don't ever want my hair to be as short as yours.' Lilli tucked her short brown hair behind her ears as she spoke, reassuring herself that she was not as deprived as Gabriella.

'Then if you brush and comb it well every day, you won't have to have it cut.'

Gabriella gave them both a reassuring hug and went to find Riccardo. He was hunched in the old chair in the studio, a sketchpad on his knees. He looked up from his drawing as she entered. 'It's not as bad as I'd imagined,' he said. 'I can see the shape of your skull and it makes your neck look longer. You must sit there and let me draw you.'

'Did Mama tell you my hair had been cut?' She sat down on a stool nearby.

'Yes and she told me why. She and Hanna told me everything, but not the little ones. They thought the girls would be too frightened if they heard the whole story.' He drew with swift strokes in charcoal, then told her to turn so he could draw her in profile.

'I have to see Bela too,' she said. 'You know he saved me?'

'I'm glad he did. You should go to him when I've finished. He doesn't want to talk about it any more.'

She was thoughtful. 'I suppose it's a horrible shock, to suddenly leap from shooting down birds to killing a real man.'

'Please talk to him. I want him to pose with his slingshot so I can work out how David looked, killing Goliath.'

She knew the story from the scriptures, of course. 'And is that going to be another painting?'

'Mama says I can only paint in the chapel if my pictures have a link to the Bible. I'm recording the events of our time, but if I can turn them into holy pictures, she won't object.'

'I can see why she thinks that. The chapel is consecrated, after all.'

'And as I've run out of canvases, the only way I can do more paintings is either to paint over work I'm not happy with or cover the walls of the chapel with frescoes.' He asked her to turn round again, so he could capture the back of her head, saying, 'The shadow of your hair points down the nape of your neck. It's a lovely shape.'

'So I suppose my shorn head will appear in something as well? Who will I be? A shaven criminal? A leper?'

'No, I don't think so,' he mumbled. Then he lifted his eyes, looked straight at her and said, 'Samson had his hair cut off by Delilah, didn't he?'

Gabriella shrieked with laughter. 'So I'm going to be a man?'

'Maybe. Though Samson would have been big and strong. But it helps me visualise the way he would have looked with less hair.'

When he had drawn her from every angle, Gabriella went to find Hanna in the kitchen and asked where her son might be. 'He's watering the garden,' she said. 'He's very quiet and withdrawn, but I think he'd like to see you.' She was halving small tomatoes and laying them cut side uppermost on a metal tray, then giving them a light sprinkle of salt. 'Here, take these with you on your way and put them out in the sun.'

Gabriella picked up one of the wide-brimmed straw hats kept by the open back door. Her bare head would need protection now it no longer had a thick cap of hair. She took the tray and placed it on the courtyard table in full sun. Come the winter, when tomatoes were no longer available, these dried fruit would be an important part of their diet, adding flavour and colour to stewed meats, soups and sauces. She thought how fortunate they all were to have a resourceful, skilled woman like Hanna, who was encouraging Mama to learn how to adapt, so they would hopefully not go hungry.

As she passed through the archway of the courtyard gate, she could see Bela. He was no longer watering, but sat slumped against one of the cypress tree trunks, his head on his bent knees, enveloped by his arms. She approached him and spoke in a soft voice: 'I'm not disturbing you, am I?'

His head jerked up and she saw his eyes were red and puffy. He didn't speak clearly, he just grunted, so she knelt beside him in the shade and removed her hat. She could tell from his look that he too was shocked at the sight of her shorn head. 'It's alright,' she said. 'My hair had to go. I really don't mind.'

'I do,' he said. 'It was so beautiful.'

'But this way, I can disappear more easily. We don't want anyone suspecting a boy with a slingshot and a girl with long red hair, do we?'

He shook his head. 'Mother wants me to stay in hiding here for a while. She's hoping no one will remember seeing me shooting pigeons. But I'm not scared. I'd do it again, if I had to.' He spoke with fierce determination, but she could see his eyes were brimming with tears.

'Thank you for what you did. You saved me. He might even have ended up killing me so thank you.' She grasped his hand and shook it.

He looked down at their clasped hands and began to cry. Not huge sobs, just trickling tears and trembling chin. 'I wasn't sure I could do it, but I knew I had to. He was so much bigger and stronger than me. It was the only way I could think of to help you.'

'I know. If you'd tried to pull him off me, he probably would have shot you. I'm glad you didn't risk your life.'

'I knew he had a gun. I could see his holster strap when he was marching you towards that alleyway. I thought if he attacked you, I wouldn't have a choice.'

'Bela, I know you had to make a difficult decision. I understand that it isn't easy to kill a human being, but you had to do it. So please, never feel guilty, never have any regrets. Just remember that you saved me and I will be eternally grateful.' She threw her arms round him and hugged him tight. She'd thought of him as a boy, barely older than Riccardo, but his actions had been those of a grown man.

At that point he finally smiled. 'And do you know, the funny thing is, when I finally got back here yesterday, the first thing my mother noticed was that I was empty-handed! She wanted to know why I was so useless when she and your mother had returned with sacks of flour, polenta and rice. She started to tell me off!'

Gabriella laughed, making him laugh too. 'And now I hear Riccardo wants to record your heroic deeds in a fresco. He wants you to be David, the slayer of Goliath.' She pulled a face. 'The big question is, who is going to pose for his Goliath?'

SIXTY-FOUR

FLORENCE

30 July 1944

Mama came rushing back into the palazzo very shortly after going out to buy more supplies. 'People are evacuating,' she shouted. 'Everyone living near the Arno has been told to get out. I think we should leave too.'

'But we're not that near the river and the cellar is all prepared. We should be safe down there,' Hanna said.

'Everyone is saying they're preparing to blow up the bridges before the Allies get here. I think it's going to get very dangerous in the city. We should get out of the centre right away.'

'They won't destroy the Ponte Vecchio, will they?' Gabriella pictured the beautiful medieval bridge, lined with goldsmiths' shops that looked like little jewel boxes.

'They've promised they won't because it's such a landmark of the city, but who knows what may happen?' Mama looked so worried. 'I'm going to pack my jewels. What's left of them. I can't leave any valuables here.'

Gabriella watched her going and said, 'But where should we go? If we can't stay in the city centre, perhaps we should camp in one of the public gardens?'

'The Boboli,' Hanna said. 'That has a lot of open space and fresh water. And I hear they are letting people shelter in the Pitti Palace up there.'

Gabriella knew the gardens, filled with fountains and sculptures, but would camping out in the open be safer than sheltering in the palazzo cellar or in the chapel? And would the gardens be crowded with terrified citizens, all panicked by the imminent conflict? Then, briefly, her thoughts turned to Stefanina. She guessed her friend lived in the centre of the city, but she could imagine her refusing to run and hide, preferring the heat of the battle to the cool of the Boboli fountains. 'What do you think we should take with us? We'll need food, won't we?'

'We'll be limited in what we can carry and we'll have to think what can be cooked on an open fire. I think rice and polenta will be the most useful foods.'

'And we've still got the wheelbarrow. It wasn't destroyed by Riccardo's flaming dove of fire, it was just scorched. We can pack blankets and cushions in that too.'

'I'm going to go out for a short while to see what news I can pick up,' Hanna said. 'I'd like to be sure we really do have to leave before we abandon the preparations we've already made.'

Gabriella went to find Riccardo. He was sketching again and Bela was standing in front of him, his arm and slingshot outstretched as if he was about to shoot a target. 'Have you heard?' she said. 'We may have to leave the city centre. Mama is packing already and Hanna has gone out to check whether this is really necessary.'

'I don't have many possessions, so I can help carry things,' Bela said, relaxing and dropping his pose.

'I must take my sketchbooks; my drawings and notes record everything that's happened.' Riccardo said. 'I'd like to take paints too, but I think I'll have to leave the oils behind and just take my watercolour palette.'

Gabriella thought how pale and pinched he looked compared to Bela, who was muscular and tanned from his days of working in the garden. Bela's upper lip showed the first shadowy signs of his maturing moustache. And then she heard the little girls' voices from under the table in the studio.

'We don't want to leave here,' Lili said, crawling out from their hiding place.

'We like this house,' Jazmin said, beginning to cry as she emerged as well.

'Don't worry,' Gabriella said. 'It will be like going off to the country for a camping holiday. You'd like to make a camp, wouldn't you? We'll cook on an open fire and sleep under the stars. Won't that be fun?'

The children nodded but she could tell they were uncertain. Their young lives had already been so disrupted, having to leave their home in Hungary and then not being able to settle in Austria. The three months of living at the palazzo, playing in the extensive garden, had been a brief time of relative normality and peace for them and now they might be about to lose this haven too.

When Hanna returned, she confirmed that many residents, but mainly those nearest to the river, were already moving out to the gardens and hills surrounding the city. 'I agree with your mother,' she told Gabriella. 'I think it would be wise to depart while we can. The streets could become very dangerous. We shall be better prepared if we don't have to flee at the very last moment.'

Over the next couple of hours, they made plans and packed bags and bundles they could easily carry. 'I think your idea of decamping to the Boboli is the best,' Mama said. 'If the city is bombed, there'll be no electricity or water. At least those gardens have fresh water, so we'll all manage somehow.'

The sun was high in the sky when they left the palazzo. Gabriella wondered if they would ever see their home again. Would it survive if the Allies had to bomb the city to chase out the Germans? She knew what devastation airborne bombs could wreak, having seen the destruction after the bombing back in late September and the wreckage around the railway lines that were attacked in March. She hoped they would be able to return to the palazzo when it was all over and find it just as they left it, dusty but intact.

They all carried luggage, even the two little girls. Bela insisted on pushing the heavy wheelbarrow, laden with small sacks of rice and polenta covered with vegetables and blankets. Everyone soon grew tired and thirsty as the day grew hotter by the minute, but Mama insisted they must get to the garden before it became overcrowded. Everywhere, people were trudging with weary steps as they carried bundles on their backs, in baskets and cases, or pushed small handcarts through the cobbled streets.

As they approached the Ponte alla Carraia, to cross the river, the queue of refugees slowed and Gabriella saw that the German guards positioned at either end of the bridge were checking every group and every person before waving them through. *This is where my long hair would have helped*, she thought, remembering how she had dazzled the young soldiers with its vibrant lustre and colour. She instinctively put a hand to her head to check her scarf covered her head completely. Her hair was already starting to grow back, a light golden fuzz, but she still bore more resemblance to a newborn baby than a girl of fifteen. How Stefanina would have laughed to see her now, she thought. What a joke, she'd have said, how are you going to turn their heads now? And then, still laughing, she'd have bent her dark curly head to capture her thick mane in her scarlet hair ribbon.

But these soldiers didn't look as if their heads would be easily turned. They may have been young, but their faces were stern, their words harsh. When one old woman refused to open her sack, a soldier split it open with his knife, causing her flour to spill. She screamed and cried, but he pushed her away as she tried to hold her precious cargo together.

As Gabriella and her family were let through, she looked back and realised why the guards were being so officious. Down below the bridge ramparts she could see other soldiers, placing metal boxes with wires on the steep, muddy bank of the Arno. She looked to her left along the river to the Santa Trinita and saw that too was being prepared with explosive equipment. So it was true after all. The Germans were planning to blow up all the bridges of Florence.

By the time they finally reached the Giardino di Boboli, Lili and Jazmin were near tears with tiredness and thirst. Bela's shirt was soaked with perspiration and Riccardo was exhausted from carrying the heavy bags of artwork and materials that he had refused to abandon. But their spirits lifted as they walked into the gardens through the entrance beside the Pitti Palace, past the sculpted grotto where the legendary Vasari Corridor began, then saw the green lawns, the shady trees and the pools topped with fountains.

'It's like we've left hell and arrived in heaven,' Riccardo said, being dramatic as usual.

'More like the Carnevale di Venezia,' his mother said, gazing around at the sight of picnickers sitting on the grass, under trees, lying on blankets and drinking wine. 'We went many years ago. It was quite debauched.'

'You rest here for a while,' Hanna said, indicating a patch of shade further away from the relaxed groups on the grass. 'I'm going to see if there is space in the palace itself. I'm sure I heard that they are letting people sleep inside.'

'No, don't,' Mama said. 'I think it will be healthier for us to stay outside in the fresh air. Who knows what will be happening inside the building? There will be no sanitary facilities for large numbers. It will be a midden in no time. We're better off out here.' She laid down her bags and her shoulders and knees sagged as she lowered herself onto the grass.

Gabriella was glad they were going to stay outside. Bela's sisters would be happier playing on the grass and splashing in the fountain pools. Riccardo was already unpacking his books and settling down to sketch. He'd gulped water from one of the flasks they'd brought with them and was drawing the entire scene spread out on the slopes of the gardens, capturing the tired families, the crying children, the many weary faces. Then peace descended as someone began strumming a tune on a guitar and others sang.

After resting for a short while, Gabriella helped to spread blankets and cushions out on the grass so they could sit comfortably. And once Mama and Hanna had laid out a lunch of plump sun-ripened tomatoes gathered that morning, raw baby courgettes and fresh crunchy bread, it felt as if they had all been blessed with another good day of life, at least for that moment.

SIXTY-FIVE

FLORENCE

November 2019

By the time they returned to the main house from the chapel, Gabriella was sitting at the courtyard table with cups of coffee. The morning chill had passed and the sun was warming the worn stones of the walls and paving. 'Come and join me,' she said as she spotted them. 'I hope you got everything you needed.'

'Yes, thank you. It was wonderful to see his early pictures. All of them contained elements that we can recognise in his later, more mature work.' Sofia pulled out a seat for her mother and sat down next to her. 'They've helped me to understand how his style originated and then developed. His paintings really are all grounded in his early years here.'

'Aah, yes. Those formative years made a deep impression on him. It was hard for him, for all of us. We went from being children one moment to bearing the full weight of adulthood the next.' Gabriella sighed and rubbed her hand over her close-cropped head. 'He suffered much pain, but I'm glad the result was such a magnificent catalogue of work.'

'Speaking of which,' Sofia said, 'I'd really like to share my photos with Phoebe Ackroyd at the London gallery. I know she'll be extremely interested in these early works. She might even ask if she can come over to view them for herself. Do you think that would be possible?'

'Oh, you wouldn't like her nosing about,' Isobel said. 'She'd be wanting to take professional photos and hanging around for ages. She's only in it for what she can get out of it.'

'I'll have to think about it, but I'm sure I can take care of any enquiries.' Gabriella seemed amused and not at all daunted by the prospect of the controlling curator.

'You mustn't agree to anything that makes you feel uncomfortable,' Sofia said. 'But I do think that the discovery of these early pictures completes the story about my father. It would be marvellous to be able to share them with everyone who appreciates his work.'

'I am delighted to hear you say so. It comforts me to think that my mistakes may have contributed to his greatness and that Riccardo's legacy is so highly valued.' The sun was edging past the palazzo and Gabriella picked up her sunglasses to shade her eyes. 'I still feel the need to make amends.'

'Then there is perhaps one other thing you might be able to help me with,' Sofia said. 'It's too much to ask of you right now, but when I return, I'd like to send you a copy of the exhibition catalogue so you can read how I tried to describe his paintings. Now I've learnt so much more about his past, I know I was way off the mark!'

'My dear, I already have the catalogue here. I sent for it, knowing the exhibition was happening and that I wouldn't be able to attend. I have followed his career avidly.' Gabriella gave a tiny, gentle laugh. 'I did find your interpretation rather amusing. What you thought was a white swan was a nun from the convent who saved the Giardino baby when she enveloped him in the folds of her habit. That baby is alive and well and today he is an eminent lawyer in New York. Sadly, none of his family survived to see his success. But his survival and his creation of an extended family bring me joy, when I mourn for his long-departed parents and siblings. It is a degree of triumph over evil.'

Sofia pulled a face at her mistaken interpretation. 'I'm sorry I got it so wrong. Then could you help me rewrite the descriptions? I'd love to do his pictures justice.'

'Of course I will help. I would enjoy making a contribution to his reputation.'

'And I've one last question...'

'Oh, here we go.' Isobel rolled her eyes. 'I've told you before, he numbered them because he was bloody arrogant. Couldn't be bothered to give anyone a clue as to what he'd painted.'

'Mum, please, let me.' Sofia put a restraining hand on her mother's wrist. 'I wanted to ask if you have any idea why he never gave his pictures titles, let alone descriptions. Why did he only give them numbers?'

Gabriella nodded in reflection. 'I fear you are too late. He was the only person who could truthfully answer that question, but I think it was perhaps because he couldn't express in words what the subjects of his paintings meant to him. They were too painful, based on such terrible, shocking events, that he could never bring himself to explain verbally what had happened. His only way of coping was to paint, over and over again, what he had witnessed. I don't suppose it gave him any deeper understanding of those times, but it was important to him to commit his feelings to canvas and record events in his own way.'

'Yes, I can understand that. But in that case, given that he allocated a chronological sequence of numbers to the paintings and we have accounted for the whereabouts of those that weren't released from private ownership for the exhibition, why does there appear to be one missing?'

'You think one is missing? Which one?' Gabriella removed her sunglasses and stared at Sofia and Isobel with red-rimmed eyes.

'Number Sixteen. Every painting is numbered, all the way up to his last completed work, Number One Hundred and Eighty-

Two. But we have no record of a Number Sixteen. Do you think there ever was one?'

Gabriella's head drooped and she was silent. Sofia could see her breathing had quickened. She began to wonder if this was all proving too stressful for such an elderly lady. But after a moment, Gabriella spoke and looked up. 'It is here. It lives here with me. It reminds me every day of how I let him down. It is my lasting shame and also my deepest joy.'

'So it actually exists?' Isobel gasped and then covered her mouth. 'You've had it here all along?'

'He came back once. Just the one time. He brought it with him, saying that he had painted it for me, to help me remember.' Her hands trembled as she reached for her sunglasses and replaced them. 'But I will always remember. I can never forget and nor could he.'

'Typical,' Isobel said. 'Just like him to be overly dramatic and make someone else feel guilty.' She shook her head impatiently.

'Oh, but I was guilty. I was the one at fault,' Gabriella said, her voice wavering. 'I look at his picture every day and I am reminded.'

'Please don't distress yourself,' Sofia said. 'But would you allow us to see this painting?' She was concerned for this elderly lady, aware how deeply affected she was by the retelling of her past.

'Yes, my dear, but first I must tell you what happened and why I have never been able to rid myself of my shame.'

SIXTY-SIX

FLORENCE

3 August 1944

Every day they waited for signs that the Allies had arrived and the Germans had departed. From their safe vantage point up on the green hills of the Boboli Gardens, whenever distant shots rang out, heads whipped round to look and chatter ceased for a moment while everyone tried to see and hear what it meant.

In the hottest part of the day, most of the refugees lay down to sleep after, if they were lucky, a meagre lunch. The waters of the fountains were used for washing and drinking and little children paddled in the pools. In the evenings, small fires were lit to boil water for tea and ersatz coffee, while women made rough flatbread from polenta and stirred thin soups in pots over the embers.

As food began to run low, boys and women ventured into the nearby parts of the city to buy whatever they could find. And on this particular day Gabriella walked down the slopes of the gardens with Bela and Riccardo. 'We mustn't separate this time,' she said. 'We must stick together – and we're not going anywhere near the river.' As they left the park, they emerged on the outer edges of the Oltrarno district. Even though it was early in the morning, the city was already much hotter than up in the cool green gardens where they slept. The walls of the buildings and the cobbles of the streets radiated the previous day's heat and Gabriella knew they couldn't stay out long.

They walked straight ahead towards Santo Spirito in the hope that the pedlars and stallholders usually gathered there would be trading. There were a few, but there was very little fresh produce. Gabriella could only afford two eggs, some overripe tomatoes and an onion. Everything was much more expensive than it normally was and she felt annoyed that dealers were taking advantage of the shortages. She felt pity for those who could not pay these inflated prices and had to steel herself to walk past the hollow cheeks and ragged, dirty clothes of people holding out unwashed hands.

They were about to start walking back to the Boboli Gardens when they heard shouting from a nearby alleyway at the side of the square. Two fascist soldiers were marching towards a truck, gripping the arms of a girl with black curly hair tied with a scarlet ribbon. Gabriella's heart slipped with a sickening jolt as she recognised her. She stood still, unable to move, watching the guards roughly dragging the young woman to the vehicle, her bare feet scraping on the rough gravel of the square. And although there was some distance between them, Stefanina caught Gabriella's eye. She gave a mocking laugh and yelled, 'Bella ciao, partisano!' Gabriella didn't dare to echo her stirring words; she knew she should stay silent to protect her brother and Bela. Any such cry from the gathering crowd would have provoked a visceral response from the guards.

'Do you know her?' Riccardo asked, coming close to her side when he noticed how his sister was staring at the uncowed girl, who was still laughing defiantly.

'Yes, she's a good friend.' Gabriella couldn't believe the cunning Stefanina had been taken.

'Maybe I can try to help her,' Bela said, putting his hand in his pocket where his slingshot lived with various pebbles.

Gabriella barred him with her arm to stop him removing his weapon. 'No, you mustn't. Look, there's two of them and a driver too. We daren't do anything. They'd shoot us on the spot. We wouldn't stand a chance.' She continued staring in horror as the men stopped at the rear of the truck. One of them stood back from Stefanina and spoke to her harshly and she spat at him. She spat right in his face. He wiped the spittle with his hand, dried it on the breast of her red dress, then slapped her so hard her head jerked to one side and hung down.

Such wild, irrepressible spirit, Gabriella thought, mesmerised by the gripping drama. It was so painful to watch, but she was proud of Stefanina's courage. *She hasn't lost her fight. But she can't win, not with two of them.* Gabriella wished she could have created a distraction, giving Stefanina a chance to escape, but she couldn't risk the lives of the two boys standing beside her. She kept watching, feeling Riccardo and Bela holding their breath too, as her friend was thrown into the truck. The soldiers jumped in after her and the vehicle left at speed.

'I wonder where she's going now?' Riccardo said. 'She's very beautiful.'

'She is,' Gabriella said, knowing he was already memorising her vibrant friend and would draw his impression of her on their return to the camp. 'She is fearless too. I only hope she survives and we can meet again one day, when this is all over.' She took a deep breath, willing herself to stay calm, to stem the tears, to show that she too could be brave like Stefanina.

'I'll remember how she looked and draw her later. Then one day I'll paint her so she'll live forever,' he said.

'I wish I could have helped her,' Bela said, still holding his weapon in his pocket, itching to put it to good use.

'It would have been foolish to even try this time,' Gabriella said, still trying to quiet her racing heart. 'But thank you for thinking about it.'

'How old do you think she is?' Riccardo asked.

'Maybe only a year older than me. I'm fifteen. Though I look younger now, I think, with my cropped hair.'

'You do. And I still think you look like a boy – when you're not wearing a scarf, that is.'

'Or a dress! I still wear dresses, remember!' Gabriella was about to aim a cuff at his ear, but withdrew her hand in time, thinking of his injury. Though long healed, it was still fragile and wept whenever he knocked it by accident. 'Come on, we must get back now, before Mama and Hanna are frantic with worry.' She tried to turn her mind away from whatever might have befallen Stefanina and concentrate on the supplies the family urgently needed.

They'd begun walking back the way they'd come when they saw a small group reading a notice pasted to a wall. Pausing to peer over their shoulders, they studied the official order issued and signed by the commander of the city of Florence, the head of the German occupying forces.

It is forbidden for anyone to leave home and walk in the streets... all windows and doorways must remain closed... German patrols are instructed to shoot people on the streets or looking out of windows...

'It comes into effect from 2 p.m. today,' Gabriella said. 'Thank goodness we came out early. But we've hardly managed to buy anything and from now on we won't be able to come out on the streets again.'

'We can stay out a little longer,' Bela said. 'It's not even nine yet. We could go a bit further and see what else we can find.'

Gabriella thought for a second. She was tempted to leave immediately, because this new edict would unnerve civilians and enemies alike. But, knowing that movement would be restricted from early afternoon, she decided he was right: 'We must still stay together, but we'll just go around the next two streets and leave to go back by ten at the very latest.'

When they found that a nearby baker was still selling fresh bread, she was glad she had followed Bela's advice. Every customer was limited to one loaf per person, but when he saw Gabriella with her two hungry boys, the baker relented and allowed them one each. 'Thank you,' she said. 'We won't waste a single crumb.'

'Make sure you don't,' he said. 'Once the electricity goes off I won't be baking any more. I'll only be able to sell flour then!'

'But you've heard that no one is allowed out of their homes from this afternoon?'

'True, but that could yet change. And everyone needs bread to live.'

They thanked him and continued walking the streets, but when they came to a crossroads, they saw fascist guards ahead. 'They're the ones we saw earlier,' Riccardo said, so they hung back, wary of going any further.

And as they and a few passers-by stood and watched, they saw the soldiers slipping a noose round the neck of a young woman and hauling her up on a rope slung over a lamppost. A slender girl with curly black hair, wearing a red dress.

Gabriella gasped and covered her eyes with her hands, but she couldn't move. She peered through her fingers as the body jerked with the tightening of the noose and the head lolled. 'Don't watch,' she whispered to the boys, unable to stop looking at the horrific scene herself.

'I have to look,' Riccardo said in a dead voice, choked with tears. 'I have to remember how it looks. Why have they hanged your friend?'

'Because she was brave.' They watched in silence as the soldiers tied the rope securely to the post and gave it one last tug that made Stefanina's body twitch like a strung puppet. The soldiers laughed and marched off, leaving her dangling as a warning to other independent, courageous young women that their youth and their beauty were no protection from punishment.

'I can't bear to see her like that,' Gabriella said. 'It's going to get so hot. It's not right to just leave her hanging there.'

'I could cut her down,' Bela said, reaching in his other pocket for the sharp knife he used to clean the pigeons he shot.

'Wait a moment. They will shoot you on the spot if they see you. We must stay here for a while till we're sure they won't be coming back.'

They stood in the shade until they thought it was safe. The early morning trade was dwindling and the baker had pulled down the shutters on his shop, having sold out of fresh bread. Soon the street was empty and quiet. 'Now,' Gabriella said. 'Before they come back.'

The sad trio ran across the street into the bright sun that had crept over the rooftops. Flies were buzzing, some crawling in the corners of Stefanina's closed eyes and on her lolling tongue and feeding on the trickles of blood running down the inside of her legs. Gabriella brushed the black flies away, ripped the scarf from her own head and covered her friend's face. Bela sliced through the noose round Stefanina's neck and lifted her in his arms. 'Now where do you want to go?' he asked, cradling her like a baby.

'We're near one of her compatriots. Follow me and let's pray that he is there.' Gabriella realised they were near via Toscanella, where she had first met Stefanina again and had her first lessons in flirting.

They rounded the corner and approached the locksmith's shop. 'I'll go in ahead,' she said. 'Make sure he's at home. Sit here in the shade and pretend that you're tired and she's fallen asleep.' Gabriella dashed over the road to the little shop and pushed the door handle, but this time it was locked. Well, of course it was. Who was going to want keys from him at a time when bread was the most valuable commodity in the city? She knocked and rang the bell and waited.

Eventually she heard a window open above her. She stood back from the door and looked up. Enzo peered out: 'Who is it?'

'It's me. Gabriella.'

He looked puzzled for a second and she realised he didn't recognise the strange shaven-headed creature knocking at his door. The once-Titian temptress now looked like a beggar on the streets.

'You shouldn't be here,' he called down. 'Go home and lock your doors.'

'Our mutual friend has suffered a serious accident,' she said. She didn't want to shout and rouse the whole neighbourhood. Who knew who might be listening and who might betray them? 'It happened nearby, so I wondered if you could help.' She waved across the street, directing his gaze towards the sad group slumped in the shade by the wall.

'You'd better come in then,' he said and closed the window. Gabriella heard the thump of his feet on the stairs inside and the door was soon unlocked. He peered up and down the street and beckoned them in. 'She's dead, isn't she? I always knew she'd push her luck too far one day.'

'I don't know what made them arrest her. We saw them taking her away and then we saw them hang her.' Gabriella gave a sob. 'She didn't deserve that.'

'No, it shouldn't have ended like that.' He heaved a sigh. 'She won't have told them anything, she was far too strong for that.'

'They just left her hanging there and we had to cut her down. We couldn't leave her body out in the hot sun.'

'The flies... I saw the flies...' Riccardo said.

'Come upstairs, all of you. There's more room.' Enzo locked the shop door and led the way up the narrow stairs to the table, where Stefanina had once laughed and downed glasses of rough wine as she demonstrated how to captivate the gullible young soldiers.

'Lay her down here,' he told Bela and the boy gently placed her on the table. Enzo removed the scarf covering her face and stroked her cheeks and her curly hair. The glow of life was fading from her burnished skin, replaced by the greyness of death. 'Such a waste,' he said. As he straightened her legs, his eyes caught Gabriella's and she shook her head. She knew he had noticed the blood that had trickled from above and they both knew they shouldn't speak of it.

They all stood around the table in silence, each of them paying solemn respect to Stefanina in their thoughts, until Gabriella said,

'We didn't know what to do and then all I could think was that you were very close by. I'm sorry if it wasn't the right thing to do.' She disentangled Stefanina's frayed scarlet ribbon from her hair and retied it in a jaunty bow, the way she had worn it in life.

'Don't worry about that. I'll look after her now. You should all get home. There's still time, but you don't want to be out much longer. They'll shoot anyone out on the streets this afternoon.'

'We know,' Gabriella said. 'We read the notice just before we found her. We've left home and are camping up in the Boboli Gardens.'

'Up there, eh? Maybe I'll find you there later tonight. She's got to be laid to rest somewhere. May as well be there. Near her friends.'

Bela looked baffled and Gabriella wondered how that could possibly happen if there was going to be a curfew from early afternoon. But Enzo could look after himself and now he had to look after Stefanina too.

SIXTY-SEVEN

FLORENCE

3 August 1944

'We were beginning to grow sick with worry,' Mama cried as the weary group returned. 'Did you have any luck?'

They gave her the bread and other goods, but when Gabriella burst into tears, her mother misunderstood and said, 'Don't cry, dear, you've done very well to get this much.'

As she crouched on the grass and sobbed, Riccardo said, 'She's sad because her friend is dead. We saw her being hanged.'

Mama gasped and put her hands to her breast as if praying. 'In God's name, what is happening to our world? You poor children.'

'I cut her down from the lamppost,' Bela said, sinking down onto the grass. He wasn't crying, but he was red-eyed and his voice choked. 'I carried her to the locksmith's shop and laid her on his table. He will have to deal with her now.'

'What's all this?' Hanna scurried across from where she had been washing clothes in a nearby fountain, carrying wet dresses over her arms to dry in the sun. Lili and Jazmin skipped behind her, wearing just their knickers, wet hair dripping onto their skinny shoulders.

'Here, children,' Mama said, handing each girl a chunk of fresh bread. 'Run back to the pool and eat it there.' They ran away giggling with their food and she added, 'This is not for their ears.'

Bela took over and explained again what had happened and by that time Gabriella had recovered sufficiently to tell the women about the German edict. 'We won't be able to find any more supplies. This is all we were able to get. From this afternoon, no one can be out on the streets.'

'They will even shoot anyone looking out of a window,' Riccardo added.

'Then we must plan our meals carefully,' Hanna said, immediately practical, after spreading the wet dresses out on bushes in the sun. 'We need to think how we can make our supplies last.' She and Mama checked their stores and began making plans to use the remaining fresh foods first. 'And after that we shall have to be content with polenta,' she said with a laugh.

Fresh bread smeared with the juice of a cut onion was shared out with the last of the tomatoes, then they all lay down on the grass to sleep. It was the hottest part of the day and all around them families were dozing in the shade. Bela lay next to his little sisters, who fell asleep immediately after their morning of games in the pool with other children. Riccardo was the only one who didn't try to sleep. He was busy sketching, his face tense with concentration on his grim subject.

Gabriella lay down on her cushion, but she couldn't sleep. Every time her eyes closed, she saw that dreadful sight again. Why did they have to snuff out that vibrant personality, that infectious laugh, that bold smile? It didn't make sense, even though she knew Stefanina was involved with the partisans and would have always been a target for the Germans. She tried once more to drift into numbing sleep, but then she heard the bell. The clock at the Pitti Palace chimed the hour twice. The deadline had come. From now on, they could not leave this haven of greenery.

As the afternoon wore on, Gabriella lost count of the times she heard distant shots. Not continual firing, but clearly the Germans were alert to any movement by the residents of Florence. Did someone dare to look out of a window or venture through a door onto the open street? Maybe some residents hadn't read the edict on the posters and were unaware that they should be hidden away.

Standing on the hillside terrace with its extensive view of the city rooftops, she could also hear but not see armoured cars patrolling the supposedly deserted streets. When it grew a little cooler and everyone woke from their siesta, she and Hanna played with the children, distracting them by teaching them songs from Gabriella's childhood. Riccardo even agreed to leave his work and show the girls how to draw comical cats, dogs and mice, while Bela gathered sticks to build another fire for their supper.

When the sky grew pink and gold, the air became a little cooler. The hill was dotted with campfires as groups prepared simple meals of soup, rice and polenta. Snatches of songs meandered through the campers and children played until they dropped with tiredness. Soon darkness had fallen and only the flickering fires lit the hillside. Mothers encouraged children to curl up together and sleep and soon the gardens began to fall quiet.

Gabriella lay with her eyes open, watching the bats flitting across the moonlit sky. They emerged at roughly the same time every night and she thought how reassuring it was that nature continued with its cycle of life at all hours, despite the disruption to human lives. Now and then, she heard a shot or the roar of a truck from far below, but up here on the hillside all was peaceful.

But soon after the clocks of nearby churches rang the hour of nine, she heard soft singing and footsteps. Men's voices, singing the words of 'Bella Ciao', Stefanina's favourite song, the rousing anthem of the partisans. Gabriella sat up, trying to see who it was. Riccardo must have heard it too, for he was sitting up, and then Bela stood, looking from side to side. 'Where's that coming from?' Riccardo asked, walking towards the path that came winding up from the grotto.

'Be careful,' Gabriella said, following him. 'We don't know who it might be.' But a moment later, in the half-light, she recognised Enzo and Marcello. They carried a long bundle between them and she realised immediately why they were here. It wasn't a bunch of kindling for their fires, it was a body, the body of Stefanina, wrapped in a white sheet.

She ran towards them and her hushed voice joined them in the words of the song as they walked higher up the hillside towards a wooded area overlooking the city. Bela and Riccardo joined their procession, along with a few individuals from other groups camped nearby, who recognised the tune and knew the words and knew what was about to happen. They all sang, *Oh, partisan, carry me away... If I die as a partisan, you must bury me... bury me up in the mountain... under the shade of a beautiful flower.*

By the light of the moon and with the help of a small lantern, they dug a grave. Gabriella couldn't tell whether the spot they chose was under the shade of a beautiful flower as the song requested, but it was in shade, it was on a hill and not a mountain, and Stefanina was among friends, not hanging alone from a lamp-post with only flies for company in the fierce heat of the day.

'Thank you,' Gabriella said, shaking Enzo's hand, once her friend had been laid to rest and the grave was filled. 'She will be peaceful up here.'

'I had to come back when I heard,' Marcello said. 'She was so brave. And in the words of our song, she is *dead for our freedom.* She died for us. We must always remember that.'

SIXTY-EIGHT

FLORENCE

3 August 1944

'I thought I heard singing,' Mama said, yawning, when they returned to their camp. 'I must have been dreaming.'

Riccardo began to explain, but Gabriella tapped his arm to stop him and said, 'It was that group over there. It's a song of freedom. We weren't asleep, so we joined in for a while.'

'Well I'm glad you didn't fully wake us.' Mama lay down again, but immediately sat up with a fright, as at that moment they all heard massive explosions coming from the direction of the city centre. The sounds were distant, yet they all thought they could feel the shockwaves in their hearts, as if the very soul and air of the city was shaken by the fearful noise of detonation.

'Heavens above,' Hanna screamed, jerking awake and looking around. 'Was that thunder?'

'No, they must be blowing up the bridges,' Gabriella said. 'You saw how they were placing explosives when we crossed the river the other day.'

'Please God they don't destroy all of them. How will we ever get home again?' Mama was on her feet, as were many people around their camp, all trying to see what was happening to their beloved city. But in the dark they couldn't see anything below the gardens but pricks of light in tenements as citizens throughout Florence awoke from the briefest of sleeps in terror, wondering how they would survive until the Allies arrived.

'They won't blow up the Ponte Vecchio, surely.' Riccardo was holding his mother's hand, like a much-younger child would do. 'Please say they won't.'

'They promised they wouldn't,' Gabriella said, moving closer to them. Hanna's arms were around her smallest children and her older son. Everyone was awake and anxious.

When the explosions subsided, groups of worried refugees tried to settle down, calming children, trying to return to sleep. But two hours later they heard further eruptions and rest became impossible for all but the smallest and the very oldest. The thunderous sounds continued until shortly before dawn and as the sky began to lighten they could see columns of smoke rising above the rooftops of the city. Adults stood in the highest part of the Boboli Gardens, trying in vain to determine exactly where the smoke was coming from. Was it all the bridges or just some? Had other important landmarks in the city also been destroyed?

And as the sun began to rise, there came the sound of cheering in the streets below. Gabriella and the boys wanted to run down the hill to see what was happening. 'It must be the Allies arriving,' Bela said. 'Let's go and greet them.'

'No, you don't,' his mother said, holding him back, even though he was now taller than her. 'It might not be safe.'

'And you're not to go either,' Mama said, turning to her children. 'We'll stay here until we know more. We'll hear soon enough, look.' She pointed out older boys from other families, running down the hillside. 'They'll be back before long with news.'

Although it was frustrating and she longed to be among those cheering and greeting the Allies, Gabriella knew they were both right to be cautious. But she couldn't help imagining the celebrations on the street, with flags, dancing and tears of joy at their liberation. The sounds of celebration seemed very close, near the Porta

Romana at the western end of the gardens, but soon she also heard rapid gunfire not far away. From the shelter of the Boboli it was impossible to tell who was shooting whom. Mothers kept their children close by them, comforting little ones frightened by the noise and busying themselves in making simple breakfasts of whatever they had to hand: stale bread rubbed with ripe tomatoes or soaked in tea, pieces of fruit and refried polenta.

Gabriella distracted Lili and Jazmin by telling them folk stories she remembered from her childhood, but every time they heard another shot they huddled closer to her, their eyes wide with fear. She longed to walk up the hill towards the trees to check that the grave dug last night was not disturbed, but she was afraid of drawing attention to the place where Stefanina now lay. Riccardo was engrossed in drawing his recollections of the previous day's events, and when she turned to him to see the latest sketch, he said, 'It wasn't fair. I keep thinking it was my fault, like with the others.' And she knew that his guilt ran deep and would never leave him, just as she knew it would never leave her either.

Bela was restless. He paced around their little family group, his catapult swinging from his hand. It was clear he longed to run down the hill to join the action below. Hanna was irritated by his pacing and said, 'If you can't keep still, go and make yourself useful. Go and hunt for kindling. We'll need more for a fire very soon.'

He grunted in reply and sloped off towards the trees. Gabriella stood up, saying, 'I'll help him. Everyone will be thinking the same thing, so we'd best collect dry wood before it all goes.' She ran after Bela and soon caught up with him. 'I'm feeling unsettled too,' she said. 'It's so hard to just sit there waiting when we know the Allies are here at last. I'm longing to see them.'

'Me too. I'd join the partisans if I could. I expect they're sniping at the Germans now. I might not have a gun, but you know how deadly my slingshot can be.' He looked at her. 'Do you think your friend ever shot anyone?'

'I don't think so. But I know she delivered guns to the resistance at least once. And I'm sure she'd have liked to use one herself, she was so spirited.'

'I wish I'd met her before... you know, before, when she was alive.'

'You'd have liked her. She was so funny and so cheeky. Beautiful too.' Gabriella fell silent, remembering that final evening of laughter in the square before the guards started firing at random. It had been so brief, that time of feeling she belonged and that these carefree young people, male and female, were her true friends. And last night, when Enzo and Marcello crept into the gardens with their burden, singing a last farewell, she had again felt united with people she understood and who understood her.

'I wish I could join them too,' she said. 'Perhaps if Stefanina was still alive, she and I would be down there in the thick of it, helping in some way. They don't always let the staffettas join in the fighting, but we ran messages all over the city and sometimes delivered vital equipment.'

'So that's what you were doing on the days when you weren't around, when I was just digging in the vegetable patch.' He laughed and shook his head. 'Wonderful.'

'We could, because we were safe. If you'd tried to join us you'd have been more at risk. Young German soldiers' heads are easily turned by pretty girls, but not by tall, strong boys with lethal slingshots hidden in their pockets.'

'You know I didn't expect to kill Bruno. I thought it would just stun him and give you a chance to get away.' He withdrew into himself for a moment. 'But I'd do it all over again, if I had to.'

She studied this bright, sensitive boy, who'd put himself in danger by saving her honour and her life. He too had a burden that would stay with him, just as she and Riccardo had dark, weighty baggage. Could any of them come through this war without scars that might never heal?

They reached the trees and, without agreeing to do so, both walked towards the scene of the previous night's burial. For a moment they stood, staring at the freshly turned earth, then, without speaking, they both gathered handfuls of dry leaves to disguise the grave. When it was quite covered, Gabriella said, 'But I want to remember where it is. We may find we can't come back for months, years even, and then it might be difficult to know exactly where she lies.'

'I can help,' Bela said, pulling his knife out of his pocket, the same knife that had sliced the noose around Stefanina's neck to set her free. He turned to the trunk of the tree with branches hanging over the grave and scored the bark with the letter S and the date – 3 August 1944.

'Perfect. Now we'll always be able to find her.' Gabriella ran her finger over the tree's bark, feeling the carving weep tears of fresh sap. *Stefanina would have liked this*, she thought, holding back her own tears.

'How do you think they managed to bring her here last night, without being shot?' Bela looked puzzled. 'The curfew started in the afternoon.'

'Enzo said a friend knew a way into the Vasari Corridor. He didn't say where exactly, but it would have let them walk right over the heads of the Germans.'

After collecting dry twigs under the trees, they began slowly walking back down the hill to their camp with bundles of kindling and Gabriella thought to ask Bela about his past: 'Why did you come to Italy?'

He was quiet, retreating into a dark place again. 'We left Hungary before it got really bad. But my parents said it wouldn't be safe to stay any longer. We weren't there originally. I was born in Austria, but I don't remember it very well. My parents moved when I was younger, when the girls were babies.'

'Was there fighting there too? Is that why you left?'

'My father was arrested. He was sent away and we don't know if he is still alive.'

'What had he done to get arrested?' Gabriella immediately pictured the men at the station, her father among them. Bruised faces and bloody noses on many.

'He did nothing apart from being himself.' He turned to look at her. 'You don't understand, Gaby. My father is Jewish, but my mother isn't. The Germans don't like that.'

'I know they have a hatred of the Jews, but they wouldn't harm you or your mother and sisters, would they?'

'But my parents thought they might. The Germans have a name for people who are part Jewish like us. They call them *Mischling*. They might have sent us away as well. People are dying, Gaby. They are not sent away to work, they are sent away to die.'

'Do you think that's what's happened to your father?'

He shrugged. 'We don't know. I hope not. He was a good man.'

And they walked in silence the rest of the way, each with the thoughts that weighed so much more heavily than their bundles of kindling.

SIXTY-NINE

FLORENCE

November 2019

Gabriella sighed and her head sagged wearily as she finished her story. 'So much sadness. And when the Allies arrived, that wasn't the end of our troubles. More people died in the streets of Florence from starvation and thirst that September than during the whole time of the German occupation. Their bombs meant there was no water and the fighting made it impossible to go and find supplies. By the time it was quieter and we were able to venture out, there were bodies lying on nearly every street, dead from lack of food and water – and of course some had been shot. The carnage was horrific, with corpses rotting in the heat, nibbled by rats and stray dogs. And those still alive were desperate to wash away the lice that had thrived on deprivation.'

'It must have been dreadful for all of you at that time,' Sofia said.

'But there were moments of great happiness too. When Uncle Federico finally returned with my father, we heard what important work they had been doing, helping to save Italy's great treasures. So many paintings and artefacts had been spirited away to Germany, but they had kept much of our art and antiquities safe in the hidden cellars and icehouses of distant country homes. And afterwards, they both worked with the city's art galleries and museums to restore order. I remember my father saying that when the bricks encasing Michelangelo's *David* were removed, the curators wept for joy to see it was unharmed.'

'But I still don't see why you say you felt shame. By then you had done so much to help your family and you'd also assisted the partisans. You shouldn't have been feeling guilty.'

'Oh, but I did,' Gabriella said. 'How could I not? I could never forget how stupid I had been, how I caused so much trouble for Riccardo and our parents.'

'But you were young too. It must have been very hard at that time. And those awful girls were horrible to you. No wonder you were easily persuaded that Bruno was on your side.'

'I was a silly, impressionable girl.' Gabriella shook her head, still astonished by her own youthful gullibility. 'I should have been more careful. Riccardo and I thought we were just playing a game, but nothing could be taken lightly in those times.'

'But you did so much later, to put it right, to make amends.'

'I suppose so, but I should have owned up earlier to Riccardo when I could see how much he blamed himself. It damaged him more than you can imagine. When I finally told him how the notebook had ended up with Carisi's cohorts, his face froze and his eyes turned to ice. It was just before he went away to art school. He said, "I'll never be able to forgive you." I remember him staring at me, his lips tight, not smiling. I cried for days when he left.

'But I know he also felt he had grown careless. His notes were hard to understand in the beginning, but once he began reversing the order of the letters, the code was instantly readable. When I gave Bruno that notebook, deciphering it was child's play.'

'But did you really never try to talk to him again?' Isobel's intense stare was drilling into Gabriella.

'I made a few attempts, but the damage was done. He was so withdrawn into himself. We were no longer close. Oh, the family sometimes did things together and he had wild moments when he was a little like his old self, but he was so wrapped up in what was happening all around us. And gradually, especially after Stefanina's death, I had become closer to Bela. I didn't tell him what I had done either, but we protected each other. And eventually, as you will have realised, we grew to be adults who shared terrible memories, but then, when we married and shared our lives, we could heal by creating and sharing good memories.'

'I can see now how those years had an enormous impact on Dad's mind and his work,' Sofia said. 'It's there throughout everything he created. So, who else knows about this painting? The one Riccardo gave you?' She was acutely aware of its immense significance and how valuable it was, given the reaction of the art market to her father's other works. The thought that it was kept here, unprotected, uninsured, guarded only by an elderly lady, made her nervous and she was anxious to secure its future.

'My family have always been aware of its existence, but they are not the slightest bit interested. It has no meaning for them.' Gabriella rose with difficulty from her seat, lifting herself with both hands on the arms of the chair. She turned and began walking into the house with stiff, slow steps. 'Come with me, I will show it to you.'

'Mum?' Sofia extended her hand to Isobel, who seemed reluctant to follow. 'Come on, we've got to see this. We might never have another chance.'

Gabriella led them to a bedroom on the ground floor, saying, 'This was my room when I first came to live here with my parents, when we left Rome, and I've slept here ever since.' It was furnished with an old-fashioned rosewood bedroom suite and a pure white, figured coverlet lay across the large bed, arranged with pale green brocade cushions.

Sofia looked eagerly for the picture and didn't see it at first because it was so small, much smaller than anything else her father had painted. Was it small because he had had to bring it here in person, or because he had wanted to control the horror, reduce it down in size until it felt controllable?

It wasn't hanging on the wall, but stood on top of a tall chest of drawers, at eye level, propped on a stand that might have once been used for a large book, maybe a Bible. It was angled so it could be seen from the bed and she realised that from there, it could be seen last thing at night and first thing every morning.

'Here we are,' Gabriella said, gesturing as if giving them both a personal introduction to this hidden piece of work. 'I look at it the moment I wake and before I close my eyes to sleep. Now you can see it for yourselves.'

Isobel and Sofia stood close together, at a slight distance from it at first, then they drew nearer to study the details of the dark painting. As well as the familiar symbols they were so used to, it contained other elements. There appeared to be a train with wooden trucks, a railway line on which wheeled iron beds and a wheelchair were travelling, and a dark curly-haired girl in a red dress on a swing, with a scarlet ribbon tied around her hair. And a smiling boy with a severed ear, his arms outstretched, pushed the swing away from him. Peering at the details, Sofia realised that the necklace round the girl's neck was formed of glistening black flies, strung side by side, like beads of jet.

'This is so like him,' Sofia murmured. 'Every part of it is so distinctive and screams out that this is one of his.'

'I recognise it and yet I don't,' Isobel said. 'He's put so much into it, as if this one painting had to say it all for him.'

'It's disturbing, but beautiful.' Sofia tried to absorb every element. 'May I take a photo?' She turned to Gabriella, who was sitting on the end of the bed.

'I'm not sure. This painting has special meaning for me. I need to think whether I can bear to share it.'

'I won't then, if you're not comfortable.' Sofia looked back at the framed canvas. 'But in that case, can you tell me what it means?'

Gabriella nodded and said, 'He came to see me soon after he graduated, before he began teaching. He said he had painted this for me, to pay me back for what I did and to summarise all we had shared. He told me then that he would never give his work titles. "I am never going to explain," he said. "I will use numbers, but there is one number I will never be able to use in public. It is too painful. So I am passing the burden on to you. This is Number Sixteen." And that was all he ever said about it.'

'But do you know what he meant by that?' Isobel sounded impatient. 'What is so special about that number?'

'At first I couldn't understand. He never said any more about it. He left soon afterwards. He could not bear to be here ever again.' Gabriella made herself more comfortable on the bed, lifting her legs and settling herself back against the pillows and cushions.

'But you worked it out, didn't you?' Sofia was desperate to know more.

'I studied it for a long time and then I realised its significance. How many vehicles do you see on the track?'

They studied the picture for a moment, then Isobel said, 'Fifteen... no, counting the wheelchair, there's sixteen.'

'That's right. Sixteen elderly Jews were removed from their nursing home in Florence and transported to Germany. Frail, old people who should have been allowed to gently end their days with dignity, loaded onto a truck and shipped out of the country. Their lives ended in Germany.'

'That's so dreadful. You told us how you'd witnessed that awful scene.'

'And can you see the platform number next to the train engine? It's very small, but I can assure you it's there.'

Sofia stared at the picture until she found it. 'Oh my goodness! It's Platform Sixteen. He put that in a lot of his paintings.' She turned to Gabriella with a look of surprise.

'Until the rail tracks were bombed, all the deportations of Jews and partisans departed from Platform Sixteen at Santa Maria Novella station, here in Florence. After that, they were sent off by truck, first to Turin and then on to Germany and beyond. There is a memorial on that platform still, dedicated to those who never returned.'

'It's a number that meant horror for him, isn't it?'

'A very significant number. Riccardo and I saw the prisoners being shoved onto cattle trucks at the station. Our father was very lucky to escape that fate.'

'I'm beginning to understand so much more now.' Isobel was wiping her eyes. 'He hid so much from us.'

'But there is still more. The girl, that carefree happy girl, swinging, full of joy in her red dress, that is Stefanina. But he never saw her sitting on a swing hanging from a tree, he saw her swinging by the neck from a lamppost. He saw her hanged and left to rot in the hot sun, for the flies to infest.'

'And she was your friend. So tragic.'

'She was only a year older than me at that time. She seemed older, being so bold and brave. But there was only a year between us. She was just sixteen.'

The intake of breath from both Sofia and Isobel was audible. They both turned back to look at the picture. The laughing girl laughed back at them, defiant and daring, so alive in his painting of her.

'Riccardo didn't really know her in life. He hadn't met her before he saw her arrested and then hanged. But he thought she was beautiful and he began drawing her likeness as soon as he could. We let him get on with it, we knew it was the only way he could deal with his sadness. He has captured her vitality, even though he saw that only briefly. And look at her feet. Can you see the bloody grazes on her toes? That's from when the soldiers dragged her across the square, tearing her feet on the gravel. There was more blood too, from their abuse of her, but he was sensitive enough not to paint that.'

'Poor Dad. He was very mixed up, wasn't he?'

Isobel was weeping. 'I wish I'd known. The times when I was impatient... he should have shared his feelings with me...'

'Mum, don't upset yourself. Don't you see, at last we've been given an opportunity to understand. I know it's very sad, but it's really important information.' Sofia held her mother close and they both sank onto a small couch set in front of the French windows. 'I feel sad too, but more because I now know how tormented he must have been throughout his life.'

'He took it to heart,' Gabriella said. 'Always he did. So passionate about everything. But perhaps that is what made him such a great artist.'

'I think that's true. Without the impact of these experiences, what would he have painted? Still lifes? Landscapes? He certainly wouldn't have had these shocking images swirling around in his head, would he?' Sofia was gazing at the picture again. 'Gabriella, I know this is a very personal painting for you. Please believe me when I say I truly understand that. But I also feel that if we are to honour his legacy, then this picture is like... well, like the missing link. It deserves recognition.'

Gabriella roused herself from her comfortable pillows. 'You mean you want other people to see it, don't you?'

'I just feel it would be marvellous for it to be shared as part of the whole sequence, the whole series of paintings he created that all relate to the experiences that left such a mark on him. Can you see that?'

Isobel looked up. 'I feel pity for him now, like I never did before.'

'I could never part with it,' Gabriella said. 'You can take a photo and share that, but I could never part with it permanently while I'm alive.'

'Could you ever see yourself putting it into an exhibition, on temporary loan?' Sofia stood to take a photograph and clicked her phone several times.

'Not in my lifetime, perhaps, but eventually, yes. In fact, I will bequeath it to you.'

'Oh my goodness, what a generous offer. I would treasure it.' Sofia checked the photos she'd taken and stood back, looking at the painting. 'But in the meantime, it would be wonderful if we could talk about incorporating a photo of it into a book about my father. I just know there will be enormous interest in this find and in the early frescoes. Would you feel comfortable with that, at least? I think it would be a way for you to respect his legacy and in a way atone for what you still feel you did wrong. What do you say?'

Gabriella looked down at her jewelled, gnarled hands, then held her head high. 'I would be proud to collaborate with you on a book about Riccardo. It would be an honour.' She eased herself off the bed, steadying herself with a hand on the bedside table. 'And finally, I wish to give you something now as well. You may have to wait some time for the painting, unless I die while pruning my roses.' She laughed. 'But I have something that will suit you, that I no longer have use for. Do you see that hatbox on top of the wardrobe? Can you lift it down for me and place it here on the bed?'

Sofia was baffled, but reached up for the round cream box with a piped black rim and placed it as she was instructed.

'Now lift the lid and see what we have here.' Gabriella was smiling. 'I can tell it will fit you perfectly.'

Inside was a coil of shimmering blue pleated silk, studded with tiny jewel-like buttons. Sofia lifted up the rippling column of slithering fabric to reveal the slim, full-length dress that carried a scent of the past, of negroni cocktails, dancing under a full moon, of love and decadence before all became defiled.

'I want you to have it,' Gabriella said. 'My family don't appreciate such things. My granddaughter says it smells too old! But it is my last treasure and I can tell it will suit you.'

'Mum, look,' Sofia said, holding the dress up against herself. 'I love it. Such colour and the scent is wonderful.'

'It smells of your grandmother, my mother. The perfume is Acqua di Santa Maria Novella. She wore it all her life. The station may have the same name, but holding this fabric to my nose always reminded me that not everything with that title was evil. There was still beauty if you knew where to look. Remember that when you write about your father. He saw the ugliness of the time, but he found beauty too.'

Sofia suspended the dress over the round hatbox and allowed

the silk to drip through her fingers and coil into it like a snake, a precious jewel of a snake devoid of venom. 'It's beautiful, utterly beautiful.'

'You will look enchanting in it, darling,' Isobel said, dabbing her eyes. 'Oh, how I wish your father could see you wearing it.'

Sofia sighed. 'I wish he could too. I miss him more than ever now we know the truth about his past.' She turned to her mother and Gabriella with a bright smile that belied her sorrow. 'But you know what, your stories have made me realise his legacy has to be my life's work. In a sense he will still be telling me how to run my life, but I have to do it for him. There must be a book and then one day, when all the paintings are reunited, when they are all together again, I'll organise another retrospective exhibition to explain his extraordinary career.'

'You must, darling,' Isobel said. 'But this time I'll help you. And you must wear this dress on the opening night, in honour of Riccardo and Gabriella and all who lived and suffered during that time.' She paused, looking thoughtful, then said, 'And I think you should call the exhibition *Painting by Numbers*.'

A LETTER FROM SUZANNE

Thank you so much for choosing to read *The Girl with the Scarlet Ribbon*. If you did enjoy it, and want to keep up to date with all my latest releases, just sign up at the following link. Your email address will never be shared and you can unsubscribe at any time.

www.bookouture.com/suzanne-goldring

I hope you enjoyed *The Girl with the Scarlet Ribbon* and if you did, I would be very grateful if you could write a review. I'd love to hear what you think and it makes such a difference helping new readers to discover one of my books for the first time.

I really appreciate hearing from my readers – you can get in touch through my Facebook page, through Twitter or my Wordpress website.

www.suzannegoldring.wordpress.com

facebook.com/suzannegoldringauthor

twitter.com/suzannegoldring

BACKGROUND TO THIS BOOK

Of course the very best background research for any story not set on home territory is to visit the location. There can be no substitute for hearing the local accent, eating the food of the region and picking up the scents. And so in November 2019, before the whole world became the strange, fearful place that we have all experienced for two years, I flew to Florence with the intention of exploring the city and finding a story that would fit this beautiful location. I travelled with my lovely daughter Jen, to whom this book is dedicated, for without her insights maybe I wouldn't have found the tale that became *The Girl with the Scarlet Ribbon*. And if, as originally planned, my husband had been my travel companion, instead of my curious and imaginative daughter, would this novel have emerged in this form?

The itinerary followed by my present-day characters, Isobel and Sofia, traces the steps that my daughter and I took during our stay, even down to particular restaurants and the opera. We walked everywhere and didn't travel by cab until our last afternoon, when it was time to return to the airport for our flight home. We ate ribollita, grilled octopus and pasta with sausage ragù. We drank Aperol spritz, prosecco and Chianti. We breathed the perfumes in the sparkling, mirrored haven of the Santa Maria Novella pharmacy and caught the scent of truffles in the Mercato Centrale. I hope that all that painstaking but enjoyable research has helped to bring this story to life.

However, as with any historical novel – and this is only partly historical – I could not know exactly what life was like for the residents of this lovely city during the war and particularly during that one year of German occupation. Research can only take the writer so far and after that there has to be an element of 'maybe' and 'what if'. But I can say that I did find an eyewitness report of the arrival of German troops by parachute and that residents thought at first it was the Allies. I can also confirm that a family did indeed keep a lamb they were reluctant to slaughter in their courtyard and that a nun hid a Jewish baby within the folds of her habit when the convent was raided.

It is also true that a notorious group of fascists and criminals, known as the Carita Gang, collaborated with the Germans in hunting for partisans and Jews. Under the leadership of Major Mario Carita, who encouraged his daughters to witness interrogations, some of the gang members boasted the title of The Four Saints. They rooted out their victims with the help of paid informers and conducted their brutal interviews in the Villa Triste, which was also the Gestapo interrogation centre. I can't know exactly what those daughters may have seen and to what degree they participated, but records indicate that the prisoners were mutilated in the way I have described.

I hope that I have captured something of the determination to survive in writing about the hardships of that time. I strongly suspect that, if anything, the deprivation was greater than I have described. However, the eyewitness accounts I have been able to find refer to the monotony of the diet, more than the lack, and often mention references to supplies arriving from farms in the valleys, along with vegetables grown in gardens and eggs laid in courtyards. The chaos that ensued following the arrival of the Allies brought more deaths through starvation, thirst and sickness than the whole period of German occupation. And although it must have been a terrifying time, eyewitness accounts again convey an impression of temporary bucolic respite, when families camped in the Boboli Gardens, where children splashed in the fountain pools and mothers stoked campfires to cook for them.

The real Vasari Corridor gave me the idea of a new secret escape route through attics and over roofs. And when we walked across the Ponte Vecchio, the only bridge that was not destroyed by the Germans, we thought of Mussolini ordering the new windows above us to give Hitler the best view of this beautiful city. When he looked down upon the River Arno flowing through the heart of Florence, he could not have known that the password for the clandestine Radio Cora contacting the Allied Forces and Italian resistance was 'the Arno flows in Florence'. Such a simple password that conveys the love of the partisans for their city, so I felt I could borrow it for my brave girls.

I hope to return to Florence one day to drink more Chianti and eat plenty of good pasta. I want to walk the length of the Vasari Corridor and look down upon that turbulent river to think about the brave men and women who fought to protect their magical city. I hope I have captured something of their courage.

RESEARCH

Walking the streets of Florence, visiting the churches and piazzas and of course sampling the food, was the best form of research, but I also found the following immensely informative:

- *SAS Italian Job* – Damien Lewis
- *Partisan Diary: A Woman's Life in the Italian Resistance* – Ada Gobetti
- 'Teaching Fascism' – Harvard Library Bulletin
- *Progress and Trends in Italian Education* – Anthony Scarangello

- *Chewing the Fat: An Oral History of Italian foodways* – Karima Moyer-Nocchi
- *Il Trittico* – Giacomo Puccini (programme printed by Teatro del Maggio Musicale Fiorentino)
- theFlorentine.net
- *Jamie Cooks Italy* – Jamie Oliver

ACKNOWLEDGEMENTS

I am immensely grateful for the support and encouragement of writing friends and colleagues, particularly the Vesta girls, Carol, Denise and Gail. I am also egged on by the Elstead Writers Group and the Ark Writers, who all have their say when we regularly share our work.

I feel very lucky in having the enthusiastic support of my lovely editor Lydia Vassar-Smith, who told me I had to write this story when I returned from Florence excited by the discovery of the wine windows and the station platform. She certainly didn't know it would lead to the hunt for a missing painting, but she allowed me to have an exciting adventure in the process. And I must also thank my agent Heather Holden-Brown for her calming reassurance whenever I thought I might be getting lost on that journey. And lastly, thanks are due to the whole Bookouture team, who make my books happen and complete the journey from idle thoughts to publication. I feel very fortunate.

Made in the USA
Las Vegas, NV
10 July 2022

51327212R00219